CRITICS AND READERS PRAISE
LABYRINTH

"Readers will cheer kick-butt Sherlock all the way to the action-packed finale."

—*Publishers Weekly*

"The twenty-third installment in Catherine Coulter's FBI Thriller series comes out this summer, and you're going to want to grab a copy."

—*Bustle*

"Catherine Coulter is one of the bona fide rock stars of the thriller genre, and her last book, *Paradox*, was as good as anything she's written. *Labyrinth* promises to be another 'white-knuckled' thriller, which means Coulter's fans better get their preordering on nice and early."

—*The Real Book Spy*

"The things you can count on in a Catherine Coulter book are a complex story line with plenty of action, intrigue, and unexpected twists and turns. *Labyrinth* has all that and more. . . . With white-knuckled pacing and shocking twists and turns, this is another electrifying novel that will sink its teeth in you."

—*Fresh Fiction*

"Great characters with an interesting story make for a really enjoyable read. . . . I couldn't put this book down it was so good."

—*Red Carpet Crash*

"I began *Labyrinth* Wednesday afternoon and finished it Thursday night! I loved it. I was riveted until the end. Can't wait for the next one!"

—S. Campbell

"*Labyrinth* is a thrill ride from start to finish. Coulter will not disappoint. The interwoven twists and unexpected turns of this fascinating book kept me on the edge of my seat. I couldn't put the book down and finished reading it in two days!"

—M. Gagne

"I just finished *Labyrinth* last night and absolutely loved it. You are really a master storyteller. I love that you always have multiple story lines to keep us on our toes. Thank you so much for a fantastic read."

—S. Burian

"I read *Labyrinth* and what's not to like?! It's adrenaline pumping from the very beginning. Your writing has always been wonderful."

—D. Burgos-Mirabel

"You got another winner with *Labyrinth*. Nothing like creating total chaos by page ten. I liked the transition back and forth of the two stories going on at the same time. I really enjoyed *Labyrinth* very much."

—T. Muller

PARADOX

"Pulse-pounding . . . Coulter fans will have a tough time putting this one down."

—*Publishers Weekly*

"Action is nonstop. . . . Perfect reading for the beach and beyond."

—*Booklist*

"Catherine Coulter remains one of the very best at what she does, and *Paradox* is some of her very finest work yet. . . . Eerie, unsettling, and breathlessly terrifying."

—*The Real Book Spy*

"Each and every Coulter book is out-of-this-world good, but *Paradox* is the very best book, to my way of thinking, that ever came out of her brain. This book simply blows your mind away. It's a captivating, intriguing, hold-on-to-your-britches book. Simply put, this is the best book of the year."

—P. L. Berry

ENIGMA

"Bestseller Coulter is at the top of her game in her twenty-first FBI thriller. . . . Twists and turns galore in both investigations ensure there's never a dull moment."
—*Publishers Weekly*, starred review

"A master of smooth, eminently readable narratives."
—*Booklist*

"*Enigma* is a new seductive and menacing thriller that sets new standards. . . . This must be next on your reading list if you love to read thrillers."
—*The Washington Book Review*

"I give *Enigma* five stars. I couldn't put it down. Another page-turning thriller."

—A. Konieczka

"I just finished *Enigma*. You've done it again! A fabulous read with enough twists and turns to keep the adrenaline meter on HIGH! Congratulations on another success. I really enjoyed this book and can't wait for the next."

—N. LeComte

THE FBI THRILLERS

Deadlock (2020)
Labyrinth (2019)
Paradox (2018)
Enigma (2017)
Insidious (2016)
Nemesis (2015)
Power Play (2014)
Bombshell (2013)
Backfire (2012)
Split Second (2011)
Twice Dead (2011): *Riptide* and *Hemlock Bay*
Whiplash (2010)
KnockOut (2009)
TailSpin (2008)
Double Jeopardy (2008): *The Target* and *The Edge*
Double Take (2007)
The Beginning (2005): *The Cove* and *The Maze*
Point Blank (2005)
Blowout (2004)
Blindside (2003)
Eleventh Hour (2002)
Hemlock Bay (2001)
Riptide (2000)
The Edge (1999)
The Target (1998)
The Maze (1997)
The Cove (1996)

A BRIT IN THE FBI THRILLERS (WITH J.T. ELLISON)

CATHERINE COULTER

LABYRINTH

POCKET BOOKS

NEW YORK LONDON TORONTO SYDNEY NEW DELHI

Pocket Books
An Imprint of Simon & Schuster, Inc.
1230 Avenue of the Americas
New York, NY 10020

This book is a work of fiction. Any references to historical events, real people, or real places are used fictitiously. Other names, characters, places, and events are products of the author's imagination, and any resemblance to actual events or places or persons, living or dead, is entirely coincidental.

First Pocket Books paperback edition August 2020

POCKET and colophon are registered trademarks of Simon & Schuster, Inc.

For information about special discounts for bulk purchases, please contact Simon & Schuster Special Sales at 1-866-506-1949 or business@simonandschuster.com.

The Simon & Schuster Speakers Bureau can bring authors to your live event. For more information or to book an event, contact the Simon & Schuster Speakers Bureau at 1-866-248-3049 or visit our website at www.simonspeakers.com.

Manufactured in the United States of America

10 9 8 7 6 5 4 3 2 1

ISBN 978-1-5011-9366-8
ISBN 978-1-5011-9368-2 (ebook)

IN MEMORY OF A VERY EXCEPTIONAL
FBI SPECIAL AGENT
MICHAEL M. (MICKY) ROMAN

1967–1998

ACKNOWLEDGMENTS

To the Prince of editing,
my very special Other Half,
whose abilities never fail to astound me.

Thank you,
Catherine

LABYRINTH

1

Sherlock had the next hour planned out to the minute. A quick stop at Clyde's Market for mozzarella cheese for Dillon's lasagna and some Cheerios for Sean's breakfast tomorrow, then thirty minutes at the gym: fifteen minutes on the treadmill and some quick upper-body work, that is if she managed to avoid Tim Maynard, a newly divorced firefighter who kept putting the moves on her. She was bummed she couldn't be with Dillon at the gym as usual, sweating her eyebrows off, but she'd been tied up in a meeting about the Mason Springs, Ohio, middle school murders. She thought of Agent Lucy McKnight, who'd been in the meeting with her until she had to run out to throw up. Lucy was four months pregnant now, nearly over the heaves, she had announced when she'd returned to the meeting, and everyone had applauded. Sherlock, Shirley, the CAU secretary and commandant, and Agent Ruth Noble were giving Lucy a just-beyond first-trimester party this Friday evening at Shirley's condo. Not a baby shower, too early for that. Their gift to her would be two pairs of pants with elastic waists. Sherlock flashed back to her own pregnancy with Sean, how happy and terrified she'd been. Lucy had a good man in Agent Coop McKnight. What a wild ride the two of them had had before they'd hooked up.

Sherlock had only enough time to jerk the wheel left, fast and hard, before the black SUV struck her passenger side. The impact hurled her Volvo into a parked sedan, and then spun her into the oncoming traffic. The world sped up, blurred into insanity. As if from a great distance, she heard horns honking, screaming metal, yells. Her Volvo struck the front fender of a truck, glanced off, hit a sedan trying to swerve out of her way, ricocheted off yet another swerving car. Her head slammed against the steering wheel an instant before the airbag exploded in her face. She heard a sharp *thunk* and saw only a flash of what looked like a body flying across the hood of the Volvo, and bouncing off her wildly spinning car. Her brain registered splattered blood on the windshield—she'd hit someone. He'd come out of nowhere. She looked at all the blood, so much blood. Hers? The person's she'd hit? The world turned round and round, a whirling kaleidoscope of colors and shapes, until they ended when the Volvo's rear end slammed into a fire hydrant. Her head was thrown violently forward into the bag and she was out.

2

Justice Cummings ran hard out of the alley between two brick buildings and into the street, looking back over his shoulder at the man and woman who were chasing him. He was a geek, not a runner, and he was surprised they weren't closer. It had been a fluke he'd gotten away from them. They'd been slowed down by a homeless man who'd shuffled between them, his head down, mumbling. Justice didn't know who they were, but they had to know he was CIA. There was no doubt in his mind they were out to take him, or worse. But why him? Why now? His brain squirreled around. All he could think of was the bizarre chatter he'd been picking up on the Russian dark web, some new kind of covert surveillance technology they were interested in, chatter his bosses hadn't thought worth pursuing. But why attack him? Besides, how could anyone outside the campus have found out about anything he did? He never spoke about his work when he left Langley, he knew the rules.

He was vaguely aware of shouts and screams as he ran all out into the street to get away from those people. He never saw the wildly spinning Volvo until it struck him, sent him airborne. His face smashed against the windshield, and he kept flying, the force of the impact bouncing him over the hood. He landed on his side, not a foot from a car sitting sideways in the street, the driver yelling out the window toward the still-spinning car. Adrenaline rushed through him. He couldn't lie there, even though blood was spewing from his face and pain seemed to be everywhere. They'd catch him. He managed to jump up and run hobbling through the gauntlet of screeching and stopped cars to the other side of the street, pushed through the gathering crowd, all staring, not at him but at the growing mayhem. He looked back and saw a car slammed into a fire hydrant, saw the windshield was streaked with blood, his blood. But he was alive, he could move. He didn't know where they were, and maybe they'd have a hard time getting to him through the growing chaos of mangled cars, blaring horns, and throngs of people running.

A moment later he was alone in another

alley next to a Korean restaurant, the smell of kimchi and the fetid odor of garbage from the two dumpsters mixing with the smell of blood on his face. He ran behind the far dumpster, pulled off his hoodie, and ripped off a sleeve to press against his nose. It ached fiercely, probably broken. His breathing was ragged and too fast. He tried to calm down, but it was hard. He was afraid and he hurt all over. He kept the sleeve pressed hard against his nose and waited. His ribs hurt and his left hip felt like it had been twisted sideways, but he could still move. He looked to see blood running down his leg, and just seeing it, recognizing his leg was hurt, made pain blast through him. He ripped off his other sleeve and made a tourniquet, tied it above the wound. He didn't know how bad his injury was, only hoped to stop the bleeding. He stood there, panting, trying to deal with the pain. In twenty minutes he had gone from thinking he'd be having a cup of coffee with a nice woman he'd met at Langley who'd never shown up at the café she herself had chosen, to running for his life. Was it all a setup? She'd been part of a plan? He realized he knew next to nothing about her except he'd thought her pretty and very nice. But he'd been lucky, he'd gotten away, only to run full tilt into a spinning car and bounce over the hood, and maybe that was lucky, too. Wonder of wonders, he hadn't broken all his body parts, only his nose, and hopefully the cut on his leg wasn't bad. Yes, he'd call that big-time luck. He wiped the blood from his face, hoped he wasn't only smearing it enough to scare people.

He knew he had to leave the alley. The man and woman must have seen him flying over the hood of that car, and they were probably still looking for him, maybe thinking he'd been too injured to get very far. They'd come again, work their way through the chaos to find him. It had to be about his work, a foreign government, maybe. What could they possibly want from him that was worth a kidnapping in broad daylight? Or worse. There were CIA protocols to follow, an emergency number to call. But someone had betrayed him, maybe someone at Langley had set him up. Would they be the ones who came for him? Who could he trust?

Justice felt pain building in his ribs, felt his leg throb, and his nose was on fire and still bleeding, but he wasn't about to go to an ER, that would be the first place they'd look. He thought of calling his wife, but no way would he put her and their kids in danger. He could hunker down at home, it was empty, his family wasn't there, but they'd know where he lived. So he was on his own until he didn't hurt so much and had time to think this through. He had to move, but Justice knew he couldn't make it far on foot. He called an Uber and set the pickup point on a street three blocks away, and thankfully saw the driver would be there in five minutes.

Blood kept oozing out of his nose. All he could do was keep pressing hard as he slipped through the crowds of people leaving work, all hurrying, many of them focused on their smartphones, none paying him any attention. He kept looking back, but no one was following him. He'd lost them. He began to feel hope.

3

Four blocks away, Savich was walking to his Porsche after a hard workout, his muscles pumped and warm, and feeling pleased with himself. He was whistling, tossing the key fob into the air, catching it. He felt good, but he always felt good after working to his limits. He looked at his Mickey Mouse watch. Sherlock would be arriving soon, he had to get home to get the lasagna together. He climbed into the Porsche, pressed the starter. He knew she'd bring the extra mozzarella cheese for the lasagna that was defrosting, and maybe some ice cream for the cherry pie she'd made the previous evening, one of Sean's favorites. He thought of Sean's birthday list and laughed. His boy, who'd just learned how to ride a bike

without training wheels two months ago, had said
what he really wanted was a Schwinn three-speed.
Yeah, like that would happen. Fortunately, he
also wanted Steph Curry sneakers. Did somebody
make Steph Curry sneakers for little kids? Probably so.

He was buckling his seat belt when his cell
belted out Gilbert Hillman's "Shining on the
Moon."

"Savich here."

"Agent Savich, this is Officer Ted Malone.
There was a car accident. Your wife, Agent Sher-
lock, is in an ambulance on the way to Washington
Memorial. I'm sorry, but I don't know her status."
A slight pause. "It looked bad, sir. You need to
hurry."

His world shrank instantly to a single black
point. He roared out of the gym parking lot, wove
between startled drivers on Wisconsin, and quickly
picked up two police cars, sirens blaring. Finally,
a vicious left brought him to the hospital's emergency room entrance. He slammed on the brakes
and jumped out of his Porsche in front of the ER,
his shield held high as officers jumped out of their
patrol cars, their guns drawn, yelling at him.

"FBI," he yelled, "car accident, my wife." He
threw the nearest officer his keys. "Please move my
car." Before they answered him he was through the
doors.

The place was a madhouse, but that was no

surprise, it usually was. Savich threaded his way through the crowd of humanity to the counter.

"My wife, Agent Sherlock, was brought in—a car accident. What can you tell me? I'm—"

Savich wasn't aware he was sheet white, his hands shaking, but Nurse Nancy Baker was. She said, her voice matter-of-fact, "I know who you are, Agent Savich. I'll take you to her. Come."

"Is she hurt badly?"

Nancy paused, laid her hand on his arm. "I'm sorry, Agent Savich, I don't know the particulars, but the doctor's with her. She'll tell you." She wasn't about to tell him his wife had been unconscious on a stretcher, her beautiful curly red hair soaked with blood, more blood streaking in rivulets down her face. She'd recognized Agent Sherlock immediately, she'd been in a number of times, not as a patient but as an FBI agent, usually with her husband. More than that, she was well known, the heroine who'd saved countless lives at the hands of a terrorist at JFK several months before.

Savich followed her, weaving through men, women, and several children, some upright, some in wheelchairs, some being comforted by relatives. They walked through swinging doors into a large space with curtained-off cubicles on each side, surrounding a central nursing station. Here it was a controlled chaos, the doctors, nurses, and techs moving fast, their faces intent and focused.

From behind the curtains, Savich heard

moans, a cry, and low voices speaking urgently or trying to soothe, one voice nearing hysteria, another calm and deep, reassuring. A doctor.

The nurse pulled back the nearest curtain and stepped aside.

Two nurses and two doctors were bending over Sherlock. The female doctor looked up, frowning. "Who are you?"

Savich immediately held up his FBI creds. They always gave him instant access. "I'm Agent Dillon Savich. She's Agent Sherlock. I'm her husband. Talk to me. What's her status?"

The woman straightened, walked to him, lightly laid her hand on his arm just as the nurse had. "I'm Dr. Loomis. That's Dr. Luther." She nodded toward a young man who was bending over Sherlock, lightly palpating her belly. "He told me about who she is and that you'd be coming. We have some urgent tests to do now, but I can tell you she's got a gash over her temple that will need stitches, multiple contusions on her arms and chest. Nothing appears broken, but we'll need X-rays to be sure. There are no signs of internal bleeding, but again, we need tests to confirm.

"She was unconscious when she got to us, but she's awake now, though still confused. She smiled up at me and said her head felt like it was kettle-drumming. That's a good sign, as you doubtless know. We're about to take her for a CT brain scan and they'll scan her chest, abdomen, and pelvis as well, our protocol for trauma of this sort. I'll know more soon. Perhaps you'd like to go to the surgical waiting room on the second floor? It's more private, less intense than the ER waiting room. I'll come see you there. Agent Savich?" She squeezed his arm. "Are you with me?"

Dr. Loomis knew he was scared senseless and would stay scared until she was willing to swear on a stack of Bibles his wife would recover. Sometimes even that wasn't enough. She would be scared to death, too, if it were her husband or her daughter lying there.

"I want to see her, a moment only. I—I need to see her."

Dr. Loomis stepped aside. "Only a moment, they're ready for her in CT."

Sherlock's eyes were closed. She lay perfectly still on a steel-framed gurney, most of her clothes cut off, the two nurses and the doctor surrounding her. So many bruises, cuts, and abrasions, as if she'd been thrown every which way. One of the nurses was speaking low to her, holding her hand as she pressed a strip of gauze over the cut on her temple. He swallowed when he saw all the blood—her hair was black with blood.

The other nurse moved aside at a nod from the doctor and Savich stepped in to lean over her. He lightly kissed her cheek, tasted her blood. He wanted to weep. "Sherlock? Sweetheart? Can you hear me?"

She opened her eyes and stared up at him, her eyes vague, not quite focused on his face. "Are you here to tell me you've got to cut me open now?"

"No cutting for you. You're awake and that's good. They're going to take excellent care of you. You were in an accident, but you'll be all right."

"An accident," she whispered. "What happened?"

"I don't know yet, but your Volvo saved your life. Doesn't matter, your next car's going to be a Sherman tank."

"We really need to take her now, Agent Savich, it's important," Dr. Loomis said from behind him.

He leaned down, kissed her again, and straightened. She was simply staring up at him, her mouth opening. He lightly laid his finger over her lips. "No, don't talk. You can tell me everything later. I swear, you'll be all right."

She looked up at the blurred face above her. All the people hovering around were wearing white, so much white. She didn't understand why, but in that moment, it didn't seem to matter. "Stay with me," she whispered, and closed her eyes again.

Savich held Sherlock's hand as he walked beside the gurney out of the ER down a long hallway. She squeezed his hand once and his heart stuttered. He couldn't stand seeing the smear of blood on her cheek, the blood matted in her hair beside the pressure bandage they'd placed on her head. No, she would be fine, her breathing was slow and steady. They pushed through another door, down another hallway, and through a door marked COMPUTED TOMOGRAPHY.

"Time to leave her with us, Agent Savich," Dr. Loomis said at the doorway. "I promise I'll come speak to you as soon as I can." She paused, then said, "Try not to worry, all right?"

He leaned down, lightly cupped Sherlock's face, kissed her mouth, and straightened. They wheeled her in and the door closed in his face. Savich stood staring at the door, aware of low voices, machines beeping, people hurrying past him. It seemed no one walked in this place, and for that he was grateful. He stood in front of the door, unable to move. He realized there was nothing he could do, and he hated it, hated feeling helpless. Slowly, Savich walked up the stairs past two nurses talking about a patient who'd thrown a bedpan at an orderly, to the second floor surgical waiting room. It was empty. Well, who would want to operate at nearly seven o'clock in the evening? Only for emergencies, like Sherlock. He had to stop it, there was no talk of surgery. Not yet.

It had been only a matter of months since Savich had spent time in that waiting room. Nothing had changed. It was small and square, its walls painted a light green, with three eye-level Monet water lily reproductions, lamps on side tables, and year-old magazines stacked neatly on a coffee table.

A new Keurig machine held the place of honor on a table in the corner, pods of coffee and tea piled in a basket. He sat down, immediately jumped back up, and began to pace. He stopped, took a deep breath. He had to get it together, there were things he had to do. That steadied him. He pulled out his cell, called Gabriella. He told her what had happened, where he was. He heard Sean in the background. "Put him on, Gabriella, and please listen, this is what we're going to tell him for now."

He said simply to his son, "Something has come up, Sean. Your mother and I won't be home until late. Eat your dinner, ask nicely if Gabriella would like to play Captain Carr with you or maybe watch those clips of Steph Curry shooting three-pointers in China again. Go to bed when she tells you to. No whining, okay? You promise?" Of course, Sean wanted to know if they were chasing bad guys, and Savich, an excellent liar, spun a fine tale about three bank robbers on the loose, nothing to worry about. Finally, he said to Gabriella, "Don't worry, I'll keep you posted. Thanks for staying with him."

There were others to call, but he simply couldn't do it yet. He slipped his cell into his jacket pocket and eased back down on a surprisingly comfortable chair. He looked straight ahead at nothing in particular, and prayed.

Savich was still sitting, his hands clasped between his knees, when Metro detective Ben

Raven, a longtime friend, hurried in. "Ted Malone, one of the officers at the accident site, knew you and I were friends and called me. Savich, the nurse in the ER said Sherlock was getting tests, no word yet on the results." Ben plowed his fingers through his hair. "Of course, you already know that." He sat down beside Savich, laid his hand on his shoulder.

"Thanks for coming, Ben." Savich looked at his friend. "It's strange. There's nothing I can do, only sit here like a zombie and wait. And wait. I don't think they ever run out of tests. Her hair was soaked with blood, Ben, it was black."

"You know as well as I do scalp wounds bleed bad. It doesn't mean much."

Savich shook himself. "Yes, I know. Do you know what happened? Who hit her?"

4

Ben said, "An SUV ran a red light, swerved suddenly, and broadsided her passenger side, sent the Volvo into a spin. She ended up rear-ending a fire hydrant."

Savich saw it clearly in his mind. She'd had an instant of awareness, and then *wham*—the rest would have been a blur. He'd bet Sherlock didn't even know exactly what had happened. She was an excellent driver, but spinning backward into a fire hydrant? *Shut it off.* He had to know more, had to see. "Do you have photos of the accident?"

Ben hesitated and Savich merely stared at him. "All right." Ben pulled out his cell and scrolled down, past a dozen shots of Callie, his wife, smiling that wonderful smile of hers, tickling their baby daughter, Taylor, who was showing all her gums she was laughing so hard. He stopped and handed his cell to Savich. "There are several videos witnesses forwarded to us, so, if you wish, you can watch some of what happened after the accident. Since Sherlock is well known, you can bet people will upload some videos on YouTube." He handed Savich his cell and watched him stare at the totaled Volvo, the fire hydrant rammed into its rear, the smears of blood across the windshield.

"That's not her blood, Savich. The blood on the windshield is on the outside, which means the Volvo struck someone when it was out of control."

The next shot was of two paramedics lifting an unconscious Sherlock out of the driver's side. Then a video of a woman somewhere in her thirties, her hair in black tangles straggling down nearly to her shoulders, wearing a brown trench coat, of all things, in the middle of summer. She was limping slightly as she walked past a paramedic and away from the smashed front end of a big black Escalade. She was holding her arm, and looked to be talking a mile a minute.

Savich felt killing rage, swallowed. "This woman's the one who hit her, isn't she?"

"Yeah."

"And you're telling me she walked away? With what? A broken arm and a limp?"

Ben said, "Yes, and some bruises. She's downstairs in the ER with two officers, along with one other person who was hurt. The woman's name is Jasmine Palumbo, age thirty-six. She works as a security engineer for the Bexholt Group, going on eight years."

Savich nodded. The Bexholt Group was a communications security company owned by Garrick Bexholt, headquartered in Maryland.

"Witnesses told Officer Malone how Palumbo came barreling through the intersection like a bat out of hell. Palumbo swears she didn't see the red light, didn't see Sherlock until it was too late, said she tried to stop, but maybe her brakes failed. We'll check out the brakes. Sherlock saw her coming at the Volvo passenger side at the last second and instinctively jerked the wheel left, so she was hit at an angle, and that sent her into a parked car, then into a spin. Thankfully there wasn't a lot of traffic in either direction, but still, in all she clipped a Tesla, a Ford F-150, and two sedans before spinning backward to smash into the fire hydrant. The airbag saved her life.

"As for Palumbo, the paramedic told Malone he thought she would be fine. Still, they're doing a tox screen, checking to see how badly her leg and arm are injured. After she hit Sherlock, she swerved and crashed into a kiosk, injured a couple of passersby and the man selling newspapers. She'll pay a hefty fine for reckless driving, but she won't go to jail unless she was on drugs or drunk. It'll be ruled an accident. I don't know anything more yet. I'll forward her insurance information."

"What about the blood on the windshield, Ben?"

"Now, there's a question I can't answer yet. All we know for sure is that according to a couple of witnesses, a man ran out into the street in front of Sherlock as she was spinning and she struck him. He was thrown up onto the hood and into the windshield, bounced off the other side. It wasn't her fault, of course. But after that bounce, he disappeared, seems to have run off. There was pandemonium, as you can imagine, people calling 911, rushing to help, shooting videos, you name it. So far he's not on any of the videos. We don't know who he is."

"You have a description?"

"We know it's a man, age undetermined, but young enough and fit enough to run fast. He looked like a tourist—hoodie, jeans, sneakers, a watch cap. We have people out looking for him, checking with other ERs to see if he took himself to one. One woman told Officer Casspi the guy was running out of an alley between two buildings, looking back over his shoulder, like someone might be chasing him.

"Obviously he has to be hurt, what with the hard impact, all that blood on the windshield. Maybe there was someone chasing him, they picked him up and hauled him away? Don't know yet. No one's reported seeing anything like that, but again, all the attention was on Sherlock.

"I have two men backtracking him, checking

to see if there was a robbery, anything hinky to set someone after him. If he did manage to walk away on his own, there'll be a blood trail. I hope. We should find him soon."

Ben saw Savich's hands clench, flex. "Listen, Savich, when Palumbo is cleared from the ER, the officers will take her to the Daly Building until her tox screen comes back. I'll have control." Again Ben touched his shoulder. "A favor, Savich, don't get involved with Palumbo, it'll keep things cleaner. It sounds like she wasn't paying attention, probably looking off at something, got distracted. If she was high, I'll clap the irons on her myself and haul her to a cell."

Savich managed a ghost of a smile. The two men sat side by side, quiet now. Savich couldn't get the image of Sherlock's beautiful hair soaked with blood out of his mind. He wasn't about to call her parents until he knew more. He swallowed, he had to call his boss, Jimmy Maitland.

Within twenty minutes FBI agents began to arrive, among them Davis Sullivan, Lucy McKnight, and Shirley Needleham, the CAU secretary, with Mr. Maitland at their head. Ben had to repeat what had happened three more times. When Dr. Loomis walked in an hour later, the surgical waiting room was full, everyone coming to their feet when she appeared in the doorway. She smiled at them. "Agent Sherlock's CT scans were completely normal, except for the superficial injuries. No intracranial bleeding, no broken bones, no sign of internal bleeding. She suffered a concussion, of course, and a cut on her head we stitched, and as Agent Savich knows, there are considerable upper-body contusions and bruising. But with some luck, she'll be fine." Given the photos a police officer had shown her of the crash, Dr. Loomis was amazed Agent Sherlock survived, but she didn't say that. She knew Agent Savich, probably all the agents in this waiting room, had seen the photos. She added, "Given the severity of the accident, she's very lucky. Right now, she needs quiet and rest. We won't know more about how bad her concussion is until tomorrow morning, when any remaining symptoms could manifest themselves. I'll review what we can expect privately with you later, Agent Savich. I want to monitor her closely throughout the night, so I prefer she stay in the ICU. If you wish to stay with her, I'll have a cot brought in for you. As you know, the cubicles are small and I doubt you'll get much sleep.

"As for the rest of you, alas, I can't offer you the five-star accommodation we're offering Agent Savich. I can assure all of you she will get the best of care." She smiled really big. "After all, she's famous, isn't she? The heroine of JFK."

Dr. Loomis looked at all the relieved faces, some smiling back and nodding at what she'd said.

Agent Davis Sullivan raised a finger. "May we see her in the morning?"

Now, this young man could raise a flutter, Dr.

Loomis thought, not immune. She said, "Check with Agent Savich first. He'll let you know if visiting tomorrow is a good idea." She turned to Savich, who still looked white around the gills, and something else, too. He was angry. She didn't blame him. She'd heard the woman who'd struck Agent Sherlock's car was downstairs in the ER. She'd walked away with a sprained arm, now in a sling, and nothing but bruises on her leg. Didn't that just figure? "Agent Savich, I'll send an orderly in to take you to her."

When she left, everyone started high-fiving and talking at once. Savich shook Ben's hand, started to thank everyone for coming, but when a skinny young black orderly with thick glasses and a goatee showed up, he only nodded and left. The orderly had to double-time it to keep up. Savich knew exactly where the ICU was, he'd been there often enough over the years. He couldn't help himself, glanced at the man's name tag and asked, "Did you see her, Malcolm?"

Malcolm wasn't deaf to the fear in Agent Savich's voice. "Yes, Agent, I did. She's sleeping, not unconscious. There's a big bandage around her head, so it looks worse than it is. One of the nurses said all her curly hair would cover the stitches over her temple. Is her name really Sherlock? As in the Baskerville Sherlock?"

"Yes, and surprise, she loves dogs."

Malcolm left him in front of a curtained cubicle in the ICU with a small salute. Savich pulled back the curtain to see a nurse fussing over

Sherlock, taking her blood pressure, her pulse. She straightened, nodded to him. "You're her husband, Agent Savich, right?"

He nodded. "How is she?"

"Her vitals continue to be in the normal range. I'm hoping she'll sleep most of the night, even with the frequent checks. If anything worries you tonight, give us a holler." She shook his hand, nodded to the stingy narrow cot snugged into the small space. "Good luck with that. I'll see you again soon."

Savich stood over Sherlock, simply listening to her slow, even breathing. They'd cleaned the blood off her face and put her in a light blue hospital gown. The bandage around her head was in layers, like a turban. He remembered when she'd been hurt in San Francisco before last Christmas, her head had been covered with layers of white bandages then, too. The leaching fear flooded back, drowning him. He touched his fingertips to her hair, still stiff with dried blood. He looked at the bruises on the top of her shoulder from the seat belt, bruises he knew looked worse than they were. An IV line snaked into her wrist from a bag of liquid, probably saline to keep her hydrated. Nothing they could give her for the concussion. She was pale and still, a lifeless model of herself. It scared him to death. She was always on the move, always ready to take on anything thrown at her. She was vital, a dynamo.

Savich leaned down, lightly kissed her mouth. He stood by her bed for a very long time.

5

WEDNESDAY MORNING

She opened her eyes and saw his face again, only inches above hers, beautiful dark intense eyes framed by black eyelashes. She remembered he'd stayed with her, holding her hand, as she was being wheeled—somewhere. He was utterly focused on her. Why did he look worried? Then pain struck inside her head out of nowhere, pain so sharp she gasped. She no longer cared if the angel Gabriel was standing over her, she was only aware of the pounding pain. She tried to raise her hand but felt a hard tug. She saw a needle sticking out of her wrist tethered to tubing.

What had happened? Where was she? Well, given the needle in her wrist, she was in a hospital, but— Her brain twisted, turned inward, and she no longer cared if she was on Mars. The pain in her head was like nails hammering into a board. She whispered, her voice insubstantial as candle smoke, "My head—it hurts, really hurts. What's happening?"

She closed her eyes against the pain, heard him call out, "Nurse, come quickly. She's awake and in pain."

She felt his fingers lightly touch her cheek. "Hold on, help's coming." His hand moved to cup her chin, and it distracted her for a moment. His low, deep voice sounded close to her cheek. "The pain only now started?"

She opened her eyes, closed them again real fast, whispered, "Yes, and it's bad, like a jungle drum pounding a battle cry." Raw fear struck through her. She was dying, she couldn't survive this pain, no one could. She felt his hand squeezing hers. "Hold on," he said again, "they'll be here soon to help you."

"I'm dying, aren't I?"

"No, you're not dying until the next millennium, then maybe another decade or so after that. Hang on, sweetheart."

Sweetheart?

A nurse hurried into the cubicle. "Good, you're awake. Let's take care of the pain first. Dr. Loomis expected you might have a bad headache this morning. She left orders for a very nice drug for you, Dilaudid. Not enough to knock you out, we can't have that. I'm injecting it into your IV right now. Breathe normally. That's it. You should feel better very quickly, only a couple of minutes."

The three of them waited silently. The couple of minutes seemed an eon to Sherlock, until finally she began to ease.

The nurse leaned down. "Better? Was there pain anywhere else? Or only your head?"

Sherlock had enough control to give this some thought. She whispered, "I feel achy, little jabs of pain here and there when I move, mainly in my chest and arms and my shoulder, but that's better now, too." She felt another ripple of pain in her head, but it wasn't nearly as bad. Still, she closed her eyes and lay very still. She whispered, "It's the oddest thing. I feel like I'm ready to float to the ceiling. Should I hang on to something?"

Savich took her hand. "I've got hold of you. If you float up, I'll bring you back down. Or maybe I'll float up with you."

"Thank you." She blinked, opened her eyes. "I know I'm in the hospital. What happened? Did someone mug me?"

"No. Another driver slammed into you at the intersection of Prior and Williams, and sent the Volvo spinning. You ended up rear-ending a fire hydrant."

"The man who hit me, is he all right?"

"It wasn't a man. Last I heard she walked away with a sprained arm and bruised leg."

"A woman hit me? A woman? But women don't drive crazy like that."

"This one did, for whatever reason."

"Did I hurt anyone?"

"A few people were injured, but not seriously. Don't worry. We'll talk more about it later."

The nurse said, "That's right, no more talk about the accident. I'm Joan Marlow, I'll be taking care of you today. I'll bet you're thirsty, right?"

"Yes."

"Let me check you out first, then water." She took Sherlock's pulse, listened to her heart, shined a penlight into her eyes, asked her to follow the light to the right, then to the left. She had Sherlock grip her hands and move her legs. She studied her face a moment. "Any nausea?"

She thought about it, then, "No."

"Good. Dizziness?"

"No, but I'm afraid to move. I feel sort of balanced on the edge and I don't want to take the chance of falling off."

"I understand. Is the pain in your head down to a dull throb now?"

"Yes, it's amazing. I'd like a liter of that wonderful drug, please. Maybe a bit more would send me floating right out the window."

The nurse laughed. "A lot of people like it, too many like it too much. Now you get some water, only a bit." Savich held out his hand and she handed him a plastic cup of cool water with a flexible straw. He moved in close, held it to Sherlock's mouth. She hesitated a moment before she sucked on the straw. She kept sucking until Nurse Marlow patted his shoulder. "That's it for right now. You can have a bit more in fifteen minutes."

Sherlock closed her eyes a moment. "Thank you."

"Any nausea from the water?"

She opened her eyes, saw her nurse had a comfortable older face, kind eyes. "No nausea. Your name—Joan Marlow. Wasn't she an actress?"

Joan grinned, patted her arm below a small bandage covering a cut. "Close. You can thank my parents, well, mainly my dad. Now, I promised to call Dr. Loomis when you were awake. She's already downstairs, on rounds. She should be here shortly."

"This is wonderful. I don't feel any pain at all, but I don't want to float anymore, I want to snuggle down and sleep for a year."

Savich leaned down, lightly kissed her nose. "Don't go to sleep yet, okay? Wait up for Dr. Loomis. See, you have a magic button to press whenever you want more painkiller." He closed her hand around a small device, saw her fingers tighten around it, and smiled. He wouldn't want to let it go, either.

"If someone tries to take it away, I'll hurt them." Was that still her own voice, sounding all low and easy?

She heard the nurse chuckle. "I don't blame you."

He was holding her hand, his flesh warm. She felt his fingers lightly touch her cheek. "Don't worry about Sean. I told him last night we were hot on the trail of some bank robbers. I'm sure Gabriella embellished to make us sound really heroic."

Such a mesmerizing voice, an actor's voice, deep and resonant, but his words made no sense. She blinked, focused on his face, licked her lips. "Was I mugged?"

The nurse said quietly, "Don't worry, the repetition isn't uncommon with a concussion. She might ask this same question again until her brain sorts things out."

And so he said, "No, you weren't mugged, you were in a car accident," and repeated what he'd told her before, adding, "I'm sorry, but your Volvo's totaled. Do you remember anything that happened?"

Her Volvo was totaled? She saw a shocked face, wild fear, and then nothing. A door slammed shut in her mind and she felt trapped inside, something she didn't understand. She could only lie there, helpless. "The woman who hit me, I saw her face for a moment. She was surprised, then afraid." She paused, trying to bring it back, but no go. "I don't remember anything else."

"It's all right. It's amazing you remember that much. Your brain got slammed around even with

the airbag. It will take a while to fill in the blanks."
Maybe she'd never remember the accident, which
might be better.

She had to know, simply had to, but it was
frightening to say the words. She whispered, "Why
are you here?"

She watched him cock his head. "Where else
would I be? You scared the bejesus out of me, out
of a lot of people. Last night, nearly everyone in
the unit was here, including Mr. Maitland. Don't
worry, I spoke to your parents and my mom last
night, assured them you're all right. And of course
to Gabriella. I told Sean you and I were chasing
bank robbers." He didn't mention the calls he'd
gotten from the *Post* and the local TV stations.
Videos of the spectacular accident and its aftermath had gone viral. The reporter from the *Post*
said there were half a dozen on YouTube. Savich
had referred all calls to the media liaison at the
Hoover.

"Parents?"

He lightly patted her cheek. "Well, sure, no
choice. They're very worried, but I told them
not to fly back, you'd be fine in a couple of days.
They'll probably call you later today. You slept
through the night, even when the nurse came in to
check on you. She was surprised you did and very
pleased, said it was the best thing for you."

She was silent, then slowly raised her vague
summer-blue eyes to his face. It was time to spit

it out, time to know, though she was afraid to say it out loud. But she had to know. She whispered, "When I first saw you last night, I thought you had beautiful eyes and awesome eyelashes. Looking at you made something stir in me, something familiar, comforting, but it faded away. I know you're not a doctor, yet you were here with me whenever I was awake. You're very handsome and kind and I love your voice. But here it is, I don't know who you are. And who is Gabriella? Who is Sean?"

6

At first her words made no sense. Then they did, and Savich felt them like a punch to the gut. She didn't know who he was? He'd seen memory loss after head trauma, most cops had, but this was different. This wasn't a stranger, this was Sherlock. Not only didn't she remember the accident, she didn't remember him. It nearly broke him, but he knew he had to keep it together, had to keep calm. It was only temporary. It had to be only temporary. He managed a smile. "I'm your husband, Sherlock. Dillon Savich."

She frowned, never taking her eyes from his face. "Sherlock? My name is Sherlock?"

"Yes. Lacey Sherlock Savich."

"You're my husband?"

"Yes, I am."

Everyone called her Sherlock? Not Lacey? How strange. Sherlock, now she'd have to get used to her odd name. She stared up at him and he saw a flash of fear, then a hint of a smile. She whispered, "If I were Stacy instead of Lacey, the alliteration would rock the world."

For an instant he saw his Sherlock, saw her smile, heard her humor. She was in there. "Yes, you'd be a triple S."

"Where did I get a name like Sherlock?"

Don't let her see how freaking scared you are. "Your father, Corman Sherlock, is a federal judge in San Francisco. I understand defense lawyers try to avoid cases in front of Judge Sherlock. Your mom is Evelyn. Since the first of the year, she practically runs Davies Hall—that's where they have classical music, symphonies. They're both very worried about you." Was he telling her too much? If he squeezed her hand to reassure her, would he frighten her? After all, she didn't know him. He was handsome? He drew a breath. "We have a wonderful little boy, Sean. He's nearly five years old, and a pistol. Gabriella is his nanny, really one of the family."

Sherlock heard the words, understood them, and she knew they should make her feel something, remember something, but they didn't. The life those words painted belonged to someone else. She suddenly saw a large room with workstations, men and women talking, she heard typing on keyboards, laughing, someone calling out a series of numbers, and then a door slammed in her brain again. A memory, but then it was gone, simply gone. The world began spinning, she was in a car and it was spinning round and round, and then there was nothing, only blankness.

She gasped. His arms were around her, this stranger's arms, yet somehow familiar and strong. He smelled good. His breath was warm and sweet against her cheek, his voice reassuring. "It's all right. Don't worry. Everything will straighten out." He kissed her forehead, only a light touch, but it froze her.

He felt it, knew he was scaring her. Well, he was a stranger to her. He eased her back down and lightly stroked her hands.

She forced herself to calm, focused on his face above hers. This man was her husband? He looked tough with the black beard scruff, like he could derail a train with a punch. His dark eyes were nearly black.

"I bet women are all over you. Do I have to beat them off with a stick? Maybe punch a few of them?"

He had to grin. "I guess you've protected me a couple of times."

Humor. She recognized he was trying to keep it light, keep her fear at bay. She studied his face. It was hard to get the words out. "We're really married?"

"Yes. Nearly six years. You became pregnant very soon after we married." He paused. "Whenever I forgot and said the word 'pregnant' in front of you, you had to run to the bathroom and hurl. And something I'll never forget, whenever I slipped up, you punched me."

She pictured herself hugging a toilet, wasn't sure if it was a flash of memory or a simple visual from his words. "Please show me a photo of Sean."

Savich pulled out his cell, showed her a short video of Sean playing basketball with Marty Perry, his best friend for years and years, he'd say. A small boy and girl were kid-shrieking, trash-talking each other like they'd seen on TV, and then she heard a woman's voice calling out, her own voice, "Come on now, guys, I've got my special lemonade ready for you." The camera panned toward her and she saw a young woman wearing shorts and a cutoff top, her curly red hair in a fat ponytail, flip-flops on her feet and pink toenails. The kids were running madly toward her and she hugged them both and turned to walk up the steps into a house, a kid on each side of her, talking nonstop.

She swallowed, aware he was looking at her, waiting. For her to suddenly remember everything?

"The little boy, that's Sean?"

"Yes. He loves computer games, Captain Carr and his sidekick Orkett this week. Of course, he loves basketball, would do anything to meet Steph Curry, though he claims he's going to be tougher and shoot more threes. He's always running around with our Scottie, Astro. Sean's smart, a kindhearted kid, and he likes to tell people Marty's going to be his future wife. Well, one of them."

Oddly, that sounded okay, sounded natural. "That woman, it's me?"

"Yes. You make lemonade from our own Meyer lemon tree. You're as kindhearted as Sean and you're beautiful, as you saw. And smarter than you have a right to be."

She remembered the large room. "Do I work?"

"You do more than work. You and I are both FBI special agents. We're at the Hoover Building, in my unit, the CAU—the Criminal Apprehension Unit. I'll tell you all about it later. I think that's enough for now. Time for you to let your brain relax. Don't worry too much, everything will come back. A little time, that's all you'll need."

She was a cop? A federal cop? Did that mean she was tough, like he was? The large room with all the working men and women—that was where she worked? Probably so. The person she was before the accident knew all those people, but the person she was now had no clue. He didn't want her to be too worried? Like that was possible.

"She—I—have red hair. Really curly?"

He lightly touched a curl hugging her cheek. "Yes, and lots of it, beautiful stuff. And summer-blue eyes. You're a knockout, Sherlock. You saw that yourself on the video."

"Are my toenails still pink?"

"You changed to coral last week, to end out the summer, you told me, to prepare your toes for the final leap to fall red."

"I'm sorry," she whispered, and closed her eyes. She wanted to cry. She whispered again, "I'm sorry."

7

MORGANTOWN, VIRGINIA
REDEMPTION HOUSE
WEDNESDAY AFTERNOON

They called her Athena, at her own request. Of course they knew her real name, but no one called her by that name when they had to communicate or when they met here to work at Redemption House, their headquarters in rural Virginia. She said the code name was an added level of security, one she'd picked herself: Athena, goddess of war.

Nikki Bexholt, Athena, looked at the three people standing in front of her, every one of their faces grim. She'd selected each of them carefully, some for their expertise, some because of their unquestionable loyalty to her. Jasmine Palumbo, her team leader, a supervisor in Bexholt's client security division, stood tall and straight, with her arm in a sling, guilt radiating off her in waves. Cricket Washburn, supervisor of campus security at Bexholt, managed only an occasional furtive glance toward her. And Dr. Craig Cook, her most precious asset, the shining star in Bexholt's R&D division, a rare inventive talent, an electrical engineering genius. He was her brain trust with his bald head and his Fu Manchu mustache he hoped made him look less like a nerd, but didn't. He'd actually been excited about snatching Cummings off the street, undoubtedly pictured himself as a debonair badass. Now he looked more scared and miserable than Jasmine or Cricket. Well, he wasn't a trained operative, and he never would be. It had been her mistake to think otherwise, a mistake to think any of them were more than the rankest amateurs. But she realized what they needed now was reassurance, her word this was only a minor mishap. They needed some spine, something that seemed at the moment to be in short supply.

She said in her usual cool, clipped voice, "It wasn't only you who failed, Jasmine. Our assessment of Cummings, and of the risks involved, was flawed. I thought with a quick injection, a forty-five-minute drive in Jasmine's SUV, we could get Cummings here without a problem, and believe me, once we had him here, we'd have convinced him there was no choice but to cooperate. I'll admit, it wasn't the best-laid plan, but what's done is done.

"We have a situation now, and we need to deal with it. Be thankful you weren't arrested, Jasmine, and fortunately your injuries aren't too severe."

Jasmine Palumbo lightly rubbed her arm through the sling. At least it no longer ached like a rotting tooth with the oxycodone on board. She pulled back her shoulders, ready to accept the ax belonged on her own neck. "Still, I blew it, Athena, it's all on me. I was watching from my car, on my way around the block, expecting to pick up Craig and Cricket holding up Cummings between them. I couldn't believe it when I saw Cummings running full tilt out of the alley, no sign of Craig and Cricket, and I panicked, thought I could head him off. I didn't see the light turn red, didn't see the Volvo until it was too late. I was told the woman driving the Volvo is recovering in Washington Memorial, a concussion the worst of her injuries."

She swallowed. "To make it worse, it wasn't just any driver, like some student or housewife from Foggy Bottom. No, the woman I hit is FBI Special Agent Lacey Sherlock, the one who topped the media charts several months ago. Believe me, I was public enemy number one to the cops at the Daly Building. They were ready to throw me in solitary and flush the key."

Athena shook her head, laughed. "Jasmine, regardless of your screwup, it could have been worse. You could be the one in the hospital. Good news is it's been ruled an accident and you're not in jail. Nor do they have a way to connect you with Justice Cummings. Of course, we have no way of knowing where Cummings is, and the last word from Artemis is the CIA doesn't know, either. She's got people out looking for him. If she finds him first, she'll make sure he's brought to us, as originally planned. He's either badly hurt, or he's hiding—from everyone, the CIA included. It would be best if we were the ones to find him, people."

Cricket Washburn said, "We know Cummings has to be hurt. We saw his blood smeared all over the FBI agent's windshield." She plowed nervous fingers through her short spikes of blood-red hair. "I don't know how he was able to move quickly enough to hide from Craig and me, but he managed it. On the opposite street, we saw a few blood spots, but they soon disappeared. We searched the whole neighborhood, but we couldn't find him."

Jasmine said, "At least Craig and Cricket had their sunglasses and hats on the whole time. They won't be identified, even if the police check the cams in the area, try to run facial recognition."

Craig said, "I've tracked down the names of some of the people Cummings knows, but we haven't found out yet where his wife and children are. No one's been in his house in Fairfax. Ellie's there, as you know, waiting for him to show."

Jasmine said, "If he's gone to ground, maybe to some cheap motel where he paid with cash, we have almost no hope of finding him. Not unless he goes home to fix himself up, pack some clothes, and take off again. Then Ellie will see him."

Craig said, "I might be able to access the traffic cams, at least see what direction Cummings went after he was thrown off the hood, but that's not going to be much help. The truth is, Athena, unlike the CIA, we don't have the resources to find him."

"Well, if the CIA finds him first, Artemis will contact me immediately," Athena said. "In any case, Cummings has no idea who you are or why you chased him. If he surfaces on his own and goes, say, to the police, then it'll be a different ball game. Oh yes, Artemis has arranged quite a surprise for him at the CIA."

Jasmine, twisted with guilt, said, "Still, it's my fault we don't have Cummings. I'm very sorry, Athena."

Athena said, "Jasmine, Craig, Cricket, it's over and done. Let's review how things stand." She held up one finger. "Metro knows your name, Jasmine, and that you're employed at the Bexholt Group. You and I will go over how to handle the police or anyone else who interviews you. I know someone will, given you struck an FBI agent. They might check your background from all the way back in Hannibal, Missouri, to find out your father's in prison for bank robbery. But you can tell them you're estranged from both your parents, and none of that will matter. Your record is clean, you have a professional degree and a responsible job." A second finger went up. "We need to be prepared for either Metro or the FBI identifying Justice Cummings as the man who left his blood on the scene. The FBI will jump on it with both feet if they find out he's CIA, a federal employee who was being chased by parties unknown, and is now missing." She leaned forward, splayed her palms on the table in front of her. "If they do, Artemis will see to it they get nowhere near finding out what he was working on. That we can't allow. No way will they find out we are already negotiating a price with the Russians about your smart wall, Craig, and that Cummings is missing because he stumbled across it. Obviously, if I'm wrong, if Artemis is wrong, it could be the end."

Athena paused. "So, we all need to go to work as usual, continue as if nothing has happened. This will still turn out all right. Artemis has her end covered. We'll continue to look for Justice Cummings.

"There is something else you should know. Agent Sherlock's husband is Agent Dillon Savich. Yes, I see you've heard of him as well as his famous wife. He's very high-profile and he's smart. We cannot underestimate him. You can count on his being interested because his wife was involved in the accident. We have to be careful he gets nothing.

"People, there's no turning back now, for any of us. We need to have everything in place by Monday."

When Athena was alone again, she walked to the window and looked out over the rolling Virginia hills, dotted with houses and thick copses of maple and oak. She took several deep breaths. It would be all right. She was not going to let this man Cummings destroy what she'd planned so meticulously. She'd waited too long, and she'd worked too hard. It would be all right.

8

"I came as soon as I could," said Dr. Emanuel Hicks as he walked into Sherlock's private room on the third floor, her new home after being released from the ICU. He was a renowned psychiatrist and hypnotist, and an Elvis impersonator in his spare time. Luckily for the FBI, he was very happy to be in his tenth year at Quantico. He was tall and skinny as a parking meter, had to wear a pillow strapped to his belly when he was Elvis.

"I appreciate your coming," Savich said, and shook his hand.

"I'm very sorry about all this, Savich." Dr. Hicks looked at Sherlock, sound asleep and breathing easily. He took in the small bandage on her head, her pallor, her stillness. She looked peaceful, but he knew the Sherlock he liked and admired was locked away. As for Savich, Dr. Hicks knew how hard it had to be for him to keep it together. Were it his own wife, Mary, lying there with no clue who he was, who *she* was, he would be scared spitless. But Savich needed him as a professional now, not as a longtime friend. He said in a practiced, calm voice, "Since I have privileges here, I was able to look at her chart before I came in. You know there are excellent neurologists and psychiatrists on staff here at Washington Memorial."

"I don't know any of them," Savich said simply. "I know and trust you. She's been asleep about an hour now since they gave her a sedative to keep her still in the MRI." He paused, then, "As I told you, Dr. Hicks, she doesn't know who I am, who Sean is, who she is. I hope I handled it right. We talked and I saw glimpses of her, but she doesn't remember anything." He stared toward her, wanting to touch her, to kiss her, to tell her to come back to him. He felt impotent and hated it. "I'm a stranger to her. The doctors didn't find that out, I did."

Dr. Hicks laid his hand lightly on Savich's shoulder. "I grant you they could have done a more thorough neurological exam a few hours earlier, but they were more concerned with her physical injuries, with making sure her life wasn't in danger. It was good you were with her when she realized she didn't remember, rather than someone who didn't know her."

"That's one of the reasons I asked you here. I wanted a friend as well as a doctor to see her, someone who knows who she is. What she is."

"I understand, and it's my pleasure. Now I need to wake her up and do an exam, and frankly, it would be better if I'm alone with her. When I'm done, I'll go check the MRI, and then we can talk. She's going to recover from this, Savich, I can promise you that already."

Those few steady words calmed him. But Savich didn't want to leave. Dr. Hicks looked after him as he finally walked out of the room, his steps lagging, then he looked back at Sherlock. Dr. Hicks couldn't imagine how it felt for her to have no memory of self or anyone else close. He touched his fingers to her wrist. The pulse was steady and slow. Good. He pushed up his glasses and bent over her, lightly shook her awake.

Twenty minutes later, Dr. Hicks walked into the family waiting room. Savich was on his feet in a flash. "How is she? What do you think, Dr. Hicks?"

Dr. Hicks said quickly as he walked into the room, "She'll be all right, Savich, as I told you. When I woke her, she didn't know me, of course, but she accepted I was a doctor and a friend, and cooperated nicely with her neurological exam."

Dr. Loomis said from the doorway, "You must be Dr. Hicks." Both men turned to see her walk in, her hand outstretched. "Your fame precedes you,

Doctor. I'm Dr. Andrea Loomis. Sorry I couldn't catch up with you earlier. And Agent Savich," she added, nodding to him, "insisted he wanted to call you in."

Dr. Hicks smiled and shook her hand. "I've had a chance to examine your patient and take a look at the MRI you ordered for her. I don't know if you've reviewed it, but it appears to be normal."

"Yes, it is." Dr. Loomis looked over at Savich and said to both men, "As Agent Savich knows, we were quite surprised by how long her amnesia has lasted following the accident. She suffered a bad concussion, of course, lost consciousness at the scene for quite some time."

Dr. Hicks nodded. "Agent Savich has seen severe concussions in the course of his work, and many of the consequences. I was telling him Agent Sherlock and I spoke while I was examining her. I am very pleased to say her anterograde memory is intact, so she's not confused, and she's not complaining of dizziness or nausea at the moment. Her balance is good. She seems to be left only with headaches, and of course, the post-traumatic amnesia." He said to Savich, "I know she is your wife and that makes this very hard, but believe me, Savich, Sherlock will remember, her brain will sort itself out again and recover naturally."

"When?"

"In my experience, all the concussion symptoms usually resolve in a few days or a week.

Perhaps as soon as she wakes up again. Sometimes it takes longer for the headaches to go away, but they become less severe. Do you agree, Dr. Loomis?"

Dr. Loomis said, "Yes, we all hope and expect her amnesia will clear up soon. I know concussions are scary, and it's impossible to predict exactly what will happen and when, but both Dr. Hicks and I are optimistic, and so should you be, Agent Savich. It's a matter now of your being patient—difficult, I know, but there's really no choice. She will heal when she heals, and there's nothing we can do to speed it up."

Savich said, "It wasn't only that she didn't know who I was or who our son, Sean, was or that she is an FBI agent. I even showed her a video. She didn't recognize herself. You both think she'll recover from all that?"

Dr. Hicks said, "Yes, I do, even though that kind of amnesia is unusual. I expect she'll recall the narrative of her life first of all. She might remember the distant past before last week. It might take even longer for her brain to lift the fog surrounding the accident, or perhaps she never will remember what happened. As Dr. Loomis said, we have to be patient." He laid his hand on Savich's shoulder. "You know all this. I'm sure you've spent much of the day reading about it."

Dr. Loomis's cell sounded loud and sharp. She looked down, frowned, and said quickly, "In fact,

Agent Savich, there is little reason for us to keep her in the hospital much longer. She can return home with you so long as you're there to watch her yourself. I would be surprised if any of her symptoms worsen at this point, but if anything concerns you, bring her back to the hospital. I'm being paged to the ER. I'm sure I'll see you later. Dr. Hicks, a pleasure to meet you."

When they were alone again, Dr. Hicks said, "All right, Savich, talk to me, tell me why I'm here. I know you're worried about her, but that's not all of it."

"All right, if she still can't remember when she wakes up, could you hypnotize her, help her piece her memory back together?"

"Ah, naturally, you would try to sort through every possibility. I could hypnotize her, of course, but I'd much rather err on the side of caution than plow ahead and try to attempt to force her to reconnect with all those memories before she's ready. There's a chance I might do harm. Her brain's been badly shaken, shocked, and though the scans show no visible damage, there is damage nonetheless, too subtle to be seen. The brain is a wonder we barely understand, and it will repair itself without me. So let's leave hypnosis off the table for the time being. We need to give her time, Savich, we need to simply wait."

9

GAFFER'S RIDGE, VIRGINIA
WEDNESDAY AFTERNOON

Carson DeSilva didn't want to die. When she awoke, her head pounding from the blow, she found herself propped up against a concrete wall. She couldn't move. She held still until the pain began to lessen. She saw her legs were straight out in front of her, her ankles bound tight with duct tape. Her arms were pulled behind her, her wrists taped together, with more duct tape, she imagined, and her hands and arms ached fiercely. She forgot the pain in her head as terror from the attack froze her. Her world shrank, turned dark, and she knew deep down more violence was coming. She would die, simply die, and no one would know. She was only twenty-eight years old and she'd be dead, simply gone. Forever. Despair slammed deep. She wanted to scream, howl at the unfairness of it all, but she didn't have enough spit in her mouth to make it worthwhile.

Stop it, Carson! You can figure this out, you always do. Don't you dare give up or I'll disown you. It was her mother's voice, usually bright as Christmas bells, but now it was low and persistent in her ear—*Carson, get yourself together, handle the head pain, you can do this, get yourself free, you have no choice.*

And so she forced herself to take deep breaths to slow down her galloping heart. She could handle the pain in her head. She could do this. Her mother was right, she had no choice.

She looked around. She was in a basement—a concrete floor, naked pipes overhead, an ancient refrigerator against the far wall maybe fifteen feet away, beside the dozen wooden stairs leading up into shadows. Luckily, he'd left on the naked low-watt light bulb overhead or she'd be blind as well as duct-taped. She saw a stainless steel double sink on the far wall, shelves above it lined with cobwebbed mason jars and defunct tools, other odds and ends of past life. She shuddered at the thought of what was in those decades-old jars. There was nothing else, only the overwhelming stench of stale dead air. Was this basement in his house? The man who'd attacked her? Yes, she knew who'd struck her down, even though he'd bashed her on the back of the head. It was the same man she'd heard thinking at her loud and clear as she'd stood in front of Ellerby's Market, two bags of groceries in her arms. She'd nearly stumbled over with the shock. It was amazing, impossible, that it was happening again right in front of a grocery store in the small Southern town of Gaffer's Ridge, of all places. She'd only just arrived from New York for a few days' stay to interview a Nobel Prize–winning scientist for her employer, Aquino Communications. It was as if he'd been inside her head, or she inside his. It had happened to her a few times before, always unbidden, always unexpected. She'd gasped with shock at what she'd heard, and whispered, *"The girls—what did you do to the girls?"* He'd have had to be blind not to see her alarm, deaf not to have heard her words.

He'd stood frozen, staring at her. *"What?* What did you say?"

Her brain kicked back in with red danger signals and she'd managed to say in a level voice, "Nothing, nothing important," and hurried away. He hadn't tried to stop her. Had he believed he'd spoken aloud and she'd heard him? Carson had piled the groceries into her Toyota and driven to her small rental cottage four blocks away, hardly knowing whether to believe what had happened. But she had to believe it, the impossible had happened, she'd actually heard him thinking. She had to put the groceries away, then she'd go to the sheriff—and tell him what? *I heard this man thinking about the three teenage girls I'd already heard were missing, and he thought their names and remembered Amy had died hard?* Would the sheriff lock her up for disturbing his peace? Haul her off to the psych ward of the local hospital? And what if the man hadn't killed those missing girls? But then how would he know Amy had died hard?

She had to go to the sheriff—no choice, let the chips fall where they may. But he'd been faster. Now she was here, duct-taped and tied against the cold wall of a basement, probably in his house, and this wretched, beyond-weird nightmare could end up killing her.

Her mom shouted at her again: *Get it together, you're being pathetic. For heaven's sake, stop feeling sorry for yourself and figure out how to get yourself free so you can fight. You've got to get out of here before he comes back, because when he does, if you're still tied up, he'll kill you, maybe rape you for good measure. He knows you somehow guessed he was the one who disappeared those three teenagers, probably killed them.*

He'd thought all their names—Heather, Latisha, Amy—and he'd seen them, like perfect snapshots, and she'd seen them, too, lying motionless on beds, unmoving, blankets covering them. He'd thought of them only by their first names and, oddly, with the tenderness of a lover.

Seeing the three girls was horrible, she couldn't bear it. Carson thought she'd pass out from the soul-grinding fear if she didn't get hold of herself.

She had to push herself away from the three girls' faces.

Carson Estevao DeSilva, use your brain.

She took a deep breath, sucked in the stale air. First, how to get out of duct tape, the modern world's holy of holies for repairing everything under the sun? She worked her wrists, her ankles, but there was no play at all. She leaned her head back against the rough, cold concrete, closed her eyes, and thought. It hit her square between the eyes. She saw herself when she was ten years old, doing a forward flip off the balance beam, and, wonder of wonders, nailing the landing. She'd been a limber little monkey until a torn labrum had ended it. It was so long ago, but she still worked out hard, but—*no, no negative thoughts*—she could try. No, more than that, she would do it. She was her mother's daughter.

Carson inchwormed herself away from the wall. When at last she was flat on her back, she lifted her hips and brought her bound hands beneath her butt. Now for the hard part. Limber was one thing, contortion was quite another. She still couldn't reach the duct tape on her ankles.

She heard something, froze. Was he back? Would he open the basement door and come down any second? Would he kill her, like he had the three teenage girls? With his bare hands around her neck, choking her until she was gone? Carson didn't move, barely breathed, listened for all she was worth.

Nothing more. Maybe it was only the house settling, but still she knew she had to hurry. She dug in her heels and lifted her hips again as high as she could. She gritted her teeth, ignored the awful cramping in her legs, and twisted and bent until finally she managed to work her legs through her arms. She was breathing hard, clammy with sweat, but she'd done it, her arms were in front of her. She lay there panting, thanking her mom for the gymnastics lessons and her hard-nosed coach. She'd swear she heard her mom shout, *Move!*

Carson went to work with her teeth, tugging gently on the duct tape seam at her wrists. Slowly, she peeled it back further and further. He'd wrapped the tape three times, he wasn't taking any chances. When the last layer fell to the concrete floor, she shook her numb hands, then rubbed them against each other like Lady Macbeth, until finally she felt pins and needles. Now for the duct tape on her ankles. As her hands strengthened, she was able to work faster. She couldn't believe it, but finally, she was free. She slowly stood up, nearly collapsed, and leaned against the wall, breathing hard. She stamped her feet, leaned down to rub her calf muscles, willing the feeling to come back.

She had no idea how long she'd been unconscious, if it was still day or early evening. He'd gotten to her so fast. She'd turned to open her front door, thinking she was going to call her mom first, tell her what she'd seen and ask her advice—and felt a sudden flash of pain on the back of her head where he'd struck her. She touched the lump with light fingers, and thankfully didn't feel any blood. She ignored her head and continued to work until she could feel her feet, and her legs were waking up. She walked a few steps, weaved a bit, and stamped her feet again against the concrete floor. Finally, she was good to go.

She wanted to run up the basement stairs and keep running, but he could be up there, waiting. She'd been concentrating so hard on contorting her body to get free, it was possible she hadn't heard him. Or maybe the basement was sound-proofed. But if he was up there, wouldn't she hear him thinking, like before? She didn't know. Maybe it had been only a onetime thing. Better not blast out of the basement, not without a weapon. She saw an old jagged water pipe overhead, looking nearly ready to fall down. She jumped for it, but it was too high. She found an ancient three-legged stool in the corner next to the refrigerator and pushed it over beneath the pipe. Now, the trick would be not to fall off the stool and break her leg. Slowly, carefully, she managed to balance on it. When one of the stool legs started to wobble, she grabbed the pipe with both hands, steadied herself, gently eased her weight back onto the stool, got her balance again. She saw the jagged pipe was screwed into another pipe, so all she had to do was twist it free. Easier said than done, even with the pipes looking older than her grandmother. She didn't have much leverage, but she was strong. She twisted again, but no movement. She pulled off her T-shirt, wrapped it around her hands, and tried again. Finally, she felt the pipe give.

She twisted until it fell off into her hands. It was more than a foot long with edges sharp enough to plunge into a man's throat. How had the pipe gotten so rusted? It didn't matter. She carefully climbed off the stool, pulled her filthy T-shirt back over her head.

She had her weapon, and even better, she had hope. She filled herself with cold rage at this monster who'd brought her here to kill her, who'd probably murdered three teenage girls. She began to climb the basement stairs, listened to the old wooden boards creak beneath her weight, loud as the crack of a fired gun to her ears, too loud.

She walked to the top of the stairs, tried the door handle. To her relief, it wasn't locked. Slowly, she pushed the door open. And froze.

"Well, hello there. What a surprise to see you up here."

10

GAFFER'S RIDGE

Special Agent Griffin Hammersmith wanted some sleep after the best Reuben sandwich he'd ever had in his life—well, the best since the Reubens Jenny had made him back when they were students at Penn State years before.

Maybe he'd take a nap after he walked back to Jenny and Aimée Rose's house on Cedar Lane, but for now, walking and breathing in the sweet clean mountain air felt fine. He took a look back at Jenny's Café, always bulging with tourists in the summer and with locals year-round, from 7:00 a.m. when the doors opened. She closed at 2:00 p.m. most days because, she'd told him, she and Aimée Rose wanted a life and she didn't want to lose her chef in training, Alfredo Smith, who wouldn't deal well alone with a dinner crowd. Griffin stretched tired muscles, rubbed his neck, saw Kyler Park ahead, and thought about curling up and zoning out on one of the wooden benches. It had been a long drive from Washington, but he'd made it in under four hours even with all the traffic, thanks to his new Range Rover with enough horses under the hood to start a ranch. Savich had insisted both he and Ruth take some time off after they'd closed a particularly bizarre case with the small police department in Picken's Creek, Arkansas, an hour south of Little Rock. It had been a hairy case—he'd nearly lost Ruth to a crazed, drug-addled teenager, but they'd managed to take him down. He wondered if she'd told her husband, Sheriff Dix Noble of Maestro, Virginia, and her two teenage stepsons about what had happened. Knowing Ruth, she probably hadn't.

"Hey, gorgeous! Wait up, you forgot your tablet."

Griffin turned to see Jenny's partner in business and in life, Aimée Rose, striding through a knot of happy tourists toward him, his red-leather-covered tablet in her outstretched hand. He'd been showing them shots of his new condo in Capitol Hill. Aimée Rose's very feminine, soft name made him smile, since she was tougher than a heat-seeking missile, brooked no nonsense, and was as full of dreams as Jenny. She loved to tease and she loved to dance, and with a skillet and a stove, she'd whip up an omelet to make the angels weep. She was dressed in skinny jeans and a light blue T-shirt that said GIVE ME LIBERTY OR GIVE ME SPAGHETTI, neither rhyme nor reason to that, but it got a laugh.

Aimée Rose gave him his tablet, patted his face, sighed dramatically, and placed her hand over her heart. "It's started, Griffin. Already two local girls and a tourist want to know your name and cell number. I told them, alas, you were gay. Maybe I was trying too hard not to smirk, so I don't think they believed me. Since you'll be with me and Jenny most of the time, we should keep you safe from roving packs of teenagers, or worse, the cougars. But beware of anything moving in the shadows, one might jump out and tackle you, take you right down."

Griffin rolled his eyes. "Yeah, right."

Aimée Rose punched his arm. "Jenny told me you never even noticed, even in college when girls would nearly throw themselves in front of you." She gave a laugh. He knew she was having fun, so he twirled a nonexistent mustache and said, "How about I start a line, lead them right into the café."

She laughed again. "Nice offer, but really, we don't need any more business. Be back to the house by seven, okay? Jenny's making you her never-to-be-forgotten spaghetti and meatballs and crunchy garlic toast you said is as good as Agent Sherlock's."

She gave him a wave over her shoulder as she strode away, a tall woman with a long step. Jenny had told him Aimée Rose never merely walked, she always moved fast, as if she had to put out a fire.

He'd known Jenny Wiley since their freshman year at Penn State, and Aimée Rose Wallberger since their senior year when she'd transferred to Penn State from Dartmouth. It had been love at first sight for Jenny and Aimée Rose.

He walked through Kyler Park, forced himself not to sit on one of the welcoming wooden benches and take a snooze. He stopped to watch kids playing tag football, and walked again with couples strolling along the paths shaded by cedars and walnut trees and the ever-present oaks, basked in the colors and scents of wildly blooming flowers. He came out on Winchester, stopped and admired the row of Victorian houses lining the street, and as always, the backdrop of the towering Appalachians in the distance. Gaffer's Ridge had been turning into a picture-perfect postcard town for hikers, campers, and antiques shoppers alike over the past fifteen years. B&Bs sprang up every month, according to Jenny, and small boutiques had nearly filled up the three-block downtown. Local merchants were happy to welcome the tourists, upgrading their shops and stores to take advantage. The town was picturesque, hilly, and thick with oaks, chestnuts, and a dozen white wooden church steeples spearing into the blue sky. There was even talk about founding a community college. And now they had Jenny's Café. Jenny joked she and Aimée Rose were getting so rich, even with their shortened hours, they might have to retire at thirty-five and move to the South of France. Griffin imagined they'd grow tired of fun and games after six months and open a restaurant in Cannes.

He saw Beauregard's Antiques across from the park and thought of Anna, her face clear in his mind, how she loved eighteenth-century English antiques, hiking, and white-water rafting as much as she enjoyed bringing down drug dealers. She would have enjoyed Gaffer's Ridge, but now she'd never see it. She'd left for Seattle months ago. She was no longer his fiancée, she'd broken it off. *My mom has Alzheimer's. I've got to go to her. I'm transferring to the DEA, Seattle division. I'm sorry, Griffin, sorry for everything.*

He knew her mother's condition wasn't all her breakup with him was about. He knew what the real reason was, and there was nothing he could do about it. And he'd tried. Over the months, Anna, his tough-as-nails DEA agent, had become over-the-top jealous of any woman who came within ten feet of him or even nodded to him. She hadn't believed his promises that he loved her and no one else, and their arguments had escalated. She'd never accused him of sleeping around on her, but Anna was convinced that one of the many women she saw with him would be the first one. She questioned him constantly about the women agents in the CAU—all three of them married, one of them, Lucy, now pregnant, but none of that seemed to matter.

When she'd left for Dulles with three suitcases and a cat carrier, a moving van set to follow her with all her superbly wrapped antiques to Mercer Island, Griffin had realized he felt sad but also relieved. There would be no more accusations, no more questioning the women he'd spoken to or met that day, no more inevitable fights, no more dreading to go home. He felt like a weight had been lifted off his shoulders. And now, standing across from an antiques shop, he realized he didn't miss her. To be honest, it was Monk he missed, her three-year-old soft-as-silk Himalayan who slept on his chest, purring loud as a tank.

He'd walked all over Washington for weeks, looking for a place to call home, and finally found what he wanted, a condo on Capitol Hill, three blocks from Garfield Park, where he could run every morning.

Now, six months later, he'd driven to Gaffer's Ridge for a short vacation, to rest and relax, and maybe nap away some afternoons. Griffin began to walk again, tried not to torture himself anymore with Anna's jealousy—*That face of yours—women line up to get close to you, and don't try to tell me you don't love it.*

He closed his eyes a moment, shut out her angry voice. No, he was going to think about the furniture he wanted for his still nearly empty condo, nothing fancy, since the down payment had taken a sizable bite out of his savings. He turned onto Berger Lane, running northeast toward the mountains. The houses thinned out, the yards grew bigger, and everywhere, trees crowded in—he recognized some poplars, elms, cypresses, and oaks, but there were so many more he didn't recognize, vivid greens against the blue sky. And there were the mountains, always the mountains, in the background. He didn't see a single B&B or tourist this far from the center of Gaffer's Ridge. The day was warm, the sun bright overhead. He filled his lungs with the clean sweet air, no trace of a car or factory.

HE'S HERE! THE PIPE, I HAVE THE PIPE. I'LL FIGHT!

Griffin jerked around at the woman's panicked voice. What? She had a pipe? He realized her yell hadn't come from the street, it was almost as if she were next to him, but where was she? He looked at the ancient gray clapboard house to his left. He saw no sign of anyone, no car in the driveway.

He waited, but she didn't yell anything more. Had he imagined her voice? He had been tired when he'd arrived in Gaffer's Ridge, both Ruth and him worn to the bone from their case. No, he hadn't imagined anything. He ran to the front door of the gray clapboard house, pounded on it. He didn't hear anyone. Or anything. He turned on the sagging wooden porch, stared toward the yellow-painted cottage catty-corner from him on the other side of the road.

11

Carson gripped the pipe two-handed in front of her like a gun and stared at the man who stared back at her. He looked surprised, and mad. He also looked strong, too strong for her to take him down. He was wearing the same clothes he'd worn when she'd first seen him earlier—a black T-shirt that showed off his pecs, tight worn jeans, scuffed boots. His hair was the color of a wheat field, his eyes, oddly, a dark brown beneath thick brows.

He looked from the jagged-edged pipe in her hands to her face. To her shock and fury, he grinned at her. "Now, isn't this a surprise? If I'd been a minute later, you would have managed to walk right out the front door. And here I thought

I had you all tied up, ready to send out in a big FedEx box. Where'd you get that pipe? And how did you get free of the duct tape?"

His surprise had morphed into a sneer, into dismissal of her as any kind of threat to him. She waved the pipe in front of her to keep him back, matched his smirk, laced her voice with derision. "You didn't do a very good job of it, did you? I'll even teach you about duct tape later, if you're not too stupid to understand."

Anger pulsed hot in his eyes, then died, and he shrugged. "It doesn't matter now, does it? So you managed to get free, but you still weren't fast enough. Or maybe you were planning to wait for me behind the front door? Catch me with that pipe when I came through? Doesn't matter, but I really do want to know how you got free of the duct tape."

Keep him off-balance, keep talking until you figure something out. She gave him back a shrug. "Call me Houdini. You want to try to take me again? Come on, give it your best shot. This time you can't get me from behind, this time you have to face me." She waved the pipe at him. "Did you hit Heather, Amy, and Latisha on the back of the head like you did me, you puking coward? Did you tie them up in your basement with your almighty duct tape? Did you rape them, torture them before you killed them? You know what you are? A pathetic monster who needs to be put down."

She saw disbelieving panic score his face, felt waves of shock pouring off him. "Shut up or I'll wring your skinny neck. I'm not a monster! I'm not a coward."

She managed a full-bodied sneer. "I said 'puking coward.'"

He was breathing hard now, shaking his head back and forth. "How do you know about Heather, Latisha, and Amy?"

"I'm psychic."

WHERE ARE YOU? TALK TO ME!

A man's voice blasted in her head. Carson froze. She couldn't believe it, was it happening again? Was it possible someone had heard her thoughts as she'd heard this man's? No, impossible, she was losing it. No one could have heard her yelling at herself in her head. Still, she focused inward and screamed again in her mind.

I'M IN A HOUSE. I HAVE TO BE CLOSE! HELP! HE'S HERE!

He stared at her, mouth open, and she saw stark fear in his eyes. Had she looked different somehow? Had it frightened him?

His hands balled into fists. He shouted at her, "What you're doing—stop it! You're not psychic, you stupid woman. Only my— Never mind. No, it's all make-believe, like zombies and vampires. What you are is a liar—you've got to be." He stared at the waving, jagged pipe she was tossing back and forth, and looked suddenly uncertain. He said slowly, "Your face when you saw me—it was like you were looking into me. How do you know the girls' names? You heard someone say something, didn't you? Some gossip about them? But when you looked at me—*how did you know?*" His voice had climbed an octave. She felt roiling waves of fear and confusion pouring off him, and rage. There was no doubt in her mind, he wanted her gone, he wanted her never to have seen his face. He wanted her dead.

HE'S LOSING IT—HELP ME!

She waited, praying, but she heard nothing. Had she really heard a man's voice? Or had she dreamed it up because she was so scared? She had to face it, there was no one to help her. It was up to her and her pipe. She couldn't get past him to the front door. He'd be on her in an instant.

He whirled around to the front door, then jerked back. "Why are you looking like that? Like you're looking at someone, talking to someone, but not really? There's no one there! What are you doing?"

"I was talking to someone close, someone on his way to help me." She saw it clearly—he was afraid. In that instant, he was afraid of her. She had to use his fear against him or she didn't stand a chance. She said with an eerie singsong voice, "Who am I talking to? How could I be talking to anyone? You said it yourself, no one's there and I'm a liar."

He screamed, "Who's there, who's close?" He

whirled around again, panting now, but no one was there. He was shaking when he turned back to her. "No, you're a liar, you've got to be a liar. You're not psychic."

"Of course I am. It's like calling 911. Help's on the way. When he gets here I'll tell him how pleased you were with yourself, picturing Heather and Amy and Latisha in your sick brain, reliving those moments when they were crying and help-less. Did it give you a rush, you worthless creep?"

Had she pushed him too hard? He was stand-ing four feet from her as if frozen. Then he yelled, "There's no such thing as real psychics! There's only those crap TV shows with make-believe psychics who are supposed to see everything, except they never see the face or the name of the killer. It's stupid. Tell me how you knew. Did that stupid old gossip, Turley Maybeck, say something to you? Nosy old biddy. She's always hated me."

She realized in that moment he did believe in psychics and that was why he was so afraid. "So Turley Maybeck knows what you are, too? She knows you're a murderer?"

"Shut up! I looked in that tote bag of yours. Your driver's license says you're from New York. Your name's Carson DeSilva. And you've got a stupid middle name—Estevao. I haven't ever seen you before. Why are you here? Tell me!"

Maybe she could rattle him so badly she'd have a chance at taking him down. It was obvious he didn't know what to do. He had no weapon, he looked panicked, confused.

She called up the monotone singsong voice again, near a whisper this time. "I saw everything. I heard what you were thinking when I faced you standing on the steps of the market. You were spewing your thoughts to me so loud a deaf dog could hear you."

"No, I didn't. I never do that. I'm not supposed to." He broke off, stared at her. "But I saw something in your face, heard you whisper. You couldn't have been inside my head, you're not special, you're lying."

She was now sure he knew all about psychics. He was shaking his head, back and forth, and she felt the fear crawling through him, fear of old faded memories, of a blurred face, a woman, and with her a young girl, both seated cross-legged on sand at a lake, by a brightly burning fire, and the woman was speaking words that made no sense. Carson felt his shock—oily and cold—and she felt his fear of that woman, of what he couldn't understand. Alarm was flooding through him now because he was afraid of her, too, afraid because she wasn't helpless like those three girls he'd killed. Carson wasn't pleading with him not to kill her.

He whispered, "You couldn't see what I was thinking, you couldn't. Tell me who told you or I'll kill you right now."

12

—

Carson kept waving the pipe back and forth in front of him like a metronome, kept her voice hypnotic. "I told you, moron, you were shouting your thoughts so loud anyone listening could have heard you. I saw the three girls, heard you say their names, like you were their boyfriend, their lover. And isn't that stupid, since you're way too old for three young girls? How old were they? Fifteen, sixteen? Young girls, teenagers, so guess what that makes you?"

"Shut your stupid mouth!"

"Maybe you dreamed about dating them? Now that's a joke, isn't it? Or maybe you wanted revenge on their parents?" She dropped her voice to a whisper. "Or are you insane?"

"Shut up!" Rage poured off him like roiling black clouds crashing into each other. He was shaking his head wildly back and forth. "This shouldn't be happening. I don't understand how you saw what you saw, how you got out of the duct tape—but I can't let you leave here. And you're too old, way too old."

"Yeah, I'm too old. There's no chance I could make the junior high cheerleading squad. Hey, I've never met a pedophile before." Had she gone too far?

"I'm not a pedophile!" To her horror, he casually pulled a gun from the back of his jeans.

A GUN! HE'S GOT A GUN!

Griffin approached the yellow cottage, took in the new black Chevy SUV in the driveway, and ran flat out. He didn't have his Glock, but it didn't matter. He burst into the house, and this time he yelled aloud, "Down! Now!"

Carson hit the floor.

Griffin whipped around to the man. "Put down the gun! FBI!" The man fired wildly toward Carson and kept firing even as she rolled, his bullets slamming into the front wall and blasting wooden shards from the front door. Griffin's leg was already in motion. His foot struck the man's wrist and he heard the bone snap. The gun went flying. The man screamed in pain and rage, grabbed his hand, then tried to dive after the gun spinning away from him across the old oak floor.

Carson rolled up on her feet and leaped at him. She brought the pipe down hard on top of his head. He shuddered, slowly sank to his knees, fell onto his side, and then his back, his arms flung out. He tried to raise his hand to his head, moaning, and stared up at her. Then his eyes closed and his head lolled to the side.

Carson stood over him, panting, the pipe still held at the ready. Her hands were shaking, she was trembling so badly, but it didn't matter, she really wanted to hit him again.

Griffin said in his calm FBI voice, "No, that's enough. You did good. But no more." Griffin went down on his knees beside the man, pressed his fingers to his throat. He looked up at her. "There's a pulse." He rose, smiled at her, stuck out his hand. "Agent Griffin Hammersmith, FBI. That was quite a whack you gave him. Your timing was perfect." Griffin picked up the gun. It was a German Walther, an older model but still a fine weapon, a deadly weapon.

Carson straightened, drew a deep steadying breath. Still holding the pipe in her right hand, she shook his hand with her left. She said simply, "I can't believe you actually heard me. And you did. And isn't that crazy? I'm Carson DeSilva. Thank you. That kick, it was amazing, so fast, so hard you broke his wrist." She'd bulleted out her words, but now he watched her take another big breath, get a grip on herself. She said slowly,

"I didn't want to die, and—then there you were, loud in my mind. I didn't believe it, couldn't believe it. You're really an FBI agent? Here, in Gaffer's Ridge? In this neighborhood? At the exact moment I was sure he was going to kill me? And you heard me, you really heard me?"

Griffin laid his hand on her arm. "Yes, I heard you, loud and clear, loud enough to break my ear-drums. Listen, you did great, Carson. Everything's under control now." Griffin felt her excitement and her adrenaline blast at him. At least she wasn't going into shock. He said easily, "I've heard the name Carson before, but well, that was a Carson on my high school football team. You're the first female Carson I've met. Sorry it took me so long to find you, but at first I couldn't tell where you were."

"Since I didn't know, I couldn't tell you." She drew a deep breath. "I think he murdered those three missing young girls. He was going to murder me, too."

Jenny had mentioned the three missing teen-agers to him. He stared at Carson. "I want to hear all about this while we're waiting for the police." Griffin took the man's wallet out of his pants, pulled out his driver's license. He took his cell out of his shirt pocket and dialed 911.

She touched his arm. "Can't you wait to call them? Maybe he'll die if we wait a while. He really is a monster, it'd save the taxpayers a lot of money."

Griffin was charmed, but alas. "Not a bad idea, but sorry, FBI, remember? And I really don't like to kill people, even passively. Let's go out on the front porch. We'll leave the door open so we can see him if he moves."

An older woman with a smoker's voice and a drawl so thick he could barely understand her answered on the third ring. "Yeah, so talk to me and make it fast and to the point. I'm busy. What's your problem?"

That sounded friendly. "I'm Special Agent Griffin Hammersmith, FBI. I have an injured man at 237 Berger Lane. His name is Rafer Bodine."

He heard a quick indrawn breath, then, "Rafer, you say? How injured? How did you come to be with him? Did you hurt him?"

13

"He's had a blow to the head, and appears to have a broken wrist. You need to send the sheriff, along with an ambulance. We have reason to believe Rafer Bodine is responsible for the disappearance and probable murder of the three teenage girls who are missing from the area, and the kidnapping and attempted murder of Ms. Carson DeSilva."

There was a whoosh of breath, and the voice turned hard. "Don't you lie to me, boy. That's a crock, and you know it. You, an FBI special agent? Carson DeSilva? Now that surely sounds like a made-up name to me. What sort of game you playing, calling 911? Interrupting the smooth march of the law? Interrupting my afternoon tea?"

"Bodine needs an ambulance and the sheriff,"

Griffin said again, his voice calm, patient, though he wished he could reach through his cell, grab the idiot woman around her neck, and tell her to stop smoking.

"All right, all right, boy. You can bet the sheriff will be there when he can, he's gotta come from Wilfred Hoag's place, had to go over and pull the old codger out from under his tractor, the paramedics are with him. This isn't good, isn't good at all. Don't you move a muscle and believe me, you'd better pray Rafer don't die from that blow to the head. You got that?"

"I surely do." Griffin stared at his cell as he punched off. "That was odd. I guess Rafer is a popular guy. Or maybe the 911 operator is his mother."

Carson swallowed a laugh. A laugh—amazing. She shrugged. "It's a small town. Sure the 911 operator knows him, but I bet everybody knows everybody. Gotta say, though, what you told her sounds pretty unbelievable."

Griffin went back inside to see Rafer Bodine still lying on his back, awake now, pressing his right wrist against his chest, gasping out curses. Griffin went outside to Carson. "Why don't you tell me what happened while we wait for the police?"

They sat side by side on the porch in view of the open front door, Griffin silent to give her time to settle, waiting for her to tell him what had happened. She'd nearly died, and that was a lot for anyone to take in. He felt a hot breeze on his face, heard oak tree branches rustle and a bird he couldn't identify let out a mellow chirp.

Carson drew a deep breath, flattened her palms on her legs. "I thought it was all up to me, either put up or die. But you were there on the street and you heard I was in trouble, I mean you didn't hear a noise—you heard me. Several times I believe I've heard what someone was thinking, but nothing like this, not someone actually hearing me. Again, Agent Hammersmith, thank you. Has this ever happened to you before?"

He nodded. He thought of Savich. "Yes, but it's not something I plan to talk about to the sheriff. Let's compare notes later. What's important now is the man lying inside the front door, cursing us nonstop. Rafer Bodine looks like a good old boy, doesn't he? Macho, tough, beard scruff, the kind who enjoys kicking butt, no provocation needed. Now tell me what happened before the sheriff gets here."

She began with her hearing Bodine's thoughts outside the market, then waking up in the basement, and finally freeing herself because, thankfully, she'd been a trained gymnast. "—I dropped to the floor when you blasted through the front door and shouted at me." She stopped, drew a deep breath. "Again, thank you."

He smiled, marveled at her. "You must have scared him spitless when you looked at him that first time. He knew you were dangerous to him, he understood what you'd seen and heard. The missing teenagers—Jenny said one had disappeared every month for the past three months, too many to be runaways. She said a lot of people were beginning to talk about a serial killer, the parents with teenage girls were keeping a tight rein on them, never letting them out alone, particularly here in Gaffer's Ridge. This was where the first teenager, Heather Forrester, lived, then up and gone, no clues." He took her hand. "I do believe you might have caught a Serial."

"Is that how you say it? It makes it sound even scarier. You think the Gaffer's Ridge mayor will give us medals?" She paused, took another deep breath, looked back to see Rafer Bodine still clutching his broken wrist to his chest, moaning louder now, in between curses. "It's true I freaked him out, but even so, he's still too big, too strong. In the end I wouldn't have had a chance, even if he hadn't pulled out that gun."

Griffin said, "You can put the pipe down now. You don't need to worry, I've got his gun." He nodded at the Walther stuffed into his belt.

"Sorry, not yet," and she gripped the pipe even tighter. "I can't, not until he's behind bars, then I'll consider letting it go."

He smiled at her, shook his head. "I guess I don't blame you." And for the first time he really looked at her. Before, he'd seen a tall woman in skinny jeans and a dirty white T-shirt, sneakers on her feet. But now he really saw her. Even with her streaked blond hair falling out of a ratty ponytail and smudges of dirt on her face, he saw her chiseled features fit together perfectly, set off by a stubborn chin that probably helped people look past all the rest and take her seriously. Her chin, and the fierce intelligence in her hazel eyes. He watched her push back a hank of hair, hook it behind her ear, where it didn't stay. She pulled the ponytail free, efficiently gathered all the hair together, and rubber-banded it again.

"Are you a model?"

She jerked, grinned at him like a loon, showing perfect white teeth. "No, goodness, a model? Me? As in walking a runway? I'd trip over my feet, not to mention I like to eat too much. I'm a writer for *American Democracy*, a monthly news and business magazine. I'm here in Gaffer's Ridge to do an interview with a Nobel Prize laureate." She paused a moment, stared at him. "I see you're not bad-looking yourself. And here you are an FBI agent. What are you doing in town?"

"I'm supposed to be taking a rest. Well, I guess that's over."

"You want to tell me how you found me? How I could hear you in my head, answering me? Do you do that a lot?"

"Nah. Hearing what other people are thinking rarely happens to me. My opinion? I think most people have natural shields. Occasionally, I'll pick up flashes of anger, or joy, but rarely anything specific. With this guy, Rafer, all I picked up from him was fear and confusion. You definitely spooked him."

Griffin turned to look back at Rafer Bodine. Blood snaked slowly down the side of his face from the blow from the pipe. How long would it take the paramedics and the sheriff to get here?

"He's trying to get up." Carson jumped to her feet and ran back into the house, Griffin on her heels. Bodine had managed to lurch up, and Carson smashed her foot down on his chest. "Stay down, you monster! The sheriff and the paramedics might not want me kicking you again."

Rafer spat at her, not a good idea because he was on his back and the spit landed on his chin. He tried again to pull himself up. "You bitch, you caved in my head!"

"Yeah, I did, and if you keep moving around I'll do my best to kick your ribs into your back, sheriff or no sheriff. I only wish I had on my boots, not these wimpy sneakers, then you'd be smart to say your prayers. Don't forget, there's always the pipe," and she waved it at him.

"You'll regret this, both of you will."

"Yeah, yeah, blah, blah," Carson said.

He stared at her out of pain-glazed dark eyes, licked his lips. "You were just like my granny and my ma. Granny's dead, last year, finally, but Ma, she gets that same weird, distant stare like she's looking into someone's head or talking to someone who's not there. It's not right. I didn't mean to do it, I didn't mean to! It's evil, you're evil!"

Griffin said, "What, exactly, didn't you mean to do?"

14

"Nothing, I didn't mean anything."

Carson went down on her haunches beside him, but not too close, a full-blown sneer on her mouth. "You say I'm evil? Now, that's a joke, Rafer, coming from you. You murdered three young girls, and you would have murdered me, too. I'm tempted, really tempted, to whack you in the face with my trusty pipe and send you to hell, where you belong."

"I didn't kill anybody!"

"Then what do you mean you didn't mean to do it? Answer Agent Hammersmith. Do what exactly?"

"Nothing!"

"Don't hit him again," Griffin said. "I want

him to think about spending the rest of his miserable life in prison."

She cocked her head up at him, slowly rose. "Well, I've heard it said Red Onion prison is lovely this time of year. Or maybe Pennington Gap, another vacation spot."

Griffin was pleased. There didn't seem to be a wimpy bone in this woman's body. Rafer Bodine didn't react. He was quiet now, eyeing the pipe, which meant he wasn't completely stupid. Griffin said from behind her, "Let's go back outside and wait. Mr. Bodine knows enough now to lie still and keep quiet."

When they were seated on the edge of the porch again, Griffin said, "I've never heard of anyone being able to bring their bound wrists out from under their butt. You'll have to give me a demonstration."

"Maybe," she said, but Griffin could see that was the last thing she ever wanted to do again. He said, "You're sure you never saw Bodine before this morning when you came out of the grocery store?"

She shook her head, but didn't answer because they heard the sirens. They watched a white Crown Vic with SHERIFF on the side in bright green letters careen into the driveway a half minute later, an ambulance on its rear bumper. Griffin gave her his hand and together they stood watching.

Two more sheriff's cars pulled up onto the grass, even though there was no reason to, this far out of town. A deputy got out of each car, and they waited, their hands on their guns, until the sheriff hauled himself out of his Crown Vic and raised his hand.

The sheriff was a big man, in his midfifties, had probably been good-looking before he'd gained too much weight. Still, he had a thick head of salt-and-pepper hair. To Griffin's surprise, he drew his gun, shouted, "Don't you two move a whisker! Marv, Haddy, get inside and see to Rafer! I'll take care of these two."

The paramedics ran past Carson and Griffin into the house.

The sheriff waited silently until one of them called out from the front door, "Rafer's going to be all right, Sheriff, banged on the head, but he's awake, cursing a blue streak. Looks like it's true, he has a broken wrist. We'll get him splinted and bandaged up a little, get him over to community hospital."

"Good, good," the sheriff called. "I'll be in in a minute."

Griffin said, "I told your 911 operator about his injuries and that he was all right."

Carson said, "Agent Hammersmith didn't have any handcuffs with him, Sheriff, but we've been keeping an eye on him."

The sheriff stopped six feet from them, his gun, a Beretta, still aimed at Griffin's chest. "Fayreen said you claim to be an FBI special agent, said she didn't believe you for a second. What's this all about? You'd better pray Rafer's not bad hurt. All right, tell me right now who you are and why you hurt Rafer."

Griffin started to pull his creds out of his pants pocket when the sheriff shouted, "Easy! You be careful, hear, or I'll have to shoot you."

Griffin pulled out his creds with two fingers, held them up. "Sheriff, I'm Special Agent Griffin Hammersmith, FBI. This is Carson DeSilva from New York. We're both visitors to Gaffer's Ridge. Like I said, this man—Rafer Bodine—is dangerous. He kidnapped Ms. DeSilva, held her prisoner in his basement. I suggest you warn the paramedics."

The sheriff walked to within six inches of Griffin's face, grabbed his creds, backed away, his Beretta still aimed at him, even though Carson was the one holding the pipe.

"You got a gun tucked into your pants. Hand it over, boy, butt first."

Griffin handed the Walther to the sheriff, who eyed it. "This here looks like Rafer's gun."

"Yes, it is. I took it from him."

A thick eyebrow went up. "We'll get to that. First things first." He studied Griffin's creds, waved them in his face. "Looks to me like this could be a fake ID. You can be sure I'll check it out thoroughly." He stuck Griffin's creds in his pocket. "I've never seen a lawman who looks like you do, more like you could be here to scam some old ladies out of their pensions, and sure enough, that would make you good at forging credentials. I can't see you putting Rafer down, you don't look tough enough." The sheriff stepped back, lowered his Beretta, but kept it in his hand. "Listen to me, boy, no way Rafer would hurt our paramedics, known Marv and Haddy all his life. Now, I'm sheriff of Gaffer's Ridge, been protecting this town for over twenty years."

"Sheriff." Griffin gave him a curt nod.

Carson said, "Agent Hammersmith looks tough enough to me, Sheriff. You should have seen him kick Rafer Bodine's gun out of his hand. I would have cheered if I wasn't so scared."

The sheriff snorted. "He took Rafer by surprise, that's all. Rafer'd break his pretty face in a fair fight."

Griffin studied the big man, his eyes so pale a blue they were nearly silver, his thick eyebrows salt-and-pepper like his hair. He was seriously out of shape, the buttons pulling over his big belly, his holster fastened to a big leather belt. He looked familiar, and why was that?

The sheriff flipped a large hand toward the cottage. "This here is Rafer's house, used to be his uncle Cauly's, but he got himself killed jumping his Harley over too many trucks, so now it's Rafer's. I don't know either of you. I don't know why you're even here in my town, claiming Rafer was going to kill you, claiming he killed those three missing teenagers. We all know Rafer better than that." He turned to Carson and spat at the ground in front of her sneakers. "And you, a woman, you claim you hit him on the head with a pipe? All right, this fellow here said your name's Carson DeSilva."

"Yes."

The sheriff shrugged. "Well, not your fault, then, is it? No accounting for what names people pin on their kids. First, I want to know why you're making all these bizarre accusations. Fayreen told me everything the boy here said, and I don't mind telling you, she was pretty upset by it all."

Carson looked him dead in the eye, knowing there was no way she could tell him the truth. He'd lock her up for sure. "I overheard him talking to himself, muttering about the three young girls. He even said their names, and said 'Amy died hard.' Then he looked up, realized I'd overheard him. He caught me by surprise at the house I'm renting, before I could get to you at the sheriff's station, he hit me on the back of the head, brought me here, and tied me up in his basement. I got loose and managed to hit him on the head with this pipe when Agent Hammersmith kicked the gun out of his hand. It all sounds pretty straightforward, Sheriff, but let me tell you, it was close. Rafer Bodine was planning to kill me, and he would have killed Agent Hammersmith if he'd been able."

To her astonishment, the sheriff laughed, then spat again, this time barely missing her sneaker. "Well now, missy, that's some story you're spinning. You're actually claiming Rafer's a murderer, killed those poor missing girls? And you're claiming he was going to kill you because you overheard him talking to himself, out loud? That's crazy, makes no sense at all."

This wasn't going well. Carson had to keep going, no choice. "Yes, I think he killed the missing girls, he said their names—Heather, Amy, and Latisha. As I told you, he knew I'd overheard him muttering about them, and that's why he was going to kill me, too."

The sheriff looked at her like she was a bug to be stepped on.

"You know what, girl? I agree with Fayreen. That's some wild tale. It's time to introduce myself. I'm Sheriff Booker Bodine."

15

Carson couldn't get her brain around it. "You're saying you're this madman's father?"

The sheriff raised his Beretta, then slowly lowered it again. "Watch your mouth, missy. Rafer's my brother Quint's only son, a fine boy, born and raised in Gaffer's Ridge, not a crazy bone in his body. He runs his pa's lumber mill and hires out to take tourists rafting on the Snake River. He's a prominent citizen of Gaffer's Ridge, you might say. It's not helping you calling him names like that. Who knows what people will think? I do know his granny would be royally pissed if she were still alive. You're lucky she passed to the hereafter last April."

Carson said, "If his granny were alive, I bet

she'd be royally pissed. I mean, her own grandson tying up women in his basement."

The sheriff continued studying them, slowly shook his head. "That isn't what I meant, missy, and you know it. What you said, that's plain nonsense. You'd best shut your mouth. Listen to me, Rafer's the apple of his parents' eye, he's his pa's heir."

His hand stroked the gun as he spoke. Griffin held very still. This overweight man with the hard face and silver eyes looked ready to shoot them dead right there, if he could get away with it. He wondered who in the family had enough power in this town to get this man elected sheriff. But the sheriff he was, and it wouldn't help if Griffin told him what he thought of him. The fact was, he and Carson were the strangers here, and Rafer Bodine was this man's nephew. It was time to try for conciliation. He squeezed Carson's hand.

To his surprise, she gave a slight nod, and said immediately, "I know this must be difficult for you, Sheriff, and I'm very sorry." She stuck out her hand. "Actually, I'm Dr. Carson DeSilva, and I've only been in Gaffer's Ridge a day and a half. But what I told you is the truth."

She held out her hand, but he didn't take it. He eyed her up and down. "Are you a real doctor, or one of those make-believe doctors who spout crap nobody cares about?"

She gave him a lovely smile. "Make-believe, spouting crap."

He frowned at her. "Don't smart-mouth me, missy. I figured as much. Don't think you can get me to fall for your wiles, no matter how pretty you are, dirty or not. You expect me to believe a stranger talking nonsense about an upstanding Gaffer's Ridge citizen like Rafer? And where's your proof? All I'm hearing is your word, and it don't sound believable at all. I mean, Rafer's been friends with Buddy Forrester since they were boys. He's known Heather her whole life. You believe he'd kidnap his friend's kid sister? It's crazy.

"And why'd you come here anyway? Are you one of those tree huggers who like to come here to hike and camp? Or are you here looking to buy one of those fancy old furniture pieces my wife is always looking at?"

"You mean antiques?"

"What else could I mean? You look like one of those people here for that old crap. Shysters back in Richmond clean out their attics, spin all sorts of tales, and dump it here for you nut heads to go crazy over. Stuff's junk, you ask me."

"No, Sheriff, I'm not here to go antiquing."

"All right, both of you tell me why you're here in Gaffer's Ridge."

Carson said, "I'm here to interview Dr. Alek Kuchar. I was planning to contact him tomorrow."

The sheriff arched a thick brow. "You mean that old buzzard scientist hunkered down in my mountains near Pilchard's Bluff? That Alek Kuchar?"

"Yes, that Alek Kuchar."

"Maybe he used to be famous, but why would anyone with half a brain want to interview that weird old gobspit now?"

Carson went stiff all over. Was he trying to rile her, get her to give him an excuse to take her in?

When she finally spoke, she managed to keep her voice calm and smooth. "Actually, Sheriff, Dr. Alek Kuchar is a brilliant physicist, a Nobel Prize laureate, and, I might add, beloved for his philanthropy. He lost his wife last year and moved here to recover from his grief."

The sheriff grunted. "Maybe he was well known in that pissant country he comes from, whichever one that is. He isn't here, that's for sure. But enough of that. Let's get to it before I go in and check on Rafer. Why don't we start by you handing over that pipe?"

Carson gave it to him. He hefted it in his hand, studied the jagged edges. "You claim you hit Rafer on the head with this pipe? And this fellow here was with you?"

Time to mix truth with lies. "I was very lucky Agent Hammersmith was nearby. He heard me yell from inside the house, and came in through the front door. He kicked the gun out of Rafer's hand. Then I hit Rafer on the head with the pipe."

"Sounds to me like you two are the attackers, this being Rafer's house, not yours. And all these wild accusations about Rafer wanting to kill you, about him killing those missing girls? What do you think he's going to say about that? Neither of you move, you hear me?" He called out to the two deputies still standing at attention some twenty feet behind him, "Brewster, Jewel, keep an eye on these two, don't shoot them if you don't have to. I'm going to speak to Rafer." Then he walked straight at Carson. She instinctively moved to let him pass and watched him walk into the house.

Carson hugged herself. She said, her voice bewildered, "I don't get it. You're a fake FBI agent? I'm a make-believe doctor? Griffin, what's wrong with him? I mean, he's the frigging sheriff. I know he's Rafer Bodine's uncle, and this has to be a big shock to him, but he's still the sheriff, he's the law here. He has to act, doesn't he?"

Griffin looked after him. "I've learned a psychopath can hide in plain sight and no one ever suspects him. But you know what? His family always knows. Always. And his uncle? Maybe Sheriff Bodine doesn't realize what Rafer is. Sorry, Carson, but we're not going to be able to count on the sheriff. Let me make a call before he comes out again." Griffin slipped his cell out of his pocket, pressed in Savich's number.

Carson whispered, "What is this, an alternate universe? Do you think he's going to toss us in Gaffer's Ridge's hoosegow?"

That's exactly what Griffin thought.

"Savich."

"Griffin. I'm in Gaffer's Ridge. I've got a

big problem here with the local sheriff. He's not accepting my credentials and I'm with a civilian, a woman, I can't protect. It's not looking good. I need your help. Can you come?"

"On a scale of one to ten, how bad?"

"Might be inching up to a ten."

A pause. "I'll try to be there tomorrow, if I can." Another slight pause, then, "Sherlock's been in a car accident. She'll be fine, but I can't leave her yet. Tell me what happened, Griffin."

Griffin saw the sheriff coming out of the house, staring toward them. He talked fast until the sheriff roared, "You give me that cell phone!"

"Is that the sheriff? Okay, do as he says, hang up. I'll make some calls, see if I can throw my weight around. I hope you didn't do anything to make me regret it?"

"Nope, I was a Good Samaritan."

"Enough, boy!" The sheriff grabbed the cell and both Carson and Griffin could see he was weighing whether or not to smash it. He didn't. He slipped it in his shirt pocket.

Marv and Haddy came out of the house, the larger Haddy with Rafer Bodine slung over his shoulder in a fireman's carry, his head and wrist bandaged. Weren't they worried about other injuries? Weren't they trained? They watched Marv lean into the ambulance and slide out a gurney. Rafer was quiet, maybe from drugs—or maybe because of a warning from the sheriff, his uncle?

16

The ambulance careened backward out of the driveway, tires screeching, and took off down the street with its sirens blaring, even though Griffin hadn't seen a car pass by in the neighborhood.

Sheriff Bodine motioned to his deputies. Both men stepped close, flanking. They were watchful, obviously on edge. The sheriff said, "Time for you two to come to the station and take another stab at talking your way out of attacking my nephew. I'm going to take your statements and Rafer's, too, once he's able. If I were you I'd call a lawyer. We have two in town, but one of them is a female and she only does wills and such. Not a real lawyer, like missy here isn't a real doctor. The other's a man and he knows what's what. My dispatcher and 911 operator, Fayreen, can give you their numbers.

"Rafer was in a lot of pain from the blows you gave him, but the gist is he said this was a home invasion, pure and simple." He eyed Carson. "Rafer's young, appreciates a pretty young woman, especially a looker like you. He lets you into his house without a qualm. Maybe you intended to scam him, but he realizes you're not for real and so you called your pretty boyfriend here to pound him? More believable than that tale you tried to sell me. Spiteful, I'd call it.

"As for you, *Agent* Hammersmith, I'll be checking out those credentials of yours when we get to the station. I suspect they're forged and I'll have the pleasure of sending you to jail. Are the two of you going to come willingly or shall I cuff you?" He shot a look at Deputy Jewel, whose name was embroidered over his left front shirt pocket. Jewel was young, sweating and scared, the hand holding his gun visibly shaking. *Settle down*, Griffin thought. *No need to panic.* To his surprise, the young deputy seemed to relax a bit. The other deputy, Brewster, was older, with sparse gray hair, thin lips, and hard eyes. Griffin pegged him for a bully, probably violent when he drank too much. This was the man to watch.

Sheriff Bodine said, "So where's your cars?"

Carson said, "My car's back at my rental house."

"And your car?"

Griffin said, "It's parked at Jenny Wiley's house."

"Now that's interesting, but not important right this minute. So both of you walked here, didn't want people to notice a car, right?"

Carson said, "Look in the basement, Sheriff. You'll find the duct tape Rafer used to tape my wrists and ankles."

"Every man has duct tape in his basement." Sheriff Bodine looked at Griffin. "You gonna say he knocked you out, too? Dragged you here to his house to kill you? Duct-taped you, too?"

"Dr. DeSilva was a gymnast, got her hands under her butt, that's how she got free. Me? I was taking a walk, enjoying the park and the town. I heard her yell for help and came running. I've been in Gaffer's Ridge less than a day, Sheriff, here to visit friends."

"Yeah? What friends?"

"I'm staying with Jennifer Wiley and Aimée Rose Wallberger, longtime friends from college. They own Jenny's Café. As I told you, I left my car at their house."

He eyed Griffin up and down, gave a loud bray of laughter. "Not that either of those two *ladies* would give you a second look, no matter if you look like a fricking movie star. Let's go. Jewel, you and Brewster follow close. Be alert."

Griffin said, "Sheriff, what about Rafer Bodine? Are you detaining him? Is one of your deputies going to follow the ambulance and guard him?"

The sheriff stared at Griffin, slowly shook his head. "You don't need to worry about Rafer. Quint's boy isn't going anywhere. I told you, Gaffer's Ridge is his home, our family's been here for generations. This is where he conducts his business. There's no place for him to go." He flicked a look at Carson. "It's you two who are the strangers who could run, not Rafer, you two accusing my own blood of murder."

Carson couldn't help it, she said, louder this time, "Sheriff, I told you, he's very probably a serial killer, no matter he's your nephew."

Sheriff Bodine gave her a disgusted look. "The two of you get in the back seat. Now." Once he'd pushed them inside, the sheriff shut the door. There was a mesh partition dividing the front from the back. They heard the door locks click. The sheriff eased his bulk into the front seat, pulled out his cell, pressed a number. "Fayreen, I'm bringing in those two strangers." He listened, then said, "Yep, the one who called you declaring he was an FBI agent. What they're claiming will make your eyes bug out. Get ahold of Judge Pinder. He's gotta be the one to decide what to do with these two." He punched off, slipped the cell back into his pocket.

Carson said to Griffin, "I know what Alice must have felt, but Gaffer's Ridge isn't any Wonderland."

17

Nikki Bexholt tied her white obi belt over her white gi, and slipped on her zori sandals. She looked up when she saw Claire Farriger, her practice partner for the past four years, walk in and change into her own gi, fasten her black belt, and retrieve her ebony wooden bokken sword from her locker. Nikki's own white belt was her constant reminder she still had a great deal to learn before she could make the leap to black. Claire was her superior and her mentor in aikido, and at forty-six, she was in her prime. Nikki tried not to feel jealous of her, a constant battle. Claire had accomplished so much. She'd been a highly successful CIA field operative, spoke fluent Russian and Serbian, and had hop-scotched her way up the CIA ladder to become the assistant director of the CIA for Europe and Eurasia analysis, second-in-command, reporting to the director of the CIA. She'd confided to Nikki she wouldn't be allowed to become director, all politics, she'd said. It was the same for Nikki—she knew she'd never be allowed to take the reins of her family's business, the Bexholt Group. It wasn't about politics, it was about her vile father, who believed a woman couldn't do the job. It was that shared fact, being unjustly cut off from what they each richly deserved, that had brought them together, and in the end set everything else in motion. Nikki picked up her own red oak bokken, the Japanese wooden sword they used for training, balanced it in her hand. She wanted ebony, like Claire's.

The only other woman in the locker room finished changing, nodded to them, and left.

Nikki waited for the door to close, then said, "Any word on Cummings?"

Claire shook her head, walked to the mirror, pulled out her comb, and smoothed her hair back into a ponytail, difficult since it was still too short. "I don't know why I ever cut it," she said. "I should have left it longer like yours."

"Claire, what about Cummings? You're not any closer to finding him, are you?" She paused, her voice hardened. "You promise you'd tell me if your people get close, right? Remember our deal. He does not die. You get him to me somehow, and I'll talk him around."

Claire laughed. "And you're fully prepared to inform him of the consequences if he doesn't do what you tell him? That there are files in his computer the CIA will believe he copied and sold? That he'll be charged with espionage?"

"Yes," Nikki said, her voice steady. "I think he'll cooperate once I make him realize he has only two choices: leave the country a rich man or spend most of his life in federal prison. I don't like it, but at least he'll be alive. And eventually his family can join him.

"You've told me his wife wasn't happy with his earnings at the CIA. When you bottom-line it, going along with us is the best solution for him."

Claire looked at her, slowly shook her head. "You think everyone can be bought?"

"In my experience in the business world, yes. You swear you won't kill him?"

Claire shrugged, slipped an elastic band around her stub of a tail, and slowly turned. "Yes, I'll keep to our agreement, for now. And no, we haven't found Cummings yet, and yes, you'll get him when we do. One thing, Nikki—excuse me if I don't call you Athena—you know, of course, Agent Sherlock's husband is Dillon Savich."

"Yes, I know. And I've cautioned my people."

"The FBI doesn't yet know whose blood was on her windshield, so we're ahead of them." Claire paused, sighed, rubbed her palm over her fore-head. "So much brouhaha about Cummings, it's exhausting." She'd already told Besserman, Justice Cummings's supervisor, to go in-depth into his computer. They'd find the little surprise she'd left for them. It would make it harder to turn Cummings over to Nikki, but so be it. The whole idea of leaving Cummings alive was nonsense. But she couldn't forget, Nikki wasn't like her.

"Has something happened you haven't told me about, Claire?"

"I'm just getting tired of Lance. Talk about exhausting. He's gotten too possessive. I'll have to clip his wings."

They were in the middle of a crisis that could turn on a dime and destroy all their plans, their futures, and Claire was concerned about her longtime lover, her personal assistant at the CIA, getting too possessive? Nikki could only stare at her. She remembered the first time they'd met. The CIA had accepted her father's bid for installing a specialized firewall for a CIA project and Nikki had wangled it so she was put in charge, not her brother. She remembered she'd been fascinated with Claire, never tiring of hearing about her assignments in the field, the constant risk of being discovered, the knowledge that death could land on your shoulder at any time. They'd gotten close, and Claire had shown her risks could be taken for the right rewards. When an engineer who worked for her at Bexholt, Dr. Craig Cook, made the breakthrough with his smart wall, her mind bloomed in directions she hadn't known she was capable of. She'd thought immediately of Claire, and they'd worked out their plans together after a session at the dojo. Nikki had the means, and Claire the experience and the contacts. All they had to do was convince Dr. Cook and a few Bexholt employees to join them.

Nikki said, astonished, "You want to clip Lance's wings? Now? You told me you needed him to do jobs for you, Claire, told me he would do anything you ask him to do. So let him be possessive for a while longer. Set him out to find Cummings."

Claire straightened, tightened her obi, and nodded. "Yes, you're right, of course. I've already set him on finding Cummings. How are the preparations going at Redemption House? Are we ready for the bankers, ready to start making money on Monday?"

"Yes, but I do worry about Savich. I can't see him giving up if he gets involved, not when his wife nearly lost her life in that accident."

Claire walked to Nikki, took her face between her palms. "Little sister, it will be all right. I'll eventually have to let him come see me, and I'll handle him. No question. We're almost there, so stop your worrying, and let's go get warmed up."

18

GAFFER'S RIDGE
WEDNESDAY AFTERNOON

The Gaffer's Ridge sheriff's station on High Moon Street had gotten a paint job and a new roof the previous year to show the tourists the townspeople cared about law and order. But the station was still what it was—a 1950s box-style concrete building, with two skinny windows in the front.

Sheriff Bodine and his deputies marched Griffin and Carson through an empty hall with benches along the walls to a high counter presiding over a central room behind it, topped with an ancient computer, a printer, and two telephones. No one was there.

The sheriff stopped and whispered, "Fayreen, get in here."

The young deputy, Jewel, said behind them, "Fayreen's got mother-in-law ears. She can hear a guy chewing tobacco in the men's room."

Brewster nudged him with an elbow. "Shut up, Jewel."

Sure enough, a heavyset older woman came barreling out of a door opposite them. She was about the same age as the sheriff, and wore a deputy's brown uniform a size too small, the buttons pulling over her healthy bosom. Her gray-brown hair hung straight and long, nearly to the middle of her back, and she even wore a woven band holding it back. It was a hippie look that stopped there. She wore a boatload of 1970s-style makeup, from fire-engine-red lipstick to black eyeliner. "Sorry, Booker, had to use the facilities and refresh my lipstick." She said toward Griffin and Carson, "I'm Fayreen Hertle, I'm the dispatcher here, and the sheriff's right hand." She pointed a finger at Griffin. "And you're the critter who hurt Rafer, aren't you?"

Sheriff Bodine said, "He sure is, and the girl here helped him. What do you think, Fayreen? Bonnie and Clyde pretending to be real folk?"

She looked Griffin and Carson up and down. "He's eye candy, for sure, and this one? Even looking like a mutt, dirty and her hair all squirrelly, you can see she's hot. How'd she get so dirty? Did she try to escape?"

"Nah, she's got claims against Rafer, says she's

dirty because he had her duct-taped in his basement."

Fayreen snorted. "Yeah, right. As if anyone would believe Rafer would hurt a fly. Listen, Booker, there's a man holding on the telephone. He refused to hang up, says he's Special Agent Dillon Savich of the FBI and he wants to talk to you." She shot a sneer at Griffin. "Says he's this fellow's boss, wants to clear up any confusion you might have."

"Yeah, well, he could be this guy's cousin, for all we know. Tell him I don't have the time. He can leave his number if he likes." He sounded quite pleased with himself.

"You got it. My pleasure," and Fayreen marched to the big front desk, picked up one of the phones, and turned away. Griffin wanted to grab the phone but knew he couldn't. When she hung up, the sheriff said, "Call Tommy Denmark, tell him Judge Pinder's out fishing for bass on Commodore Lake and I need him here as a witness."

"On it, Booker."

The sheriff led them back down the short hallway and into a nicely furnished office at the back of the building with two large windows overlooking the parking lot. Beyond the dusty lot sprawled the ever-present mountains, blurred with low-lying haze. There was a big antique partner's desk with two chairs facing it and a beautiful mahogany credenza behind it, one photo on top showing the sheriff, a striking-looking older woman, and a young man and woman, big smiles on their faces. A rich black leather sofa sat against the far wall, a coffee table with a dozen perfectly aligned magazines on top, flanked by four matching leather chairs. There wasn't a coffee stain anywhere. The AC was set on freezing, and felt wonderful.

Carson said, "I thought you didn't appreciate antiques, Sheriff." She nodded toward the impressive desk.

The sheriff grunted and eased his bulk down into an oversize black leather chair that creaked beneath his weight, motioned them to the two chairs in front of the desk. The deputies, Jewel and Brewster, stood at attention by the door, arms crossed, trying to look intimidating. Griffin wanted to laugh but didn't.

"My wife," the sheriff said. "She told me a fancy office impresses the tourists. The mayor agreed but said I had to pay for it myself." He fell silent, gave them the rheumy eye, began tapping his blunt fingers against the desktop. Once again, he said in a whisper, "Fayreen, get in here."

A moment later, the door opened and she was there, a notebook and pen in her hand. "I'm here, Booker, ready to take down what these two jokers have to say. When I called Tommy, I think I woke him from a nap, but he was excited about coming over to be a witness for your interview. Well, I hear him already. I'll bring him in now, all right, Booker?"

The sheriff nodded, resumed tapping his heavy fingers on the desktop. They waited in silence.

Fayreen came back into the room followed by a vampire-pale older man, so pale Griffin wondered at first if it was makeup. He had longish ink-black hair with no gray, and dark-rimmed glasses. Of all things, in this blistering heat, he was wearing a black suit, white shirt, and black bow tie. Why didn't he fall over with heatstroke? Griffin wondered if he was the local mortician.

Booker rose. "Come in, Tommy. I want you to listen to these two, they've got a story to make you shake your head in wonder at the strangeness of human nature." He didn't introduce Carson or Griffin, simply waited until Mr. Vampire and Fayreen sat down on the leather sofa, the fat cushions whooshing under their weight. Finally, he said, "This is Mr. Thomas Denmark, one of Gaffer's Ridge's councilmen. He's going to be our witness."

Griffin started to open his mouth, knew in his gut it wasn't a good idea, and kept quiet. He wished he'd somehow fallen into a bizarre dream, but knew it wasn't a dream, and he wouldn't be jerking awake anytime soon.

The sheriff said, "I know Fayreen didn't have

time to tell you much, Tommy, but we're holding these two for questioning and we're about to interview them. I wanted to be sure you folks over at city hall know we're doing everything by the book until Judge Pinder gets back." He turned to Carson. "Now, missy, I want you to tell Fayreen and Councilman Denmark here all about what you're saying happened today. Take your time, so Fayreen can write it all down. Be clear and don't get hysterical." He added to Griffin, "When she's done, we'll get to you, boy."

The words *occasionally telepathic* wouldn't ever cross her lips, not in this town—well, not in any town, not even with her aunt Casey or any of Carson's friends. Carson cleared her throat, ready to go through it all again, with only slight adjustments. "I was coming out of the market—"

"Which market?" Fayreen said. "We got two, you know. Booker always says to get all the specifics you can think of, so's we can check out what you tell us."

"Ellerby's Market," Carson said, and looked more closely at Fayreen Hertle, realized she looked a bit like the sheriff. A cousin, a sister? Did the sheriff's family run Gaffer's Ridge? Great, just great.

"All right, get on with it." The sheriff began tapping his large fingers against the desktop again.

Carson stared at those heavy tapping fingers and said, "He was coming toward me—Rafer

Bodine, although I didn't know his name at the time. He didn't see me. His head was down and he was talking to himself, but still, I heard him clearly. He was talking about the three missing teenage girls." She ignored the looks of patent disbelief and plowed ahead. She told them how he'd even said their names—Heather, Amy, and Latisha—how he'd hit her on the head. She spoke slowly, fluently, describing how she'd escaped and how she'd managed to unscrew the jagged pipe and gone upstairs to find him there, back to kill her. "I screamed bloody murder. That's when Agent Hammersmith came crashing through the open front door and kicked the gun out of his hand, and I ran at Rafer and hit him on the head with the pipe."

19

Three faces stared at her, more with disdain now than disbelief, as if Carson hadn't even managed to spin them a good tale. No Oscar for her. She stared back. She'd told them all of it calmly, in a clear timeline. She wondered how they'd be looking at her, what they'd say, if she'd told them the truth, all of it. Without doubt they'd cart her away to the funny farm. She waited. She became aware Mr. Vampire was staring fixedly at her, like she could be a tasty blood donor. She looked at his thin fingers, nails too long for a man, and tried not to shudder. He really was white as new sheets, and his black-framed glasses magnified his eyes. He cleared his throat, but didn't smile. So he wouldn't show his fangs? He said in a surprisingly deep voice, "Ms. DeSilva, you're Portuguese, is that right?"

"What? No, I'm an American. And like most Americans, my ancestors came from elsewhere. In my case, my dad's parents came from Portugal, thus my Portuguese last name. And I'm *Dr.* DeSilva. Are you from Copenhagen, Mr. Denmark?"

He blinked at her, gave her a rictus of a smile. "You're very fast, Ms.—Dr.—DeSilva. Are you a medical doctor or an academic doctor?"

"My field is journalism. I'm thinking about writing an article on police behavior in small towns. What do you think?"

"We're not here for your sarcastic comments, missy," the sheriff said.

Mr. Vampire only blinked again, a habit, she supposed, and gave her another pained smile. Again, he didn't open his mouth. Fangs were a real possibility. He gave a small nod, said to the sheriff, "May I question her, Booker?"

"Feel free, Tommy."

His magnified eyes focused on her. "Tell me why you came to Gaffer's Ridge, Dr. DeSilva."

"I came to interview Dr. Alek Kuchar, a Nobel Prize–winning physicist. Perhaps you've heard of him?"

"Oh yes, he's something of a hermit, I understand. Now, let's speak more about what you think you heard Mr. Rafer Bodine saying as he was walking toward you. It was more like mumbling, wouldn't you say? Not really speaking aloud, not in the middle of Gaffer's Ridge, in a public place, in front of a grocery store, actually confessing to kidnapping? Don't you think that sounds a bit hard to believe, Dr. DeSilva? A bit far-fetched?"

Well, yes, actually. She kept her voice smooth and controlled. "Nonetheless, he was talking to himself, not mumbling, and I heard him clearly."

Was Councilman Denmark looking at her neck? Was she getting hysterical?

"And you said you and Special Agent Hammersmith had never met until you screamed for help, when, you claim, Rafer Bodine drew a gun on you?"

"Yes."

Griffin saw the pulse in her neck pounding. He said, "Let me add when I ran into the house, she was already poised to take a run at him with the pipe, to save herself."

Calm, calm. "I would have tried, yes. But if Agent Hammersmith hadn't come, there's no question in my mind Rafer Bodine would have shot me, probably buried me with the three girls."

"All right, boy, since you think it's your turn, you can start at the beginning, too. Like with who you claim to be."

When Griffin finished repeating who he was and what had happened, he said, "Maybe you can get Rafer to tell you where he buried the girls.

Even if he doesn't, you have enough, Sheriff, to investigate him thoroughly. You can find out if Rafer Bodine has an alibi for the dates each of the girls went missing. You can ask if anyone ever saw any of the girls with him, whether he knew them. You can begin at his house, in his backyard. If you don't have access to a cadaver dog, the FBI can help. The FBI can also assist you in the investigation, with all our resources.

"Even now, that house is open, unsecured. Rafer could have some of his friends destroying important evidence right now. I'm sorry this man's your nephew, but you are the sheriff, and that means you can't ignore the facts."

"Your facts," the sheriff said, sitting forward, his hands now fists, "they're ridiculous accusations, nothing more. And she's not claiming he actually admitted to murdering the girls, are you, missy?"

"No, not in so many words."

The sheriff smiled, said to Griffin, "Ah, I'm beginning to see what might have happened here. She was obviously in Rafer's house with him, don't know exactly why, but I imagine the two of them may have been having an argument, don't know about that, but I'm having trouble not yelling at her myself. If you are an FBI agent, you probably misunderstood and broke in. Rafer must have fired his gun in self-defense when you came at him, all physical like that, in his own home. If there's a crime here, it's that you broke in and assaulted him."

Carson looked ready to rise out of her chair and leap on him. Griffin grabbed her hand. He said, "Whatever you may think, Sheriff, you have a lead on the three missing teenage girls now. You have a suspect."

Councilman Denmark cleared his throat. "Sheriff Bodine, may I give you my preliminary thoughts?"

The sheriff nodded. "Go ahead, Tommy."

Mr. Vampire sat forward, his hands flat on his bony knees, and cleared his throat. "There are some serious accusations flying around here about Rafer. There appears to be no proof of anything, except those accusations. I have to agree with the sheriff. We know Rafer, but we don't know you two. Are you who you claim to be, or are you lying con artists of some sort? I think Judge Pinder is going to have his hands full with you."

Fayreen patted Mr. Vampire's knee. She put down her pen, sat forward. "I agree, Booker. Listen to me, you young yahoos, Rafer's a lovely boy, always has been. High spirits, sure, he's a Bodine, the boys and girls in the Bodine clan are all high-spirited. But what you two have accused him of, it shows me you didn't do your homework."

"What Fayreen is saying," the sheriff interrupted, "is that if you had a brain, you'd realize your accusations won't cut it, not here in Gaffer's Ridge. I think that's enough for now. We're going to check out your stories, and we're going to wait for Judge Pinder." Sheriff Bodine rose. "Thank you for coming, Tommy. As for you two, our deputies are going to make you feel at home in our cell."

Griffin said, "May I have my one call first?"

"You already had your call back at Rafer's house," Sheriff Bodine said, and he smiled.

20

Savich slipped his cell back into his pants pocket, then turned to face Sherlock. Her eyes were clear, thankfully, and there was only a single Band-Aid covering the cut over her left temple. She was looking at him steadily, a half question on her face, a look he knew well. "We have an agent—Griffin Hammersmith—he's in trouble in a small town in western Virginia called Gaffer's Ridge." He saw a flash of recognition in her eyes. "You remember Griffin?"

"I don't know, but when you said his name— does he look like a god?"

"Yes. It's his cross to bear."

She cocked her head at him, a long-standing habit. "What happened to him?"

Savich told her what little Griffin had said before the sheriff took away his phone. "So I called the sheriff, but he wouldn't speak to me, his dispatcher told me he didn't have time, and she hung up on me. Whatever's going on, Griffin wouldn't have called if it wasn't serious."

"You sent him to this Gaffer's Ridge on a case?"

"No. He was taking a short vacation to visit a couple of friends from college who live there and own a restaurant downtown, Jenny's Café."

"Are you going to call them? Maybe they know what's going on."

"You don't miss a step, do you? I will now. I need to find out more about the situation before I call Bettina Kraus." At her blank look, he added, "Bettina's the SAC of the Richmond Field Office, took over from Walt Monaco. She's tough as nails and the prettiest smile you've ever seen. She's a good leader, fair to a fault, and what's best—she's got a sense of humor." He pulled out his cell, got the number for Jenny's Café. A woman's harried voice answered on the second ring. "Sorry, but we're closing in fifteen minutes so we can't take you now."

"Is this Jenny? Jenny Wiley?"

"No, this is Aimée Rose Wallberger. Who are you?"

"I'm FBI Agent Dillon Savich, Griffin's boss. Griffin called me, said he was in trouble. Have you spoken to him?"

"Trouble? How could that be? I saw him only a couple of hours ago. He was perfectly fine, going for a walk around town to keep himself upright and not nap away the afternoon. He was really tired. He's expected for dinner with Jenny and me at our home at seven o'clock. Jenny's already there, cooking his favorites."

Savich told her about Griffin's call and his own follow-up call to the bizarre woman at the sheriff's station. "I believe this Sheriff Bodine has taken him and a woman whose name I don't know to jail, apparently for no good reason. Griffin was worried, especially for the woman. The sheriff refused to speak to me and his dispatcher hung up on me. Before I call the Richmond Field Office, get them over to Gaffer's Ridge, can you tell me about this sheriff?"

Aimée Rose stopped wiping the long counter in the kitchen. "This is bizarre. I can't imagine what happened. All right, the sheriff's name is Booker Bodine and he's a pompous moron, and a bigot as well. But here's the thing, he's the sheriff because his family, the Bodines, are fixtures here, they've practically owned Gaffer's Ridge for generations. The sheriff's father, Calder Bodine, was sheriff before his son. The largest bank is owned by Quint Bodine, the sheriff's brother. He's the rich one, also owns a car dealership, a half dozen retail stores, and lots of land with mineral rights he leases out for big bucks."

"What has Sheriff Bodine done to qualify as a moron and a bigot?"

"He hates that Jenny and I are gay and live together openly and don't keep it in the closet, where he thinks such perversions belong. But he loves Jenny's Mexican food as much as everyone else in town, so he doesn't sneer at us when he comes to get fed. As far as I know, and I would know, he doesn't talk trash about us around town, either. He wouldn't dare. But I'm sure as I can be if Jenny's Café wasn't so popular and say instead we owned one of the antiques stores, he'd be busy trying to run us out of Gaffer's Ridge, tarred and feathered with signs around our necks. I suppose I have to give him credit for running a tight, peaceful town. Hardly anything bad happens here, no drugs, no gangs, no violent crime.

"Now, Agent Savich, you said Griffin's in jail, with a woman? That's crazy. He doesn't know anyone in town other than Jenny and me. Listen, let me call Jenny, close the café, and get over to the jail, see what's going on."

"Another moment, Ms. Wallberger. You said nothing bad ever happens?"

"Sorry, my head's spinning about Griffin. Something terrible happened three months ago—a young local girl named Heather Forrester disappeared without a trace. Turns out two other girls—all of them sixteen, or close, I think— have disappeared a month apart from two other towns in the area. They're all still missing, maybe kidnapped or dead. So far as I know there are no clues as to who did it. Our customers with teenage daughters are really scared. We mentioned the missing girls to Griffin, but how could he know anything? He only just got here. So why is the sheriff pissed enough to put him in jail?"

Her voice had risen an octave. Savich said, "I don't know yet, but the sheriff will have a reason. Call and ask if they'll let you see Griffin and get back to me. Tell him I'm calling Bettina Kraus. I'll try to be there tomorrow."

He punched off his cell, looked over to see Sherlock listening to his end of the conversation, an eyebrow arched. "Dillon?"

He felt a leap of hope, she saw it and quickly shook her head, whispered, "I'm sorry. I used your first name because I heard Agent Noble call you Dillon. And since you're my husband, I figured I did, too."

"Yes," he said. "You do." And he told her what he knew about Agent Griffin Hammersmith.

He watched her take it all in. "You had a flash of memory of Griffin, that's a good start."

"Yes, but I didn't recognize the agents who visited."

"Like I said, seeing Griffin is still a good start."

She hoped so. She found herself looking at him again, really looking. He was a big man, tall and fit, muscular, no doubt about that, with his hard face, dark eyes, and thick black hair, a little too long. If she saw him on the street she'd think he was hot, maybe turn around, slip her phone number in his pocket. And this man was her husband. She'd slept with him, had a child with him, fought with him, played with him. In her mind, such as it was at the moment, that meant she could trust him. She looked at his hands—like the rest of him, they were large, competent, but his fingers— "Why do you have scars on your fingers?"

"I've whittled since I was a kid, it's part of the package."

"Are you good?"

He blinked. "Some people think so." He wanted to tell her about his grandmother, the painter Sarah Elliott, and his talented sister, Lily, a cartoonist, but he didn't want to overload her with information.

"How long have we been married?"

She'd already asked him that, another sign of concussion. He said again, "Six years in November. You were pregnant right away with Sean."

"But I'm an FBI agent, how could I let that happen?"

He laughed. "It's still a mystery. We woke up one morning and evidently something happened during the night, and then we were parents." He gave her a sexy grin.

She started to smile at him, but she didn't know him. She drew back. "You know I didn't mean it that way. Listen, I heard your side of the conversation on your cell. If this Griffin is in trouble, of course you need to go to this Gaffer's Ridge, and I'll come with you."

He stared at her, swallowed, and shook his head.

She bulleted it out fast, before he could speak: "Dillon, here's the thing. I don't want to stay here by myself. You heard Dr. Loomis, she said I could leave. You're the person I must know best, the person who knows me best and cares about me. I trust you. Staying together with you feels right. I want to get my memory back, and being with you could help me remember.

"You told me I'm a good agent and we work together. So let's go to this Gaffer's Ridge and rescue Griffin Hammersmith."

He was silent, and she gave one last push. "Really, I feel fine, it's only my ID brain that's offline."

He spoke before he thought. "No, absolutely not. You were hurt, Sherlock." It was odd, but even as he said that, he knew he'd lose this round. She didn't realize it yet, but Sherlock could be the captain of a debate team. And she was right, they'd be together, he'd tell her more about their life. He could keep an eye on her, protect her. Savich knew he'd worry constantly, but then again, he'd worry constantly no matter where she was.

He walked to her bedside, bent over, and settled on a kiss to her forehead. He felt her stiffen, and absorbed the blow. He kept his voice light and easy, his expression never changing. "All right, we'll leave tomorrow morning, if Dr. Loomis clears you. I'll take Sean over to my mom's, tell him it's an early birthday present for both him and his grandmother. Would you like to see him before we go?"

She stilled, then slowly shook her head. "I want to, but I don't think it would be good for him, Dillon. You've told me he's very smart, so he might very well guess something was different about me and ask questions." She swallowed. "I don't want to take the chance of scaring him or leaving him with doubts." It was an adult decision, but still, she hated it. If she saw her small son, would she recognize him? Would everything come rushing back? No, probably not, but maybe by the time they returned, she'd remember everything.

Savich said, "I'll tell him you've got the flu and don't want to infect him. He'll stay with his grandmother until you're not contagious. How does that sound?"

"I don't know. I don't know him."

Savich swallowed. "He'll buy it, plus the early birthday present for him and his grandmother. Now, it's a four-hour drive to Gaffer's Ridge. The Porsche—that's my car—can shave that down some."

Sherlock blinked. She saw a red Porsche, clear as could be. She said, "You love that car. It's blast-out red and it drives cops wild to see it whiz by and not be able to give you a ticket when you have the siren on the roof." She drew back, whispered, "I saw it, I saw the Porsche, I heard the siren."

She'd seen his car, of all things. He said, smiling, "Excellent. It's been quite some time since we've had the siren on the Porsche." It was an old memory, but that didn't matter. He wanted to ask her what she was thinking—about herself, about him, about the bizarre situation they found themselves in—but he realized it would be for his sake, not hers. And so he smiled at her again and said nothing.

21

Fayreen grinned as she slid the two dinner trays under the bars on the dark green linoleum floor.

"Imagine your girlfriend making dinner for the two of you. Jenny said it was your favorite, and then she asked me all sorts of questions I didn't answer. They've been waiting to see you." She checked her watch. "Deputy Brewster should be done with them any time now, making sure they're not carrying any weapons or phones. He already checked your spaghetti, no telling what she could have stuffed under those meatballs." She turned to Carson. "Mrs. Clapper—she rented you your house—found your purse on the front steps. She gave it to me. I don't like to be without my purse myself, so here you go, all except your cell phone. We're going to keep that for you. She said your bag of groceries was spilled all over your front porch. She put the stuff away for you, didn't want the nonfat milk to go off."

Fayreen forced Carson's big black cloth messenger bag through the bars. "Thank you," Carson said to her retreating back. It seemed to her that spilled groceries, a handbag on the front steps were big clues something had happened to her. Evidently not. Carson unzipped her handbag and began looking through it—recorder, small notebook, her current paperback mystery, makeup bag, rental car keys, small brush, the usual odds and ends. She realized she basically carried her life around with her.

But there was one big thing missing. "He took my wallet, Griffin. Rafer Bodine took my wallet. I remember he told me he'd looked at my driver's license, knew my name. I'll have to ask for it back, if they admit they found it. Everything else is here." She pulled out her makeup bag and checked her mirror. She burst out laughing. "I surely do look squirrelly, Fayreen was right about that. Goodness, Griffin, why didn't you say something? I could have at least finger-combed my hair, maybe washed my face in that bowl over there, though I don't see a water faucet."

"That bowl is the toilet," he said, and grinned at her appalled look. "Don't worry, I don't think we're going to have to spend the night in jail. Like

I told you, my boss, Dillon Savich, must have called the SAC in Richmond by now—"

"What's a SAC?"

"That's special agent in charge. Bettina Kraus is the SAC of the Richmond Field Office. She's a mover and a shaker. I predict she'll be here pretty soon and she's going to bring the cavalry. She's involved in Civil War reenactments, so who knows what she'll bring." He looked down at his watch. "I spoke to Savich about two hours ago, so half an hour, more or less."

"You mean you're so important an FBI field office is going to assemble a team to come rescue you?"

"Yep." No need to tell her Savich would have called in the troops if a summer intern was in trouble. "Carson, you don't look all that bad, really. If you have a Kleenex, you might wipe your face off. Just here." He pointed to his left cheekbone.

He watched her spit on a Kleenex and scrub at the dirt on her face. She brushed her hair quickly and pulled it up in a ponytail, tying it expertly with a new elastic band from the depths of the messenger bag. He saw a notebook and a beat-up paperback, and that was only the first layer.

He watched her dab on a bit of pinkish lipstick, look over at him, and smile. "Well? Would I still scare chickens and small children?"

He grinned. "I think small children are safe, but I've got to be honest here, I'm not sure about the chickens."

"Har har." She zipped her messenger bag. "That was very nice of Fayreen to bring me my bag. Maybe she likes me after all." She looked toward the toilet. "Well, maybe not."

They fell to the amazing spaghetti with Jenny's special sauce and managed to get halfway through before Fayreen appeared with the two deputies and unlocked their cell. "You're lucky," she said. "Sheriff Bodine said you can speak to your visitors, said he didn't want to give you one more thing to complain about to Judge Pinder whenever he gets back. Twenty minutes, no longer." She looked over at Carson. "You cleaned up, did you, missy? Well, the two of you look so perfect and buffed up, makes me wonder if you're waiting for the TV vans to roll up any time now, drum up publicity for your movie? That's what I'm guessing this is all about."

Griffin said easily, "I suggest you contact the sheriff again, Fayreen. I'm expecting a squad of FBI agents in about"—he looked down at his watch—"twenty minutes. Believe me, you don't want to face them alone."

Did he see any doubt in her eyes? He didn't think so. She said, "Now, that sounds like another whopper to me. I mean, where are your wing tips? And your black FBI suit and white shirt and buzz-cut hair?"

"Do you wear your uniform on vacation?"

"Don't get smart with me. And you stop

trying to scare me with talk of the FBI coming. It won't work. I'm not about to bother Booker with your tall tales. He's eating barbecue with the family tonight, the whole family. Rafer's daddy and mama will be there, that's Mr. Quint and Mrs. Cyndia, trying to figure out what this is all about, after, of course, they go to the hospital to visit their poor boy."

Griffin shrugged. "Up to you, but don't say I didn't warn you."

"I'm going to take you to the interrogation room. It's not comfortable like Booker's office. You walk in front of me and don't try anything funny."

Griffin raised an eyebrow. "Interrogation room? You have so many criminals running around in Gaffer's Ridge you need a designated interrogation room?"

Fayreen shook her head, curled her lip at him—an amazing feat, really—and directed them down a short hallway that gave onto the station's central room. She pointed right, to a room labeled INTERROGATION, and opened the door, waved them in. "Sit down and don't even think about trying to run. I'll bring in your visitors."

Griffin and Carson walked into the room, Jewel and Brewster on their heels. The room at least larger than the cell Griffin and Carson were sharing.

Fayreen said from the doorway, "Here they are, all worried about you."

"I don't believe this," Jenny said, and ran over to Griffin to hug him.

Brewster stepped in front of her. "Step back, Ms. Wiley. No touching the prisoners. All of you, sit down, keep your hands on the table where I can see them."

Jenny looked Brewster up and down. "These hands make your tacos. Be nice to these hands."

22

Griffin nearly burst out with a laugh, but not Aimée Rose, she was nearly sputtering. "Come on, Brew, you think we're here to bust them out of jail? And what is this 'Ms. Wiley'? You've eaten more meals Jenny's cooked for you than your wife has. Carollee told me so herself." Aimée Rose shut her mouth then, better not to rub salt in the wound. Word was Brewster was a bully, mean as a snake, and he sometimes knocked his wife around after a bender, but who knew what would set him off?

Brewster said from between seamed lips, "Don't you call me Brew, like I'm a damned beer. I'm Deputy Sheriff Brewster."

"Why not?" Jenny asked. "Everyone else does, like they call Jewel FJ—Family Jewels."

Jewel's face turned crimson.

Jenny said, "It's all right, it's all in good fun."

Griffin grinned. "What about the sheriff? Does he have a nickname?"

Brewster wanted to flatten the pretty boy. He couldn't right then, but he was going to talk to Carollee for sure, ask her what she'd been saying about him. He'd probably have to rearrange her thinking a bit. He felt Jewel's hand on his sleeve, shook it off. He looked down at his watch. "You're only running out of visiting time, shooting off your mouths."

Griffin nodded. "You gentlemen can leave now." But they didn't, probably on Sheriff Bodine's orders. They stood by the door, their backs to the wall. Griffin ignored them, said to Aimée Rose, "Come on, babe, time to calm down. Last thing I need is for you guys to be tossed into our cell with us. It really isn't big enough for four of us, and there's only one john."

Jenny looked ready to burst. "Don't you dare joke about this, Griffin Hammersmith. It isn't funny, it's fricking outrageous. You know your boss called Aimée Rose, told her about your call to him? He asked her all sorts of questions about the sheriff. Why didn't you call us?"

Griffin glanced over at Jewel and Brewster. "I'd hoped Savich could deal with the sheriff without any fuss. Plus, the sheriff took my cell."

Carson sat forward, raised her voice. "Griffin

said the Richmond Field Office should be here soon to bust us out."

Brewster straightened up like a shot. "What'd you say?"

Griffin said, "Don't worry, Brewster, as long as you don't resist, I doubt they'll shoot you or throw you in your own cell." He shrugged. "But I could be wrong."

"Lying little punk," Brewster said under his breath, but not under enough.

Jewel's young voice broke a bit when he whispered to Brewster, "Maybe we should call the sheriff, warn him the Feds are coming?"

"Don't pee your britches, Jewel. Pretty boy here is trying to scare us, that's all. This is only one more of his lies."

Jenny said, "Agent Hammersmith isn't lying. Wait until the FBI wagons pull up, you're going to be in big trouble. And Brew, you can forget coming in for your tacos and meatloaf. You're no longer welcome in our eating establishment."

If Griffin wasn't mistaken, Brewster stared at her with horror, shaking his head. "No need to be unpleasant, Jenny, I'm only doing my job. Really, only doing my job."

"Then you'd best be careful how you treat Agent Hammersmith."

Brewster opened his mouth, probably thought about his meatloaf and tacos, and shut it.

Jewel swallowed, his prominent Adam's apple

bobbing up and down. He shot another scared look at Brewster. "But why would he lie?"

Brewster called out, "He thinks he can rile us, worry us enough to let him go. Not going to happen, so stop your twittering. As for you and the girl, the sheriff said you two are going to stay in jail until Judge Pinder gets back with his walleye and bass and decides what to do with you. But like everyone knows, you never can plan on anything with him."

Griffin said quietly, "Deputy Brewster, do you have any idea how many laws you've broken, interfering with a federal officer? Do you have any idea what I could make happen to the lot of you, beginning with Sheriff Bodine?"

"Nothing's going to happen," Brewster said, and took a step forward and raised his fist. He shot a look at Jenny, stepped back. "The Bodines won't let anything happen, you watch."

"Brewster—"

Brewster ignored Jewel. "So you keep a civil tongue in your mouth, boy, or I'll show these visitors out right this minute and put you two mutts back in your cell."

Jenny ignored him, leaned forward. "Griffin, if your boss hadn't called Aimée Rose, we wouldn't have known where you were." She shook her head in disbelief. "Except, of course, this is one of the first places we'd have come if we couldn't reach you, hoping for help from the sheriff to find you."

She pointed at Carson. "Okay, now, who is she and why are you two together?"

Carson waved her hand. "I'm Carson DeSilva and I can talk, too. Actually, I ate a late lunch at your café yesterday right after I drove into town. The guy at the gas station told me you were putting Gaffer's Ridge on the map with your cooking. I've got to say that was an outstanding Reuben sandwich, maybe the best I've ever had, and I live in New York so that's saying something. And why am I telling you that? Sorry." Carson stuck out her hand, heard Brewster snarl, and drew her hand back. "Griffin's told me a bit about both of you. It's a pleasure to meet you. It's true, you two could outcook the White House chef."

"I think Jenny could, but I'm still learning the finer points," Aimée Rose said. "So you like our cooking and you somehow hooked up with Griffin today. What happened?"

23

While Carson told them, without mentioning telepathy, of course, Griffin watched Jenny's face. Jenny usually looked serene and calm as a Madonna, as if nothing could faze her. She was small and round, with thick dark hair in a ponytail, sweet until someone bad-mouthed someone close to her or her cooking. Then she could turn mean as a Doberman. She was also smart as a whip. Aimée Rose was a good seven inches taller, outweighed Jenny by thirty pounds. Her hair was a short cap around her head, raven black this week, and she looked as tough as one of Griffin's hiking boots. But, still, he'd always thought Jenny was the tougher of the two.

Carson spoke fast, knowing time was running short. Griffin realized Jenny was studying Carson as she spoke, her eyes cool, assessing. Then Jenny turned to him and slowly nodded. Good, Jenny believed Carson. He trusted her judgment of people.

Griffin picked it up. "I heard Carson yell, but I couldn't tell which house she was in. Luckily, I was nearly out of town and the houses were farther apart, and not that many. Still, she had to yell again before I found the right house." One of Jenny's eyebrows shot up, only her left eyebrow, a move he'd tried to master since college and couldn't, a move he'd always admired. She knew about his gift or curse, depending on his perspective at the moment. He wondered if she suspected Carson's shout wasn't out loud. She didn't say anything, but he knew Jenny would ask about it later.

Aimée Rose said in the direction of the deputies, "May I use my cell phone?"

Jewel looked agonized. Brewster said, "No. Not while you're with these two. Can't have you sending messages to their criminal buddies while you're in here. If you want to call them a lawyer, wait until you're out of the station. But good luck reaching Junior Rippetoe, he never works after five o'clock." Brewster grinned. "Like the sheriff said, Judge Pinder will be here when he gets here. He'll decide what to do with these two for putting poor Rafer in the hospital."

"Putting Rafer in the hospital!" Carson looked ready to spit she was so angry.

Griffin put his hand on her arm, said quietly, "Let him say whatever he wants. It won't matter." He looked down at his watch. Soon now they'd see SAC Bettina Kraus's very pissed face.

"Yeah, that's what you managed to do, with pretty boy's help." He gave her a hard look. "You, an out-of-town nobody."

"You think I'm a nobody? Well, maybe I am, but I happen to work for Ritter Aquino in New York at Aquino Communications." Her chin went up. "Mr. Aquino is my boss."

"Really?" Aimée Rose said. "You work for the big kahuna? On Madison Avenue? Their head-quarters is at the center of the communications universe, right?"

Carson nodded. "Yes. And as I told Griffin and the sheriff, I'm here to interview Dr. Alek Kuchar." She turned to Griffin. "Sorry, but there's been so little time to tell you anything about myself, my job, or my background. Mr. Aquino and my father have been friends since childhood, so I've known him all my life. I've been one of Mr. Aquino's primary speechwriters for three years now, and doing my own writing, too. This trip? It was my father's idea I should come interview Dr. Kuchar. Uncle Ritter agreed, thought it would add to my chops."

Griffin stared at her. Ritter Aquino had

enough firepower to get her out of this himself—in fact, he was a nuke, an EMP, who could put out every Bodine light in the area.

He picked up a wave of uneasiness from Carson. She was fretting, wondering if she should tell them something else or not. He took a guess on what it was. He said, "Your father and Ritter Aquino go back a long way, you said. Tell us about him."

Griffin's not going to like this. I should have told him earlier. Okay, chin up and do it. "My dad's Vincente Paulo DeSilva, of the DeSilva family of organized crime fame centered in Newark, New Jersey." She clasped her hands so tightly in front of her, her fingers turned white. "Listen, my dad's not part of the DeSilva family organization, even though he's been hassled about it by every local politician and national law enforcement agency. Nothing ever comes of it, ever. He opted out of the family when he studied journalism at UCLA, to get away from all of them."

Brewster looked like his face would split, his grin big enough to show a gold molar. "Well now, Jewel, the sheriff was right. Looks like we've got us a real connected criminal here. What gall."

"I thought I was a movie star," Carson said.

"So you're a connected movie star, girl."

"That's Dr. Girl to you."

"Shut your yap. The sheriff's going to love this. You're mobbed up. No wonder you tried to murder Rafer, it's in your blood. Jewel, we've gotta tell the sheriff he's got himself a baby rattler."

Jenny said in a clear voice, "Vincente DeSilva is a journalist and he also writes biographies. *Beast Killer*—that's his most famous one—is about Genghis Khan. I've read it," she added to Carson. "Your dad's a very good writer."

"Thank you."

Griffin said, "Add me to the readership list, Carson. He is very good."

She leaned in close, whispered so the deputies couldn't hear her, "Unfortunately Dad's in Vienna, researching his next book. Uncle Ritter would help us if I call him. He'll blow a fit, then get all icy cold and measure Sheriff Bodine for a coffin."

Griffin sat back in the uncomfortable chair with its uneven legs, crossed his arms, and said, "Let's hold Mr. Aquino in reserve, see what the FBI manages first."

Brewster said to Jewel, his eyes narrowed on Carson, "This Aquino fellow, he's a big shot in what? Communications? You mean he talks on the news?" He laughed at his own joke, looked down at his watch. "I gave you more time than you're supposed to have. Sheriff Bodine said twenty minutes and I gave you twenty-seven. I wanted to hear if you could tell your story the same way twice, girl. Now, you can count on me calling the sheriff, telling him the score."

Griffin said, "Of course, I could call Sheriff

Dix Noble in Maestro. Dix can be quite a load, his wife, Ruth, too." He added to Carson, "She's an FBI agent, sometimes my partner. As with Aquino, we'll hold off for a while. I don't know how many agents are coming, but I'll wager the sheriff's leather sofa they're not going to need backup." He glanced at Brewster. "Maybe you want to tell Sheriff Bodine to get ready for a tsunami."

"You aren't scaring anybody, boy. Jewel, get these two back to their cell. If the girl here wants to use the facilities, she can call out." He checked his watch. "At least we're getting overtime."

They heard Fayreen yell, "Precious Lord above, don't shoot me!" Then a woman's voice Griffin recognized: "Hold yourself perfectly still and stay quiet."

The cavalry had arrived.

He whispered to Carson, "That's Bettina. You're going to love her."

24

They heard a squawk from Fayreen, then sputters and shouts. The door to the interrogation room burst open and there stood SAC Bettina Kraus, her Glock strapped to her thigh, holding an HK MP5, a submachine gun that would scare any sane human being. She was wearing riot gear—an army-green multithreat body armor system and flak jacket with FBI stenciled in big yellow letters across the front. Her pockets were filled with extra magazines, a radio, flex-cuffs, and naturally, a cool pair of sunglasses. Trust Savich to tell Bettina to come bristling with attitude and weapons. In her jeans, dark blue T-shirt, and scuffed black boots, her salt-and-pepper hair pulled back in a short tail, she looked as mean as a pissed-off mother-in-law. Griffin couldn't have scripted it better himself.

Two more FBI agents stood behind Kraus in full riot gear like hers, their MP5s in their hands, their bulging biceps on display in their blue short-sleeved T-shirts. They stood tough and silent as boulders. Griffin knew them both. David Foxx, aka Slick, liked to play the badass, though he had a wife and three young daughters who ruled the roost at home. Griffin had played horse with DeAndre Watkinson at his neighborhood basketball court. DeAndre was nearly six and a half feet tall, and had a vicious scar bisecting his left cheek. Luckily, he wasn't a very good outside shooter, and Griffin had won forty dollars off him their last game.

Brewster, the idiot, put his hand on his Beretta.

He thought better of it when Slick tapped him on his shoulder. "Moron. Don't you move another muscle."

Kraus said, "Slick, DeAndre, take their weapons."

Slick and DeAndre simply stood directly in front of the deputies, eyed them up and down, absolutely no expression on their faces, and held out their hands, waggled their fingers. "Sidearms, now, butts first."

Brewster swallowed, handed over his Beretta, and nodded to Jewel, who quickly followed suit. DeAndre and Slick slipped the Berettas into their flak jackets and took up positions on either side of them, their MP5s pointed to the floor.

"Now," Kraus said, "stand down. Do not move. Do not open your mouths unless I tell you to. You would not like the consequences."

Kraus gave Griffin a big smile. "I believe we have containment, Agent Hammersmith. Glad to see you in one piece. You're well, I hope? No fingernails pulled out? No bruised kidneys from these two fine specimens?"

Brewster yelled, "Hey, wait! We didn't do anything!"

Kraus slowly turned and gave Brewster the stink-eye. "No more warnings. Keep your mouth shut."

Brewster's mouth worked, but he wisely kept quiet and looked down at his scuffed boots.

Jewel cleared his throat. "Ma'am? May I speak?"

"What? Make it fast. Don't waste my time."

"We didn't lay a hand on either of them, I swear, ma'am, Agent Ma'am."

Griffin caught a smile on Slick's mouth that didn't, however, reach his cold eyes.

Kraus said, "Griffin, you okay?"

"Fingernails still intact, but no telling what they would have got up to."

"And who is this?" She turned to Carson, an eyebrow up.

Carson stared at this awesome woman, cleared

her throat. "I'm Carson DeSilva. I met Griffin today. He saved my life, kept me from being murdered."

"That isn't true!" Brewster yelled. "Rafer's a good man, never hurt a flea, ask his ma, his pa, his pa's brother, ask anyone in town, well, except for fighting sometimes at Five Star Bar, but everyone's always fighting out there."

DeAndre picked Brewster up by the neck and swung him around. "Keep your mouth shut, little dude. Nod when I put you back down."

Once Brewster's feet touched the floor, he swallowed, rubbed his neck, and nodded.

Kraus smiled. "Good to hear Griffin can be useful when he's not on the clock."

Brewster was scared, but he knew he had to man up. Jewel was too young and he'd probably already peed his pants. Besides, he knew to his bones Jewel would tell everyone in town what happened if he folded like a two-dollar tent. He drew himself up as straight and tall as he could. "Ma'am, sirs, I'm a sworn officer of the law. My questions and observations are justified. You're wearing what look like official uniforms and combat gear, but you can buy that stuff on Amazon. I'm going to need to see your identification. And I want to know why you came busting into our sheriff's station looking like you're ready to take out Al Qaeda."

Kraus smiled at Brewster, surprised he was showing some backbone. "Do you, now?"

Brewster gripped his mojo in both hands and took a very small step toward Kraus. "Ma'am, I don't know who you are, but you don't have any business here in our station. We are the law here in Gaffer's Ridge. What did you do to Fayreen?"

Kraus handed Brewster her creds. "Fayreen? She's in your cell. As you can see, Deputy Brewster, I am Special Agent Kraus, FBI, from the Richmond Field Office."

His hand shook as he looked down at the FBI credentials, but he couldn't let the sheriff down, or his life would be hell. He swallowed, licked his lips. "How do I know these aren't bogus, like his?" He nodded toward Griffin.

Bettina's voice remained smooth, steady, interested. "Why in the world would you think Agent Hammersmith's creds are bogus? You could have easily called to verify his FBI status."

"He's a murderer if Rafer doesn't make it, both of them are. Him and the gal over there tried to kill poor Rafer. And look at them, they don't look like cops. We thought they were con artists, and poor Rafer got in their way."

"Hmmm." Bettina gave both Griffin and Carson the once-over, nodded. "I agree, they're both too pretty for their own good. But why didn't the sheriff allow Agent Hammersmith to call his superior in Washington? Why didn't your sheriff speak with Agent Hammersmith's boss?"

Brewster saw the alligators gliding toward

him, mouths open, teeth ready to chomp. He cleared his throat. "Sheriff Bodine thought the fellow who called him was this Hammersmith's cousin. Fayreen hung up on him."

Kraus blinked, looked astonished, though Griffin bet Savich had already told her everything. "I would have to say your sheriff is neither very bright nor is he professional. Now, here's what you are going to do, Deputy Brewster. You're going to call Sheriff Bodine, tell him his presence is requested in—" She looked down at her black-banded iWatch. "Ten minutes, no more. After I've spoken to him, I'll decide whether or not to take all of you into federal custody. You've broken enough laws to paper your cell in the Pennington Gap federal prison."

25

Brewster knew serious when he saw it, he recognized it from the same look on his mother-in-law's face. Mother Maude, as he was told to call her, was meaner than he was, and this woman was close. He pulled out his cell, punched in a number, and turned his back to whisper into the phone. "Sheriff, Brewster here. A whole battalion of Feds came busting into the station, in war gear, with submachine guns, FBI written all over their jackets. So I guess the good-looking fellow wasn't lying. The lead Fed, the SAC they call her, is a girl, ah, woman. She said you gotta come now."

They watched Brewster's face turn white. "There's nothing Jewel and I can do, Sheriff. We have no armament, they took our Berettas. I told you, they have submachine guns. You've got to come, Sheriff."

They heard what sounded like curses, but couldn't make out any words. Brewster hung up. He was sweating profusely. "Sheriff Bodine is on his way."

Kraus nodded. "So perhaps this Sheriff Bodine has a brain after all. Slick, DeAndre, take the gentlemen's cell phones and escort them to the jail cell to keep company with Fayreen. Have Agent Cutler watch them, tell her we're expecting the sheriff in a few minutes. Aren't there any other staff in this office?"

"Well, ma'am," Jewel said, "there's five more deputies, but two have the flu, two are on vacation, you know, since it's summer and all, and one is coming in a bit later for the night shift, at ten o'clock, but Bobby's usually late."

Brewster wanted to take this FBI woman's throat between his hands and squeeze, but he managed to swallow his bile. "Ma'am—Agent Kraus, we're deputies of Gaffer's Ridge. You can't put us in our own jail cell. It isn't right."

"Tell you what, Deputy, we'll let a federal judge decide what's right. You had Agent Hammersmith occupying your cell with his companion here, unlawfully, I might add. A tight fit for the three of you, but you'll manage."

Slick, who'd been staring at Carson, snapped to when Kraus nodded toward him.

Slick shoved Brewster's shoulder. "Get yourselves moving, boys."

Jewel said, "Ye-yes, sir. Sir, ma'am, we were only doing our jobs, watching over these attempted murderers like the sheriff told us to. Deputy Brewster's right, he and the girl over there tried to kill the sheriff's nephew. Fact is, ma'am, Rafer's in the hospital, maybe barely hanging on. He could be dying, they both attacked him, ma'am, they admitted it."

Griffin smiled at Jewel. "Actually, if Rafer Bodine dies, it'd be the first fatal broken wrist I've heard of."

"She smacked him on the head with a pipe!"

"Indeed she did, an excellent shot," Griffin said. "Agent Kraus, this man in the hospital, Rafer Bodine, may be a serial killer. To date, three sixteen-year-old girls have gone missing, one of them from Gaffer's Ridge, the other two from towns in the area. So, even with a headache and a broken wrist, Rafer Bodine could escape. I doubt the sheriff put any guards on him."

Kraus nodded. "Slick, when we're through with the sheriff, find out what hospital he's in and head over there with DeAndre and guard this Rafer Bodine."

They heard Jewel say to the agents as he and Brewster were marched out of the interrogation room, "Fayreen won't like using the john in the cell, what with us in there with her."

Brewster said, "She can hold it. I don't care who they are, Sheriff Bodine will get us out fast enough."

"Live in hope," DeAndre said, and gave a sadistic laugh. "Move along, boys."

Griffin said, "Agent Kraus, that was an awesome incursion. You're my hero."

Carson punched his arm, looked at Kraus. "No, you're my hero. Thank you." Carson stuck out her hand. "Thank you for coming."

"You're very welcome. Agent Savich thought it would be a good idea to come looking like Delta Force to scare the crap out of them. I can't wait to meet this Sheriff Bodine."

Carson said, "Maybe at first you think he's another good old boy, but I'd say the sheriff is scary, and I'm from New York. You want to dismiss him, but behind his eyes, there's something you don't want to deal with." She looked down at herself, over at Griffin. "I couldn't believe it—he looked us up and down, saw how dirty we were— well, not Griffin, but me—and still he called us movie stars."

Kraus looked from one to the other. An eyebrow rose. "Imagine," she said.

Griffin said, "You haven't met the other characters in our traveling show—these are my good friends, Jenny Wiley and Aimée Rose Wallberger."

Jenny said, "It was a treat to watch you, Agent Kraus, and a pleasure to meet you. What would you say to my feeding spaghetti to you and your team after this is all straightened out?"

"And I've already made my special caramel pecan cheesecake," Aimée Rose said.

Kraus said, "If that would be spaghetti with meat sauce, you're on."

Aimée Rose said, "Jenny makes her meat sauce from scratch, of course, lots of garlic and butter."

Kraus looked down at her iWatch. "We haven't got long before the sheriff arrives. Agent Savich gave me the overview of what happened, but I need all you can give me in five minutes, Griffin. Ms. Wiley and Ms. Wallberger, I need to ask you to leave now. I'm not expecting any violence, but we can't take the chance of having you here when the sheriff arrives. We'll see you later for that meal you promised. I'm thanking you in advance."

Once Jenny and Aimée Rose had left, Carson quickly recounted what had happened as she had so many times already, with no mention of te-lepathy.

Kraus nodded. "Very succinct. I must say you and Griffin have had an exciting day. I have a lot of questions, but they can wait until after we meet with the sheriff." She looked at the big round clock on the wall. "Ah, about time for Top Dog to walk through the door." Kraus grinned as she checked her MP5. "Ms. DeSilva, you called the sheriff scary?"

Griffin said, "It's actually Dr. DeSilva. And she did, yes. I'm not so sure."

Kraus nodded, smiled. "Noted."

Carson said, "Yes, trust me, there's more to him than meets the eye. 'Scary' is as good a word as any."

Kraus nodded again, said to Agent Vickie Lynn, "Tell Higgins to come inside and line everyone up in the outer room, combat ready, and look eager to form a firing squad. I think I hear Sheriff Bodine."

Griffin grinned. "Showtime."

26

Griffin watched Sheriff Booker Bodine from the narrow front window as he screeched his Crown Vic to a stop at the curb, slammed the car door, and marched into the station, his hand hovering over his Beretta clipped to his belt. His face was set, his mouth working—was he talking to himself? Griffin saw no fear, only rage in his eyes, and a big barbecue stain on his shirt. Then he stopped, looked around, saw the FBI van, and drew a deep breath. Good, he realized he was going up against something more powerful than he was, something he couldn't control. Griffin watched him square his shoulders, thrust out his chin.

Sheriff Booker Bodine was met by six hard faces, three men and three women, all in FBI flak jackets, holding submachine guns at the ready in their gloved hands. An older woman with her hands on her hips stepped forward, her smile as cold as her eyes. Behind them he saw Hammersmith with DeSilva beside him, next to the water fountain, their backs to the wall. He didn't see Fayreen, Brewster, or Jewel.

So the pretty boy had juice. He'd managed to bring the FBI in force into his town. Hell's bells, as his mother would say to his father when she was pissed. This crew looked tough, probably as soon shoot him as say good evening. He let his hand flit over his Beretta anyway.

He stared at the tall, fit woman with her short salt-and-pepper hair slicked back from her face, no makeup, and aviator glasses. Was she trying to look like a man?

He smiled at her and tried his best to sound like God. "I am Sheriff Booker Bodine. Who are you?"

Kraus handed him her creds. "I'm FBI Special Agent Bettina Kraus, special agent in charge of the Richmond Field Office."

Booker studied her ID, handed it back to her, and swallowed bile. "I would like to know why you have invaded my station house and why you look ready to go to war." He stabbed a finger at Griffin and Carson. "And why those two are out of their cell where they were rightfully placed. They're being held for questioning, and I have every right to do that." Out went his chin.

None of the agents changed expression.

Kraus said, "First, Sheriff, I would like to know why you refused to accept Agent Hammersmith's credentials and incarcerated him instead, and why you didn't call to verify his identity. And why you haven't placed a guard on a man accused of kidnapping Dr. Carson DeSilva. This man, Rafer Bodine, I understand is your nephew?"

Don't throw your weight around, Booker, Jess had told him before he'd left. *Be calm and logical, better to butter the bread and pour on the honey.* He pointed to Griffin, said in a calm deep voice, "Ma'am, Agent Kraus, this man does not look like an FBI agent. However, if you say he's legitimate, who am I to say? But it makes no sense to me you'd let him into law enforcement. And that girl—"

Griffin said, "Sheriff, are you really referring to Dr. DeSilva?"

Bodine looked like he wanted to shoot Griffin right this minute, or choke him, but he sucked it up, raised his chin even higher, and pointed to Carson. "That woman shouldn't be free. She's a danger to our law-abiding citizens. Look, Agent Kraus, I had good cause to throw them in jail. They put a young man in the hospital, a man well known and well liked in Gaffer's Ridge."

Kraus said, "I understand Agent Hammersmith and Dr. DeSilva told you what this young man did, this young man who also happens to be your nephew?"

"Yeah, sure I listened to their lame story. It was full of holes and inconsistencies and flat-out lies. I didn't believe a word of it and neither did anyone else who knows Rafer. So look, it appears I will have to release Agent Hammersmith if you vouch for his identify. I will, however, keep her"— he tossed his head toward Carson—"under lock and key. By her own admission, she struck Rafer Bodine on the head with a pipe, a blow that could have killed him. It is my right and my responsibility as sheriff of Gaffer's Ridge to protect my town and its citizens. So you may escort Hammersmith out of here, since you have no reason to stay."

Kraus wasn't going to waste her time arguing with this little tin god. "Sheriff, here's what's going to happen. I am sending two agents to your hospital to keep guard on Rafer Bodine. As of this moment, the FBI is opening an investigation into the kidnapping of the three teenage girls and of Carson DeSilva. Kidnapping, as you perhaps know, is a federal crime. In view of your conflict of interest, your involvement in this case seems counterproductive. Further, the DOJ—that's the Department of Justice—"

"I know what that means!"

"Most Americans do. Now, the DOJ will determine if your behavior warrants prosecution."

Booker looked ready to explode. Then he pulled back his shoulders, stretched himself to his full height. "I have been sheriff in Gaffer's Ridge for twenty-two years and my daddy was sheriff before me for nearly forty years. I have worked hard to keep my town orderly and crime free. Ask anyone—there is hardly any trouble here in Gaffer's Ridge."

Kraus said, her voice dry as dust, "Except for the missing teenage girl from your town, Heather Forrester, three months ago."

"Ma'am, Agent, I am as certain as I can be our poor Heather was taken by an outsider. Probably one of those fool hikers saw her, took her. Or maybe it was someone from one of the other towns who are missing a teenage girl. No one I know in my town would harm a hair on Heather Forrester's head. I've been doing all I can, but there's absolutely nothing to go on, no ransom note, not a single clue. Obviously, it's not Rafer, his family is rich, plus he's been friends with the Forrester family since he was a child." He tossed his head toward Carson again. "But she's new in town, claims she's here to interview that nut case Alek Kuchar, a weird dude who's been hiding in the mountains. The guy's crazy, so I don't see how—"

Kraus raised her hand, cut him off. "Sheriff Bodine, here are your choices: If Agent Hammersmith allows you to assist the FBI in our investigation into the three missing girls, you and your deputies will follow his orders to the letter. You will in no way impede, obstruct, or attempt to sabotage any part of his investigation or I will report your actions to the DOJ. If you agree, you may remain as sheriff of Gaffer's Ridge, temporarily, despite your clear conflict of interest. Let me stress it is up to Agent Hammersmith to decide whether he wishes to include you and your deputies.

"Your second choice: you can hand me your weapon and your badge now, leave this office immediately, and face federal charges. Let me be absolutely clear: if you in any way interfere with Agent Hammersmith's investigation, he will arrest you for obstructing justice."

27

Griffin waited to see what the sheriff would do. Bodine looked like his guts were twisting, looked ready to spit nails, but he managed to say calmly enough, "I have known Rafer all his life. He wouldn't hurt a fly."

"We're not accusing him of hurting a fly, Sheriff," Kraus said patiently, "but of kidnapping and the attempted murder of Dr. DeSilva. And he's going to be a major suspect. I have received a nod from Agent Hammersmith, so now it's up to you. Will you give Agent Hammersmith your full cooperation? Or leave?"

Booker yelled, "You want me to actually work with this prick? This puffed-up pretty boy who doesn't know anything, doesn't know this town or anyone in it?"

Kraus said nothing, merely stared at him, no expression on her face. Bodine stopped, looked back and forth from her to Griffin. Griffin saw the moment he believed her. The moment he realized he could and would lose his job and be charged with the crime of impeding a federal agent, that he'd be a laughingstock when word got out, and it would. He looked at Griffin, and for a moment Griffin felt sorry for him. For Bodine to have to take orders from him, it had to gall him but good.

Griffin watched him slowly nod.

"Say your agreement out loud, Sheriff Bodine."

"I agree to work with Agent Hammersmith."

"To be specific, you'll do exactly what Agent Hammersmith asks, follow his instructions and his timeline expeditiously, and give him your full cooperation. You will guarantee to provide him with unbiased information, you will not obstruct justice in any way. State your agreement aloud."

It looked like it was gutting him to say the words, but he got them out. "Yes, I agree to work for Agent Hammersmith, do everything he says, my deputies as well."

Kraus nodded. "If I hear you are trying to sabotage Agent Hammersmith in any way, I will have a warrant for your arrest from a federal judge this fast—" And she snapped her fingers. "Do you understand me, Sheriff?"

He nodded.

"Out loud, please."

"Yes, I understand you."

"Good. So now it's up to you. I'll have two of my agents available to Agent Hammersmith if he needs them. You will provide him with any office space he requires. You will now return Agent Hammersmith's and Dr. DeSilva's cell phones, all their identification and personal belongings. Rafer Bodine's house is out of bounds to you until our FBI forensic team is through."

Bodine said, "Your forensic team won't find anything at Rafer's house. It's her word against his and they'll see there's no proof."

In that moment, Griffin knew the sheriff had already seen to removing evidence, including the most damning, the duct tape. On his own initiative? Griffin didn't know. He did know he wanted to meet Rafer's parents, Cyndia and Quint Bodine.

Kraus ignored him. "The forensic team will be at Rafer Bodine's house tomorrow morning to go over the basement where Dr. DeSilva was held. Special Agent Higgins will be staying there tonight to avoid any more disruption of the scene than has already happened.

"You may now release Deputies Brewster and Jewel and your dispatcher. Let me warn you, Sheriff, your deputies' behavior reflects directly on you. One sneer from any of them, one act of insubordination, they'll be visiting your jail cell and you will be the one to turn the key."

The AC was on high but Bodine was sweating, two huge circles beneath his arms. Carson was very pleased. They watched him walk to Fayreen's desk, stiff anger in every step. He took their belongings out of one of the drawers. "Rafer's gun is in the evidence locker, if you want it. It was his grand-daddy's gun. Old Ansel taught him how to shoot when Rafer was twelve, taught him how to use the gun in self-defense, and only in self-defense." He took the keys and disappeared through the door to the cell.

"Stand down, guys. Good show." Kraus turned to Griffin. "You sure you're all right with this plan?"

Griffin thought asking the sheriff to actually cooperate would be a near-perfect minefield. "Yes, but the fact is I doubt we can trust him, even though we do need him for the moment. He knows the people and the area."

Kraus said, "Agreed. And arresting him now might cause more trouble than it's worth." She patted Griffin's arm. "I've always believed in keeping your enemies close, Agent Hammersmith."

"I'll bet the duct tape from Rafer's basement is long gone. And yes, he'll try to sabotage me, both he and the other real power in the station, Fayreen. I think we'll know soon enough what tack they'll take. I imagine he'll be on his cell phone to every one of his deputies, the wounded hero with The Man's heel on his neck.

"Is everyone hungry? If so, I'll call Jenny, see about that dinner she promised. Carson and I already ate something, but not much. We could force down a bite or two."

"Sounds good to me," Kraus said, "as soon as we get everything secure. Vickie, you can take some food to DeAndre and Slick later or I'll never hear the end of it. Oh, and don't forget DeAndre likes lots of Parmesan on his spaghetti. Lead the way, Griffin."

Griffin said, "We'll meet you at Jenny's house—it's 201 Cedar Lane. I think Carson and I will walk, enjoy the evening now that we're out of the slammer."

"You convicts are all the same," Kraus said, and grinned at him. "See you shortly. Ah, thanks for the change of pace, Griffin. You know this story will make the rounds."

28

There was next to no traffic when Griffin and Carson stepped out of the station. The evening had cooled down and the trees rustled with a light breeze. Gaffer's Ridge was closing down for the night. They walked a moment in silence before Griffin said, his voice light, "It's been quite a day for both of us, especially you. Here I was, tired from a hard case and walking around town to avoid taking a nap after Jenny fed me lunch. I was thinking of nothing more than what kind of furniture to buy for my new condo in Washington, when suddenly your voice was yelling in my head. I wanted to talk with you about your gift. When it came to you, that sort of thing."

Carson stopped, turned to face him. "So this

was why you wanted to walk. You wanted to see if I was all right with all that happened. Between us. In our brains."

He nodded, kicked a pebble from the path.

She sighed. "It's all so very weird. And no, it wasn't new to me."

"Tell me how it came about."

"I was in a bad car accident when I was seventeen, left me in a coma for a week. When I was finally swimming back to the surface, I heard someone speaking. The voice sounded distant, and it sounded somehow odd. I came to discover she wasn't speaking to me. She was thinking about dinner and what she'd make and how her louse ex-husband was picking up her daughter at eight o'clock. I couldn't believe it. It was a nurse. When I opened my eyes to see her, I said, 'Why is your ex-husband a louse?' I thought she'd faint, then I guess she decided she'd said it out loud. It's happened only a few times, and it's always unexpected. I've never been able to make it happen. I remember when I was walking down Madison in New York next to a man in a business suit. I heard all about his presentation to his boss that morning and how he'd nailed it. I couldn't help it. When I passed him, I smiled big and congratulated him on impressing his boss. He gave me a weird look and nearly broke into a run to get away from me. The last time it happened, one day last year, I was walking toward Fiftieth and Fifth to shop a sale at Saks.

I ran into this young man, a complete stranger, like Rafer Bodine. And his thoughts were as loud as Rafer's. He was insanely happy. He'd just gotten married and all he could think about was his bride. He was very graphic about it. I remember I simply stopped and stared at him. I don't think he ever noticed me. He continued on his way, nearly skipping he was so happy. I told my mom each time it happened. Bless her, she hugged me, whispered against my ear, 'Another amazing part of you, Carson. Enjoy it, use it, appreciate it, and don't let it worry you.'

"Then there was Rafer, hearing him thinking about the three girls." She sighed. "I've studied this gift you and I have. Do you know, I haven't found a single medical explanation. Sure, there are gazillions of references to people getting the 'sight' after a head trauma, but nothing you'd call legitimate research. Now, how about you?"

He said, "The first time I was maybe fifteen. I heard my mother's thoughts. I'd just walked in from school, real quiet. I wanted to surprise her, give her a little scare, when her voice sounded in my head, 'I know you want to scare me into gray hair, Griffin, but not this time. I've got a bone to pick with you.'"

She laughed. "What was the bone?"

"I honestly don't remember, but I bet Mom would. I guess this gift, or whatever you want to call it, I inherited from her. She knew it, but she never spoke of it to me. I like that your mom talked about it with you.

"And like you, I can never predict when there'll be somebody knocking on the front door in my mind. There's one other person I know who's like us. That's Agent Dillon Savich, my boss. You'll meet him and maybe another agent, who happens to be his wife." He paused a moment. "Sometime I'll tell you about how Savich and I dealt with a very scary old woman, name of Louisa Alcott, no relation to the author."

"Does Louisa have your gift?"

"Not exactly. She had a different gift— actually, she had an amazing power that almost killed us." He leaned down and sniffed at a wildly blooming red bougainvillea.

"Will you tell me what happened someday?"

"We'll see."

"I'll remind you. Now, you believe hooking up happens when the right person is in the right place at the right time. Like you were today."

"Sounds sort of reasonable. I think strong emotion may be a factor, as it was with you."

"I was knocked out and kidnapped and scared out of my mind when Rafer pulled out that gun, so I'd say I was pretty amped up. Agent Kraus doesn't know about you? About what really happened?"

"Nope. No reason to drag her into it."

"Do you know how much longer she and her agents will stay?"

"She's done her job. I imagine they'll head out tomorrow. She's leaving DeAndre and Slick—that's Agent David Foxx—to guard Rafer. Also, she'll come back if I call her, which I don't think will be necessary. Savich is coming. I'm thinking he'll be all the backup we need."

"You make him sound like Superman."

"Let's say in a fight I'd want him at my back. Like I said, Sherlock, his wife, is also an agent. He told me she was in a car accident, but apparently she's okay. She's got this amazing gift—no, a different amazing gift—she walks into a crime scene and she's crazy good at reconstructing it. It's like she can see what happened."

"Do you know, I've lived in New York all my life and never even saw a mugging? Okay, I've seen some drug deals on street corners, at least that's what I thought they were. A day in Gaffer's Ridge with its church spires and antiques shops, and this—" She waved her arms around her, eyed him. "I still find it amazing you're an FBI agent. Can you imagine what would have happened if you were an insurance salesman or a vet running an animal clinic? Hey, will you teach me how to kick like that?"

Griffin laughed. "Sure, why not?" He was glad Savich was on his way, since his gut was telling him he was going to need him. Griffin wasn't going to question his gut. When he had in the past, things hadn't worked out well.

Carson said, "You know the sheriff is only going to pretend to cooperate, right, Griffin?"

"That's exactly what I expect. Although Agent Kraus may have scared him enough to make him useful to us, at least for the short term. When I see him and his deputies in the morning, I'm going to send them to Radford and Marion—the towns where Amy Traynor and Latisha Morris lived. I want him to tell the local sheriff or police chief what's happened here, that these kidnappings are all under the purview of the FBI now. He can bring back copies of their case files and share his work with them, which I doubt he's done. Then I'm going to contact them myself, see what they've been up to, any and all the angles and leads they're following."

"And Heather Forrester, who's from here?"

Griffin smiled. "Do you know, I imagine the sheriff has done due diligence, since she's from Gaffer's Ridge. I'll review all the interviews he and his deputies have conducted, see if I need to speak to the family. But I'll bet you he's been very thorough."

"What if the other law enforcement people won't cooperate with the sheriff? I mean, I wouldn't even want to give him my name."

"Don't forget, Bodine knows these people. They'll see he's cooperating, even though he doesn't like us, even though his nephew is involved. I think that'll help us. We can also ask Agent Kraus to arrest him, and he knows it."

When they turned the corner onto Cedar Lane, they saw FBI agents lounging around the FBI van, no longer wearing their tactical gear but looking like regular folks in jeans and T-shirts. Jenny and Aimée Rose were on the front porch of their white 1940s cottage, inviting them in for dinner.

Carson stopped, breathed in deeply. "Can you smell that spaghetti, Griffin? Delicious, and after all, we did only get a taste. I hope she's got lots of garlic toast."

29

As Savich turned onto Route 60 out of Richmond and headed due west toward the George Washington and Jefferson National Forests and the Appalachians, he said to Sherlock, "Only about an hour and a half before we're in Gaffer's Ridge. It sits in a long sleeve of land between two mountain ridges, maybe fifteen minutes south of Lexington, Virginia. Not to be confused with Lexington, Kentucky." Slight pause, then, "How do you feel? Any head pain?"

"No, I'm fine, don't worry. I took two aspirin, so I'm good to go. Sean isn't worried, is he, that his mom's really sick?"

"No, he vaguely understands it's more a pain in the butt than any serious disease. And believe me, he's a happy camper now he'll get to spend several days at his grandmother's house. Talk about a huge treat. She's the chocolate chip cookie queen. He'll be fine, Sherlock, don't worry, okay? A couple of days in Gaffer's Ridge, and we'll head back."

Sherlock looked at the man who'd been her husband for six years. He'd brought her clothes to the hospital and she'd changed in the bathroom, not in front of him. She'd looked at herself in the mirror and seen what he'd told her was her usual uniform—white blouse, black pants and boots, a black leather jacket it was too hot to wear, and her credentials. He'd even handed her her service Glock and her small Glock 380, along with an ankle holster, saying, "I took both your Glocks home, no sense freaking out the nurses. They're yours. You always wear the little 380," and she'd strapped it on her ankle. It had felt completely natural. Her hair was clean, pulled back in a clip at the base of her neck, curling tendrils already corkscrewing around her face. She touched on lipstick, rubbed in a bit on her cheeks because she was too pale, and stared at herself. *Whoever you are, you've got a seriously good-looking husband. Not only is he hot, he seems nice and very concerned about you. Are you nice? Are you smart? Are you a good agent? I heard one agent say he hoped I could still read a crime scene, whatever that meant.* But she knew, deep down, she knew. But she didn't know the woman in the mirror. She said now, "Dillon, riding in the Porsche—it feels familiar."

He felt a leap of hope, shot her a sideways look. She was tilting her head to the side, it was a familiar gesture, too.

"Excellent. That's the second time you've remembered my Porsche." He paused a moment. "Remember that video I showed you? You were wearing shorts and a cutoff top, flip-flops, and said you had made lemonade for Sean, Marty, and me? I dreamed about you in that video last night. Marty wasn't there this time, but she was probably close by. You remember, she's Sean's future Number One Wife?"

"I remember, that is, yes, you told me about Marty, showed me a photo of her and her family. The video—I wish I could remember." She shook herself. "You said we've known them forever?"

"That's right." He turned on his blinker, passed an eighteen-wheeler. The driver honked, whistled at the Porsche, and gave Savich a thumbs-up.

Savich returned the wave, eyed Sherlock, and plowed ahead. "Before I could drink your lemonade, Griffin called, interrupted my dream. I sure wanted that lemonade, but he was insisting."

She cocked her head at him again, graceful, inquisitive, a look that held a wealth of meaning to him, though she didn't know it. He said, "Griffin wanted to talk to me again."

"How do you know? I didn't hear your cell phone."

Was it time to tell her? Would it make this even harder for her, or help her remember? "Sherlock, sometimes I know when people want to talk with me. Particularly Griffin. That's one of the reasons I wanted him to transfer from the San Francisco Field Office to Washington, to the CAU."

"What are you saying? That you and Agent Griffin Hammersmith are psychic?"

He shot her a quick look. She didn't appear horrified or alarmed and she wasn't laughing. She looked fascinated, like she wanted to pull the words out of his mouth.

He said, "Well, yes, you could say that. It doesn't happen often, and as I said, I appear to have a strong connection to Griffin, but he's not the only one. I don't suppose you remember the Alcott family? Griffin and I dealt with them while you were keeping watch on the JFK terrorist?"

Terrorist? She saw a flash of a man in a security line holding a grenade—and then he was gone, behind the white door, as she was starting to think of it. "I think I just saw him, I mean I saw the terrorist. What was his name?"

"Nasim Conklin. Maybe in bed tonight, I'll tell you about him. That's why people recognize you, and they do—you were on TV and you went viral. You're the heroine of JFK."

She could only stare at him, then she grinned. "A pity I didn't save the president."

He reached over and grabbed her hand, felt her still, and released her. It didn't matter. He grinned at her. "While you were worrying about terrorists, I was meeting the Alcotts. One of them had some scary abilities of her own, well, not more than Autumn Backman, but different."

The solid white door opened again and Sherlock saw a pale little girl lying motionless on a hospital bed. She drew in her breath. "I saw her for a moment. Did she die?"

"No, she woke up, her gift thankfully intact."

"Her gift? What could she do?"

"She helped me take down some very bad people." There was much more, of course, but he stopped. Sherlock had enough on her plate, he didn't want her wondering if she should call the people with the straitjackets.

She said, "I'm glad she didn't die. Why don't you call me Lacey? That's my first name, right?"

"You've always preferred Sherlock, like your father—the federal judge in San Francisco. He says it scares the criminals."

She nodded. "Yes, you told me. It's a cool name." She'd spoken to her parents, reassured them she was fine, deciding not to mention she wouldn't know them if she passed them on the street.

"Don't you like Sherlock any longer?"

"Yes, I do. It's different. I was only wondering." Act normal, no choice, but nothing was normal. She watched him punch a number into his cell phone, put it on speaker: "Griffin. Talk to me. You're on speaker."

They both listened as Griffin filled them in

on what he'd been doing. In an emotionless voice, Savich assured him Sherlock was all right and they'd be in Gaffer's Ridge in an hour.

Savich punched off, and said now, his voice matter-of-fact, "We're going to need your excellent eye, your assessment of the people we meet in Gaffer's Ridge. We're going to need you with us as a federal agent, okay?"

"I'll do my best." She looked at his profile: straight nose, high cheekbones, square jaw, and swarthy complexion, his hands on the steering wheel. He wore a wedding band that matched hers, and, of all things, a Mickey Mouse watch strapped around his wrist. He had big strong hands. She cleared her throat. "You said you'd tell me all about the JFK incident—tonight in bed. What did you mean exactly?"

Ah, there it was, the eight-hundred-pound gorilla in the car, wedged between them. He gave her a quick look. "Give me your hand, Sherlock."

She didn't want to, he knew it, but he was patient. His right hand remained open, waiting. Finally, he felt her cool palm against his, felt her fingers lightly touch his. He squeezed. "We're married, I know your body as well as I know my own. I also realize I'm a stranger to you, and you can't imagine climbing into bed with me. I want you to know I have no intention of stripping in front of you, no intention of jumping you. But we will sleep together, Sherlock. I don't snore, usually, and neither do you. You usually sleep with your head on my shoulder, or we spoon. I like both. You do, too. But that's up to you." He turned to see her staring at him, her face pale, a bit of alarm in her eyes.

"Okay," she said, but her voice was barely above a whisper, not because she was at all afraid of him but because her head was aching something fierce, and the highway was weaving back and forth in wide, dizzying loops. She felt drunk and nauseous, closed her eyes, swallowed. She didn't want to throw up, she wouldn't. She heard him speaking again, but his words didn't make sense, they were jumbled, moving and changing, like the road. "Stop the car!"

He pulled over onto the shoulder.

She opened the door and threw up. She'd eaten so little there wasn't much, mostly dry heaves. She felt his hands rubbing lightly up and down her back, holding her shaking shoulders. At last she whispered, "I'm okay now."

Savich handed her a bottle of water, watched her drink, then spit it out. She handed him back the water bottle.

"Thank you. I think it was all the curves in the highway, made me nauseous. I'm all right now, but I think I could nap."

He handed her a Kleenex, then worried. Should he turn around and take her back to the hospital? Should he have brought her in the first place? "Do you still feel nauseated? We can stop at the hospital in Lexington, let them take a look at you."

She didn't open her eyes, but reached out her hand. Instead of touching his hand, her palm landed on his thigh. She jerked her hand away. He said nothing, only took her hand in his and gently squeezed. After a moment, her hand lay quiescent in his. Finally, she said, "No more hospitals, Dillon, I'll be fine. It was the oddest thing. When you were speaking, it seemed all the words were mixing themselves up. It was like I was dyslexic, even though I was listening, not reading, and I couldn't understand you. Really, I'm okay now. Don't worry. It's the concussion, it's messing me up a little bit, but you know there's nothing to be done. Time and rest. And maybe some distraction, but only after I wake up." She tried to smile at him.

"All right, take a nap, Sherlock. I'll wake you when we get to Gaffer's Ridge." He watched her lean her head against the door, close her eyes. He knew a hospital wasn't the answer, that keeping her with him was best. She'd been right about that.

What was going on in Gaffer's Ridge would engage her, and he'd make sure she got her rest. He'd tell her stories about cases they'd had, people they knew. He eased the Porsche back onto the highway and prayed. He heard her breathing slow as she fell asleep. He wished he had a pillow or a cover for her, but he didn't, hadn't thought of it. He kept driving, slowly, heading toward the west and into the distant mountains.

30

GAFFER'S RIDGE
RAFER BODINE'S HOUSE
THURSDAY, NOON

Sherlock awoke as Dillon entered Gaffer's Ridge, assured him she felt fine, which was mostly true. She looked around at the lovely little town with its hills and dips as Savich slowly drove the Porsche down Winchester Street toward Berger Lane, where the forensic team from the Richmond Field Office was processing Rafer Bodine's house. Griffin and Dr. DeSilva would meet them there.

Savich pulled the Porsche behind the FBI forensic van in the driveway. Sherlock's eyes were bright, and that was good. "Any headache, any nausea, anything wonky, you tell me, you promise?"

She smiled at him, a real smile, and nodded. "I promise."

"Stay put."

She waited until he opened the door for her, gave her his hand to help her out. She stood quietly a moment, taking everything in. "An old house, more a cottage," she said, looking around, "but there's charm here, or there could be, if someone did something with the yard, planted some colorful flowers. I guess Mr. Bodine isn't much for regular yard maintenance." She didn't realize she was studying the scene like a trained investigator, but Savich did. They turned to a black Range Rover pulling in behind the Porsche. Sherlock said, "Is that Griffin Hammersmith? And the woman?"

"Yes, that's Griffin. I would assume the woman with him is Dr. DeSilva."

The two of them got out of the car and headed over. The man waved. Sherlock said, "Would you look at those two. I've gotta say, they're close to being the most beautiful duo I've ever seen. They should be on a red carpet."

Savich grinned. "Even women FBI agents stop and stare at Griffin in the Hoover Building. Worse, the word's out he and his fiancée are no longer together, so he's fair game. I heard he had half a dozen invitations to lunch last week. Not to mention to dinner, the movies, to see etchings, whatever.

"He and Ruth—Agent Ruth Noble— finished a hairy case in Arkansas a couple of days ago so I gave them both time off.

So that's Dr. Carson DeSilva. You're right, she's a looker, too."

She said suddenly, "Griffin has a cat named Monk." She blinked, turned to shake her head at him. "I remember his fricking cat's name, go figure."

"Alas, his ex-fiancée, Anna, is Monk's mother, so Monk had no choice but to go with her. She and Monk now live in Seattle. She's DEA."

Griffin stopped in front of Sherlock, smiled down at her, not all that far since she was tall. He saw no recognition in her eyes. He said, "I'm Griffin. You and I have been through some wars together. I imagine we'll be in a lot more before we both hang it up in the misty future. I can't imagine what you're going through, Sherlock, but your eyes are clear, the flame's still burning. Another couple of days and you'll be line-dancing again, and keeping us all safe," and he grinned at her.

Sherlock said, "I'll certainly try. Have you been in the CAU long?"

"Eight months now. I first met you at the San Francisco Field Office. Savich convinced me to transfer to the Hoover. I'd like you guys to meet Dr. Carson DeSilva, a journalist from New York."

Carson took Sherlock's hand. "It's amazing to meet you, Agent Sherlock. I wrote about you shortly after the JFK incident, along with most every other journalist in the U.S."

Savich had told her strangers recognized her. She managed a smile, said, "Thank you."

Griffin said, "I see Caleb's already here with his forensic people. Bettina and her crew met with him at the sheriff's station. She went back to Richmond last night. Slick and DeAndre are guarding Rafer Bodine, and on loan to me if I need them." He turned to Sherlock. "I know Savich has already told you a dozen times, but really, if you need to kiss us off for a while and take a snooze, holler, okay?"

Again, she only smiled.

Savich had worked several times in the past year with forensic crime scene supervisor Caleb Minter. He was tall, in his late fifties, and he was whip thin, his salt-and-pepper hair sticking up in clumps on his head. He was hyper, always moving, even his leg bounced up and down when he sat. Savich wondered what Caleb's wife thought of that constant bouncing leg. Caleb didn't know Sherlock wouldn't know him from Adam and he wasn't going to call attention to it. Savich shook his hand. "Caleb, good to see you."

Sherlock smiled at the man who could have been her father or an escaped prisoner, for all she knew.

"And you, Savich." Caleb turned to study Sherlock's face. "Heard you were in a wee bit of an accident Tuesday. It's great to see you up and about. Now, down to business. Most of the crew is upstairs, and Lotus is out with Oscar in the backyard. First, we didn't find any duct tape in the basement, or anywhere else in the house for that matter, which means someone removed it. In fact, the whole basement looked like somebody's cleaned it up. Plus, we couldn't find a computer or a router. And there's no car. We think someone took those, too."

Griffin said, "Makes sense. Rafer Bodine owns a black Chevy Uplander. A pity it was taken. There'd be proof Bodine transported Dr. DeSilva here. As for the missing computer, that's not a surprise, either. Rafer's going to claim self-defense in his own home, and without physical evidence, it's going to be hard to hold him for long."

Carson said, "As for the pipe, Sheriff Bodine took it, so maybe it's in evidence." She paused. "Or maybe he threw it away. Griffin, do you think the sheriff removed anything he believed could be proof against his nephew before Mr. Minter showed up?"

Griffin said, "Or Rafer's family. Whatever, the sheriff was the one who made the calls and set it in motion."

Minter said, "The sheriff? That's a sorry thing to hear. Now, we did find a length of pipe suspended from the basement ceiling. I'm sure we can match it to that jagged piece of pipe you managed to break off, if it is in evidence. Dr. DeSilva, amazing job of getting yourself free of the duct tape and hitting him with that pipe. Can you come down to the basement with us, show us exactly where you were?"

Carson really didn't want to go back down to that basement, but she saw Griffin looking at her, a question in his eyes. She straightened her shoulders and followed Minter down the stairs, Griffin and Savich behind her. When they stood in the middle of the basement, Carson looked around, seeing it with new eyes. "It seems so small now. I would have sworn it was larger."

Savich said, "Dr. DeSilva, one more time please, tell us what happened, show us everything you touched down here."

Carson sucked in the stale, fetid air, drew a deep breath, and told them exactly what she'd done, showed them the stool she'd used to reach the pipe. When she finished, her heart had stopped pounding. It was only a basement, an old decrepit basement.

Minter said, "We'll see if we can pull some fingerprints from that pipe if it is indeed in evidence at the sheriff's station, and not disappeared like everything else. We do have good evidence you were in the basement, in any case. Let's go back upstairs, there's something else I want to show you."

When they were once again in the small entrance hall, Minter drew them into a loose circle around him. "Look here at the bullet holes. We found some 9mm bullet fragments, so we'll be able to show where the shots came from. Did the sheriff also take the Walther?"

"Yes," Griffin said.

Minter said to Carson, "Can you paint us a word picture, Dr. DeSilva, of what happened between you and Rafer Bodine once you came up the stairs?"

Minter's two forensic techs came downstairs and introductions were made, then Minter nodded to Carson. She began to talk. She was a journalist, she was used to telling a story. She told them nearly word for word what she'd said and what Rafer Bodine had said. "—Griffin kicked out his leg and his foot clipped Bodine's wrist, broke it, you could hear the bone snap. Bodine dropped his gun and I jumped forward and hit him on the head with the pipe."

There was a loud bark, followed by Oscar the cadaver dog barreling into the entrance hall.

Savich turned and smiled, went down on his haunches, and rubbed the three-year-old beagle's ears. Oscar tried to lick any part of Savich his tongue could reach, his tail wagging so fast his rear end shook. Like Astro, Oscar loved an ear rub, so Savich kept stroking, added a rub down Oscar's back. Lotus, Oscar's person, handed Savich a couple of dog treats. As he fed them to Oscar, he said to her, "Oscar didn't find anything, Lotus?"

Lotus, aka Kiley Lu, shook her head, making

her long, straight sheet of black hair swirl around her head. She was small and slender, and someone once said she was as delicate as a lotus blossom, and the name stuck. "There are no bodies buried in the backyard. Oscar is thorough."

Griffin said matter-of-factly, "Then Rafer Bodine buried them elsewhere. He'll have to tell us if he wants a deal, but I hope it won't come to that."

Carson said, "Or Heather and Latisha could still be alive, prisoners somewhere." She cleared her throat, but it was so difficult to say the words. "But not poor Amy. Like I told you, Rafer said Amy died hard, but he didn't say what exactly happened to her." Carson realized she was breathing too hard, too fast. "Sorry, but I want to hit him over the head again."

No one spoke, but Carson realized they believed all three girls were dead. Finally, Sherlock said in a clear voice, "Yes, I agree with you, Dr. DeSilva. It's up to us to find Heather and Latisha. I'm very sorry about Amy. Griffin, where do the girls live?"

Griffin said, "Amy Traynor is from Radford, a small town south of Gaffer's Ridge. We won't notify her family until we're absolutely certain she's dead. She was the second teenager taken. Heather Forrester was the first, from Gaffer's Ridge, three months ago. Latisha Morris is from Marion, on the edge of the national forest."

Lotus said, "If you give us the place to look, Oscar will find Amy Traynor."

At the charming Victorian Gaffer's Ridge Inn on Winchester Street, Savich and Sherlock were shown to a large corner room on the top floor by the owner, Mrs. Carmody, who was huffing by the time they got to the third floor. She proudly showed them the amenities, told them this was her most superior room, and left.

Sherlock walked to the large double window and stared out at the miles of thickly forested hills and the distant mountains, lightly veiled in a thin summer fog. She saw green planted fields closer in, cut by flat roads, and the houses lining them were small white dots. There was a series of framed photos set up at eye level on the walls, all of Mrs. Carmody's pets through the years, and a lovely remodeled bathroom with a stack of white towels and a big shower stall. She was grateful Dillon hadn't said anything even though she knew he'd seen her stare fixedly at the queen-size bed.

They met Griffin and Carson for lunch at Jenny's Café. There was only one empty booth in the large room, kept open by Aimée Rose for them. They were aware of stares from the locals, and even the tourists began to realize something was different about their group.

Griffin and Carson had told them pretty much all they knew by the time they finished their burritos. When the last piece of apple pie was eaten, Griffin said, "Let's go pay a visit to Rafer Bodine."

Carson said, "I can't wait to see how he plays this," and she popped her knuckles.

31

Everyone piled into Griffin's Range Rover for the short ride to the community hospital near Lexington. The skies were blue, dotted with cumulus clouds. The temperature wasn't quite as brutal, dialed back a bit by a fresh breeze, and the AC in the Range Rover worked like a champ. Griffin told them about his meeting with Booker Bodine that morning. "Of course, he wanted to shoot me, but he's not a stupid man, he knew he had to at least appear to cooperate. I didn't rub his nose or his deputies' noses in any of it, didn't accuse him of taking evidence from Rafer's house or calling Rafer's family so they could take care of it. I didn't think it would be worth it, not without real proof. I told him and his deputies to talk to law enforcement in Marion and Radford, let them know what's happening, bring back copies of their files, which, amazingly, Booker hadn't read and didn't have. We'll see if he does as he's told. My guess is he won't do anything overt to mess up the investigation since one of the girls is from Gaffer's Ridge. As for how he'll deal with me, we'll see."

Carson nodded. "Yes, a tire iron at night to the back of your head has probably occupied his thoughts. But you know, I'm thinking he has to at least wonder if Rafer did kidnap the girls."

Griffin looked at Sherlock in his rearview mirror. She was pale, silent, looking out the window. He wanted to ask her if she was okay, but caught Savich's eye and kept quiet. He asked instead, "Savich, do you think we could get Dr. Hicks out here to interview Rafer Bodine?"

"Sure, Dr. Hicks would love it, but I strongly doubt Rafer Bodine would allow him to pull out his gold watch."

Sherlock listened only vaguely as they discussed how to move forward with the investigation, how to best utilize Slick and DeAndre, the two agents from the Richmond Field Office now taking turns guarding Rafer Bodine. Finally, the two aspirin she'd taken at Jenny's Café got her headache under control.

It was as if he knew. Savich turned in his seat. "Better now, Sherlock?"

She nodded. "I was thinking about bringing

Sean here before it gets cold. Camp out in the forest, go for hikes, cook him hot dogs over a fire." She hoped her enthusiasm didn't sound put on because it wasn't.

Savich said, his eyes on her face, "Sean loves s'mores. Maybe after we're through here and Carson's had a chance to run over Rafer Bodine a couple of times with her rental car, we can visit for a weekend." He was pleased to see she smiled.

They pulled into the parking lot of the community hospital a few minutes later. The hospital was a square three-story concrete building built in the eighties, surrounded by parking lots on all sides. It was framed by distant tree-covered mountains and set in a forest of the ubiquitous pines and oaks, and an occasional chestnut and beech, a beautiful setting, soothing for both body and soul. Inside it was bustling, since it was the only hospital in a sixty-mile radius.

They were directed through the lobby to a bank of elevators to take them to the third floor. "I know it's strange," the grandmotherly woman at information had said, "that room 415 is actually on the third floor, but what happened is the hospital CEO had them skip the three hundreds because of a scary dream he considered a portent, so there you have it." She shrugged, rolled her eyes. "We all make do."

They spotted Slick, aka Special Agent David Foxx, halfway down the wide corridor, sitting outside the partially open door, a *Sports Illustrated* magazine on his lap. He said hello to Griffin and Savich, then stood a moment and stared at Carson. "You clean up well, Dr. DeSilva."

"Thank you, Agent Slick. You, too, although I miss the awesome impact of the riot gear."

Slick smiled, then turned to Sherlock. The FBI grapevine was the fastest in the land, and he'd found out quickly enough she had amnesia from the accident Tuesday. Imagine waking up next to someone you didn't know and not recognizing your own kid. It had to be hard on both of them. He studied her face a moment, took her hand. "I'm Agent David Foxx, Richmond Field Office. You can call me Slick. I'm very glad to see you up and moving, Sherlock." He gave her a grin. "I gotta say, you don't look too pitiful after your accident, but I guess the big guy here has been waiting on you hand and foot. How do you feel?"

Sherlock stared up at the man with his charming smile and cop eyes, and said, "I'm better, thank you." Nothing else.

Slick nodded. "Most of us have heard about the guy who struck your windshield while you were whirling around like the teacup ride at Disney. Is he all right?"

Savich said, "He hasn't been found yet, Slick. People have turned in cell phone videos from after the accident, but none are clear enough to run facial recognition. They're running his blood, hoping he's in the DNA database. We all hope he's not too badly injured."

Sherlock swallowed. Twice now she'd seen the huge smear of the man's blood on her windshield, heard the heavy thump of his body when he struck the hood. But this time the image didn't simply disappear behind the white door as it had those times. It faded slowly, and she realized it was more like a memory, not a flashback. Didn't that mean her memory was mending itself? But why hadn't she seen his face? She smiled up at the stranger who evidently knew her. "Will you tell me sometime how you got the nickname Slick?"

"Ah, there's a story. I might need permission from Savich to tell you. And maybe my wife. And maybe my kids. The dog'll be okay with it."

"I wish we had the time," Savich said, "but things are happening fast. Fill us in on what's happened here."

Slick pulled out a small notebook. "Last night at eight o'clock, Sheriff Booker Bodine, his brother and Rafer Bodine's father, Quint Bodine, and a lawyer by the name of Harmon Jobs came to see Rafer. The lawyer closed the door, said he and his client were entitled to privacy. They stayed for thirty minutes. I heard the sheriff tell Rafer as they were leaving that he'd be going home soon. He looked pretty pleased with himself. Rafer's dad, Quint Bodine, looked pissed, didn't say anything to me. As for the lawyer, his card said he's from

Richmond, from the firm of Pringe, Weldon and Hayes. I looked them up, they're big into criminal defense.

"As for Rafer Bodine, he was bitching non-stop—his head hurt, his wrist was killing him. He was claiming to anyone who'd listen that you, Griffin, kicked him in the ribs, in the leg, in the kidney, just about everywhere. He wanted to press charges for police brutality. However, after his visit with the sheriff, his dad, and the lawyer, he's been quiet, not a word out of him." Slick paused, looked over at Carson again and did another double take. He was married, blessed with three girls, all hellions, but as his brother always said when his wife wasn't in the vicinity, he wasn't dead yet, and DeSilva was a knockout. He said, "Dr. DeSilva, before the lawyer closed the door, I heard Rafer telling his uncle he wanted you arrested for hitting him so hard on the head with that pipe you nearly killed him. He claimed both you and Griffin were laughing as you slammed your boots into him."

A thick lock of blond hair curled around Carson's cheek and she tucked it behind her ear. "It's a bummer, but I was wearing sneakers."

Sherlock spurted out a laugh. "I can't wait to meet this putz."

32

Rafer Bodine was sitting up in bed, his wrist in a cast, looking fit, truth be told. He sneered at Hammersmith, the one his uncle Booker called the pretty boy, and wished he could have another go at him. Who cared if he was FBI? Were these some of the people with machine guns who drove their armored truck into Gaffer's Ridge—his town—and took it away from his uncle Booker? And all because Booker couldn't get his mind around Mr. GQ being a federal cop? Rafer understood the way his uncle's mind worked—sometimes he saw what he wanted to see, believed what he wanted to believe, but in this case, Rafer knew the reason his uncle had hauled them to jail. He'd quickly called Rafer's pa, and taken charge. Last night when Booker and Rafer's pa and ma had visited the hospital, he'd told Rafer not to worry, there was no proof he'd done anything to Carson DeSilva, and Rafer knew he'd gone through the house himself, made everything they shouldn't find disappear, including his SUV and computer.

Rafer eyed the agents as he raised the bed. No way was he about to look up at these bozos. They were staring at him like he was a loser. He shrugged and said, his voice indifferent, "What do you lot want? My lawyer told me I don't have to talk to you, so forget it." He stopped when the woman, DeSilva, came forward to stand beside Mr. GQ. She looked bright and shiny as a new penny, as his grandma used to say, her thick blond hair loose to her shoulders, most of the beautiful stuff hooked behind her ears. She wore small diamond studs. He had to admit she was as beautiful as Charlize Theron, and everyone knew he'd worshipped the actress for years, even recorded her perfume commercials on TV. It didn't matter how DeSilva looked, screw the top-notch packaging. He hated her for the crawling fear she'd made him feel, the fear that had made him panic. She'd known some-how about the girls, and then he'd really messed up, and all because of what he'd seen on her face, seen in her eyes. His brain had screamed at him, *She knows, she knows, she knows it all.* He'd felt instant corrosive fear because he'd believed to his soul she was dangerous, believed she was like his mother. His mother called it a gift, and said it was only for the special few, like his sister, Camilla. He remembered how his mother went on and on to his father about how fast Camilla was learning to do things even she couldn't do. And he'd known for the longest time he had no gift, known there was nothing special about him, known they were disappointed in him, whispered about him. No, he wouldn't think about his sister.

He forced himself to look away from DeSilva, to the man and woman standing behind Hammersmith, both looking at him with mild interest at best, both spit-shined in their cool black clothes, all sharp and hard, doubtless more FBI agents. Well, maybe not the girl with the curly red hair, but where were the freckles? He couldn't see any. Was she that white all over? He wouldn't mind checking that out for himself, then maybe, well, who knew? He stared hard at her. "You're an FBI agent, too?"

Sherlock gave him her patented sunny smile, not realizing it was her trademark. She appeared to give his question some thought. "I'm told I am. Actually, I don't remember, but I will soon."

"What does that mean?"

"Not important. Now, I understand, Mr. Bodine, you were involved in the kidnapping of three teenage girls, very probably murdered them. Amy Traynor—we know she's dead—that's what you let on to Dr. DeSilva. But what about

Heather Forrester and Latisha Morris? Are they still alive?"

Rafer's lawyer had told him to keep quiet, and he'd meant to, but her question made him yell, "That isn't true! Don't believe anything she says, she's lying. She claims she read my mind. Can you imagine anyone taking that seriously? You know it's nuts, she's nuts." He saw his lawyer's stern expression in his mind's eye, and shook his head. "I've got nothing more to say."

Sherlock said, "At least tell us why you kidnapped those sixteen-year-old girls. Did you rape them? Have there been other young girls, but from farther away, nowhere near Gaffer's Ridge so they couldn't be traced back to you? Were all of them sixteen? Are you a serial killer, Mr. Bodine?"

Rafer felt bile rise in his throat. He wasn't about to sit here and let her spew this crap at him. He managed to keep his voice calm. "I didn't kill anyone. I wouldn't ever hurt anyone. The lot of you, go away. Leave me alone. Get the nurse, I want pain meds. My lawyer said you have nothing on me, I'll be going home soon. Uncle Booker told me all about your takeover, but there's no way that'll last for you. You'll see." He stared at Savich. "Who are you?"

"I'm Agent Savich. It's all very straightforward, Mr. Bodine. Help us find the missing teenagers, tell us where you took them, and it could save your life."

Quiet, keep your mouth shut, that's what his pa had said, too, last night after the lawyer laid it out. He said, "You've got no proof, you've got nothing at all. Go away."

Sherlock cocked her head at him. "Help me to understand, Mr. Bodine. If Dr. DeSilva didn't read your mind, if she didn't scare you witless, then why did you knock her unconscious, take her to your house, and duct-tape her in your basement? Surely you and your lawyer have come up with a story, an explanation, right?"

"I didn't! I never touched her, I don't even know her. She's fricking crazy. You should be locking her up."

Sherlock said, "Does your family know what you've been up to? Are they involved? Or are they covering up for you out of habit? Are you a screwup Mr. Bodine?"

"No! My family is none of your business."

"Oh, but they are, because someone not only removed your car from your driveway, this same someone probably also removed your computer and the duct tape. Which makes me wonder, how does a guy make do without any duct tape?"

"Very funny. Look, I came home and walked in and there she was holding that pipe, ready to brain me." He flicked a look toward Griffin. "And that one, that pretty boy, came running into my house and attacked me. They're probably sleeping together and he's lying to protect her."

His wrist hurt, his head hurt, and he was scared to his bones, but no way would he let these four see it. He looked over at Carson, managed another credible sneer, coated it with sarcasm. "You're a journalist for this big shot in New York City, and everyone knows you people make up stuff all the time." And then to Griffin, "So, are you going to charge me? My lawyer says even if you do, you can't hold me for long. There's no proof I did anything wrong."

Carson still wanted to leap on him, but instead she took another deep breath, even managed to smile at him, watched him jump. For the first time in her life, she tried to hear what someone was thinking, but there wasn't anything to hear.

Sherlock said, "Tell us, Mr. Bodine, what did you mean—Agent Hammersmith won't last for long?"

He held it in, shook his head.

Sherlock studied Rafer Bodine. He was a fairly good-looking man, early thirties, and probably tall, but she couldn't tell with him in bed. His hair was blond, more gold, really, with some wave to it, a bit on the long side. She'd bet he moseyed when he walked. She wished she could see a monster behind those dark brown eyes, but she didn't. What she saw was anger and fear, and petulance. She said to get him talking again, "Mr. Bodine, we hear your family has been in Gaffer's Ridge for generations, that many of you run successful businesses here. Is this true?"

Rafer stared at all the curly red hair, the pale face, the incredible light blue eyes. He said slowly, "Maybe I'll tell you, if you tell me if you're white all over. Or are you sick?"

"Your father, Mr. Bodine," Sherlock said without pause. "Isn't he the president and owner of Gaffer's Ridge First City Bank? His name is Quint Bodine?"

Rafer looked at the four faces, then back at her. "You call yourself Sherlock? That's dumb. A girl can't be Sherlock."

"Your father, Mr. Bodine?"

Why not? It was common knowledge. Why would the lawyer mind? "That's right, he owns a lot of things, not only the bank but some of the stores in town, like the dry cleaners, and two gas stations, and a whole lot of land. My pa signed over a share of the lumber mill to me three years ago and I run it. I'm a respected citizen around here, not that you strangers would know anything about that."

"And your mother? What does she run?"

He said with no hesitation, "She runs the family. No one screws with her. She'll fix you in ways you can't imagine, she'll fix the whole lot of you. She doesn't need anyone else. I'm not talking anymore. Go away." He seamed his lips and looked away from them.

Sherlock said, "That sounds mysterious, Mr. Bodine. Are you saying we should be afraid of her?"

He turned back to look at Sherlock. He didn't see how it could hurt to tell her the truth. He said simply, "She'll shine you, she'll shine all of you." He turned his head away from them again, stared out the window, and really did stop talking.

"You'll see us again soon, Rafer," Griffin said as they left.

33

Elton John's "Rocket Man" blasted out of Savich's pocket as they crossed the parking lot to the Range Rover. Savich pulled out his cell and listened as they walked, asked questions, and punched off. He motioned them to the car, turned, and made a call, this one longer. When he got into the Range Rover, he said, "Hold off starting the engine, Griffin. You guys need to hear this. That was Detective Ben Raven, Metro, in Washington. Sherlock, the man who struck your windshield and disappeared—they had no luck with the local ERs, no matches with missing persons, you know the drill. But we got lucky. They put a rush on DNA testing and the results just came back. Now the disturbing part—the man's DNA was in the database because he's a CIA analyst, thus a federal employee. His name is Justice Cummings. Ben went to Cummings's house, found it empty. One neighbor told Ben he saw the wife and two kids get in the car and leave Monday morning. He said they sometimes head to a cabin in the Poconos for a vacation, sometimes to her mother's, he couldn't be sure, didn't know where in the Poconos, maybe one of the neighbors knew. Without the husband? Ben asked him. The neighbor shrugged, said he'd heard the guy was a spook and no one ever knew what the dude was up to."

Griffin held up his hand. "Whoa, a CIA analyst running into a car in the street and disappearing? If that had anything to do with CIA covert activity, especially here in the States, it'd take a presidential order to get anything out of them. Even with a personal call from the president himself, given the CIA culture, getting them to tell us what this analyst was up to would be like prying open a tuna can with a Q-tip."

Carson stared at him. "I understand they're secretive, they have to be, but with you guys? The FBI?"

"To give you an idea of how the CIA operates, Ben Raven called Mr. Maitland at the Hoover, who called Cummings's supervisor—group chief— at Langley. All he got out of the group chief, a Mr. Alan Besserman, was stone-cold silence, then an 'I'll look into it' and a curt thank-you. Since

Cummings hit an FBI agent's windshield, namely yours, Sherlock, Mr. Maitland is ready to crack the whip, although where exactly he'd crack it is a question. He spoke of going over Besserman's head to his boss, Claire Farriger is her name, the assistant director of the CIA for Europe and Eurasia analysis. He told me he'd get back to me if she deigned to see him, so he wants us to be ready to come back to Washington." He added to Sherlock, "Mr. Maitland wants the CAU to lead up the investigation. I told him we needed another day here in Gaffer's Ridge. He has Agent Lucy McKnight in charge for now. She already tracked Cummings taking an Uber from several blocks from the accident to Alexandria, where he destroyed his cell."

Griffin said, "I'll bet the CIA is working as hard as we are to find Cummings before his disappearance hits the media, and it will, too juicy not to, particularly since he struck your windshield, Sherlock."

Sherlock was thinking her world was awfully strange, being FBI, hitting a CIA analyst who had, oddly, simply disappeared. How often did something like this happen?

Griffin said, "We don't have much time, so we need to move fast. What about Rafer Bodine? Sherlock, you're a fresh eye. What did you think of him?"

Sherlock said thoughtfully, "He's scared, he's angry, but here's the thing—I didn't see evil in him. I know that's an odd thing to say, but being that scared and angry isn't what you'd expect from a serial kidnapper. Is it, Dillon?"

"No," Savich said. "I don't think Rafer is alone in the girls' disappearance. Carson, you said he seemed really sorry Amy died?"

She nodded. "Yes. And he seemed really frightened yesterday at his house, too, frightened of what I could do, or might do. Then today he spoke of his mother fixing us—'shining' us."

Griffin said, "Jenny never spoke of anyone being afraid of Mrs. Bodine. Maybe they keep it a secret and it was the only threat Rafer could think of. So who's involved? Rafer's mother? His father? For that matter, is Sheriff Bodine part of this? And that's why he behaved as he did? To try to contain the damage?"

Savich said, "I know one thing. We don't have time to put together a task force. We have to find those girls fast. If they're still alive, what we've done has already put them in more danger. I think we should go speak to Mrs. Bodine right now. Take it right to her face, see what she says."

Griffin nodded and revved up the Range Rover.

34

They drove from the hospital back toward Gaffer's Ridge through beautiful rural countryside, a single road cutting through flat green farmland, with copses of trees dividing the fields. The mountains were closer here, tree-covered with a soft and hazy fog lacing over them, impossibly magnificent. Griffin turned onto an unmarked single-lane road that immediately wound upward. Pines and oaks were summer full, their branches so thick over the road they nearly met to form a canopy. The temperature was cooling and Griffin cut the AC. Everyone opened windows and breathed in fresh, sweet-smelling air.

He said, "Last winter when I was driving across the country to Washington, I stopped in Gaffer's Ridge. Jenny and Aimée Rose and I hiked for a week, didn't matter when it snowed. I couldn't get over how clean the air was, how the sun glistened off the snow. No cars, only the outdoors and the trees. It's gorgeous country, endless mountains make you feel like you're standing on the earth's backbone."

Savich said, "Katie Kettering, the sheriff of Jessborough, Tennessee, says the same thing—the mountains are forever at your back, like a neighbor you can always count on." He turned in his seat and said matter-of-factly to Carson, "Griffin told us about the gift you have. Did it surprise you?"

As if he were talking about the weather. Carson cleared her throat, saw Griffin nod at her, said to Savich, "I've been told it's a gift—well, that's what my mom calls it. Like I told Griffin, it's always a shock, makes me crazy when it happens. Luckily, my mom didn't haul me to a shrink when I told her. She believed me."

Griffin asked, "What did your father say?"

"No way would I ever tell Dad. I can see his writer's brain latching onto it, making me the subject of his next book, or maybe he'd try to fit me in with his current project—on Freud. No, thank you. But with you, Griffin, it was the first time I've actually communicated with someone. I guess it's a gift, since if we hadn't connected, I might be dead and buried with those poor girls."

Griffin said to Savich, "Carson and I talked

about this last evening. I told her it's sometimes like that with you and me. Well, on occasion."

They stopped talking to let Griffin navigate the sharp switchbacks up the narrow single-lane road. It sometimes passed a mere few feet from a sheer drop, and there was only the occasional turnout dug into the side of the mountain to allow an oncoming car to pass. But they saw no traffic, not a single car or truck. He said, "Jenny told me this is a private road, mostly a private mountain, really. She said she didn't know of anyone who came here.

"She told me the Bodines are treated like royalty, well respected by the locals, but not exactly liked. She added no one ever crosses them, or appears to want to. Then she paused a second, and warned me to be careful."

Sherlock said, "I'm wondering how Mrs. Bodine would fix us—what she actually does to 'shine' someone."

Savich said, "That's one of the reasons I want to meet her, to find out what this 'shining' means." He remembered how Blessed and Grace Backman could control most anyone they wished to control—they had their own word for it, 'stymie.' He turned and smiled at Sherlock. She started, then looked wary. It went straight to his gut, but he said nothing.

Griffin pulled the Range Rover to a stop when the road simply ended. They saw a large sign on curved metal hanging on a freshly painted white gate, EAGLE'S NEST. There was a weathered dark wooden call box next to it.

Griffin said, "Why would someone want to name their property after a Nazi hangout in Bavaria?"

Carson said, "My dad told me Hitler disliked Eagle's Nest because of his fear of heights, and who cares? Sorry."

Griffin leaned out of the driver's side window and pressed the call button. A woman's deep voice answered. "What do you want, Agent Hammersmith?"

Griffin looked for a camera but didn't see one. He raised an eyebrow at Savich as he said into the call box, "Since you know my name, ma'am, you probably also know why I'm here. Just to be sure, we're FBI and we'd like to speak to you about your son, Rafer. You are Mrs. Cyndia Bodine?"

"Of course I am. Yes, I see you brought some reinforcements. Wise of you." The gate buzzed open.

Wise of him? Griffin pulled through, looked back to see the gate close behind them. "I don't see any cameras."

"I don't, either," Carson said. "Guys, I really don't want to be shined. Whatever that means can't be good."

Savich said, "We'll see if she tries anything. Too bad for her son, Rafer, but it appears he can't shine anyone or he surely would have tried it on you, Carson."

The road didn't widen when Griffin was through the gate. It narrowed a bit. At least the asphalt was new and the curves were less sharp, which was something. There was no railing on the cliff side, only stout-looking gnarly bushes planted every three or so feet. Carson said, "Those bushes are meant to keep your car from going over the edge? They look sturdy, but I doubt they'd stop a rabbit on a bicycle."

Sherlock laughed, and was very glad Griffin hugged the mountain.

In five hundred feet they reached a flattened clearing near the top of the mountain, at least two hundred feet wide. In the back, on the very edge, stood an ultramodern structure of glass and painted black wood. Beside it was a huge garage. Across the way were what looked to be a guest house and storage sheds, and around all of it was a wide, perfectly landscaped yard, bordered by a thick forest.

35

GAFFER'S RIDGE
EAGLE'S NEST
THURSDAY AFTERNOON

Carson breathed in the crisp cool air as she climbed out of the Range Rover and looked around. "They simply scraped off the top of the mountain to give them as much flat space as they wanted. Everything seems perfect, not a blade of grass growing too high or where it shouldn't. No stray yard implements, no dead flowers in a pot—everything's perfect. Look at all the out-buildings, neat and freshly painted. Flagstone steps shiny and clean. And would you listen—not a sound. Except for the leaves dancing in the breeze. It's like a perfect painting, no messy life to disturb it."

Griffin said, "There had to be more here when Rafer was a kid, maybe a basketball hoop on one of the four garage doors. It's too quiet, makes me itchy."

Savich studied Sherlock for a moment. She was still pale, but he didn't think her head was hurting her any longer. "Let's let Mrs. Bodine wait for us a while, wonder why we're not coming to the door. Before we go in, you should all know what MAX coughed up on the Bodines of Gaffer's Ridge last night." He grinned. "Not one of the Bodines has a single felony, not even a parking ticket. There are two living brothers: Booker Bodine, the sheriff, and Quint Bodine, the bank owner, the one with the business smarts evidently, and all the money. The brothers married their cousins—two sisters, Cyndia and Jessalyn Silver. Quint and Cyndia's only daughter, Camilla, disappeared when she was a teenager, a suitcase and her clothes with her. She didn't leave as much as a letter to explain why. As far as anyone knows, she has never been heard from since that long-ago night. The story was in the local newspapers at the time, part of the family's efforts to find her. The papers mentioned private investigators, but there was nothing to suggest they ever found her. Rafer was five years younger than his sister.

"Booker Bodine, the sheriff, and Jessalyn have two children of their own, a boy and girl, Miller and Dixie, both in their twenties, both work for their uncle Quint at his bank, both unmarried."

Savich paused when he saw a woman come

out through the large mahogany front door. Good, she couldn't stand waiting for them. And that meant she was worried. He stilled, felt her reaching out to him. A show of power? Or was it the illusion of power, which was a power in itself? He looked at Griffin and Carson, saw Griffin had grown quiet as well.

She called out in what sounded like a smoker's voice, "My husband told me you'd be showing up here. I told him I'd rather think you'd want to speak to him, not me, but he shook his head, told me no, you would come here. Sure enough, here you are, though you didn't call ahead and no one asked you. So, come in, I won't stop you." She turned on sandaled heels and walked back into the house.

Carson said quietly, "Mrs. Bodine seems straightforward enough, if a little on the rude side. But not scary."

Griffin said, "Don't underestimate her. She could be dangerous." He looked toward the house. "Be careful, all of you."

Sherlock said, "Mrs. Cyndia Bodine, dangerous? She looks like an upper-middle-class housewife ready to meet a friend in town and go antiquing. I guess I was expecting a long braid, a tie-dye dress, and bare feet, maybe some hoop earrings, but here she's wearing sexy sandals and capris. How old is she, Dillon?"

"She's fifty-five, her husband, Quint, is sixty-three. Odd she said her husband told her we were coming here."

They walked up wide wooden steps, across a porch, through the large open door, and into a vast entryway covered with big ochre-shaded Italian pavers. The entryway gave onto five wide steps leading down into a great room at least forty feet long and thirty feet wide, with floor-to-ceiling windows stretching from one end to the other on the far side. French doors opened onto a wide deck with an incredible view of the mountains. There was a mammoth white stone fireplace at one end of the room. Persian carpets were scattered here and there over a shining oak floor. There were burgundy leather sofas, chairs and coffee tables, a seven-foot grand piano. The furniture was oversize to fit the scale of the enormous room. At the other end of the great room was a dining area with a long glass table, a dozen chairs around it, a large bouquet of roses set in the middle. Behind the dining area was an open archway, probably leading into the kitchen.

Savich said, "You have a lovely home. Do you call it Eagle's Nest for a reason?"

"Don't worry, there's no Nazi subtext here. This was the site my husband's father picked out for their family home when he was a young man. He liked the fact an eagle had made its home here before him. Of course, we've completely rebuilt and expanded the house to my own liking."

"And where did you hide the cameras by the gate? We couldn't see them."

She gave Savich a small, satisfied smile and a brief wave of her hand. "Of course you didn't see them. What good would they be if you could see them?"

Griffin asked, "Is your husband here?"

She shook her head. "You must already know he's a very busy man, many demands on his time. He trusts me to deal with you. Naturally I know why you're here. And I know of Agent Hammersmith, my brother-in-law described him perfectly. As for you other two, give me your names and tell me exactly what you want. No, not you, Dr. DeSilva. Booker described you to me as well." She stared at Savich.

He introduced himself and Sherlock and handed her their creds, but she waved them away.

Cyndia Bodine cocked her head at Sherlock. "Agent Sherlock, an odd name—but I'm sure you find it effective."

"Perhaps I do. Mrs. Bodine, we would like to speak to you about your son, Rafer, and three missing teenage girls."

Mrs. Bodine seemed to look inward for a moment, her eyes going darker. Then she blinked. Sherlock looked thoughtfully at this woman with her dark eyes, green maybe, but hard to tell, and black hair pulled in a fat chignon at the back of her head, thick lustrous hair, with not a single gray strand she could see. The woman was very lady-of-the-manor, but—not quite. Something about her made Sherlock jittery.

Cyndia Bodine said, "Agent Sherlock, you really shouldn't be here. You belong in bed. Another couple of days, I'd say."

Sherlock felt her heart give a leap, but said only, "Why do you say that, ma'am?"

"I have eyes in my head. It's obvious to me your pallor isn't natural or normal. Perhaps you've been in an accident of some sort?"

36

"I'm an FBI agent, ma'am, made of sturdy stuff. I have no problem being here. We've been told your husband, your brother-in-law Sheriff Booker, and your lawyer visited your son at the hospital last night."

Sherlock saw a flash of—not anger exactly, more like contempt, in the woman's eyes. Those dark inward-looking eyes scared her, she admitted it. She felt her small 380, snug in its ankle holster, her Glock in its belt clip. She was glad Dillon had given them to her. But what good would a gun be against something you couldn't see?

Cyndia Bodine waved them toward the sofas in the vast great room. "I suppose you should sit down." Once seated, she said, "I'm not worried about my son. He is innocent of any wrongdoing. Rafer wouldn't hurt any living creature, it's not in his nature. He's a good boy, strong and resilient. Trustworthy. Our lawyer, Mr. Jobs from Richmond, assures us Rafer won't be spending a day in jail. There is no evidence he is guilty of anything, except protecting himself in his own home. Would any of you like some tea?"

Sherlock doubted any of them would want to eat or drink anything this woman offered. She said, "We're fine, thank you."

Cyndia Bodine didn't sit, she moved to stand by the fireplace. "My brother-in-law, the sheriff, has told me your story, Dr. DeSilva—your claim you heard Rafer talking to himself about those three poor missing teenage girls. All the rest of your wild tale, too—you were kidnapped by my son, he duct-taped you in his basement—" She shot a look at Griffin. "And of course the exciting break-in by Agent Hammersmith. I must say, it sounds like a B movie. Still, it's inventive. I have wondered why you would make up such a tale, but I've decided I really don't care." She shrugged, added, "However, I will give you some advice. I strongly recommend you don't try to foist your story about hearing my son mumbling out loud about the three missing teenagers outside Ellerby's Market on anyone else. Our lawyer assures us you would be ridiculed in court."

Carson sat forward, realized her hands were

fisted on her legs, smoothed them out. "Doesn't it concern you, Mrs. Bodine, that your son was going to murder me? To keep me from going to the sheriff, which, as it turns out, would have been a big joke on me?"

"Come now, Dr. DeSilva, it seems to me you're already a proven liar, on record claiming you heard Rafer talking aloud to himself. That certainly wasn't true. I'm also informed the FBI forensic team has gone over Rafer's house and found not a shred of proof of your accusations. Give it up, Dr. DeSilva, give it up and go home. Go back to New York. Forget about Gaffer's Ridge, forget your interview with Dr. Alek Kuchar. Yes, Booker told me. Give Alek a call, send him a text, not that he'd answer you."

Carson couldn't help asking, "You know Dr. Kuchar?"

Cyndia Bodine said, "Of course. He and I share tea now and then, here or at his cabin. It's only a quarter of a mile that way." She nodded vaguely toward the west. "He's a fascinating man, but very damaged. In any case, Alek won't want to talk to you, especially if I ask him not to. Believe me on that."

Griffin said, "Mrs. Bodine, even if we can't prove your son kidnapped those girls, he will still go to prison for kidnapping Dr. DeSilva, and for attempted murder of the two of us. Those will be federal charges. I'm an FBI agent and a very credible witness."

To his and Carson's surprise, Cyndia Bodine laughed, shook her head. "Come now, Agent Hammersmith, what would you expect him to do when you attacked him? And she hit him on the head when he was down? No, don't bother to spin more tales to me." She moved from the fireplace to a burgundy leather chair and sat down, crossed her legs and began swinging her long, narrow foot like a metronome. Sherlock found herself staring at that foot, and her pretty light blue toenails.

"I was very glad Agent Hammersmith and I incapacitated him," Carson said. "I was afraid, ma'am, he had come back to kill me."

Savich saw Cyndia Bodine's dark eyes go inward, heard her begin humming deep in her throat. Then she blinked, looked at each of them. "I will say this only one more time. My son is not a murderer. A dozen, two dozen people, will testify to that. So stop your lies, Dr. DeSilva. Go home."

Gooseflesh rose on Carson's arms. What was Cyndia Bodine thinking when she seemed to look inside herself, as if she'd gone off somewhere? Carson was sitting across from a fifty-five-year-old woman with a youthful face, wearing a lavender summer top over white capri pants, light makeup, nothing at all to set off her large eyes. She wasn't classically pretty, but what she had in spades was presence, gravitas. She was more than a well-to-do rich man's wife who knew her own importance.

She was something else entirely, and it scared Carson to her bones.

Savich said in his deep, matter-of-fact voice, "Rafer told us, ma'am, that you'd fix us, that you'd 'shine' us. I've never heard the word 'shine' used that way. What did he mean, exactly?"

"I'm his mother. What mother wouldn't try to 'fix' anyone who threatened her child? 'Shine' you? Come now, what drama. Rafer was having you on, nothing more. I can see from your ring, Agent Savich, that you're married, and so is Agent Sherlock. Perhaps to each other, if I have it right? Tell me, what would you do to someone who threatened your child? Wouldn't you do anything to protect him?"

Savich wasn't about to let her see he was impressed. She was arrogant enough, utterly convinced they were only temporary annoyances. He sat back, crossed his arms. "We all have our lives, our families. As for your family, Mrs. Bodine, all the members sound fascinating. Has your family always lived here in Gaffer's Ridge?"

She looked at her watch, shrugged. "No, not always. I myself am a descendant of Mariah and Elija Silver of the Grantville, Tennessee, Silvers. My family has been celebrated in those parts for generations. My sister and I both married cousins, brothers actually, and, of course, moved here to Gaffer's Ridge, where we have lived now for many years."

She looked down at her watch again. "My husband will be home in three hours and fourteen minutes and I have errands to run in town. Is there anything else?"

Carson stared at her. "Ma'am, how can you be so exact?"

"Long years of marriage and habit, Dr. DeSilva. My husband is always punctual." She looked again at Sherlock. "Would you like an aspirin? For your headache?"

"No, ma'am, thank you, I'm fine." No need to tell this woman she'd kill for two more aspirin.

Cyndia turned back to study Carson. "Before I had Rafer, I had a daughter nearly as beautiful as you, Dr. DeSilva, but she ran away. She was a teenager with all the usual teenage angst and rebellion, and one day she was simply gone." She broke off, then said, "Her hair was as dark as mine, but her eyes weren't a dark green like all the women in my family, more a dark gray. She was still so young, but already quite striking. Her name is Camilla, after her grandmother, who lived with us before she died. She was very independent, always anxious to fly free. She was driving at twelve, no matter what we said, and, as you now know, the road to Eagle's Nest is difficult. I suppose you could say she was wild, undisciplined, but she laughed and danced under a full moon, nearly to the edge of the cliff. But then one night, she packed a suitcase and left. I have searched for her, and waited many years, but she hasn't contacted me. I wish I knew why she left in the first place and what she's doing with her life."

Sherlock said, "Was your daughter disturbed in some way?"

Cyndia splayed her hands in front of her. "Of course not. I still have some of her birthday cake in the freezer." Her voice caught, her face shadowed. "My husband believes it's time to throw it away. Now, if that is all—"

Savich pointed to the far wall. "Your scrying mirror is very old, isn't it?"

All of them looked toward a small jet-black convex bubble mirror, its frame black as well, elaborately fashioned in the art deco style.

"Ah, so you recognize it. Very few people would know what it is. Yes, it is very old, made by my grandmother in the late 1920s." She added to the rest of them, "If you don't know, a scrying mirror is a divination tool, nothing more. Its purpose is to provide focus to the practitioner."

Savich asked, "It is my understanding scrying mirrors are always passed from mother to daughter, usually to the eldest. Isn't your sister, Mrs. Jessalyn Bodine, the sheriff's wife, two years older than you? Why is it in your possession?"

37

A deep musical voice said from behind them, "Why yes, we are exactly twenty-one months apart and yes, I'm the elder." They turned to see a tall, dark-haired woman walk gracefully down the five steps into the great room. She was striking, probably a knockout in her younger years. She was taller than her sister, with the same brilliant dark green eyes and glossy black hair, and no sign of gray. Rather than her sister's chignon, she wore her hair like a younger woman, in a ponytail, but it looked right on her. She wore boots, tight jeans, and a fitted white top, and carried a light green jacket over her arm. She gave a little wave to her sister. "Hello, Cyn, sorry I'm late. I did hurry when I heard from Booker this bunch might be coming to hassle you, but wouldn't you know—that idiot Glynis Lars hit the back of Wallace's hay truck and it overturned and blocked the road just outside of town. No need to ask, yes, she was drunk as a skunk, as usual. Poor old Wallace was sputtering at her, since he doesn't curse." She turned to look at each of them, her eyes resting a moment longer on Sherlock.

"My name is Jessalyn Bodine and I'm Sheriff Booker Bodine's wife. I know you're all FBI agents except for you." She studied Carson, said finally, "Cyn, she reminds me a bit of Camilla, despite the difference in coloring. What do you think?"

"A bit, I suppose. She's so much older than Camilla was when she left." Cyndia Bodine was quiet a moment, then made introductions, waved her sister to a chair beside her, but Jessalyn didn't take it. She continued to stand, her arms crossed. She said, "Agent Savich, I heard you ask about the scrying mirror. I gave it to my sister since she has more use for it than I. I find it interesting an FBI agent would know about such an esoteric tradition."

Savich said easily, "More use than you would have, Mrs. Bodine? Can you tell me why?"

Jessalyn laughed. "I suppose you may have heard around town the Bodines are blessed with some special gifts? Alas, neither Rafer nor my poor Booker, nor our two children, I might add, were blessed with much of anything. I married Booker anyway, even knowing he would get fat, like his father did. He entertains me, you see. I didn't want him to sell the hardware stores to become sheriff, but he wanted it so badly, wanted to leave his own mark, also like his father did." She shrugged. "I let him have his way."

Griffin stared at this woman. "How did you know he would get fat?"

"He loves his beer and buffalo wings, loved them even when he was young and fit and hand-some as Rafer." She nodded toward Griffin and Carson. "Booker should have known no one would lie about being an FBI agent. Of course, once he realized he was wrong, he behaved himself. He's adaptable, always a positive virtue in a hus-band. A pity. Usually, he's faster on his feet."

"You're admitting he removed the duct tape and Rafer's computer from his house?"

A dark eyebrow went up, accompanied by a look of astonishment. "What did you say, Agent Hammersmith? Why would he do something so ridiculous?"

Cyndia said, "Jess, you told me you married Booker because you liked his name and you could drink him under the table."

Jessalyn laughed. "I still do and I still can. It's like you knew Quint would stay skinny as a snake and make buckets of money. I gather all of you very serious people have been here for some time. Cyndia and I have errands to do. Are we all finished?"

Cyndia Bodine rose to stand beside her sister.

Savich rose as well. "Actually, Mrs. Bodine, we would like your permission to look around your house and property."

She raised a perfectly arched brow, laughed. "Tell me you're joking, Agent Savich? No? For myself, I really don't care if you wish to spend your time grubbing about my house, we have nothing to hide, but Quint would not be pleased. I'm sure he would demand a warrant, for which you have absolutely no grounds. I must say I find it incredible that you accuse my son of monstrous acts, then expect me to let you tear up my home."

She paused, took her sister's arm. "One more moment, Jess." She said to Carson, "You might as well know, Dr. DeSilva, I called you a liar because I know Rafer didn't mumble anything at all under his breath. You and that man next to you who hurt Rafer, both of you have a gift you can't claim because no sane person on the planet would believe you, so none of it will matter."

She looked at Sherlock. "You're not like these others, but you're not exactly common, there is some light in you."

Sherlock said, "Any light you see in me is very low wattage, Mrs. Bodine."

"You're clever. You notice things, things other people don't necessarily pay attention to. But your headache is worse, you need to rest."

Cyndia started to walk away arm in arm with

Jessalyn toward the kitchen, her sandals slapping on the oak floor, Jessalyn's boots making no sound at all. "It's time for you to leave. You may all let yourselves out."

"Mrs. Bodine," Savich said, "would you mind if I used your bathroom?"

"What? All right. It's down the hall to your right. The rest of you can wait outside. Jess, come with me to the kitchen. I want you to taste my lasagna sauce."

Savich waited until they were out of hearing, and said quietly, "Griffin, Carson, look around in the woods, check for possible grave sites. Sherlock, you have an excellent eye. Check out the size and shape of the buildings and the garage."

"A hidden room?"

"This would be a perfect place for it, but more than one room, I imagine, since three teenagers were kidnapped."

The house was large, at least six thousand square feet, and there wasn't enough time to do any sort of search. Savich was lucky to find Mr. Bodine's home office near the bathroom at the end of a wide, carpeted corridor. He gave Sherlock one final look, saw her walking down the front steps, and hoped she'd go back to the car if she felt ill.

Sherlock ignored the niggling headache and walked quickly to the large four-car garage. She looked through the window of the first dark-blue-painted bay door. It was pristine inside, a workbench along the back wall with tools laid out neatly on shelves above it. Four cars lined up like soldiers at attention—a new white Mercedes sedan, a black BMW SUV, a Chevy Silverado truck, and a classic baby-blue Mustang older than she was. There was road dust on the Mustang so she guessed it was Jessalyn Bodine's car. She stood back and examined the space. No doubt in her mind the garage interior should be deeper. She examined the space again, walked it off again. And stopped, her head cocked. It was strange, but now the measurements appeared exactly right. She had to hurry, Dillon would be out at any moment and they'd have to leave. She quickly examined the outbuildings—a small woodworking workshop, a toolshed with tractor, lawn mower, and gardening tools, and a well-constructed storage building with skiing equipment, odds and ends from the house, and some paintings stacked against the wall, a white sheet covering them. There was a painting still on an easel that wasn't covered. Rich vibrant colors were splashed on with abandon, it seemed to her, with no theme, no attempt to be anything but wild untamed colors themselves. Cyndia Bodine's?

She walked quickly past the guest house. It didn't look like it had been used in a long time, given the layer of dust she saw through the living room window.

She walked back to the house, disappointed, hoping the others had better luck. Her headache was gone. She felt lighter on her feet, less tired. She saw Mrs. Cyndia Bodine standing in the doorway of the entrance hall, and, oddly, Cyndia seemed to be staring at her. Where was her sister, Jessalyn?

Cyndia said to Sherlock as she walked up the steps, "You couldn't see what you couldn't see, now could you?" Sherlock felt the weight of her focus. Cyndia turned on her heel and walked back into the house and down the oak steps into the great room. She'd left the front door open, so Sherlock saw her pull open the side French door and walk to stand at the deck railing. She never looked back at Sherlock.

Where was her sister? Where was Jessalyn Bodine?

Sherlock wasn't about to let herself be spooked. What had Cyndia meant—*You couldn't see what you couldn't see?* She stood quietly a moment in the open doorway, studying the woman's back, playing the words over in her mind. She felt a sudden, sharp flash of pain in her head, like a blow from a hammer, then another, blinding pain, more agonizing than the pain she'd awakened with in the emergency room. She stumbled, pressed her palms to her temples, but the sharp battering pain kept digging into her. She felt the earth begin to spin, fast, then faster still. She grabbed at the front door, but it slipped out of her hand and seemed to move away, growing smaller and smaller until she was standing by herself in a vast space, weaving, dizzy, her head pounding so fiercely she couldn't bear it. Was she dying? She gave a small cry and went down.

38

The walls of Quint Bodine's home office were covered with glass-encased tribal masks, spears, and an elaborate ancient headdress. Savich walked quickly to a massive mahogany desk. Behind it were large French doors that gave onto a wide wooden deck with incredible views.

His pulse kicked up when he saw the top-of-the-line iMac. He pushed a jump drive into the USB port and kept his eye on the door as he booted up the computer. He watched the progress as the jump drive transferred its program to the computer's hard drive. He quickly powered down, plucked the jump drive back out, and left the office, smiling. When the computer was powered up again, the program he'd tweaked himself would hide from view, search for the computer's passwords, and allow him remote access. Unless Bodine took a great deal of care and was over-the-top paranoid, he would never know.

Done. He was past the bathroom when he heard Sherlock cry out. Then nothing.

He raced to the front entrance hall, his Glock at the ready. He saw the open front door swinging as if pushed by an unseen hand or the wind, only there wasn't a wind. He saw Sherlock sprawled on her back outside on the porch.

He caught sight of Mrs. Cyndia Bodine on the deck, her back to them, leaning over the railing, staring toward the mountains, seemingly unaware. He ran to Sherlock, heart pounding, went down on his knees, found the pulse in her throat. Her pulse was there, slow and steady. Had she fainted? The trip had been too much for her. It was his fault. He touched his fingers to her face, cupped her chin, leaned down, kissed her, whispered, "Come on, sweetheart, open your eyes. Smile up at me." He gathered her in his arms. She felt as boneless as a sleeping child, her head lolling back on his arm. He lightly slapped her face, bent close, whispered again, "Sherlock, come on, sweetheart, open your eyes and look at me. Call me an idiot for bringing you to Gaffer's Ridge, for bringing you here to this cursed mountain." He felt her move. He waited. He looked over at Mrs. Bodine, who still stood quietly on the deck, her back to them. Hadn't she heard Sherlock scream? There was no sign of her sister. Where was she?

Sherlock moaned, but didn't open her eyes. Her fingers clutched his arm. "Thank heaven you're here. My head, it hurt so bad I thought I was going to die. It wouldn't stop. I couldn't get away from it, I couldn't—" She swallowed.

"How is the pain now?"

She opened her eyes, blinked to clear her vision, and stared up into his hard, sculpted face, his cheekbones high and surely sharp enough to slash ice, and his eyes dark like night—"Are you the Prince of Darkness?"

That's what she thought, looking at him? He shot another look toward Mrs. Bodine, who still hadn't moved, and lightly stroked a fingertip over her cheek. "Do you want me to be?"

She raised her hand to touch his face, then dropped it. He caught her hand and laid it over her stomach. "I wish I knew who you were, really knew. I mean, everyone agrees you're my husband, and that means you've seen me brush my teeth and paint my toenails. I guess you've seen a lot more, too, but I don't remember any of that. You told me I don't snore. Did you say that to make me feel better?"

She was beginning to sound like herself, a huge relief. He wanted to tell her he'd kissed the small birthmark on her left hip a good thousand times over the past six years. "Sometimes you make little snorting sounds, like Sean. I'm not the Prince of Darkness, I'm your husband, and that makes me proud and happy." He lightly touched his fingertips to her forehead. "I'm in there, locked deep inside your brain, sweetheart, you're just not ready to let me back out yet. Now tell me, how's your head—any more pain?"

"No, the pain's gone, but I still feel weak—" Her voice fell off a cliff.

Savich held her against him, rocked her. Slowly she pulled back. "I think I'm okay now." She looked at the front door. "It was so strange, Dillon, I felt so good, so normal when I came back toward the house, but suddenly a hammer hit me on the head, and it was worse even than right after the accident. I was nauseated and dizzy, so I grabbed for the door, but I swear to you it began moving away from me. It got smaller and smaller."

"I heard you scream."

She stared up at him. "I screamed? I don't remember making any sound at all." She dug out a smile. "I had something strange to tell you, but I can't remember what it was now." She felt another hit of pain in her head that made her jerk, then held herself very still.

Savich turned to see Mrs. Bodine looking through the glass French door, focused on them. Her lips were moving. He gently laid Sherlock on the porch. "I'll be right back." He ran to the glass door, shoved it open, grabbed Mrs. Bodine's arms, and shook her until her head snapped back on her neck. He yelled in her face, "Stop it! Now!"

She gave a small guttural sound, shoved against him, hitting his chest with her fists. "Stop what? Are you crazy? Get away from me!"

He pinned her arms to her sides, leaned in, and said very quietly, "I'm giving you one warning, Mrs. Bodine, only one. You hurt her again and I will kill you. Do you understand?" He shook her, then pushed her away from him.

She was breathing hard, the pulse leaping in her throat. She looked at him, furious, and he felt a sudden shock of pain in his head. He formed a stark, clear picture in his mind of her holding her own head, and reflected the pain back on her. She didn't fall, but she did stagger and fetch up against the deck railing, mouth agape, shock clear on her face. She whispered, "You're very strong."

"Yes," he said, "I am. I hope you believe me—I will kill you if you try to hurt her again, Mrs. Bodine. This is your only warning. Tell me you understand me."

"Of course I understand you. Yes. You're a violent man from a violent world. You should be in jail, not my innocent son. Listen to me, I didn't touch her. How could I? She's outside by the front door, and I'm here, looking at my beautiful view. Go away, Agent Savich, all of you go away. I want you out of my house."

He left her on the deck and hurried back to his wife.

Sherlock's head didn't hurt, nor was she dizzy any longer. In fact, she felt perfectly fine lying on her back and not moving. She saw Dillon coming toward her, saw the wild mix of emotions on his dark face, quickly tamped down when he saw her looking at him. She slowly sat up. She tried to remember exactly what had happened, but there was only that blank white door again. The blasted amnesia. She hated having to pretend to be what everyone believed her to be, when she was no one at all, a one-dimensional being who lived in the present with only an occasional glimpse of someone she knew, or madly enough, of Dillon's red Porsche. She didn't flinch when he came down beside her. He cupped her chin in his palm, studied her eyes. "Don't sugarcoat it, how do you feel?"

The strange words floated through her brain, and she remembered: *You couldn't see what you couldn't see.* She raised her hand to his face. "I'm all right. Really, I feel fine. Why am I on the floor, Dillon? Don't get me wrong, I'm really comfortable. I remember you laid me on my back and left me here."

"Yes, but only minutes ago." Savich wanted to carry her away from this place, but first he had to tell her the truth. "It wasn't your concussion that made your head hurt so much, made you pass out. It was Cyndia Bodine. I guess what we saw was her 'shining' you."

Sherlock gaped at him. "You mean she attacked me psychically? From clear across the room? But how is that possible? She didn't get near me."

"She didn't need to get near you or touch you. She attacked you psychically because you're the most vulnerable of the four of us."

"Because I'm not gifted like the rest of you."

"Maybe."

Sherlock licked her dry lips, shot a look toward Mrs. Bodine still standing on the deck staring at them, rubbing her arms up and down, as if she were cold. But why would Cyndia Bodine attack her? Then she remembered the words again and repeated them aloud. " 'You couldn't see what you couldn't see.' She said those words to me because she was worried I'd see something she didn't want me to see. But what is it, Dillon? I walked around the garage, checked the outbuildings, the guest house, but I didn't see anything that set off an alarm."

They saw Griffin and Carson approaching the house. She let Dillon help her to her feet, steadied herself.

Carson called out, "Why were you lying on the porch? Are you all right?"

Savich nodded toward Cyndia Bodine. "She's

fine now. Cyndia Bodine attacked her, shined her. But she won't do it again."

Griffin said, "Where is her sister? Where is Jessalyn Bodine?"

Carson said, "She's probably in the basement, stirring a cauldron."

39

Claire Farriger stood at her office window watching rain-bloated black clouds scuttle across a starless sky. She knew it was still hot outside, the humidity near 100 percent, and rain was close now. She should leave soon or she'd get soaked. But she couldn't. What a mess Nikki had made of something as simple as picking an unsuspecting computer nerd like Justice Cummings off the street. Even at a preset location. It was Nikki who'd insisted her people be the ones to grab Cummings, that they would keep him hidden until he understood fully what was at stake, and they had his agreement. A deal breaker, she'd said. It was the price Claire paid for agreeing to work with amateurs, without field experience, without guts to do what was necessary. Keep Cummings safe? It was ridiculous. Bad enough Cummings had happened upon the chatter about the smart wall before she could shut it down. He could have ruined everything, even exposed her. She could have taken care of it herself, but Nikki and her blasted conscience insisted she and her people could handle it. She sighed. It would have been so much easier for her to arrange a fatal accident. Of course, she hadn't spoken about Nikki's massive failure the night before at the dojo. What good would it have done?

She heard a light knock on the door.

"Come."

The door opened and Alan Besserman walked in. He worked under her as a resident expert in Russian technology and weaponry, and he was Justice Cummings's group chief.

Farriger started to take a strip off him for keeping her waiting, but she saw his reflection in the window glass. He looked beyond exhausted, his suit rumpled as if he'd slept in it, his shoulders slumped—and something else. There was both fear and alarm in his pale, bloodshot eyes. Obviously neither he nor the half dozen agents she'd assigned had managed to track down Justice Cummings. Farriger closed her eyes a moment. She reviewed her options if they didn't find him before the inevitable phone call from FBI Assistant Director James Maitland. Besserman had already put him off. Maitland wasn't a man she wanted to set against her. And of course he'd have Savich with him.

She stated the obvious, without turning, "So I gather you still haven't found Cummings?"

"No, ma'am." She saw Besserman push his fist against his palm in the window reflection. "We know he took an Uber from about three blocks from the accident to Alexandria. We went through the neighborhood where he was dropped off, but no one there recognized his photo. He smashed his cell phone, as you know, so no help there.

"We've been checking cams in Alexandria, but no sign of him. If he's alive, why would he hide? Why didn't he call in? Call me? It doesn't make sense otherwise." He paused, then said in an emotionless voice, "I'm beginning to think it's possible he died from his injuries after striking that car. That wherever he was planning to go in Alexandria, he didn't make it."

"Then where is his body?"

"Hasn't been found yet."

"Does he know anyone in Alexandria?"

"Not that we could discover. We're doing a wide grid search to find him—or his body. Still no sign."

Farriger watched Besserman start to pace her office, a long narrow room. She saw him momentarily distracted by her paintings of medieval tapestries on the walls. Why was Alan being so slow? She nudged him forward. "Alan, there has to be a reason Justice ran. We backtracked him to the Blaze Café—a waiter said he was obviously expecting someone, kept looking at his watch. But he got impatient and left. The bodega cam across the street shows two people walking toward him—and shows him running away. Why was he there? Who were these people he was running from?"

Besserman stopped on a dime, stared at her reflection in the glass. Farriger slowly turned to face him. "Think, Alan. I know you like the guy, you think he's smart, and I agree he's done excellent work, but—" She said nothing more, let her silence speak.

Besserman knew what this looked like, and he didn't like it. He had no idea what had happened, but it couldn't be what she was hinting at, absolutely not. He said slowly, his voice firm as a judge, "I am as sure as I can be Justice wasn't at that café to meet with a foreign operative. Justice isn't a traitor."

Farriger shrugged. "Alan, I don't want to think it, either, but we have to consider it. Remember, you told me about the chatter he'd picked up about some kind of breakthrough in surveillance technology on Russian back channels? You brought it to me and we decided it didn't merit our attention. Well, maybe he lied to you, maybe he managed to identify the source of the chatter about 'smart walls' in Russia, and found out more, maybe someone offered him money to funnel them information. There had to be something going on to set this off. Have you finished the forensics on his workstation? His clearance was high enough that even if he didn't escalate it, he could have copied enough sensitive information to hurt us badly. Let's hope he's not trying to be another Edward Snowden."

Besserman stood tall and squared his shoulders, but still looked rather ridiculous with his mussed hair and rumpled suit. "We're still checking, but it doesn't matter, I will not believe Justice Cummings would ever contact a foreign government, would ever turn traitor. Absolutely no way, but if a Russian counterpart tracked his access back to him specifically?" He shook his head. "Still, there'd be no reason to kill him. The information was already in our hands, at least that's what they'd think."

He paused, looked pained to even say the words. "All right, let's assume he contacted someone outside channels, see where it takes us."

Farriger merely looked at him and waited. Besserman cursed under his breath. He said slowly, "If he believed the people he saw were ours and that's why he ran, he thought he'd been busted." He paused, ran his tongue over his lips. "But they weren't our people. The people he saw outside, it's possible they had nothing to do with him and he ran because—" He shook his head. "No, wait. I may be going far afield here, but there's another possible scenario. He was cheating on his wife, meeting a woman after work at the café. It's possible he ran from the people he saw outside because—" He looked frustrated because no good reason popped into his brain, except "Maybe he believed she'd found him out and thought his wife had hired a P.I. He got spooked."

She tried not to laugh. "Say you're right, then we're back to why wouldn't he call you after he got hurt? You're not only his friend, you're his chief. Or call some other friend? Why, Alan?"

"Because he's dead, that's why. He managed to get himself hidden and he died."

Farriger smiled, a tight smile, rarely seen, but it was there, showing white teeth. It was disappointing Besserman and his crew were taking so long to find the trail of sensitive documents she herself had copied from his workstation—documents they would have to believe he'd copied, something never allowed, an act to trigger a major alarm. Those copied files would incriminate, and Cummings would have no choice but to cooperate with Nikki—at least Nikki believed he'd have to, or be branded a traitor. But what Claire really wanted was Cummings dead. She hoped Besserman was right—Justice's body would turn up somewhere in Alexandria. It would solve all their problems.

Besserman stared at his boss, found her smile alarming.

Farriger said, "If he were dead, it would be sad, but at least it would mean Justice can't hurt us. But here's the thing, Alan, I don't believe he's dead, not for a New York minute. Cummings is a chess player. I've seen him play. He's an excellent strategist, his mind razor sharp. He thinks six moves ahead. So, it only follows that if he's hurt, he's still in the Washington area, somewhere smart, somewhere off our radar."

Besserman said, "Obviously he's not at home, and he hasn't been there. He hasn't used his credit cards. One of our agents did spot a black SUV idling in Cummings's neighborhood, maybe half a block from his house. When our agent finally went to talk to the woman—yes, it was a woman—she gunned the SUV and got out of there fast. Of course, he got the license plate, ran it. The vehicle belongs to a fleet run by the Bexholt Group, the big communications security company. We've had dealings with them."

He'd surprised her, he saw it, but only for a moment, then her face smoothed out again. Had he imagined it?

She said, her voice clipped, hard, "Yes, I know who they are, and yes, the CIA has been involved with them before, on a firewall installation. Do sit down, Alan. Long day, long night. A woman, you say?"

He nodded. "Was she watching Cummings's house? I'll call Bexholt in the morning, find out who had that SUV yesterday. Haul her in here and find out why she was there."

Alan hadn't moved toward the gray leather sofa. He still stood watching his boss. Farriger said, "No, don't call them, don't go see her. I want to handle this. The last thing I want is for the FBI and Metro to find out we brought someone here to question. No, I'll deal with it. Any more pertinent info you waited until the bitter end to tell me?"

"There is one other thing, ma'am, but I doubt it has anything to do with any of this, whatever this is. There's talk in his group he and his wife haven't been getting along. Bottom line appears to be she wants him to quit the agency, go private where he could earn a lot more money. But that's not unusual."

She shook her head. "Still, if there is real conflict at home, it could be a red flag."

"Justice told Pamela Snow in our office his wife and daughters left for the Poconos a couple of days ago. I suppose her leaving could mean something."

"It's late, Alan. Go ahead and send your people home. We'll pick this up in the morning. But keep me posted. He shows up, call me."

"I will. Good night, ma'am."

Farriger watched Besserman walk across the shined oak floor. She turned back to the window, heard the door quietly open and close. It started to rain, thick fat drops striking hard against the glass.

It was mesmerizing. She would wait another day until she knew more, then she would decide what the FBI had to know.

But now she had to deal with a more pressing problem—the woman their agent had spotted watching Cummings's house. She looked out at the heavy rainfall for several more minutes, then picked up her cell phone.

40

Carson groaned as she ate the meat off a barbecue sparerib. She set the bone down in a growing pile next to the mashed potatoes, leaned back, and rubbed her stomach. She looked sadly at her plate. "Two ribs left and I can't, just can't eat them, or I'll explode. Wait, there's no substance to tomatoes, is there?" And she ate the one lone tomato slice on her plate. She waved at Jenny, gave her a thumbs-up, sat back, and sighed. "The good Lord can take me now."

No one disagreed with her. Savich sipped on his favorite oolong tea, hot and strong and black as sin. On Savich's plate were the carcasses of two corncobs, stripped clean.

Jenny and Aimée Rose had kept the café open

for dinner, a first, and the place was packed. Jenny and Alfredo Smith, her sous chef in training, were in the open kitchen, Aimée Rose and two college-age servers running their sneakers off to take care of customers. The four visitors were seated at one of the best tables, by a large window looking out onto Winchester Street. Aimée Rose came bustling back, grinning widely. "You liked? Any more seconds? Sherlock? You ate well, too. Excellent."

"Everything was perfect," Griffin said for all of them. "We thank you for keeping the place open for us."

"Yep. Only look what happened." She waved at the crowded room. "We weren't expecting all these folks, but what could we do but feed them?" She rubbed her fingers together. "If things keep going like they are, I might have to buy myself a red Porsche like yours, Dillon."

Savich grinned up at her. "Nah, not red. I see you in a kick-butt black Porsche, extra-turbo-charged engine. Maybe a sign on the back: *FEAR ME*, all caps."

Aimée Rose's eyes lit up. "Oh yeah, maybe me in black leather. Maybe a whip attached to my belt. Now, who's up for fresh peach pie? It's Alfredo's specialty."

She was met with a chorus of groans. Sherlock said, "The spirit's willing but the stomach's stuffed."

When Aimée Rose took herself off, Carson

leaned toward Sherlock across the table. She took her hand. "I still can't believe what Cyndia Bodine did to you. I didn't know anyone could do that. How do you feel now, really?"

Sherlock gave her hand a squeeze. "Once Dillon realized what she was doing—from across the room—he stopped her and the pain was suddenly gone. Really, I'm fine now."

Griffin said, "Tell us exactly what happened."

Sherlock looked at the three of them, smiled, and said, "Okay, we've had our break, I guess it's time to get back to it. Here's what happened. I'd walked around the garage, made mental notes on measurements, realized they were off, and then suddenly, they weren't. I'd stepped onto the front porch when this awful pain ripped into my head. I finally blacked out."

Savich said, "I'm thinking Mrs. Bodine didn't want Sherlock to remember. But she didn't know Sherlock. She remembers Mrs. Bodine said, 'You couldn't see what you couldn't see.' We all know what that could mean."

Griffin said, "The girls, if they're still alive, are very probably being kept in that garage, or below it in underground rooms."

Savich said, "Agreed. However, if we try to get a warrant, you know we'll be turned down flat. We've got to think of another way."

Carson was staring at Sherlock. She couldn't get her head around it. "And I thought it was weird

I can sometimes tell what people are thinking. But this is way weirder, it's very scary." She paused, then said slowly, "Sherlock, you may be having trouble with your memory because of your accident, but I can see you're smart, you're insightful, and no matter what Mrs. Bodine did to you, you still remembered what she said."

Sherlock wondered if she'd ever again see herself as insightful. She said, "I don't know if I'll agree with you when I finally remember who and what I am. All right, Dillon, you've been holding out on us. Come on, spill."

Savich gave them a huge grin. "Okay, here it is. When I supposedly went to the bathroom, I found Quint Bodine's office." He pulled his jump drive out of his pants pocket. "I installed a worm on his computer. When he boots it up with his password, I'll have remote access to his hard drive without his knowing it."

Griffin could only shake his head. "Amazing, good going, Savich. Of course, nothing we find is admissible in court, but who cares? Now, about this worm you installed. It's your own design?"

Savich only smiled. "Mostly, yes. I'll take a look at it later, let you know if I find anything important. Griffin, we know Slick and DeAndre can stay to help you after Rafer's released from the hospital tomorrow. You could have them check for more missing teenagers in a wider area."

Griffin nodded. "Good idea. I'll pick up Sheriff Bodine's files tonight, read them over, see what's missing, and what information we still need. But the way I see it, Savich, it's most likely the girls are at Eagle's Nest."

"And if they're not?" Carson asked.

"Then we check records to see what other properties Quint Bodine owns. Or Rafer owns. If the girls are still alive, they have to be somewhere close."

Sherlock said, "And that's the question—why take the girls in the first place?" She raised her near-empty glass of iced tea. "Let's end this soon."

41

Savich paused at the bathroom door, his hair still damp from the shower, a towel wrapped around his waist, and watched Sherlock. She'd changed into her tiger-striped boxers and flowy top, his favorites he'd packed without thinking. Now he realized she might think they were too sexy, which they were, and it might make her uncomfortable. She was standing by the bed, her hand on the covers, unmoving, staring down.

He said quietly, not wanting to startle her, "Sherlock, please don't be concerned. I'm not going to jump you."

She slowly turned to look at him, head to toe. He said, his voice calm, trying for a bit of humor, "Usually I don't wear anything to bed, but maybe it would be best if you handed me a pair of boxers and a T-shirt from my go bag."

His black go bag was open on the bed. She picked out a pair of royal-blue boxer shorts, held them up, and suddenly saw herself laughing, watching Dillon walk away from her, a rip in his pants, his royal-blue boxer shorts on display, and she was responsible. She blinked. She held up the boxer shorts again. "Did you ever rip your pants? And you were wearing blue boxers?"

He gave her a huge grin. "When you were in the FBI Academy, I role-played a bank robber in Hogan's Alley and your job was to spot me and bring me down. During our scuffle, I ripped my pants. Believe me, you weren't the only one laughing her head off. I had to toss the pants."

"I saw you walking away in my mind, even heard myself laughing. I know you're not going to jump me. You're not that kind of man."

She stopped, walked over and handed him the T-shirt and boxers. "Thank you."

"I'll be out in a minute," he said, and closed the bathroom door.

Sherlock paused in front of a photo of a beautiful golden retriever framed on the wall beside the bed. His name was Carl, printed in gold leaf on a plaque beneath the photo. He was leaping high, catching a Frisbee in the air. She touched her fingertips to the photo. "That was an excellent catch, Carl. I'll bet you were a great dog. So, can you help me out? I'm not eighteen anymore, and that superbly built man in the bathroom is my husband. I have a child with him. What do you think, Carl? Should I consider taking him as a lover? A stranger with benefits? Or is that too wicked?" She began to laugh at herself.

Savich came out of the bathroom, heard her speaking to the golden in the photo. And waited, saying nothing, listening.

"On the other hand," she said to Carl, "I don't believe in cheating. At least I don't think I do. It's strange, but I know about some things, about how to do my hair and my makeup, what I like to eat, how to drive, even my ankle Glock 380—it's familiar to me. Ah, but people—it's people mostly who are gone. I wouldn't recognize my parents. I haven't even had a glimpse of them. And Gabriella? I know she's Sean's nanny, but nothing else. I have these brief snapbacks, I guess you'd call them, but mostly they don't mean much to me. Are people in a specific part of the brain? And that's the part that's wonky?" She sighed. "What's a girl to do, Carl? That's the question, isn't it? Would sleeping with him really be like cheating, since I don't know him? Would I feel like doing the walk of shame tomorrow morning?" She turned away from the picture. "I know so much and so little."

Savich walked to her, very gently took her arms in his hands. He hadn't touched her bare arms in too long a time, because the bruises were still vivid and had to hurt. He studied the bruises on her shoulders from the seat belt, managed to smile down at her. "I love the tiger stripes."

She started, froze, then, finally, eased. "I thought you did like the tiger stripes, well, on some level I did. I see you looking at the bruises on my arms and shoulders. They're not so bad now, Dillon. They don't hurt much and they're fading, too. Oh dear, did you hear my conversation with Carl the golden retriever?"

"Your end of it, yes. Carl didn't add much of anything."

She laid her palms on his chest, felt the warmth of his flesh through the black T-shirt. She leaned up, breathed him in, then jerked back. "Do I do this often after you shower?"

"Sniff me to make sure I've washed behind my ears? Yes, usually."

"Somehow I don't think checking to see if you're clean has anything to do with my sniffing you."

Savich cupped her beloved face between his hands. She'd loosed her hair from the clips and now it was a wild nimbus around her head. He fingered a bright corkscrew curl, wrapped it around his finger. "I think the first time I saw you, I fell in love with your hair. The amazing color—it's not red, more titian. I wanted to bury my face in all those curls." That was only the beginning of what he'd wanted when he'd first laid eyes on her at Quantico more than six years before, but it was best to stop.

She took a step back from him, pressed her palms against her head. "I hate this. I try to act normal, like I'm here and tuned in to everything, only I'm not. You probably heard me tell Carl I know how to do things, like when I saw the piano at Eagle's Nest, I knew I could play. I know who the president is, how to use my cell phone, my iPad. It's people, Dillon, it's people who are hidden away. How can I know things and yet not know people? Even you, the most important person in my life, and you're a stranger to me." She poked a finger against her chest. "All I know about who I am or what I am is what you tell me." She began to cry, silently, tears running down her face. "I've lost you and me. I've lost what we are."

He wanted to weep with her, but instead he drew her in. She didn't resist. "It's okay to cry, baby. I know everything's hard. It'll be okay, you'll see." Stupid, meaningless words. He felt her shaking with the force of her tears. He stroked his hands up and down her back. He said against her hair, his voice steady, "The truth is I can't imagine what you're going through, but I do know that here"—he laid her hand against his heart—"you'll remember. You'll come back to you and to me. Carson said you're intuitive and she's right. I've seen you shine with it. But for now you'll have to trust me to have your back. Can you do that? Can you trust me?"

She raised her face, tears still wet on her cheeks, swallowed. "I've watched how you act with other people, how you treat them. I've seen how kind you are. But I heard you tell Mrs. Bodine you'd kill her if she hurt me again, and she believed you and I believed you. You're a warrior, Dillon, and you protected me. Do I trust you?"

Her palm was still against his chest and she felt the steady beat of his heart. "I'd be an idiot if I didn't. So yes, I trust you." She gave him a crooked grin. "I look at that bed and know it shouldn't worry me. I know it's stupid, but I can't help it."

He kissed her hair, said against her ear, "We both have to be patient, Sherlock. And honest with each other. If there's anything you want to say to me, please, always say it, okay? And don't worry about the bed. I don't want to be a stranger with benefits."

She nodded against his neck. "Maybe what we need is a good knock-down, drag-out fight, yell at each other. The problem is, I can't think what to yell at you about. Do we fight?"

"On occasion."

She leaned back in his arms. "Do we fight about money? About sex? What?"

"Maybe because I'm the better cook? Well, at some things, like lasagna. You hate it when guests praise my lasagna and ignore your garlic toast and Caesar salad. Actually, it's really quite funny. But then you bring out your apple pie and everyone drools and praises you to your eyebrows, and all's right with the world again." He kissed her forehead. "But seriously, we don't fight about money or about sex." He gave her a crooked grin. "We have enough of both. We're very busy trying to raise our boy and do our jobs. When we have knock-down, drag-outs it's usually about work. I'm your boss. I give you assignments you sometimes don't agree with and you leap into the fray, no holds barred. You're ferocious."

"My boss. That's got to be tough, for both of us."

"Yes, sometimes, but usually we work well together, spark off each other."

She looked thoughtful, nodded. "Know what I think? Sounds to me like I'm the brain and you're the brawn."

He laughed. "Sometimes. I think we're each a little of both."

She said nothing for a moment, then, "I wish I could see my mom and dad's faces, see what Sean eats for breakfast."

"He eats Cheerios, one sliced banana on top. He's asking for a three-speed bike for his birthday, which he won't get, of course, but he will get his favorite birthday cake—chocolate.

"I'll show you a photo of you with your parents, okay?" He saw her chew this over. This was uncharted territory and he hated it, felt like a blind man trying to feel his way.

She nodded, rubbed her forehead. "It just hit me. I'm really pretty tired, Dillon."

Savich kissed her forehead. "We've both had a long day. Let's get ourselves some sleep." He put their phones on the chargers and switched off the bedside lamp.

They lay side by side on their backs. After a couple of minutes of dead silence, Sherlock said, "This feels weird."

"Yes, but weird is what we've got. Weird is okay for now, don't worry."

"Okay." She leaned toward him, kissed his cheek. Neither of them said anything. She wished the bedside lamp with its thirty watts was on, she wanted to see his expression, but then again, she really didn't know what she wanted to see. She whispered, "Good night, Dillon. Thank you for having my back."

42

WASHINGTON, D.C.
THURSDAY NIGHT

She'd been a moron to run from that man walking toward her SUV in Justice Cummings's neighborhood. She should have handled it, said she was surveilling a cheating wife, or even waiting for a friend. Anything at all. But like an amateur, she'd panicked and floored the SUV. Ellie Corbitt wanted to kick herself, not that it would do any good. She'd bet the man got her license plate.

She squeezed her eyes closed. She had to get up the courage to call Athena, warn her. No, easier to call Jasmine. She was responsible for letting Justice Cummings escape. She'd screwed up even more than Ellie had. But this was a close second.

Jasmine answered on the first ring, and Ellie talked fast. Jasmine was silent for a long time after Ellie had said it all. Then she let out a long breath. "This isn't good, Ellie. Whoever the man was, whoever he's working for, they'll find out the SUV belongs to Bexholt, and from there they'll identify you."

"I bet the guy who spotted me was CIA," Ellie said. "I mean, they must be looking for him, too. And the guy was dressed in a spiffy black suit, their standard uniform. If not CIA, then the FBI. Doesn't matter, either one is bad. Should I call Athena? Warn her? Jasmine, what should I do?"

"Ellie, it will be all right. For now, you stay out of sight, and do not, I repeat, do not go into work tomorrow. Call in sick, you got that? I'll call Athena," and she talked about mistakes and how everybody made them, just look at what she'd done!, and not to worry.

"Yes, I've got that, but then what?"

"I'll let you know," and Jasmine hung up.

Ellie was so scared she couldn't think straight. Sure, she was smart, committed to this wonderful project. She was so tired of scrimping to make ends meet, but the fact was, she was an accountant, not a trained operative—*Stop making excuses.* She should have called Athena directly, groveled, told her she'd panicked, that she was sorry. Now she had to trust Jasmine to handle it. Jasmine had offered up such nice forgiving words, but it didn't change the fact Ellie had let the group down. She'd compromised everyone, and the success of the project. She kept reliving the scene in Cummings's neighborhood over and over in her head, wondering what was going to happen now, to her, to Jasmine, and to everyone else. Her brain squirrelled about as she lay in bed, even tried to talk her into hopping an express train to the West Coast, or a nonstop flight to the Philippines. What would happen now? Jasmine would know what to do. Wild ideas kept tromping through her brain until she finally took two prescription sleeping pills at 2:00 a.m. They dragged her deeply under.

She never felt the bullet that slammed into her brain. She fell from sleep into death without ever knowing she'd died.

43

After breakfast at Jenny's Café, Griffin and Carson walked Savich and Sherlock to the Porsche. Savich said, "We talked about everything except Quint Bodine's computer. My worm got his files downloaded and out to me, but unfortunately we still don't have access—MAX ran into a layer of encryption behind the admin password. It could take him some time to get through it. Once we get in, I'll call the minute I find something."

Griffin said, "I wonder why Bodine would go to the effort to encrypt at all unless there's something he wants to be sure is protected."

"The fact he did encrypt makes me very hopeful he considers what's on his computer is critical. We'll find out soon. You need me, I'm a call away."

They shook hands, Carson gave Sherlock a hug, said against her ear, "Please call me if there's anything I can do for you."

Once they were on the interstate, Savich let the Porsche loose, happy to hear the engine sing hallelujah. It was a bummer, but he throttled back to just over the speed limit. He took Sherlock's hand in his. "Tell me how you're feeling today."

She gave him a real smile. "Fine, I'm fine. I can't wait to meet Mr. Maitland. Wait. Did he come to the hospital? Have I already met him?"

"Yes, but there were lots of agents there, doesn't matter you don't remember him. Now, some disturbing news from Washington. While you were in the shower, Ben Raven, a Metro detective, texted me. He got an anonymous call early this morning. They found a body at the apartment of an apparent break-in. Her name was Eleanor Corbitt. Ben caught the case. He thought she looked familiar and went back to check video cams at the scene of your accident. Sure enough, Eleanor Corbitt was there, standing on the street corner. He spoke to his LT, who called Mr. Maitland, who called me thirty minutes ago. I didn't tell Griffin about it, he's got enough on his plate. I didn't tell you right away—" He stalled.

You were concerned I might freak out, you wanted to break it to me gently after we left. She didn't say that, said only, "And the dead woman being on that corner, now, that ain't no coincidence."

He spurted out a laugh. That was his Sherlock. "You're right about that." Savich let his Porsche pass a big eighteen-wheeler at ninety miles an hour, smiling wider with each RPM. When he reluctantly slowed back to sixty, it was Sherlock who laughed.

It was odd, but Sherlock would swear she remembered the smell in the morgue—strong lemon disinfectant with a slick of something foul just beneath. It was the smell of death. And it was cold in the autopsy room. She and Savich stood over Eleanor Corbitt's body. She was thirty-six at the time of her death. She'd been a pretty woman, with long dark brown hair, a fair complexion. But now her hair was bloody, her face slack and gray. A sheet was pulled to her shoulders, showing only the edges of the Y cut. Ben Raven stood at Sherlock's elbow. Was it to catch her if she fainted?

The M.E., Dr. Horowitz, said in his clipped voice, "She was remarkably fit, in excellent health when she died. I estimate TOD around the middle of the night, say three a.m., but of course, that could be off by several hours either way. She took sleeping pills sometime after midnight so she was very probably asleep when she was shot in the head and killed instantly. If she'd been awake, there'd be signs of a struggle. And I'd say this one could have put up a good fight. No, she never even knew."

Sherlock cocked her head to the side. "I doubt she was raped."

Dr. Horowitz shook his head.

"Then why was she killed?"

Ben Raven said, "Her apartment was ransacked, looked like someone broke in, looking for money, for drugs, whatever, and her wallet and her jewelry were missing. And it could have been a robbery gone bad. That's what it's supposed to look like. But there's something you don't know. Apart from being at the scene of your accident, the woman who struck you, Jasmine Palumbo, and this woman—both of them work for the Bexholt Group, the big communications security company headquartered in Maryland. Jasmine Palumbo is a supervisor there in security engineering. Corbitt was in accounting. Corbitt had worked at Bexholt for five years at the time of her death, Palumbo for eight.

"I've had several hours to think about how this all went down. If we eliminate all of it being coincidence, it's got to have something to do with the CIA analyst who struck your car and disappeared. For whatever reason, someone eliminated Corbitt, made it look like a common crime. Was she a loose end? Was it something she knew she shouldn't know? Was it something she did? Someone saw her who shouldn't have? We don't know any of it yet."

Savich said, "Security engineering and accounting. Strange combination. And you said Corbitt was standing on the street watching the accident?"

"More likely watching her co-worker Jasmine or looking for Justice Cummings," Sherlock said.

Ben said, "My vote is she was looking for Cummings. Who was he going to meet after work at the Blaze Café? We spotted two people he probably saw outside the café before he ran. We couldn't identify them, the angles weren't right. Do you want the FBI techs to have a go?"

"Yes, send them over," Savich said.

Sherlock said, "What does the CIA say about all this? Have they bothered to share anything, like what Cummings's major responsibilities were?"

Savich said, "Of course not. They say his job description is need-to-know only. Mr. Maitland is pissed, to say the least. I imagine he'll go see Cummings's boss and his boss's boss today, try to find out if Cummings knows either Eleanor Corbitt or Jasmine Palumbo."

Ben laughed. "From what I hear the CIA keep their operations so close to the vest even they sometimes can't find them. But your Mr. Maitland, my money's on him."

Sherlock saw a bull of a man, his dark brown hair slashed through with gray strands, standing behind a big desk, leaning toward her, his palms pressed flat. Suddenly, there was a big smile, at something she'd said? She remembered him, he had indeed been at the hospital.

Ben said, "Sherlock, is something wrong?"

She shook her head, looked back down at the pretty woman who was dead at age thirty-six. What had she done? Or seen? Or failed to do?

As they walked out of the morgue, Sherlock said, "I recognized on some level I'm comfortable with autopsies. I knew what I was seeing and being told, and it didn't make me want to hurl. Have I ever met Dr. Horowitz before, Ben?"

"Yes, many times." He was pleased she'd called him by his first name, though to her he was still a stranger.

Savich said, "If you hadn't caught the case, Ben, if you hadn't recognized her, I strongly doubt a connection would ever have been made. It's Mr. Maitland's call now. Time for us to see what he's planning."

44

Goldy, Mr. Maitland's longtime bulldog gatekeeper, told Savich and Sherlock, "He's near to erupting. Go on in, see if you can calm him down. If you need the fire extinguisher, holler."

Maitland rose and kicked his desk when they walked in. "These blank-brained secretive CIA yahoos don't return my calls." He slammed a folder down on his desk. "No more frigging phone tag that doesn't lead anywhere. We're going to go see Claire Farriger. She's an assistant director for analysis. The title is longer, but you get the gist. Besserman is Justice Cummings's group chief, Farriger is Besserman's boss." He stopped, gave Sherlock a worried look. His face softened. "Sherlock, there's no need for you to come with us.

Perhaps you'd be better off going home, getting some rest?"

"Sir, would you normally suggest resting to me?"

He looked embarrassed, shook his head. "Well, no. I'd be afraid you'd hurt me. Sorry, Sherlock, I guess I'm tripping all over myself because you're hurt"—he ran his hands through his hair—"and I'm making things worse."

Sherlock patted his arm, something she'd never done before. He blinked down at her, smiled.

"Sir, what makes things worse is doing nothing and thinking and worrying and feeling sorry for myself because when I'm alone I'm a tabula rasa. I don't even know what I would normally be thinking about. I want to be of use. I'd very much like to visit the CIA."

Maitland shot a look at Savich, who nodded.

"All right, I'd appreciate your perspective, Sherlock."

Savich told his boss what he'd learned about Eleanor Corbitt from Ben Raven. "—So we have two Bexholt employees, both at the scene of Sherlock's accident, one now dead, murdered. Corbitt was in the Bexholt accounting department. The woman who struck Sherlock, Jasmine Palumbo, is in their security engineering division, a supervisor. Does the CIA know about Corbitt's murder? How could they, unless they have a spy in Metro?"

"Who knows? I'll bet there are CIA spies over at that pizza joint on Bentley Street where FBI agents hang out. But all right, it's possible we know something they don't, yet," Maitland said, and rubbed his big hands together.

Savich said, "Before we go to Langley and possibly get blindsided, Sherlock and I should pay a visit to Bexholt, see if we can't find out how these two women tie together with Justice Cummings."

"Hmmm. It wouldn't be a bad idea to get more ammunition. Okay, yes, go to Bexholt, find out what in blue blazes is going on there. I want to be armed with everything possible before we storm the CIA." Maitland checked his watch. "And, of course, it would be nice if we could find Justice Cummings."

At the elevator, Sherlock said, "Does he usually kick his desk?"

"Maybe. It could be this is only the first time we've caught him doing it."

Sherlock said matter-of-factly as she punched the elevator button, "Everything seems unsolvable right now, but I suspect it'll all be simple once we figure it out. Most things are."

He marveled, wondered if she realized it was something she'd said many times in the past. What was more, she was usually right. He lifted his hand to touch the bouncing curls, and froze. She was humming a country-western song he'd written for her at least three years before, about a man finding his mate at long last at the dollar slots.

He said, "I think you first heard that song at the Bonhomie Club. It's a nightclub run by an incredible woman, Ms. Lily. I sing country-western music there a couple of times a month. My friend James Quinlan, another FBI agent, plays the sax, makes it weep. You'll meet him soon enough."

He shut up at the helpless look on her face. He'd told her that morning that his boss, Mr. Maitland, had a fine brain and he didn't meddle. Savich had assured her she liked him, and his four linebacker-size sons. And his wife, June. And then he'd stopped cold—if she didn't know Mr. Maitland, how could she possibly know June Maitland? She didn't even know her own son. She remained too scared to see Sean, still too scared Sean would realize something was wrong. Her fear warred with her guilt.

So he talked to her about everything else—their cases, their vacations, memories they'd made together as a family. His Sean stories made her laugh, but he knew they amused her from a sort of distance. There was no emotional punch to remember. Except for the guilt.

He helped her into the Porsche, handed her his phone. "Remember I told you Mr. Maitland doesn't meddle? But this time is different. He told me his gut is doing the rumba, he knows this could be something big." He scrolled down in his photos. "This is a photo of Jasmine Palumbo and recordings of everything Ben gathered for us, including her interview when they took her in after she hit your Volvo. We're going to surprise Ms. Palumbo. I checked and she's there."

It took them only an hour to get to Coverton, Maryland, with Sherlock asking questions about the information Ben Raven had given them. She said, "When I look at her photo, I think she looks familiar. I think I must have seen her face just before she hit my car—a Volvo?"

"Yes. It makes sense you saw her face before she struck you. Why not?" He patted her hand. "*I* can't wait to see her face when she lays eyes on you."

Jasmine Palumbo stared off into space, ignoring the piles of work on her computer screen, primarily the schedules and assignments for Bexholt staff for the security installation at the Kentington Hotel. It was a top-drawer contract for top-drawer clients. The Bexholt Group would be providing communications security for a series of private negotiations between staff of the Federal Reserve and the European Central Bank, starting on Monday. She smiled as she rubbed her arm through the sling. Not broken, they said, but it still throbbed, and her smile quickly fell away. She didn't want to take any more pain meds, they fuzzed her brain. What were the odds it would all come down to an accident? What wretched luck she would drive into that intersection and into an FBI agent's car just as Justice Cummings shot out of that alley and went flying over the agent's hood. There was still no sign of that pissant idiot. Was he holed up somewhere? Dead behind a dumpster on K Street? No, she knew he was out there somewhere, injured but still a threat.

She sighed, rubbed her arm again. She'd had the formal Bexholt Group plans printed up for her scheduled meeting with Nikki and Nathan Bexholt, brother and sister, Nathan, COO, and Nikki, VP of the Bexholt Group their father had founded. She's included how the Bexholt people would interface with hotel security and with the Central Bankers' own security teams. What a joy that would be. She knew Nathan Bexholt was smart, savvy, and driven, and could barely tolerate his sister, Nikki. Not that the feelings weren't mutual. Nikki was officially in charge of the operation, and he would try to find holes in her plans to look superior, so Jasmine knew everything set out had to be perfect. If all went well, Nathan would never know what the real plans were, what they were really going to do in the meeting room.

Jasmine looked up when her door unexpectedly opened, and there stood a tall, good-looking hunk duded up in a dark suit, white shirt, and dark tie, giving her a dead-man's stare. Where was Glynn, her assistant, who guarded her door like a mother bear? She gave the man a quick study. He looked tough and professional, made her wonder what he'd look like stripped down. In the next moment, she saw a woman standing just behind him—tall, slender, curly red hair—Jasmine jumped out of her chair. "You're Agent Sherlock!" She came around her desk at a run and stopped in front of Sherlock. "You're here and you're all right. I'm so sorry I hit you, I didn't see you. No excuse, but I'm so sorry."

"Ms. Palumbo," the man said in a dark sexy voice, a nice addition to the package. Jasmine looked away from the woman staring at her curiously.

He was holding out his creds. "I'm Agent Dillon Savich, FBI, and this is Agent Sherlock. But you already recognized her."

Sherlock nodded to her, said nothing. So this was the person who'd struck her. Palumbo was tall and fit, dressed all in black. A requirement for a security engineer?

Jasmine, flustered, stepped back. She accepted Savich's creds, gave them a cursory look, handed them back. She waved away Sherlock's creds, splayed her hands in front of her. "I already knew who you were, Agent Sherlock. Again, I am so sorry."

Sherlock said quietly, "But you do have an excuse, Ms. Palumbo. You were watching for Justice Cummings. You saw him running out of the alley and he distracted you. Maybe you thought you could bring him down?"

Jasmine froze, but only for an instant. She had to keep her head. How did they know? It had to be a guess, nothing but a guess. She shook her head, looked bewildered. "I'm sorry, but I don't remember anyone running out of an alley. No, I lost concentration thinking about a security project I'm leading—for a meeting here in Washington, and I—I really don't know who this person is you mentioned. Justice, you called him?"

Savich said, "We'd like to talk to you about him, Ms. Palumbo. And the accident."

Jasmine wished she were anywhere but here, facing these two FBI agents. She'd even jump at a meeting with Nathan Bexholt and Nikki sniping at each other. She turned, walked back to her desk, and slowly sat down. She waved them to the two chairs in front of her. She knew, of course, they'd recognize a delaying tactic when they saw it, but it didn't matter. She needed time to get herself together. She had a superior brain, she could do this.

She should have known the FBI would come to talk to her, but she hadn't expected them to know about Justice Cummings and she hadn't expected Agent Sherlock. Of course she knew what Sherlock looked like from pictures and from countless videos, but in the flesh, she looked as stylish and kick-ass in her black blazer and low-heeled black boots as the male agent. She'd heard Sherlock had left the hospital, but she was back at work already?

Jasmine said matter-of-factly, "Look, I know you'd like to speak to me about the accident. I mean, I did hit an FBI agent. Again, I'm so sorry for my inattention. But I'm afraid I don't know who Justice Cummings is. Is he the man you crashed into?" Her voice came out nice and smooth, utterly sincere, even though she was still shocked at hearing they'd even considered a connection. Athena—Nikki—had been so sure they wouldn't—it was the first time she could remember her being so wrong.

Savich could see no obvious sign she was lying. She was good, steady and sincere. He settled back and said easily, "Before we discuss Justice Cummings and the accident further, tell us, Ms. Palumbo, what is it you do here at the Bexholt Group?"

Familiar ground. Jasmine felt her confidence returning. She said, "As I'm sure you know, the Bexholt Group is known for our expertise in electronic security and vulnerability assessment for our clients' communications. We do some manufacturing of firewalls, too, and some of our own R&D. I'm a security engineer here, among many others. I work in security monitoring, primarily."

"Were you at work for Bexholt at the time of the accident?"

"No, it was late in the day and I was off."

Savich said without pause, "Did you know Eleanor Corbitt was murdered last night in her apartment?"

Jasmine heard his words, but they didn't immediately make any sense. Then she gasped, shock freezing her. No, there had to be a mistake. Ellie had called her last night, frightened, and Jasmine had told her not to worry, she'd take care of it. So how could Ellie be dead? Murdered? She wanted to scream, to weep. What was going on here? She knew she had to keep it together. She looked Agent Savich in the eye. "This is horrible, unbelievable. Why would anyone kill Eleanor Corbitt? She was an accountant in our accounting division. Do you know who's responsible?"

Savich saw the shock, knew it was real. "Not yet. Tell us about Ms. Corbitt."

Jasmine shook her head back and forth. She still couldn't take it in, couldn't deal with the reality of it—Ellie dead, not just dead, but murdered. *Get it together.* "I'm very sorry to hear this, though I didn't know her well. She was more an acquaintance, you could say. This is nuts, it makes no sense. As I said, she was an accountant, for heaven's sake."

Sherlock said, "The killer waited until she was asleep and shot her in the head."

Jasmine shuddered, couldn't help it. She picked up a pen and began weaving it between her long fingers. "Do you know if it was a boyfriend?"

Stupid, stupid, the agents would know Ellie was divorced from an abusive crap-head. Ellie was leery of men at best. Jasmine's brain cleared and she said aloud, "Stupid question. Her husband abused her. She finally divorced him. Everyone in the office knew about the situation. I can't imagine she'd have a boyfriend so soon after the divorce. I heard her ex now lives somewhere in Virginia."

Sherlock said, "It was a very nasty divorce, we understand."

"From what I heard around the office, yes.

Then you suspect him? I believe his name is Brook Hughes."

Savich said, "Brook Hughes is currently in the South of France, near Cannes. Crimes of passion usually aren't like that—a bullet to the brain of a sleeping woman—more often they're loud and bloody if two people really hate each other. It looked like a robbery on the face of it, but it's more than a small coincidence given both you and Ms. Corbitt work at the same company."

Sherlock picked it up. "That and the fact Ms. Corbitt was caught on video standing at the street corner at the scene of my accident on Tuesday, staring straight at you. It seems logical to assume she was somehow involved. And did her involvement make her a loose end? Was someone afraid she might have helped us understand what all this is about?"

Jasmine splayed her hands in front of her. "What you're implying is horrible and insulting. I can't help you, Agents. I have no idea why she was there. I'm very sorry she's dead, she was nice, a good worker, but I don't know what she did after work, how she spent her evenings and with whom."

Savich said, "If you were only acquaintances, how do you know her ex-husband's name? Ms. Palumbo, where were you between midnight and four a.m. last night?"

Jasmine rose straight up, cleansing waves of anger pumping off her. "You dare ask me that? What is this? We both worked at the same company, nothing more, nothing less." *Keep it together, calm down.* She looked at Sherlock. "Is this out of spite because I hit you? You know I didn't mean to, it was an accident. Look, I was hurt, too—" She waved her sling at them. "Listen, I told you, I knew Ellie Corbitt as an employee here, that's all."

Sherlock's voice stayed calm. "Come, Ms. Palumbo, we need to know your whereabouts."

"Very well. I assume you're asking everyone? But why are you involved at all? Ellie was in Washington. Isn't that a police matter?"

Sherlock merely waited, not taking her eyes off Palumbo's face.

Jasmine shrugged. "Very well. I was home in bed, alone. No alibi." She stared at Sherlock, caught a glimpse of the Band-Aid beneath all that curly hair. "I'm very sorry about Eleanor Corbitt. I'm also very pleased you're going to be all right. You are, aren't you?"

Sherlock cocked her head. "So they tell me."

45

Booker Bodine sat stiffly in a chair across from his own desk in his own office, his jaw locked, his eyes looking down at his big watch that even gave him the time in Hong Kong. And Griffin studied him. Perhaps it was petty of him, but the sheriff's office was the only private place in the station house.

Griffin said, "I read your files on Heather Forrester's disappearance, Sheriff Bodine. You were obviously very thorough. After all, Heather's family has lived in Gaffer's Ridge for years and you know them well. Now, as for the teenagers missing from Marion and Radford, those investigations also appear quite intensive. All three reports determined the girls were kidnapped, even though there were no demands for money. All the reports indicate there's no direction to go in now, and they're awaiting further developments. You were in Marion yourself yesterday, weren't you? Did you discover anything to help us?"

Sheriff Bodine looked up from his watch. "No, I didn't. It's Sheriff Bud Bailey's town, so sure he was thorough, as was Chief Mule Lindy in Radford."

"Mule? That's his name?"

"Not until he got kicked in the head by his pa's mule when he was a kid, no harm done. Look, the reports I gave you are everything Bailey and Lindy had. Of course, there's nothing to go on, or we would have solved the case. Look here, this town doesn't run itself, I've—"

Griffin said, "Sheriff, I don't like the fact I'm sitting here at your desk any more than you like me doing it. You might get it back if you work with me. Now, answer a question for me. In Mule Lindy's report, it's noted several times Amy Traynor was a very independent girl with a mind of her own, always questioning her parents and her teachers."

"Yeah, she was known as a flat-out little hellion. But that didn't give anyone the right to take her."

"No, but it is interesting. In your report and in the Marion report on Latisha Morris, the missing girls are close to sainthood. Now, Sheriff, give me an account of what you saw yesterday."

There was just enough threat in Griffin's voice to make Booker's lips seam, but he wasn't stupid, he managed to swallow his bile. Griffin had known Booker would push him, challenge him. In his position, Griffin supposed he'd do the same.

"I met with Sheriff Bud Bailey in Marion, but he didn't have anything new to add except whoever took Latisha was real smart. Then I went to talk to Ms. Sulina Morris—she's Latisha's mother, a social worker with five kids. Latisha recently turned sixteen and she's the oldest. Ms. Morris couldn't tell me anything I didn't already know, anything that isn't in the reports." Booker shrugged. "When I told Bud the FBI was involved now, he spat in his wastebasket."

"Was this a sign of approval or disapproval?"

Booker chewed this over, thought better of lying about it. He said, reluctantly, "Bailey thought it couldn't hurt to have fresh eyes on the case. Said to tell you he was now considering maybe Latisha was tired of taking care of all her younger brothers and sisters, and had run off. Maybe there were drugs involved, but nothing solid. I think he was shooting off his mouth, wanting to impress you."

"I trust you told Sheriff Bailey you agree with FBI involvement?"

"Me? Doesn't matter what I think, does it? I can't remember exactly what I said."

Griffin said, "Let's leave the drugs aside. I saw

there was no mention of Ms. Morris seeing any strange boys around or seeing any strangers at all near her daughter."

"Look, Ms. Morris's got five kids, no husband, and a full-time job. I doubt she notices much of anything. Still, she was frantic, said her daughter has to be kidnapped or she'd have gotten in touch with her. The trip was a waste of time. My time. Nothing new, only Sheriff Bailey's lame ideas about drugs." Booker shrugged, looked bored.

"Where is Rafer's SUV? It's evidence from the crime scene. Where is it?"

Only a slight pause, then, "I asked Rafer in the hospital, and he said he didn't know, said he was going to report it stolen."

"And you know nothing about it?"

"Of course not. You know, Rafer's lawyer, Mr. Jobs, said you couldn't hold Rafer, said he was going to file for habeas corpus. Rafer's going to leave the hospital today."

Griffin knew this. Mr. Jobs had already called him, pointed out there was no evidence, presented him with a release warrant, so Griffin had agreed to his staying with his parents when he left the hospital. And he was to stay there until further notice. Mr. Jobs had grumbled, but finally agreed.

Bodine said, "Rafer didn't do anything, neither did anyone else in my town."

Why not lay it out? Griffin said, "Let me add I've met his mother, Cyndia Bodine. She's a person of interest, along with her son and your brother. Tell me, Sheriff, did you call her or your brother at Rafer's house before you brought Dr. DeSilva and me in? Did one of them tell you to remove the evidence? Or vice versa?"

Booker snapped back in his chair, his face flooded with furious color. "No, I didn't call her! I didn't call anyone!"

Griffin studied him a moment, knew he'd never get the truth out of him. He rose as he said, "Be here tomorrow morning, Sheriff."

"Tomorrow's Saturday."

"You're right. So not too early, say eight o'clock?"

After Booker marched stiffly out of his own office, Griffin sat back down, took stock. Then he picked up his cell to make sure Quint Bodine was at the bank and not at home with his son. Then he called Carson. "You said you needed to call your boss. What did Aquino have to say?"

"He thinks there's a great story here, and I can stay as long as I wish, just so I bring home the goods."

"I'll make sure the goods happen. Be ready in ten minutes. You and I are going to visit with Rafer's daddy at his bank, the grand pooh-bah himself, Quint Bodine."

He opened his cell phone to the files Savich had given him about Quint Bodine and started reading.

When Carson stepped into Booker Bodine's office, Fayreen's laser glare nearly searing her back, Griffin looked up. "I called Slick and DeAndre. Rafer already left the hospital. I told them to go back to Richmond, I'd holler loud if I ran into trouble."

Carson couldn't believe it. "He's out of the hospital? Not coming here to jail? But—but—Griffin, he kidnapped me!"

"I know. But I'm thinking his being free might work to our advantage. You ready to go see Quint?"

46

ALEXANDRIA, VIRGINIA
WAREHOUSE DISTRICT
FRIDAY MORNING

Justice Cummings woke up to humming—soft, soothing, close by. He opened an eye to see a man with a towel around his head sitting cross-legged next to him. He smelled ripe.

The man stopped humming, leaned in close to study Justice's face. He said, "I'm Dougie." He straightened his towel and smiled down at him. Justice saw the towel was more gray than white, MARRIOTT emblazoned on it. Justice eyed the grizzled man, who could have been fifty or eighty, impossible to tell. He wore a dirty Hawaiian shirt and pants once green, now more like stale guaca-mole. And that weathered Marriott towel. He had surprisingly beautiful white teeth.

"Hummer will be back with some more antibiotic cream for your leg and nose. If you don't know, your nose is offline, but I'll tell you, boy, when the swelling and bruising go down, it'll make you look tougher, less like a nerd."

"But I am a nerd," Justice said, and sucked in his breath when a mountain of pain slammed into his leg.

"A nerd's okay. I knew a nerd, a long time ago, maybe ten years, I dunno. Hummer left me aspirin to give you. All I got is Wild Turkey to wash it down. Here you go."

Justice didn't care if Dougie was giving him arsenic. He opened his mouth, felt his stomach lining burn off when the Wild Turkey hit it. He wheezed and coughed and Dougie laughed. "I guess you gotta get accustomed to it," he said, and drank down the rest of the bottle without stopping. He wiped his hand over his mouth. "Oh yeah, Hummer's going to bring you back some bottled water. I told him booze cures anything, but he said since you're hurt, you need the water to keep you hy-drated."

"Dougie?"

"That's me."

"My name is Justice. How did I get here?"

"You've been kind of out of it since Hummer found you huddled in on yourself in his doorway, and dragged you inside. Me, I prefer my box. It's too dark for me in here. We've been taking care of you ever since.

"You offered Hummer a wad of cash to hide you, but he didn't take it, so your money's still in your wallet. Not much, though. Hummer said you had some fancy ID. You're CIA and that's sure enough interesting. That's a real funny name. Why'd your folks name you that?"

"Wishful thinking on their part—they wanted me to be a judge, like my dad was. That, or a priest."

Dougie placed a lone dirty finger on Justice's forehead, tsk-tsked, then said, "Your daddy was a judge? Well, I guess everybody's daddy's gotta be something. A long time ago, my daddy was something, too, but I don't remember what now. Don't think you got a fever, but you did—maybe two days ago, but I don't remember."

"What day is it?"

"Day? Not important enough to know. You're lucky. Hummer got back last week from the world out there, or maybe it was last month sometime, time is weird, you know? Anyways, Hummer was a major in the army but nobody cares about him now and Ruth left him a hundred dollars because she had to take a necklace she found in his nest, stolen, she said, and she had to return it. Anyways, that was a long time ago, too. Then there was his friend, he had a weird name, weirder than yours. Hummer called him Manta Ray. Hummer saved his bacon, too. He was all shot up, and you know what? Manta Ray came back flying in a helicopter all the way from Ireland, and he brought Hummer a buttload of money. Hummer bought us all blankets and pillows and a grill and charcoal and steaks and three bottles of vodka. Ireland's a long way from here. It's really green there. Here comes Hummer now."

Justice's brain was squirreling around trying to make sense of what Dougie was saying. Then he let it go. It hurt too much to worry about it. Oddly, he felt safe.

Dougie sat back cross-legged and began singing "Take Me Home, Country Roads" in a sweet voice, true and soft as summer rain. Justice looked at the man striding toward him. He was military straight, tall, with buzz-cut hair. He looked fifty, maybe sixty, and he was clean. He was wearing green camouflage pants and shirt, a leather belt around his lean waist.

"I remember now, I made it here to the warehouse district," Justice said.

"Yes, you did," Hummer said. He set down a bag and stuck out his hand. "I'm Major Hummer, and this is Dougie, and you're Justice Cummings. A good name, I like it. Here's water, and more antibiotic cream for the cut on your leg and maybe it'll help your nose, too. I splinted your leg, don't know if it's broken, but if it is, at least it won't heal all crooked. Here, drink."

Major Hummer twisted off the lid of a plastic bottle of water and handed it to Justice. Justice drank most of the bottle down in one long gulp, choked and started to cough.

No one bothered to thwack him on the back, Major Hummer and Dougie simply looked at him and waited. He realized when he finally caught his breath the aspirin must be kicking in. He was starting to feel better. "Thank you, Major."

Dougie said, "I was telling him about Manta Ray. Too bad we ate all those steaks. Justice, you're looking better, not like you're going to croak it anymore." Dougie straightened the listing towel on his head. "You hold still now and let Hummer rub in the cream. Did you kill anyone?"

"Me?" Justice's voice was nearly a squeak. "Not me. I'd never kill anybody."

"That's good, but maybe not. There's lots of folk in the world out there rotten clean through."

Major Hummer's hands were gentle, a surprise, as his big rough fingers massaged in the cream with a Kleenex he pulled out of a small packet.

"Isn't bad," Hummer said, sitting back on his haunches. "Healing good. Now, let me bandage you up again, I got some sterile pads and a roll of paper towels to wrap around the pads."

After two more aspirin, Justice was feeling even better. He saw his pants, folded up neatly beside him. He was wearing only his shirt and his boxers and a thick pad of paper towels wrapped around his thigh. He vaguely remembered the Uber he'd taken to Alexandria, to a blighted neighborhood he'd passed through three years before, and then he'd walked three blocks to the warehouse district. It was desolate, derelict, the buildings falling in on themselves. It was home to a dozen or more homeless people, depending on the season, their cardboard nests propped against the buildings to keep them from collapsing. Odd how he'd remembered this place, known to his bones he'd be safe here. If his leg didn't kill him.

Justice looked at Dougie, who was humming again, then at Major Hummer on his knees beside him. "Thank you both. I owe you my life, Major Hummer. And no, I didn't kill anybody. But people are after me and I don't know who they are. I ran out into the street and slammed onto the hood of a car that was spinning around because another car had hit it. They ran after me, but I got away."

"You're young," Dougie said. "You should be able to run even with a gimp leg. I once had a daughter—I think she was my daughter, and I do remember she liked to run, but it was a long time ago. Maybe she's about your age, that's what I thought when I saw you. Had to help you, could have been my daughter. Did Ruth send you?"

"Who's Ruth? Is she your daughter?"

"No, she's not my daughter, but she's real important. I'm her snitch." Justice watched Dougie preen. "She's an actual special agent, FBI, and she's a good person. She's smart, is Ruth.

Hummer, you got your cell phone? I can call Ruth for you, Justice. She'll know what to do."

FBI? Dougie was a snitch? Justice felt like he'd fallen down the rabbit hole, but then he really looked at Dougie, realized he wasn't crazy—well, he was, but still, it did sound like this Ruth woman might indeed be FBI.

He started to say no, don't call her, but then he thought about it. She wasn't CIA, no way would this Ruth agent even know about him, no way could she be involved with the people after him.

"Let me think about it, Dougie," Justice said. "Do you know Ruth's last name?"

"I did, once upon a time, but time's slippery, you know? Names are slippery, too."

"Yes, I know. Let me rest awhile, think this through—" And Justice closed his eyes under the watch of two homeless people who'd probably been on psychotropic meds once, but no longer. They were forgotten now, left to fend for themselves, but they'd helped him. Justice heard Dougie rise. "I'm gonna get Sally, Hummer, she can come and watch him awhile. I got to get more Wild Turkey. Over at Bilbo Baggins—you know Stan the barkeep, he puts a half bottle near the dumpster for me, wrapped in the *Washington Post*."

Justice had eaten at Bilbo Baggins a couple of weeks before. He didn't know Stan the barkeep, but realized he liked him. Justice fell asleep and dreamed he was running, running so hard his side was hurting something fierce, but he knew he had to keep going or they'd catch him. And what? Kill him? He saw her face, a strong face, set and hard with purpose. Why? The woman was gone and he saw his boss's face. Mr. Besserman was standing over him at his workstation, eyeing the odd intel Justice had come across, and he was saying something, but what? Then he was running again and he saw another woman's face, frozen with disbelief, wild red hair in bouncing curls all over her head and blue eyes, yes, she had blue eyes, but somehow she was out of time. Then everything hurt, and he jerked awake, blinking in the dim light.

He heard breathing, knew someone was close, and tightened with fear. A woman's scratchy voice said, "Hold on, Justice—that's your name, isn't it? That's what Hummer told me. Okay, let me turn on some light. It's always so dark in here, but that's the way Hummer likes it even when the sun's shinin' real bright outside like it is right now. I'm Sally. Dougie was drinking his Wild Turkey Stan left him, but Hummer, he's upstairs in his nest, napping with the angels, like he always does for a while after he comes back from the world out there. Did I tell you? I'm Sally."

A flashlight came on. And he looked into the raddled face of an older woman who might have been his mother if she didn't look so derelict. She was wearing ragged clothes, her hair an improbable red with black and gray roots two inches long, but she was smiling at him sweetly. She was no threat. "Open up," she said, and when he did, she poured some more water into his mouth. "Slow—good. Now, how is your leg? Your nose?"

He thought about that. "A dull throb, but nothing bad."

"Doesn't matter. Hummer said to give you more aspirin anyway."

He dutifully swallowed the aspirin, drank more water, and lay back against what was probably a very dirty pile of—what? Blankets? He didn't know, didn't really care.

"Did you kill anybody?"

Was that their only theme? He couldn't blame them, living this hardscrabble life. "No. I didn't kill anybody. I don't know what I did, but someone sure wants me bad, someone wants to kill me."

Sally sat back, straightened her long, once-dark-blue skirt, now a dingy gray, around her skinny legs. She wore ancient flip-flops on her dirty feet. "I wish someone wanted me, not to kill me, you know, wanted me the other way, the good way." She shrugged, shined the flashlight in his eyes, then turned it off. "Gotta save the batteries. You promise no cops are gonna come here and shoot us?"

Could he make that promise if they—whoever

they were—found him? "No," he said firmly. "No one will find me here."

"Well, you can't trust the cops, now can you? But Ruth, she's good people."

Ruth, Justice thought. Ruth, the FBI agent. He slept again.

47

Griffin and Carson left Fayreen, silent and glaring, and stepped out onto the sidewalk. Griffin said, "The bank is one block over. I read up on Quint Bodine, since I doubt he'll tell us much himself. Even though Savich is focused on Sherlock and their case back in Washington, he'll still have MAX decrypt those files as soon as possible."

Carson patted his arm. "If my wife had been in an accident and had her memory wiped, I'd be distracted, too. I'd probably forget even your name, much less a bunch of files."

Griffin smiled at her, couldn't help it. Then he thought of Rafer Bodine, of what he'd done to her, or what he might have done to her—if—if Griffin hadn't been close, if he hadn't heard her, what would have happened? No, he wouldn't go there. And Rafer's mother, Cyndia Bodine. Given what she'd done to Sherlock, she was, to his mind, even more dangerous. And now Rafer was going home. "After we see Quint Bodine, I want you to know we're sticking together. If you need a bathroom break, you check in with me first, all right?"

Carson would have rolled her eyes, but he had a point. She nodded.

They looked up to see Jenny striding down the sidewalk toward them. She stopped, grinned. "I just missed you guys. I took Fayreen a lovely frittata for brunch—with my famous breakfast fries so maybe she wouldn't try to poison you, Griffin. She even thanked me, added under her breath you guys were up to no good in here, trying to ruin Gaffer's Ridge. Hey, will you be coming to the café for lunch today? There's a college kid who works at the FedEx, comes by for a slice of my meatloaf afterward every single day. He heard you kicked Sheriff Bodine out of his office and he's dying to meet you, shake your hand, probably ask for an autograph." She grinned.

"It's a plan," Griffin said. "I've never signed an autograph before."

Griffin and Carson split off from Jenny and walked the block over to Gaffer's Ridge First City Bank on High Moon Street. It was a warm day already, the sun bright overhead, the boutiques and antiques shops doing great morning business.

The bank was a square redbrick building with a sign over the double doors stating it had been built in 1909. It looked straight out of the Old West, complete with two original-looking hitching posts out front.

"I wonder if they sprinkled sawdust on the floor," Carson said as she preceded Griffin into the bank.

"How about a free beer if you open an account?"

There wasn't a western bar or any sawdust inside. The floors were highly buffed wide oak planks, and Remington-type color murals covered the walls showing a cattle drive, a rodeo scene with a cowboy doing rope tricks, and a western hoedown, with cowboys riding through on horses and women walking in long dresses and bonnets, carrying baskets, their children playing with hoops. A line of half a dozen customers waited their turn to be beckoned by the tellers seated behind a long counter made of dark oak etched with more scenes from the Old West. They heard soft music in the background, a spaghetti western theme.

Suddenly everyone went quiet.

"We've been spotted," Griffin said low, and smiled and waited until everyone in the bank had turned toward them. Griffin held up his creds. "Hello. I'm FBI Special Agent Griffin Hammer-smith, from Washington, D.C. We're here to investigate the disappearance of Latisha Morris, Amy Traynor, and Heather Forrester. We'd appreciate any help you can give us. If you or your neighbors have any information, please come by the sheriff's station." Griffin knew that in a town this size, everyone knew everything about everybody. If anyone did know anything, particularly about Heather Forrester, he hoped they'd come forward.

There was a buzz of conversation too low for Griffin or Carson to make out. Carson touched his arm and he turned to see a tall, aristocratic-looking older man, beautifully dressed in a gray three-piece suit, a pale blue tie, and black Italian loafers, stride out of a room at the back of the bank next to a huge vault. He paused, frowned, then closed the door behind him.

They recognized his son, Rafer, in him as he got closer. While Rafer would have fit into the western setting, his father looked like he'd be at home in an old-world drawing room, holding a brandy in his long, thin fingers.

All eyes were on them again when Quint Bodine stopped directly in front of them, gave a cursory look at Carson, looked at her again, then resolutely turned to face Griffin.

He said in a melodic voice, pitched low so no one would overhear, "My wife called to tell me my son has arrived home. He'll be staying with us, since his cottage has been marked with yellow crime scene tape and he was told he couldn't return. May I ask how long it will be until you'll be satisfied, finally, that you have nothing at all against my son?"

Griffin said, "Mr. Bodine, I assume?"

"You assume correctly."

"I'm Agent Hammersmith, and this is Dr. Carson DeSilva." He handed Bodine his creds. Bodine waved them away. "I know who you are." He looked at Carson. "And you. You are the woman accusing my son of kidnapping you and tying you up in his basement."

Carson nodded. "Yes, that's right. Duct tape, not rope. You left out the part where he pulled a gun on me and would have killed me if Agent Hammersmith hadn't come in and kicked the gun out of his hand."

Bodine went silent, studied the two of them. Griffin saw he kept looking back at Carson. Because she was drop-dead gorgeous? No, he had more the look of a man who wanted to strangle her with his bare hands? Make her disappear?

Quint finally said, "Come to my office." He turned on his heel and walked to some discreet stairs tucked behind an unmarked door.

That brief meeting would be fodder for gossip for days, Carson knew, giving a quick look back at the lobby with at least twenty people staring after them. If no one had heard what they'd said, it wouldn't matter, they'd fill in the blanks.

48

Quint Bodine's office didn't look like it belonged in the Wild West any more than he did. Rather than old-world, it was painfully modern, with Swedish furniture that reminded Griffin of the IKEA warehouse.

Bodine nodded toward two chairs, and moved behind his very plain blond-wood desk, with only a computer and a phone on top. He sat down in his ergonomically engineered desk chair. He said nothing at all, merely steepled his long, thin fingers and gave them an emotionless look. Carson took Griffin's cue and looked back blankly, waiting him out.

He finally said, "You have absolutely no evidence against my son. All you have is Dr. DeSilva's statement she heard my son mumbling about the three missing teenage girls, which is ridiculous on its face. Or at least, that's what you told Sheriff Bodine. Don't push this, Dr. DeSilva.

"Agent Hammersmith, I suppose you'll claim you're only doing your job. Those three girls are missing, and an investigation is already under way, has been since Heather Forrester was taken here in Gaffer's Ridge. But you've mistreated my son. You unlawfully entered Rafer's house and broke his wrist. You also mistreated my brother. You had Booker threatened with machine guns and have occupied his office so he and his deputies can barely function. Yesterday you entered my own home without my permission and your Agent Savich physically attacked my wife. Believe me, I will be discussing this with our mayor, and he with our congressman. You should know I have other ways as well to deal with you."

Griffin studied Rafer's father a moment. He saw a man who was used to power, to wielding it with no hesitation whenever it would gain him what he wanted. "Do you know, Mr. Bodine," he said slowly, "I've already been physically threatened more than once in this town. And now you give me a barely cloaked threat to use your influence. Or was your threat psychic?"

Bodine smiled, a shark's smile, with teeth. "What do you think?"

"I think you could be capable of both.

When we were at your home yesterday, your wife attacked another FBI agent, Agent Sherlock, and that is what led Agent Savich to protect her. Surely none of this is a surprise to you?"

"Of course she told me what Agent Savich said. It's absurd, my wife wasn't even close to Agent Sherlock when she fell to the porch outside the front door. My poor Cyndia was very upset."

"So you're denying what happened, what your wife is capable of?" Griffin asked.

"Cyndia is insightful, excellent, really, at understanding people, reading their emotions. Everyone who's met her knows it. It can sometimes make people wary of her, uncomfortable. Yes, some people have claimed there is more to it, that she has some kind of psychic power, but of course, she's never made that claim. It's patently ludicrous. I would hardly expect it of the FBI.

"Tell me, why is this woman with you, Agent Hammersmith? She is not any kind of law enforcement. She is in fact a journalist from New York, here, she's stated, to interview Dr. Alek Kuchar."

"That's right, Mr. Bodine," Carson said. "I was here to do an interview, and your son attacked me."

"I asked why she's here with you, today, in my office, Agent Hammersmith."

"In truth, Mr. Bodine? Here it is: I'm afraid to leave her alone in Gaffer's Ridge. Someone, probably a Bodine, might try to kidnap her again."

To his surprise, Quint Bodine drew back and laughed. It was a magnificent full-bodied laugh, an expensive brandy sort of laugh. "Kidnap her? In order to what? Sell her to a white slaver or something equally ridiculous? Isn't that somewhat melodramatic, Agent Hammersmith? I'll tell you what her coming here with you is about—it is harassment. You're out to harm my reputation and that of my family. What with your making that public announcement to all the bank customers about the kidnappings when everyone knows you believe my son is guilty."

Quint Bodine slammed his palm on his desk. "You know it's not easy to sue the FBI, but I can sue Dr. DeSilva for slander. And believe me, my pockets are very deep."

Carson gave Bodine her own shark smile. "Really? Well, my publisher's pockets are so deep you'd get lost in them, Mr. Bodine." She rose and leaned over his desk. "Bring it on."

There was dead silence. Carson drew a deep breath, calmed herself, and sat back down.

Bodine was eyeing Carson with too much interest for Griffin's peace of mind. As if he was assessing her, considering how best to deal with her, as if she baffled him.

Griffin then realized Quint Bodine had been playing them, and doing a good job of it. Griffin had to get the control. He decided he would try to goad Quint into losing it, maybe giving them more information. He sat back in his chair, swung his foot. He said with a sneer, "So you're comfortable with the knowledge your son may have murdered three young girls."

Bodine nearly levitated out of his ergonomic chair. Then he drew a deep steadying breath, even smiled. He slowly rose, shot his French cuffs, looked his fill once again at Carson, and said, "I invited you into my office, I have even been polite, answered your questions. But I want no more to do with you. It's time for you to leave. Do not come back to this bank again. You may contact my lawyer if you wish, but not me, and not my son."

He'd gotten too much of a rise out of Bodine.

Strained silence followed them out the door. Griffin took Carson's elbow as they walked back down the narrow stairs to the bank lobby, where all eyes followed them again, watching.

Griffin nodded and gave a little finger wave to the citizens of Gaffer's Ridge gathered in the Wild West lobby. Once outside, Griffin paused, looked back. "Quint Bodine knows, Carson, he knows everything."

"Yes, you're right, he does."

He stopped at the corner to let cars pass. "I didn't like the way he was looking at you."

Up went an eyebrow. "What do you mean?"

"Like you were prey."

49

LANGLEY, VIRGINIA
CIA HEADQUARTERS
FRIDAY MORNING

Savich had tried his hand once at solving the fourth clue on the *Kryptos* sculpture in front of the CIA's New Headquarters Building—the NHB—at Langley. The first three had been solved, but not the fourth. Every once in a while the fourth would hit the news, and cryptanalysts, both amateur and professional, would try yet again to decipher it. So far, the brain behind the codes, Jim Sanborn, had given out two intriguing clues. Still, no one had managed to make sense of the seemingly random jumble of letters.

Maitland waved toward it. "When you have a spare minute, figure that out, Savich."

He sounded perfectly serious. Ah, what faith. Savich only smiled.

Sherlock said, "That sounds like an order to me, Dillon. Maybe when this is all over you can amaze the world."

That drew him up. Savich looked down at her. "You really think I could solve the clue, do you?"

"Mr. Maitland seems to have no doubts and he is your boss, he ought to know what you're capable of, right, sir?"

"That's right," Maitland said. He still didn't know how to treat her, what to say, what to do. How did the two of them handle it?

There was nothing he could do about her amnesia, but it was time to remedy something he could. He grinned ferociously. "Time for me to throw my weight around." He marched into the lobby, right up to the large security desk, and held out his creds. "I'm here to speak to Assistant Director Claire Farriger. Right away."

Surprisingly, within five minutes they were facing a man with thick dark hair, maybe forty, wearing a stylish brown suit that barely contained his body builder's bulk. He introduced himself as Lance Armstrong, of all things, and Assistant Director Farriger's personal assistant. He took each of their creds, studied them like it was a final exam and they'd failed. He finally said, his voice clipped, "Many people here call me the assistant director's pit bull. They would be correct. Now, I realize you, sir, are marginally important in the FBI, but you did not call to make an appointment. Assistant Director Farriger is very busy. However, I doubt she would want me to show you out, given you are FBI, so I will inform her you are here." He turned, gave a light knock on a door off a large entryway, and disappeared inside, closing the door behind him.

One of Maitland's eyebrows shot up. "He's the admin? He's Goldy's counterpart? Looks like an ex–field operative to me." He huffed out a breath. "He's certainly more buff than his namesake, but my money'd be on Goldy. She could take him in a New Jersey minute."

Savich agreed. Sherlock only smiled, she had no clue.

Mr. Lance Armstrong came right back out and nodded. "Assistant Director Farriger will see you for five minutes. You may go in now. Please follow me."

Sherlock giggled.

It was so unexpected, Savich stared at her. She hiccupped, splayed her hands in front of her. "Sorry. He's so very formal and persnickety, like a butler, despite looking like a professional wrestler."

Claire Farriger watched the three FBI agents closely as they walked into her office, James Maitland in the lead. He looked as he always looked when she saw him on Capitol Hill—hard, no-nonsense, impatient to get to whatever work was at hand. She respected that about him, on occasion. She'd also seen him so brusque she'd wanted to punch him out. She wasn't surprised to see Agent Dillon Savich and his wife, Agent Sherlock, were with him. She'd not met Savich before, but had heard plenty, usually praise. He was much admired for his sheer doggedness. She'd even wished he'd worked with her at the CIA rather than at the FBI. Now she'd be squaring off with him. And yet again she marveled—what were the odds Justice Cummings would smash the windshield of Agent Sherlock's car? She'd hoped to avoid a direct meeting, but it really didn't matter. She knew how to treat their kind. She took the lead immediately and intended to keep the reins firmly in her hands. "Mr. Maitland? Agent Savich?" She paused, looked beyond the two men at Sherlock. She couldn't help a punch of pride at what this amazing woman had done. Farriger came from behind her desk, shook Sherlock's hand. "It's a great pleasure to meet you. I heard you were in an automobile accident on Tuesday and one of our own analysts was involved. All of America is relieved you're all right. Do sit down." She cast a glance at Savich and Maitland. "Gentlemen, you may sit, too."

Statuesque, that was Sherlock's first impression of Farriger, most likely a runner, long and lean. She was well dressed in a dark suit, white blouse, low black heels. Arrogance shimmered the air around her, and a formidable intelligence. She looked ready to handle anything the world dished up, and there was something else, something that eluded Sherlock. Was she worried? Anxious? From that moment on Sherlock never took her eyes off Farriger's face.

Farriger sat down behind a very nice mahogany desk with a shiny matching credenza flanking it. There were no photos, no plants, nothing at all. "I assume you are here to discuss my missing analyst, Justice Cummings. A terrible thing he was involved in a traffic accident, he and Agent Sherlock. But why are the FBI here?"

Mr. Maitland said, "We are involved because Mr. Cummings is a federal employee and it is feared he has come to harm. That puts him in the FBI purview."

Farriger said in a calm, clipped voice, "Obviously, it is not every day a CIA analyst gets struck by a car and disappears. Of course we have protocols in place, a number he was trained to call. We have taken precautions, of course, in case he's been compromised. And we're looking for him, out of concern for his well-being."

Savich said, "As of this morning, there is still no word of his whereabouts. Neither you nor I have any idea if he is dead in a ditch or holed up somewhere nursing his wounds or under interrogation. I find it curious he's made no contact with anyone here at the CIA, his place of employment. Am I missing anything?"

Farriger tapped her fingers rhythmically on the desktop, said nothing.

Maitland said, "I find it curious as well that he hasn't at least contacted his group chief, Alan Besserman, or you, Ms. Farriger, tell you he was hurt, or in trouble, and he needed help?"

"That is disturbing, naturally, Mr. Maitland. We will discover the reasons for his actions once we find him and bring him in, if, that is, he is still alive."

"Bring him in? It sounds like you believe he's done something wrong," Sherlock said. "He's in the Russian group, isn't he, ma'am? Is there anything related to his work that warrants investigation? Was he working with anyone outside the organization? Assets, perhaps, stationed in Moscow?"

Farriger waved her off. "Not that either I or Mr. Besserman know of. He's a talented analyst, not a covert operative. But his work is highly classified. If you came expecting a briefing about his work here, we are at an impasse. You can continue to look for him along with us, and we can brief each other if we make progress. There is nothing more I can do for you. Now, if that is all, I need to prepare for a meeting with the director." She rose.

Mr. Maitland sat back, began swinging his foot. "We already know a good deal about him. Justice Cummings is thirty-one years old. He came to you from MIT six years ago. He was immediately assigned to the Russian section, where he has excelled. He's married, two children, and his wife and children are currently out of town, their specific whereabouts still unknown."

Farriger didn't sit down again. She stood tall, looking down at the three of them, impatience shimmering off her. "Of course you know his background, Mr. Maitland, it's public knowledge. What is your point?"

Savich said, "We know he was running from someone he saw outside the Blaze Café off Elder Street. He ran into Agent Sherlock's car, probably broke his nose, since his blood was all over the windshield, as well as possibly incurring other injuries, and went flying off the other side. He kept running. Who could he have been running from, Ms. Farriger?"

She gave an impatient shrug. "It seems highly possible to us this was a personal matter. I'm sure you've checked his finances—"

"As have you," Mr. Maitland said. "We hope he contacted his wife, but as I said, we're still in the process of locating her. Have you?"

"I believe Cummings and his wife are estranged, separated perhaps. That's all we know."

Savich saw it, even though she was fast, a microexpression, then her face smoothed out in an instant. She'd been in the CIA for twenty-three years, she'd been in the field, taken courses in how to dissemble. But she'd slipped. Why was she trying to push his personal life on them?

Mr. Maitland said, "We tried to contact

Cummings's group chief, Alan Besserman, but we're unable to reach him. Is he here today?"

"I would assume he's at his desk."

Sherlock said, "Perhaps you can ask your Mr. Armstrong to check for us."

Farriger gave her a stony look, picked up her phone, punched a button, and gave instructions.

Mr. Maitland said, "I assume Mr. Besserman can tell us at least something about what Cummings was working on?"

She smiled, a sharp raptor's smile, showing lots of very nicely capped teeth. "As I said, you are not entitled to that information, Mr. Maitland. You doubtless admired the *Kryptos* sculpture—it's Greek, of course, for 'hidden.' It was chosen to remind us we collect secrets here. If we divulged what we do, what we learn, what we suspect, even to the FBI, without a truly pressing reason, it would compromise our mission, and national security with it. Now, I have a question for you. Why doesn't the FBI believe we are capable of investigating the disappearance of one of our own analysts?"

Mr. Maitland smiled. "We believe someone was out to kill him, or to take him. We believe he knows he's in danger and that's why he hasn't contacted anyone. Perhaps the people who were chasing after him found him and are holding him. Not for ransom, there isn't enough money in his family to tempt a kidnapper, so why else?

"We can't ignore he works for the CIA, gath-

ers information about Russia, their politics, their
intentions. Perhaps he found out something so
important he tried to capitalize on it. I suspect you
share that same concern, Ms. Farriger, whether
you're willing to discuss it with us or not. Someone
tried to take him in broad daylight, off the street.
Why not wait until night, when he was home and
in bed? It seems reckless, or desperate."

Farriger nodded. "Which supports my
point—this was not the work of professionals. And
a foreign agency taking a CIA employee on U.S.
soil? The blowback would be so severe, it's never
happened. As I said, I believe his disappearance is
more likely to be some kind of personal matter."

She gave him a hint of a tolerant smile. "Is
there anything else, gentlemen? Agent Sherlock?"

Farriger's phone buzzed. She picked it up,
listened a moment, said, "Thank you, Lance.

"Sorry, but Mr. Besserman isn't available for
you today."

"Does that mean he isn't here? Is he at home?"

Farriger only smiled at Maitland.

Sherlock gave Farriger her patented sunny smile
and yet again, Savich saw his Sherlock clear as day.
She said, "We have found the remains of Mr. Cummings's cell phone in Alexandria, Ms. Farriger."

Savich marveled at the fluency of that lie.

Farriger's reaction was immediate, her voice
sharp, too sharp. "It was obvious to us he'd
smashed his phone. How did you find it?"

Sherlock only smiled.

Farriger shrugged. "Can you do anything with it?"

Sherlock nodded. "I'm sure we can, our best people are working on it. We're hopeful we'll be able to get his cell history. We can help you find Mr. Cummings. We can resolve this situation together."

Farriger looked at the pale, pretty face of a woman she had to admit she admired. "I understand you have amnesia, Agent Sherlock. That must be very difficult for you. I realize you're surprised I know, but then, of course, it's my job to know—" She broke off, smiled again. "I realize you want to help, but you must understand I consider Justice Cummings my own responsibility. Naturally we're aware that as an analyst, his job is a sensitive one. With that in mind, we have to be concerned he might have been compromised." She looked at all three of them and walked around her desk, clearly dismissing them. "I will deal with it. If you can manage to access anything on his cell phone, call me. Thank you for coming. Agent Sherlock, I hope you regain your memory very soon. As I said, it—it must be difficult." She walked to the door and opened it, said nothing more.

Mr. Maitland slowly rose. "Ms. Farriger, there is one other thing, well, two other things, actually. The woman who struck Agent Sherlock's car works as a security engineer at the Bexholt Group. Strangely, the body of a murdered woman was discovered this morning. She is—was—also an employee of the Bexholt Group. You must find that odd, if not downright suspicious. Have you worked with Bexholt?"

Of course he knew they had. She said easily, "Certainly. They're a respected communications firm dealing mostly in the private sector, but there are occasional government contracts as well, including projects with the CIA. Why are you telling me this?"

Maitland shrugged. "Thought it might be of interest to you."

Farriger waited silently until they'd filed out of her office.

Lance came in to see her standing at her large window, staring out at the hills. "It rained very hard last night," she said, not turning.

"Yes, it did," Lance said. He knew this mood, she was thinking, barely aware he was even there, and that meant the problem with Justice Cummings had escalated.

He walked up behind her, laid his hand lightly on her arm. "Is there anything I can do?"

She did turn now. "You have already helped immeasurably, Lance." She nodded toward the door. "See that I'm not disturbed."

Once her office door was closed, she picked up her cell phone and punched speed dial.

"Athena?"

50

Rafer Bodine faced his mother across the dining room table, his roast beef sandwich between them. His wrist was in a cast, but it still hurt in spite of the three aspirin. The doctor had said he didn't need anything stronger, even for the headaches, the idiot.

Normally he loved the horseradish his mother smeared on the roast beef, but today he didn't notice. He was too scared and too angry at himself for being such a screwup. Without thought, he took another bite, chewed, wishing there were something he could do to stop the madness, to stop that FBI agent, Hammersmith, but he couldn't think of anything.

Cyndia said, "Rafer, tell me you believe me,

tell me you understand I had no choice but to hurt that FBI agent, to teach them all a lesson."

Rafer stared at his mother. She was concerned about what he thought, about anything? "Pa said you shouldn't have attacked her like that, with your gift. He said showing off your powers, and to the FBI, wasn't smart." He put down his sandwich, wondering if he'd said too much, looked at the cast on his wrist, winced.

Cyndia sighed, tapped her fingertips on the table. "I suppose your father is right. I should have showed some restraint. But, Rafer, they made me really mad, with all their poking and prodding, and their ridiculous arrogance—their disrespect." She shrugged, then added, her voice as indifferent as her shrug, "Well, no matter, it's over and done with."

He wished he could dismiss the things he'd done like she could. Over and done and forget it. It was only an afterthought. Instead, Rafer felt so guilty, he couldn't hold it in. "I'm sorry, Ma, look what I've brought down on you. But that journalist, she scared me so bad, I panicked."

Cyndia laid her hand lightly on Rafer's cast, pressed in just a bit until he winced. He didn't pull away, didn't say a word. He understood her need to correct him, and he accepted it. She said, her voice gentle and as cold as the mountains in winter, "I've told you and told you, never panic, Rafer. But you did, even though there was no reason to. You should have asked yourself what could DeSilva do?"

"She could have gone to see Uncle Booker."

She began tapping her fingers again and arched an eyebrow. "Yes. Now picture that. What would she tell him? That she dumpster-dived into your brain and heard you thinking about those girls? Rafer, can you imagine DeSilva claiming she heard your thoughts? Yes, I see you realize how ridiculous she'd sound. Now, Mr. Jobs assured your father and me there won't be any charges since there's no evidence. Your word against hers, that's it." She took his hand. "You know your uncle Booker called me right away and explained everything. We made certain to clear out all the evidence from your cottage that could possibly tie you to that woman. So everything is all right. The FBI forensic team didn't find a thing. I don't want you to worry about this—incident—anymore, Rafer. But you must learn to stay calm and think rationally before you act. Better yet, if something unexpected happens in the future, call me before you act."

Rafer looked down at his half-eaten sandwich, looked quickly away. No matter what she said, there was no getting around the fact he could have ruined things for them, put them all in danger. The worst was he'd upset his mother. Bad things happened when he upset his mother. His stomach cramped, viciously, then settled again. He looked back at her, wondered why she hadn't punished him. Because he'd been hurt? She was beautiful, his ma, but now she didn't look angry, she looked so disappointed, so sad. He knew he wasn't what she wanted, never had been. He wasn't much of anything. He tried to justify himself, but knew he sounded lame. "It would have been all right if not for Hammersmith showing up like that, out of the blue."

"Hammersmith. Yes, he's worrisome, isn't he?" Her voice was absent, as if she was focusing on something else entirely.

Rafer said nothing, nor did Cyndia expect him to. She sat back in her chair and studied her son. Rafer was handsome, the picture of her own father at his age. He looked like a man's man, like her own father had, but her father had been gifted and he'd passed his gift down to her. And she to her daughter, Camilla. She shook her head, to focus on the here and now. There was nothing she could do to change the past. But change the future, she was committed to that. And Rafer was vital. No matter what he was or wasn't, he was still her son, his father's son, and he was all they had.

He still looked scared and ashamed, like a little boy who'd peed his pants and had to own it. She lightly patted his arm, well above the cast. "Do you want to make this up to me, Rafer? And to your father?"

His eyes lit up, but even so, she still saw fear lurking. Of what she was going to ask of him? His mind had always been so clear to her, but now she couldn't be certain.

He said, "Yes, Ma, yes. Anything. I'll do anything for you. For Pa."

"You're a good boy, Rafer, and I love you. Now, there is something you can do for me, something you do very well. You're recovered enough to act for me, past time, really. In fact, it must be done today. It's important to me, Rafer, so you can't fail, you understand? You need to be strong, and brave. I'm going to tell you exactly what to do and you will do it."

He felt his insides turn to ice. He knew, oh yes, he knew what she was going to tell him to do. Even thinking about it made him sick to his stomach, but she was looking at him with such naked hope. And something more, something he'd felt from her forever, a sort of pressure bearing down on him, a feeling he couldn't escape, couldn't begin to fight. Even as his brain screamed at him, he slowly nodded, his eyes frozen on her face. She still looked at him with her own special kind of focus. He nodded again, licked his dry lips, whispered, "Yes, Ma, whatever you say. But what about this?" He waved his cast at her.

"I've taken the cast into account. It won't get in your way." She rose and he stood with her. She hugged him. "You're my good son, Rafer. Make me proud of you."

When Rafer left Eagle's Nest thirty minutes

later, he drove slowly down the narrow road with all its switchbacks. He thought about his life, the plans and dreams he'd had when he was a young man just graduated from high school, the future spread in front of him. Maybe he'd go to college.

Rafer laughed at himself.

None of it mattered now. This was what his mother wanted. He wouldn't screw up this time.

51

Savich slid his Darth Vader jump drive into MAX's USB port to load his access codes off the decryption program MAX had outsourced from Quint Bodine's encrypted files. With the program's massive processing speed, it was possible MAX could, if necessary, break the encryption by brute force. How long would it take? He didn't know. He watched the blur of scrolling figures, then satisfied, he rose. He looked out his office window at the agents in-house today, talking on their cell phones or typing on their computers, Ruth biting into a chocolate chip cookie from a batch Lucy had brought in. Since his door was open, he heard Ollie and Davis discussing a case they were working on. He saw Shirley, his invalu-

able secretary and organizational genius, sitting at
her large desk as usual, facing the wide windows
and glass door of the CAU unit. She fixed their
problems, made any arrangements they needed,
protected them like their mother confessor. He
saw her looking at Sherlock, a frown on her face.
Sherlock was staring fixedly at a tablet set up near
her laptop on her desk. What was she looking at?
In that moment, she looked up, saw him, and
started. Slowly, ever so slowly, she nodded to him,
not with a smile, but at least it was a sort of recognition. It was something.

He took a last look at the whirling letters
and numbers on MAX's screen, line after line of
code, then rose and walked out into the unit. He
spoke briefly to Shirley, checked up on the case
he heard Ollie and Davis discussing. He took his
time, no need to rush, until he reached Sherlock's
workstation. He looked down at her tablet and
saw a video of Sean and Marty shooting baskets
and making free throws, or trying, both children
attempting to copy Steph Curry's dribbling. They
were yelling at each other, laughing. Kid play.
Sherlock was staring fixedly at the screen. He saw a
tear slide down her cheek.

It nearly broke him. He pulled a Kleenex
out of the box on her desk and handed it to her.
She didn't make a sound, merely dabbed at her
eyes. She continued to sit quietly, not looking at
him, still staring at the softly playing video of two

happy children in a perfect childhood bubble, as they should be, enjoying themselves immensely. He saw Sean make a basket and hoot and holler, and Marty tell him anybody could make that shot, even Astro, and that set them off arguing again. He remembered that afternoon nearly two months before because he'd taken the video. When they'd hit the grass, wrestling, Astro had danced around them, leaped on them, barking his head off. Savich shooed Astro away and let the kids pummel him for a while. He remembered Marty's fingers touching his face, and her wet kiss, remembered Sean claiming Marty couldn't make a basket if her spelling grade depended on it, and Marty screeching they didn't even have spelling grades yet and he was lamer than her little brother, who couldn't even walk yet.

Savich didn't say anything, aware every agent was looking at them. They didn't know how to treat Sherlock, what to do for her. She had no clue who they were when she joined them, but she always tried very hard to put them at ease. It was difficult for the entire unit, but everyone was dealing, everyone was trying to act naturally—good luck with that.

The video stopped with his holding each kid under an arm, walking back toward the house, Sherlock's laughter behind him. She'd come out of the house, picked up the iPad, and taken over the recording.

Slowly, Sherlock closed the tablet. She looked up at him and tried to smile. "I know I should be writing up Jasmine Palumbo's interview, but I happened to be looking—" Her voice trailed off.

He lightly touched her shoulder, not quite a pat. "We shot that video this summer. I remember it was on a Sunday, early July. After the kids drank a quart of lemonade and stuffed down a dozen cookies, we took them to the Roosevelt Memorial. You showed them Roosevelt's sidekick, his dog Fala, and we walked along the Tidal Basin. There were lots of tourists, lots of kids. It was hot. We bought some peanuts. It was a great afternoon." He paused, waited, but she said nothing. He said deliberately, "After we dropped Marty off at her house and put Sean down for a nap, we made love and had our own nap. You made Sean hot dogs for dinner with mustard and sweet relish, his favorite. You made me the sweetest summer corn-on-the-cob and a three-bean salad."

She gulped. "It—it sounds wonderful."

"It was."

She raised her face to his. "I have this sudden craving for tacos."

He looked down at his Mickey Mouse watch. "Would you look at the time. Let's go upstairs and get you a taco and me a veggie burrito." Shirley gave them both a big smile as he escorted Sherlock out of the unit. When they were gone, Ollie Hamish, Savich's second-in-command, turned to everyone. "She remembers Mexican food is her favorite, at least taco craving is a good start. She's going to make it back."

Lucy eyed the three remaining chocolate chip cookies, felt how tight her pants were, and moved the paper plate away. She said, "She asked me how I was feeling several times. She's trying very hard."

Ruth Noble said, "I wish I knew what to say to her. I babble about Dix and the boys and this and that case, and she tries to look involved, but I know she has no clue who or what I'm talking about."

Her cell buzzed. "Agent Noble. Who? Dougie? What's going on?" A moment, then, "I'll be right there."

She stood, looked at her watch. "I hate to interrupt them, but this is about Sherlock's accident and the missing analyst. I need them now."

52

ALEXANDRIA, VIRGINIA
WAREHOUSE DISTRICT
FRIDAY, EARLY AFTERNOON

Savich, Sherlock, and Ruth stood over a sleeping Justice Cummings. Dougie sat cross-legged beside him. Sally was leaning against a rotted wall nearby, rubbing dirt off her elbow, her long flowered skirt covering her legs, and Major Hummer was behind them.

Dougie looked up and gave Ruth a sweet smile, fitted his towel closer around his head. "Ruth, I'm real glad you came so fast. I didn't force Justice to see you, I swear. He said you could come. But I don't know about these two. Who are they? Do you know them?"

Ruth came down on her haunches beside him. "I trust them completely, Dougie. This is my boss, Agent Savich, and Agent Sherlock. They're both very smart and very kind and they want to help. Agent Savich, Agent Sherlock, these are Dougie, Sally, and Major Hummer, friends of mine."

Dougie gave Savich and Sherlock a suspicious look, then looked toward Hummer, who slowly nodded. Then Dougie stared up at Sherlock. "Pretty hair," he said. "Not really red as fire, but a different sort of red. I think my daughter had red hair like yours, but I'm not sure anymore, it was a long time ago, you know?"

"Yes, I know." Sherlock went down on her knees next to Dougie, handed him her creds, watched him look at them a moment. Did he see well enough to read? Then he took Savich's creds, gave them a longer, harder look. "Looks real official, both of 'em, but it's what Ruth thinks that matters and Ruth says you're okay." He handed back their creds. "Like I told you, I wouldn't ever have called Ruth unless Justice said I could. That wouldn't be right. He's a good kid, Justice is, but he's a mess, doesn't know what's going on. He's hurt, and he's scared spitless. I told him he could trust you, Ruth, everybody here knows you're straight, even that day the FBI ran all around our neighborhood to find Manta Ray, carrying guns and wearing those Kevlar things. You made sure none of us got hurt." He frowned. "Ruth, that wasn't that long a time ago, was it?"

"Not long ago. You remember it just right." She patted his arm.

Savich went down on his haunches beside Justice Cummings, pressed his fingers to his wrist, took his pulse. He laid his palm on his forehead. No fever. But he looked a mess, his nose obviously broken, stuffed with Kleenex. His shirt was torn and bloody. A surprisingly clean blanket was pulled up to his waist. Savich lifted the blanket and looked at the paper towels wrapped around a wound on his leg, hoped there was sterile gauze under them. He looked up at Major Hummer in his army fatigues and black boots up to his calves. "What can you report, Major? How bad is it?"

Hummer came smartly to attention, cleared his throat. "The boy made it here, I don't know how, showed lots of grit. He deserves one of my Purple Hearts." He paused briefly, a sort of mental reboot, Savich thought. "It was Tuesday afternoon, around six o'clock, I believe. I remember I was hungry. I found him huddled in on himself, pressed against that far wall, just inside the door, near to where Sally's sitting. He was in a lot of pain. I called Dougie and we peeled off his pants. I saw the cut wasn't too bad, could do without stitches, but I was worried about infection. I bought some butterfly strips and bandages from Elmwood Pharmacy over on Gleason Street and some antibacterial cream, the kind you get over the counter. Fixed him up. He'd be awake now, but Dougie encouraged him to drink some of his Wild Turkey because the aspirin wasn't doing the job. The Wild Turkey sure did the job, knocked him right out."

Dougie said, "Ruth, I told Justice the broken nose would look good on him, make him look a bit tougher. He liked that. He said someone is after him. He's scared, did I tell you that? You'll take care of him?"

"Yes, we will. Thank you for calling me, Dougie."

Dougie reached out, touched her arm. "Really, Ruth, he's scared, more scared than I was when the FBI came hunting for Manta Ray, even though I gotta say they didn't roust any of us."

Justice Cummings opened his eyes, saw three strangers staring at him. His heart stuttered. They'd found him.

Dougie leaned over him. "It's all right, boy, you don't want to try to run, you don't have any pants on. And your boxers have blood on them from your leg. These three folks are FBI agents. That's Ruth, I told you about her. She's my friend and I'm her snitch. Remember, I asked you if I could call her? Did I tell you that? Anyways, she brought them with her, swears they're gonna help you. This here's Ruth."

Justice looked up into Dougie's dirty face, at the Marriott towel on his head, at his vague, kind eyes. He felt a spurt of hope, swallowed. His voice sounded scratchy. "You're really an FBI agent, Ruth?"

"Yes, I am. Agent Ruth Noble. And you're Justice Cummings. It's a pleasure to meet a friend of Dougie's." And she shook his hand, like everything was normal, like he wasn't lying in a derelict warehouse wearing bloody boxers. "Dougie and I go way back to my days in Metro." She introduced Savich and Sherlock. They all pulled out their creds and held them close so Justice Cummings could read them. He slowly nodded. "You're not CIA, and that's a relief. That might sound crazy, but somebody set me up, they knew where I'd be. I don't know who, and that's the problem. I don't know anything."

Savich said in an easy voice, "Do you remember running into the street? You hit a spinning car, flew over the hood?"

"I see it over and over. I was running, and looked back to see how close they were, and wham. I thought I was going to die."

Sherlock took his hand. "I was driving the car, Mr. Cummings. I know, that's quite a coincidence. I'm very pleased we're both going to be all right. Dougie and Major Hummer have taken very good care of you. We know you took an Uber here to Alexandria, and you were dropped off not far from here, and you smashed your phone, right?" At his nod, she said, "That was well done. Why did you come here to the warehouse district?"

"I remembered passing by this area several years ago. I knew nobody would come here to look for me. I didn't know what else to do, who I could trust, so like you said, I had an Uber drop me off three blocks over and walked here. I managed to get inside this building and knew I couldn't go any farther. Major Hummer found me. He and Dougie have taken care of me. And Miss Sally sings show tunes to me. Major Hummer says the wound on my leg doesn't look infected what with all the antibacterial cream he's smeared on me. It looks like I'm going to live."

Savich said, "Yes, you are. You'll be fine in a couple of days. You'll need to get your nose looked after, and your leg checked out. We will help you with that. We have a lot to discuss, Mr. Cummings. You up for it?"

Justice grabbed Sherlock's hand, held on for dear life. "You won't tell anyone, will you? You'll keep them away from me?"

"Don't worry. We won't let anyone hurt you."

"You found my cell phone? How did you know it was mine? I really smashed it but good."

"No, we didn't find it, it went offline so we figured you'd destroyed it. Justice, we haven't located your wife and kids, either. Where are they?"

"My—oh, Melissa—Mellie—she and the kids are in the Poconos, at her aunt's cabin. There's no cell service, so you have to know to call Aunt Josie's landline to reach them. I was supposed to be with them, but then she got really pissed at me. She wants me to quit the CIA and get a real job. And that's the problem. I really like being an analyst. I think I've helped our country. She called this a time-out—sounds stupid, it's what she says to the kids. She got pregnant my senior year at MIT, her senior year at Boston College, and we eloped. We had another kid two years ago—Nate's his name, his older sister is Annie, and I'm sorry, you don't care about that."

Ruth said, "Trust me, Mr. Cummings, we care about everything you care about. Go on."

"Please, call me Justice."

"He needs some hy-dration, Ruth. Major Hummer said when you're sick you gotta keep hy-drated." Dougie put the bottled water to Justice's mouth. Justice guzzled down nearly half the bottle. He was breathing hard when Dougie pulled it away.

"Thank you, Dougie."

"I remember my wife wanting me to change jobs," Dougie said, shaking his head, making the towel list to the left. He straightened it. "I don't remember what I was doing that upset her or what she wanted me to do. It was a long time ago, ten years, twenty? I don't know. Do you remember, Hummer?" Dougie craned his head around to look at him. Major Hummer shook his head, said, "Don't worry about it, Dougie. Time doesn't mean much. All that's important is what's here and what's now, and who cares in the end? There's always an end, isn't there?"

Ruth said, smiling at Hummer, "Yes, but the end isn't now, not for Justice. How do you feel now?"

"Agent Ruth, ma'am, I'm okay. My nose throbs, you know, and my leg sort of aches, but it isn't bad. Can you find out who's after me?"

Savich said, "We can and we will, but first, Justice, you'll need to help us. Who were you meeting at the Blaze Café Tuesday afternoon?"

Justice didn't meet his eyes, but he slowly nodded. "I really don't have a choice, do I? All right, I'll tell you the truth. I was really pissed at my wife for giving me that ridiculous 'time-out,' for acting like my job isn't important enough. It really is, I mean, it's about keeping us all safe. So when this pretty woman asked me if I'd like to have coffee with her after work on Tuesday, I said yes. I didn't plan to sleep with her, believe me, but I was pissed. I wanted to spend some time with someone who appreciated who I am and what I do. So we made a date to meet at the Blaze Café, but she didn't show. I waited, then walked outside, looking for her, and that's when I spotted them—a man and a woman, looking at me, but trying to be cool about it. But I'm a CIA analyst, I know all about surveillance and how it should be done, and they'd screwed up. So I ran. Took them off guard, but they ran after me. When I came out of that alley I looked back and saw them. I ran into the street and hit a car, your car, you said, Agent Sherlock, and I flew off the other side of the hood. My leg was hurt, my nose was bleeding something fierce, but there were so many people running this way and that, talking on their cells, shooting videos, total chaos, so I managed to get away. I ended up here, and Major Hummer and Dougie took care of me."

Savich said, "A man and a woman? Strangers to you?"

He flushed, nodded. "At first I thought maybe they were there because of the woman I was supposed to meet, maybe she was married and they were private investigators and that's why she didn't show up. But only for an instant. Even though they were wearing sunglasses I could tell their faces had that fixed look I've seen on faces before, giving nothing away, except they were there to take me, or worse."

Savich said, "Can you describe them to us, Justice?"

"He was wearing a ball cap. I remember thinking he was bald because all I saw was scalp around the cap—not naturally bald, I remember thinking, more like he shaved his head, but I could be dead wrong. And he had a big mustache. The woman had on a beret thing so I couldn't see her hair, it was all tucked under the beret. They were average size, I guess, and both of them were wearing dark sunglasses. The woman was smaller than he was."

Sherlock said, "Excellent, Justice. Tell us the

woman's name—the one you were supposed to meet?"

"Christy, her name was Christy Blake."

Savich pulled out his cell and scrolled to a photo, showed it to Justice. "Is this Christy Blake?"

53

Justice stared, swallowed, looked like he'd be sick, then pulled himself together. He slowly nodded. "Yes, that's Christy. She—she looks dead. Is she dead?"

"Yes," Savich said. "Her name is—was—Eleanor Christine Corbitt. She was murdered in the middle of last night."

Justice gaped at Savich, bewildered, confused. "She was—murdered? But why? What is happening here?"

Savich was aware Ruth and Sherlock were staring from him to the photo of Eleanor Corbitt on his cell, waiting for him to answer. He said, "It's likely it all ties in to you, Justice. And what happened on Tuesday. Tell us what she said to you."

"Christy said she worked at Langley, in personnel resources. She said she'd seen me off and on and thought I was cute and she always liked talking to analysts because we were all so smart and she'd heard I had a great sense of humor." He swallowed. "But—I don't understand. Why would she target me? I mean, it's not like I'm the captain of the CIA ship, I'm only an analyst. And why would anyone kill her?" His eyes grew stark. "Someone killed her because of me? Last night? She's dead because of me?"

Sherlock said, "Did you meet Eleanor Corbitt at Langley?"

"Sure. Wait, the first time I met her was in the parking lot at Langley, after work. She'd dumped her bag on the ground and I helped her clean it up. The second time we met, it was in the cafeteria."

Savich said, "She didn't work at Langley, Justice. She was an accountant at the Bexholt Group, in Coverton, Maryland."

Justice was shaking his head. "But then how did she get in the cafeteria?"

Savich said slowly, "Only employees can eat there? No visitors?"

"Not as far as I know, only those of us who actually work there. I guess a bigwig could bring a guest, but why? I mean, it's not exactly Chez Langley."

Savich said, "It looks like Eleanor Corbitt targeted you specifically, Justice, set you up to be taken when you left the Blaze Café. Can you think of any reason why an accountant at Bexholt would do this? Why she would pretend she worked at Langley?"

Justice thought back. Christy—Eleanor— was dead. She'd seemed so interested in him, genuinely interested. She'd laughed at his humor, she'd touched his arm with her fingers, leaned in close. All of it had been an act. Her real name was Eleanor Christine Corbitt, and whoever was after him, they'd killed her. He felt numb, then angry. "It doesn't make any sense. Like I told you, I'm an analyst, not one of those guts-for-glory operatives. I don't know any secrets. What do they want with me?"

Sherlock asked him, "What do you do exactly, Justice? That is, what are you working on right now?"

"I—why? Oh, I see." They could practically see his brain working through what he was allowed to say. Finally, "Look, I'm breaking some rules here, but there is something I've been occupied with that's been frustrating me. I was making my usual rounds on the Russian dark web, sites I can't really talk about. I picked up an exchange about some kind of breakthrough in surveillance technology, something that can't be detected with current sweep technology. There was talk of a sale or an auction very soon, something about a demonstration.

"I was worried enough to show the chatter to my group chief, Mr. Besserman. I believe he was concerned enough to take it to his boss, Assistant Director Claire Farriger, but he didn't actually tell me he had, so I'm not sure.

"Monday before last, Mr. Besserman came back to me, wanted to know if I'd heard anything more, but I hadn't. I remember he shrugged, said it was a ninety-nine percent chance it was nothing, only some bozo mouthing off, and we saw this sort of thing all the time on the dark web. Of course we do. It happens, not at all unusual, but I didn't forget about it. There was something about it that made me think I'd chanced to hit on something big. Then I saw something more, same source, and there was talk about 'smart walls,' which I didn't understand. What about smart walls? And I told Mr. Besserman and he told me to let it go and put me on something else. But I decided I'd pursue it on my own time. It was after that I met Christy— Eleanor Corbitt—and you know the rest."

No, Savich thought, they didn't know the rest. Not yet.

His cell rang. It was Griffin. "What's up?"

Griffin said, "We have another missing teen-ager, this one from Whytheville, not all that far away from Gaffer's Ridge. Her father said she was supposed to be with friends at a movie, but she didn't come home when she was expected. They rang her cell, but there was no answer. Her father said she and that phone were inseparable, like all teenagers today. That's when they suspected something was wrong.

"Savich, she celebrated her sixteenth birthday last Friday, makes her the same age as the other three missing girls."

"Where's Rafer Bodine?"

"That's the thing, Savich. We could have held Rafer until there was a court order, but I didn't see the point. Rafer left the hospital this morning. If he's involved in this, it's my fault."

"You couldn't have known, Griffin. Taking another girl now, with the FBI in Gaffer's Ridge, already asking questions, it's more than reckless, it's insanity. You know what to do, Griffin. We're up to our necks in alligators here. If you need outside assistance, give Bettina a call and she'll send DeAndre and Slick back. Keep me informed."

Savich punched off, said to Sherlock, "Another missing teenager near Gaffer's Ridge. Sixteen years old, like the other three."

Sherlock stilled. "Is it always like this? One horrible thing after another? All on top of each other? And we're supposed to fix everything?"

Ruth patted her shoulder. "That's pretty much our job description. Now, Justice, let's talk more about the man and woman you saw outside the Blaze Café. Close your eyes and picture them. Think back. Did they look at all familiar to you?"

54

WHYTHEVILLE, VIRGINIA
FRIDAY AFTERNOON

Griffin studied Linzie Drumm's distraught parents. Mrs. Drumm was bowed in on herself, rocking back and forth in the visitor's chair in Sheriff Cruisie's office. Mr. Drumm was pacing, trying to keep calm, but he was so angry and frightened, he couldn't hold it in any longer. He whirled to face the sheriff and yelled, "What are you going to do now? Three girls already missing—and now our daughter. Yes, she and two friends went to see a movie. Then Linzie told them she had time to do some shopping and they split up. She's not at home. Her friends don't know where she is. And all you want is to sit here talking to us?"

Sheriff Bale Cruisie listened to Donny Ray Drumm's rants. It was his job as sheriff, just as

Donny Ray fixed his Ford F-150 and did it well. His patience, however, was nearly at an end. He sat forward. "Listen to me, Donny Ray, I know Linzie. She's a cute girl, just turned sixteen, and from what I hear, she and her friends are stretching their wings. I know she likes to sneak out and see her girlfriends and go to Buffett's for hamburgers and to hang out with boys. Why should I believe it was anything more than she left her friends to go look for a good time?"

Wrong thing to say, but before Griffin could defuse the situation, Donny Ray yelled, "You idiot! You make it sound like it's our little girl's fault, like she's loose!"

It looked to Griffin like Mr. Drumm was ready to attack Sheriff Cruisie, and Griffin managed to catch his arm before he smashed his fist into the sheriff's face. He said in his calm, deep FBI voice, "Mr. Drumm, that's quite enough. Sit down. Let's all calm down."

Maybe it was Griffin's tone, but Drumm shook himself, seemed to deflate, and sank into the other visitor's chair. "Sorry, Bale, she's my little girl. She's missing, like the other three girls. Three months and no word about any of them." He looked up at Griffin. "Agent Hammersmith, does the FBI know anything yet? Do you have any kind of plan?"

"Yes, I do," Griffin said. "Now, Mr. and Mrs. Drumm, I want to show you some photos. Tell me if you recognize any of these men."

Griffin scrolled up a photo of Agent Ollie

Hamish, one of Agent Davis Sullivan, and finally, one of Rafer Bodine.

The parents studied each of the photos, shook their heads.

Griffin said, "I'd like to speak to your daughter's friends, get the exact time they last saw Linzie, and if they recognize any of these men. The quickest way is for you, Mrs. Drumm, to call her friends and their parents over to your house right away. Can you do that?"

When the Drumms left with something useful to do, Sheriff Cruisie said, "It's a start. Two of the photos look like FBI agents, right?"

Griffin smiled. "That's right. We use photos of male and female agents in circumstances like this one, sort of a lineup."

"Who's the third?"

Griffin said, "His name is Rafer Bodine, from Gaffer's Ridge."

Sheriff Cruisie cursed. "Now, that's a big surprise. I've known Sheriff Bodine and his brother, Quint Bodine, forever. Rafer is Quint's son, but of course you already know that. You sure about this? I've never heard anything hinky about Rafer."

Griffin said, "Let's say he's our primary person of interest for now."

Sheriff Cruisie turned to the gorgeous young woman who'd said not a single word since they'd briefly met. He'd have pegged her as a model, and here she was with a PhD. She was standing in front of his ancient file cabinets. "What do you have to do with this, Dr. DeSilva?"

Carson smiled at him. "I guess you could say I'm an FBI agent in training, Sheriff Cruisie. More an interested party, really."

He nodded. "Now, if you don't mind, I need to accompany you folks to the Drumms' house. I can help you with those teenage girls. I know them and their families. I can help keep all the parents calm, too."

Carson said, "I think we should get the boys in their group there, too. Could you call Mrs. Drumm, make that happen, Sheriff?"

"Will do. Also, let me print up the three photos, easier to show them around town, see if anyone's seen Rafer Bodine today." He rose, rubbed his hands together. "Can't say I'm not glad you're here, Agent Hammersmith. Everyone in towns around here has been dead worried, me among them, and to be honest, it's hard to know how to proceed. Then I got a call from Bud Bailey over in Marion and he said the FBI was now in charge. I was about to call you when you walked in. I'm glad you're here." He shook his head. "None of us have ever seen anything like this before."

The Drumms lived in a pretty yellow single-story house with a big front yard and an inner tube hanging by a stout rope from an oak branch. The property looked homey and settled, like the surrounding houses in this solid middle-class neighborhood. It looked safe. Yet a girl who lived in this lovely house had been taken. Cars with Linzie's friends and their parents were already arriving, filling the driveway and lining the sidewalks.

Griffin and Carson walked into a comfortable, old-fashioned living room, filled to brimming with parents and teens, both boys and girls. The parents were subdued, most looked scared. The teenagers, particularly the boys, looked excited. The immortality of youth, Griffin thought, and wondered when it would hit the kids that Linzie Drumm could be dead.

It took time and patience since the parents all wanted to interrupt, question their children themselves. It was interesting how the boys acted as opposed to the girls. When the questions started, they turned nervous and scared, but they tried not to show it. The girls, for the most part, were openly shocked and afraid, and huddled into one another. None of the girls or boys had seen Linzie Drumm after midday, and those who'd seen her before then had been at the movies. Some believed she'd gone home, but no one knew for sure, and her two friends said she'd gone shopping.

Griffin pulled out the three photos and the teenagers gathered around, studying the pictures, looking at one another. Two of the boys shrugged, said they might have seen Agent Ollie Hamish pumping gas at the Exxon station and coming out of Clemson's Pharmacy. The girls were excited at first, but tears hovered when they didn't recognize any of the men. It was one little girl, short and plump, with beautiful green eyes and wispy blond hair, who whispered, "I saw him."

She pointed to Rafer's photo.

Her name was Melanie Sparks. She was nine years old, there because her sister, Nina, was Linzie's best friend and one of the girls who'd been at the movies with her. Her sister told her to stop making things up and her parents joined in the chorus, and the little girl slinked back behind her mother.

Griffin waited until everyone had calmed down again, then thanked parents and kids and sent them on their way. He asked the Sparkses to stay.

"She makes things up," said Mrs. Sparks, a stout woman with her daughter's green eyes. "I'm sorry she's wasting your time, Agent Hammersmith. I'm always telling her to stop spinning tales, but she says she's going to be an actress when she grows up and she wants to practice."

Nina looked closely at her little sister. "Mel, you know this is really important, don't you? We have to help find Linzie. Tell the truth, did you really see this man?"

Melanie whispered, "Yes, I swear I did, I promise," and crossed her heart.

Griffin came down on his haunches in front of the little girl. "Tell me where you saw him, Melanie. And when."

The little girl sent an agonized look at her mother, who looked ready to blast her. Then Mrs. Sparks drew in her breath and said, "Tell Agent Hammersmith what you saw, Melanie."

Melanie looked down at her worn blue sneakers, the laces coming loose on her left foot. "I saw him at Buffett's Hamburgers a week and a half ago, maybe it was last Tuesday. Nina and her friends let me go with them after my summer camp was over for the day."

Griffin said to Nina, "Was it a Tuesday? A week and a half ago? Was Linzie with you?"

Nina had to think a minute, then said, "Yes, I remember. There were six of us."

"Go ahead, Melanie."

"He had on this cap, a baseball cap, it had a big *Y* on it, and a jacket and I thought that was weird, it was really warm, you know? He was standing next to a black truck, eating a hamburger, not sitting at one of the outside tables. Mrs. Buffett has them all under the shade trees."

"What else did he do?"

"He ate the hamburger, really fast, and you know what? He didn't toss his trash in the waste can. He dropped it on the ground. I remember thinking Mama would tell him not to be a yahoo, like she does us. He wiped his hands on his jeans, got in his truck, and drove away. That's the only time I saw him."

"Did he talk to any of the girls? To Linzie?"

"No."

"I want you to close your eyes, Melanie, picture him standing there by his truck, all right? Good. Now, did he look at the girls? At Linzie?"

Melanie looked like she wanted to cry. "I don't know, Agent, sir."

"That's okay. You did great." Griffin shook the little girl's hand. "Sheriff, we need to go speak to Mrs. Buffett."

Sheriff Cruisie said, "Good idea, someone had to take his order for the hamburger."

It was Mrs. Buffett herself, a woman of nearly eighty, wiry gray hair scraped back in a skinny bun, who'd served him. "Yep, a handsome young man, nice and polite, but he mumbled. I couldn't believe it when he tossed his wrapper on the ground, left it for us to clean up. So it turns out he was still a dirty little kid, didn't learn manners from his mama." She shook her head.

"Did you notice if he looked at the teenage girls? Did he talk to them?"

"Nope, not that I saw. He didn't make a big deal out of it since he wasn't a teenage boy, he looked them over, sort of nodded, and went over to his truck. I don't think any of the kids noticed him, too busy flirting. I'll say this for him, he kept his truck mighty clean. So why'd he throw his wrapper on the ground?"

Carson said, "Like you said, his mama didn't teach him manners."

"Ain't that the truth. You want one of my hamburgers?"

Carson turned down the hamburger, but she did buy a cup of french fries for the road, lots of salt, and walked beside a whistling Griffin to his car, Sheriff Cruisie nearly bouncing beside them.

Griffin said to the sheriff, "I'm going to take another trip to the Bodines' house, have a nice long talk with Rafer. I think they might even be expecting me."

"There's no direct evidence, though," Cruisie said, and shrugged. "I mean, who's going to convict him because he happened to be here a week ago Tuesday eating a hamburger?"

Griffin said, "It's another nail in his coffin at trial, as my former SAC in San Francisco would say. I think we'll get him, Sheriff."

Cruisie shook his head. "I don't understand why Rafer Bodine would go around kidnapping teenage girls. Like he's suddenly become a serial kidnapper? It doesn't make sense to me. I've never heard anything bad about Rafer. You must already know his family's a power in Gaffer's Ridge, but Rafer? He's always seemed to me to go with the flow, as the teenagers say. I pray to heaven he hasn't killed them. No one could stand that, no one.

"To think he's Sheriff Bodine's nephew. It would be a huge blow. Would you like me with you to talk to Rafer Bodine?"

Griffin thought about it. He wanted Carson with him, and the sheriff was more useful to him here in Whytheville. "Sheriff, let me handle this first interview. I'll keep you posted. I need you to show those photos around town, talk to neighbors and the businesses around the parking lot at Buffett's. Spread your deputies in a wider circle."

Sheriff Cruisie's shoulders squared. Like the Drumms, he now had some work to do that could mean something. He shook Griffin's hand, nodded to the gorgeous woman with him.

55

MORGANTOWN, VIRGINIA
REDEMPTION HOUSE
FRIDAY, LATE AFTERNOON

Athena looked out the window to see Jasmine leap from her car and race to the house. She burst through the front door, breathing so hard she was panting. "Athena, did you tell them Ellie's dead? Tell them she was murdered? Did you find out any more? Do the police know who killed her?"

Athena fanned her hands. "You know the most of any of us, Jasmine, since you were interviewed by the FBI. We're all as shocked and horrified as you are."

Jasmine heard Cricket sob, saw her black mascara was smeared by her tears. She looked folded in on herself. As for Craig, his eyes were red, too, from crying. Jasmine shouted, "For heaven's sake,

Athena, Ellie didn't just die, someone killed her. A robbery? Do you believe that?"

"None of us know what to believe. I do know everyone in the accounting department was interviewed. You told me two FBI agents met with you, Jasmine, asked you about the accident and about Ellie. Did they give you any idea of the direction they're taking?"

Jasmine nodded. "Yes, they wanted to know not only about the accident but also about Justice Cummings. They don't believe Ellie's murder was a robbery, they believe Cummings and Ellie are somehow connected and that's why the FBI is involved. They said they identified Ellie on video across the street from the accident. Athena, none of this makes any sense. Who would kill Ellie? Why?" She banged her fist against her palm.

"Listen, all of you. I can't tell you who killed her, or why. It's possible it was a break-in, as the news stories said. Or maybe her miserable ex-husband had her killed. You all know there was violence in their marriage and that's why she divorced him. We certainly had nothing to do with it."

Craig raised angry eyes to her face. "Fine, we know none of us had anything to do with Ellie's"—he stumbled, sucked in a breath—"murder. Obviously Cummings didn't have anything to do with it, he's got to be injured, maybe dead. What about Artemis? And for once, let's call her by her name—Claire Farriger. Her contacts may be important and far-reaching, but we hardly know her at all. She'd be capable of this, wouldn't she? I mean, you told us she was once a CIA operative, a spy. She knows violence."

"No, impossible," Athena said, but she felt the spit dry in her mouth.

Jasmine said, "Athena, I called you last night, told you Ellie was frightened she'd been seen at Cummings's house, that she could be identified. Did you tell Artemis? Craig's right, let's call her by her name—Farriger. Did you tell her?"

Athena had known Jasmine's question was coming. She wasn't about to tell them she also suspected Farriger. She had a feeling Claire would be capable of having her own mother killed if she was afraid her mother would give something important to her away. It made Athena sick to her stomach to think about it—Ellie sleeping, shot in the head. She'd always hated violence, wanted no part of it. But Ellie was gone, and she wouldn't let her death blow them apart, they were too close to success. She said, "Listen to me, all of you. I said no, it was impossible. Well, I spoke to Artemis earlier. She was as shocked as the rest of us. And no, I didn't call her last night, so she had no way of knowing Ellie was worried she'd been seen in Cummings's neighborhood.

"This is a terrible blow, but we have to continue. We're so close. We have to be ready by Monday."

Craig said, "She could have found out herself. Listen, Ellie and the rest of us agreed we were willing to break the law to make our fortunes. The device is my own invention, after all. But none of us wanted any violence. We're not killers. You've got to see this is getting completely away from us. First you talked us into kidnapping Cummings, and now Ellie is dead? My dear, sweet Ellie is dead?"

Had Craig and Ellie been lovers? Athena didn't know. But she wasn't about to let Craig, or Artemis, or anyone, blow up her plans. "Ellie was one of my dearest friends, Craig. We'll all miss her terribly. But she wouldn't have wanted us— wanted you—to quit now. She knew you were a genius, you deserved your chance. We're so close to becoming rich beyond your comprehension. Ellie wanted that, too, for herself and for us. Craig, will you be ready to go live on Monday?"

His eyes went back to his monitor, as she'd hoped. "I've already tested, Athena. The signal is still too weak. I told you we need more panels installed."

"That's already in progress, Craig. They'll finish installing them by the end of the day Saturday. When they're done, we'll be able to hear a whisper."

56

Athena walked down the short corridor, through the kitchen, and out the back door of Redemption House, the lovely colonial she'd bought several years ago for a country getaway, now their headquarters. It was set back a half mile from a little-used country road, a perfect spot, isolated enough for safety, but close enough to Bexholt to reach in under an hour.

She tossed her car keys in the air, caught them handily, and unlocked her silver Audi. She would get to Coverton and Bexholt with enough time to speak to her brother and dear daddy. She laughed. Daddy, in particular, would have a stroke if he knew what was going to happen, what she, his daughter—a mere woman—was making happen.

She turned off the AC, opened the convertible top, and sang Katy Perry's "Roar" at the top of her lungs.

Fifty-two minutes later, she parked in her personal space next to her brother's at Bexholt. Her father's space was on the other side of her brother's, his gleaming black Bentley directly in front of the main entrance to Bexholt, of course.

She walked around to the passenger side of her Audi, opened the door, and shoved it against her brother's driver's side panel. A pity about another lovely gouge in his white Mercedes.

She strode through the main entrance into the huge gold marble-floored lobby with seasonal photos of Maryland on its white walls and smoothly morphed into her alter ego, Nikki Bexholt.

Nathan Bexholt, COO and heir apparent to his powerful father, Garrick Xavier Bexholt, turned from the large window overlooking the lovely three-acre park twelve floors below. His own office had the same awesome view of the small decorative lake. His sister Nikki's office overlooked the Bexholt campus, their R&D buildings and the warehouse complex with its lines of shipping trucks, white with bright blue lightning bolts on their sides. He rubbed his neck, wished there was someone to massage the knots out, but that would have to wait. Crissy, his wife of fourteen years, was in Paris, probably on the lookout for an artist/lover with oily black hair and a concave chest who splashed red and black blobs on a white canvas. Who cared? They each had their own lives. Their two boys were at Andover, and thank heaven, in good standing. He turned to face his father, who wasn't wearing his usual *go team* expression. He looked tired, pensive.

Nathan said, "What a day. I still can't believe it—Eleanor Corbitt, dead, murdered. I sent everyone in accounting home after a Detective Raven of Metro finished interviewing, even hauled two employees out of the bathroom to speak to them. Apparently there were some FBI agents here as well." He shrugged. "Of course, no one seemed to know anything helpful. It's a pity she didn't have any close friends here at work." He rubbed his neck again. "I knew her, Dad, I knew Eleanor. She was nice, competent, always on point, on the quiet side, but really sort of intense—" Nathan paused, saw his father raise a salt-and-pepper brow, and added, "She kept her private life very private. I never heard any gossip about her after she divorced her husband, a gold-plated jerk, I heard." Nathan turned away to look out at the park. "I have no clue what she did when she left work every day. I hope whatever it was didn't lead to this."

Garrick Bexholt joined his son at the window.

"Your mother told me she saw Eleanor once in one of those women's centers she likes to support." He shrugged, added with a dash of contempt, "You know several of the women's shelters are on her endless string of charities."

Nathan frowned. "Maybe one of the husbands didn't like what Eleanor was doing, so killed her."

"Who knows?" Garrick asked without much interest. "Maybe you should pass that along to the Metro cops. Or the FBI, or whoever. Ah, here's your sister." He looked down at his Piaget watch, shook his head. "Late," he said to Nathan. "But what can you expect from a woman?"

Garrick Bexholt watched his strong-willed, outspoken daughter stride through the door, his secretary, Margo, standing behind her looking helpless. Bexholt merely shook his head, mouthed, *Go home*. Margo, no expression on her face, nodded and turned away.

Garrick kept a smile firmly in place as Nikki walked up to him, gave him a light kiss on his cheek.

"Well, where have you been? The FBI are at your office, been there at least five minutes now, waiting for you."

"Did you and Nathan speak to them?"

Garrick said, "Of course not. Why would I?"

Nathan said, "I really wasn't available when they were here. Dad's right. Why would they want to talk to us? To me? What could I possibly know? Ah, but they want to speak to you."

"Well, that makes sense. After all, I supervise the accounting department. It's a pity, but I really don't have anything useful to tell them. They can wait a bit longer."

Nathan said, "FYI. Since you were supposedly in Washington all day, I went ahead and sent everyone in accounting home. They were all either crying or sitting there doing nothing anyway. So why not dismiss them? It makes for good employee relations. I'm sure you would have done the same thing, wouldn't you?" He saw she wanted to blast him, reveled in it a moment, but instead she said, "Why did you say 'supposedly'? Of course I was in Washington all day."

Nathan shrugged. "My assistant tried to call you, but got booted to voice mail. Then she called one of the staff and was told you'd left. I asked Dad, but he didn't know where you were, either."

Garrick said, "Where did you go, Nikki? Overseeing the Federal Reserve conference is top priority, you know that."

Nikki gave a shrug to mimic her brother's. "I had some personal business to take care of, didn't take long at all. I saw you messaged, Nathan. I ignored it." She harked back to what he'd done, still pissed. He was like their father, always sticking his nose in her business. The accounting department was her business, not his, not their father's—well, it was their father's, but maybe not for all that long.

Nathan watched her chin go up, watched her eyes flash from calm to fire, and got ready for the show. She was so predictable, the little bitch. "You should have called me, asked me."

He gave her a smarmy smile he knew she hated. "As I said, no one was getting any work done. As I also said, I couldn't reach you, and it was good for employee morale." Nathan studied his younger sister's face, not much expression now, but her eyes told everything if you knew how to read them. Even when she was a little girl, he knew when she was lying to him, knew when she was trying to stab him in the back. It was a good bet, given her mood, she'd put another dent in his car door. Well, that was why he had two assistants, one of whom would get the car fixed without any bother to him. Let her pull her passive-aggressive crap, it didn't matter. Nathan had come to realize his younger sister not only disliked him, she hated him to his soul. She'd be ecstatic if *poof,* he was gone forever. In odd moments, he'd wondered if she'd kill him if she knew she could get away with it. He'd never been particularly mean to her, usually simply ignored her. He was her senior by six years, after all. As an adult, he continued to ignore her and her fake praise when she couldn't get out of giving it, her backbiting, her jealousy, her attempts to make him look bad in their father's eyes. He marveled at how blind she seemed to what his father was to his core—Garrick viewed women as underlings, to be told what to do, to give him sex when he wanted it, however he wanted it, didn't matter if the woman was his wife or not. Didn't Nikki realize he tolerated her at best? Gave her what he had to when there was no other choice? Nathan knew their father would never give her what she wanted in the end—and that was the big chair. No, she'd stay planted in any chair he gave her, forever. Nathan vaguely remembered when he was small seeing his mother stand up to her husband. He remembered the fight, the blow to her ribs, her tears and groans, then the awful silence, and at last his father's soft, cold words: *Don't cross me again, Kyra, or I'll break your ribs next time, shave off that pile of hair you're so proud of.* Nathan never said a word, not then, not to this day.

He shook his head, he didn't like to remember that night. With Nikki, his father pretended to show respect, to give her power in Bexholt, since she'd worked her butt off in every department he'd assigned her to, probably expecting her to fail spectacularly. Only she hadn't. And now she'd taken this Federal Reserve assignment—seeing that the hotel conference room, the entire floor, was secure from any electronic surveillance or simple eavesdropping. He could have easily taken care of it himself, but oddly, Nikki had begged their father to be put in charge of this one, to work alongside all the other security teams. So her father had hidden his contempt again, and let her have her way.

Most of the time Nathan found his sister tedious and annoying, but unlike their father, he recognized she was smart. As smart as he was? No, of course she wasn't, but still, he knew in the deepest part of him if he didn't stay alert, she'd try to find a way to bury him.

He grinned at her now, knowing it would drive her nuts that he hadn't answered her about sending the accounting department home. He said instead, "You sure look good in Armani black." Not a lie. She looked like a powerhouse, a champ. Nikki wasn't exactly pretty, her features were too strong, her focus too intense. At least she didn't look bland, like his wife, who for some strange reason liked to copy Nikki's clothes. But black Armani made his very pale-faced blond Crissy look like a crow—in mourning.

Nathan eyed his sister again. No wonder she couldn't keep a husband. She held even the smallest slight close to her breast, she nurtured resentment. There was never any forgiveness. She was a ball-buster, vindictive. Denting his cars, it was so typical.

When his father finally retired, if he didn't croak over his desk, Nathan would get her out of the main Bexholt campus, set her up at one of their plants in Spain. She could bust Spanish balls.

Nikki said to their father, "Everything's on schedule for the bankers' conference on Monday. The Kentington Hotel will be swarming with security, and we're making good progress on securing the conference room as well as the entire sixth and seventh floors. We've already started installing the acoustic panels and the Faraday cage."

"I was told you're covering the entire room," Nathan said. "You know that's not really needed. What, you're trying to impress them?"

"Isn't that the whole idea, Nathan? You're not jealous, are you?"

"You know their own security will examine the room for listening devices. I hope they don't ruin all your work." He paused, rubbed his hands together, and Nikki's eyes went to the backs of his big hands. She hated his hands.

"Let's have no more bickering," Garrick said. "I'm sure Nikki will do an adequate job."

Right, you bastard. She left her father and brother discussing their weekend plans to go out on the yacht with Nathan's two boys. "No women allowed, Nathan, only us men," she heard her father say when she was nearly out of his office.

57

Nikki walked swiftly down the hall to her office, stopped when she saw a man and a woman talking to each other in low voices, her admin seated only six feet away. The Feds. She would have to be careful. Jasmine had already been spooked by these two, best not to underestimate them. What were they saying to each other?

Savich said, "Mom said Sean talked her into pizza for dinner, pepperoni, of course."

"That's his favorite?"

"Well, it's your favorite and so that's his favorite, too."

"What's yours, Dillon?"

"I'm a vegetarian, so it's always Vegetable Delight for me, but Sean's a carnivore like you."

He was a vegetarian. Sherlock hadn't noticed what he'd eaten, even at Jenny's Café.

And Sean. He was the image of his father, dark eyes and dark hair, a rich olive complexion. She looked down at her white hands, wondered what part of her he had. Sean. She liked the sound, the feel of his name, but when she pushed, there was the white door, again closed. Did he have a middle name?

Savich rose. "Ms. Bexholt? I'm Agent Savich and this is Agent Sherlock." He handed her their creds. Sherlock rose to stand beside him.

Nikki pretended to study the creds, but she'd have known very well who these two were even if Jasmine hadn't told her. She'd seen Agent Savich on TV enough, and Agent Sherlock—everyone knew who she was. She returned the creds, stuck out her hand, shook theirs. "Do come into my office. Paul, please go home now."

A tall, middle-aged man with a sharp goatee nodded, smiled at Sherlock. He moved quickly to open the door for his boss, then quietly closed it after they'd all filed inside.

Should she gush over Agent Sherlock? Paul probably already had. She wanted to, but she had to remember she was the one near the top of the food chain at Bexholt, not someone they'd expect to bow and scrape.

She said, "I know you're here to speak to me about a member of my accounting department,

Eleanor Corbitt. I understand she was killed last night. We at Bexholt are all greatly disturbed and saddened. We all want to know what you're doing to find out who killed her, but I'm not certain I understand why you, the FBI, are here. Isn't the FBI only involved with federal crimes?"

Savich studied this woman while she spoke—smoothly, calmly, in charge. She was tall, fit, and dressed in black, her hair nearly as black as her suit, pulled up high on the back of her head in a sort of twist, held by a pearl-encrusted comb. The style suited her. She had a strong, arrogant face, an expressive face. Expressive? Why had he thought that? Because there was something that worried her, profoundly. Her hands were restless, her fingers tapping on the desktop, obviously a longtime habit. As if she realized what she was doing and he'd noticed, Nikki quickly motioned them to the chairs facing her desk.

She sat down, clasped her hands in her lap. Such a ridiculous habit, the finger tapping, one she'd seemed to develop overnight after the first time she saw her father hit her mother in the stomach with his fist when Nikki was eight years old. She'd started tapping her fingers after that, if she didn't pay attention, no matter the time or place. She cleared her throat. "So, what can I do for you, Agent Savich? Agent Sherlock?"

Sherlock gave Bexholt her patented sunny smile, so much a part of her it was second nature.

"We understand you and Ms. Corbitt lunched together on several occasions, that she visited your office a number of times. She was obviously closer to you than any other employee in the accounting department. She was your friend. We would like you to tell us about her."

Nikki froze. How did they know that? Jasmine wouldn't have said anything. She and Ellie had always been discreet, bordering on paranoid, yet people had noticed and people had talked. She wanted their names, and when she found out, they'd pay.

She said, her voice trembling a bit, as if on the verge of tears, "Of course I knew Ellie. She was a friend, but not really a close friend. What I mean is she was an employee in our accounting department and she did some work for me on a couple of special projects. I did find her very nice and competent. I will miss her, as will all her co-workers."

"Did you ever visit her home?"

"I remember when she bought a condo last year and was very excited about it, showed photos all over the office, but no, I never visited her. The couple of times we had a business lunch was in a little pizza place just up the road from the Bexholt campus. I'm sorry, but I really don't know about her life, you know, her outside interests, or who her close friends were." Nikki rose. "Is there anything else I can do for you?"

Savich didn't move, said easily, "We find

it interesting and a bit too coincidental that two Bexholt employees—Eleanor Corbitt and Jasmine Palumbo—are both connected to Justice Cummings, the CIA analyst who was thrown over the hood of Agent Sherlock's car on Tuesday. Of course you know it was Ms. Palumbo who caused the accident. We believe Ms. Palumbo spotted Cummings, and was trying to catch him, which means, of course, that's why the accident happened. Chasing him distracted her and she struck Agent Sherlock's car.

"As for Eleanor Corbitt, she appears to have specifically targeted Justice Cummings. She came on to him, invited him for coffee after work, but she never showed up. She even used a false name—Christy Blake. And now she's dead, murdered. You know both of these women, Ms. Bexholt. Tell us what they were doing."

Nikki sat back down, giving her time to think. Even after Jasmine had warned her about their sudden attacks, she had still underestimated these two. Jasmine had screwed up big-time, true enough, but Nikki had believed there'd be no connection made. How had they found out about Ellie setting up Cummings? And using that fake name, the name of her married sister? Inviting him for coffee? Not showing up? Evidently Cummings had told someone and that someone had told the FBI. But who had Cummings told? *Get it together, they're fishing, nothing more.* She managed a concerned expression. "It does seem like a coincidence, as you say, and to me as well, Agents, but I believe that's all it is—a coincidence. I can't imagine why Eleanor Corbitt would even be at Langley, much less want to go out with a CIA employee, namely Justice Cummings. I mean, she didn't even like men. I can't imagine who would tell you such a thing. And Ms. Palumbo wanting to chase him down? That makes no sense to me." *Shut up, shut up.* "I'm sorry, but I can't help you."

Gotcha. Savich hadn't said a word about Langley.

Sherlock said, "Do you believe Eleanor Corbitt was gay, Ms. Bexholt?"

She leaned back in her chair, folded her arms, defensive, but she managed to look at them dead-on. "I really don't know about her sexual preferences, nor do I listen to office gossip. I remember she mentioned once her ex-husband was a worthless jerk and he'd burned her out on men. It was simply my impression she didn't date. Other than that, I don't know." She shrugged.

Sherlock continued, "What if I were to tell you it was Justice Cummings himself who told us Eleanor Corbitt—Christy Blake—was the woman he was supposed to meet at the Blaze Café?"

Nikki felt her heart seize, then laughed. "So you've watched old Perry Mason shows. I remember my dad laughing, saying the 'what if' lure was exactly what Mason said to witnesses to trip them up. Sorry, Agent Sherlock. No one even knows if this man is still alive—" She realized what had popped out of her mouth and froze.

Another slip. Savich smiled at her. "So you know Cummings worked at Langley and he was CIA, and you know he's missing. That's a lot that you know, Ms. Bexholt."

"I am blessed to know people who tell me things."

"Give us names, Ms. Bexholt," Sherlock said.

Nikki shook her head. "No."

Savich picked it up. "I can also assume you knew Eleanor Corbitt lied to Justice Cummings, told him she worked in personnel services at Langley. We know she set him up. And you do as well, don't you, Ms. Bexholt? Did you plan it?"

Savich rose, laid his palms on her desk, leaned over, and said, his voice deep and steady, "You have all the money, you're the one who wanted Cummings kidnapped. Tell us why."

She grabbed her landline and dialed three digits. "I want to speak to Mr. Phelps. What? He's gone home? Very well," and she forced herself not to slam down the phone. She cleared her throat. "Bart Phelps is one of Bexholt's in-house counsels. I will have him call you on Monday. Now, Agents, if you will excuse me, I have an appointment to keep."

Savich straightened, looked down at her, and

said, his voice hard as nails, "When Mr. Phelps calls us, Ms. Bexholt, do have him tell us why you wanted Justice Cummings taken. And how Jasmine Palumbo and Eleanor Corbitt were involved. Is your father also involved? Your brother?"

Nikki roared to her feet, so angry, so afraid, she was shaking with it. "This is an outrage. I want you both out of my office now. Get out!"

Neither Savich nor Sherlock said anything more, simply turned and walked out the door. Savich was smiling when they rode the elevator down to the lobby. "That went perfectly. Ms. Bexholt is scared and furious and there's not a doubt in my mind she's up to her eyeballs in whatever this is."

Sherlock said, "Did you see her tapping her fingers? I got the feeling it was a habit and she didn't want us to see her doing it. Why, I wonder?" She shrugged. "She's strong and confident. She's also arrogant and a liar. I'd say right now she's scared spitless because she lost it a couple of times. Now you're hoping she'll make another mistake. And yes, the Armani suit was stunning on her."

He laughed, couldn't help it, paused a moment, hugged her to him. "Can you think of a why?"

Sherlock was proud of herself, she hadn't frozen when he'd hugged her. She smiled up at him. "Too many pieces to this puzzle, too many possible turns. It's like a maze—we haven't found the key to it yet."

"More a labyrinth, I think, with Nikki Bexholt waiting at the center, a modern-day Minotaur." He kissed the tip of her nose.

Sherlock said, "Did you notice that bust of Athena on the pedestal by her desk?"

He nodded. "The goddess of war and wisdom."

"I wish I'd thought to ask her why Athena."

They walked out into the warm late afternoon, Savich holding her hand. Sherlock stopped, breathed in deeply. "Smell the night jasmine." She looked up at him. "I suppose you have someone in place to follow Ms. Bexholt when she leaves for the evening?"

"You bet. I'll make a call right now, tell Lucy we're leaving."

When he slipped the cell back into his jacket pocket, he said, "All set. Let's go home and get to know our guest better."

"I'll heat up your spaghetti sauce, whip up a salad." She stopped cold. "How do I know it's your sauce?"

He tapped a finger to her temple. "A sure sign you're on the mend." They got in the Porsche and passed through the kiosk, the guard giving a nod and a thumbs-up to Savich on the Porsche.

"There's Lucy pulling up now. She begged me to take this surveillance since Coop is out of town fishing and she said she's bored to tears, wants some work to chew on."

Sherlock saw Lucy sitting at a workstation, heard her talking on the phone. Then she was grinning up at Sherlock, patting her stomach, and Sherlock was hugging her, congratulating her. The white door slammed. "But, Dillon, Lucy is four months pregnant, she can't be on surveillance, I mean—" Sherlock couldn't believe what she'd said and began shaking her head at herself. "What's wrong with me? It doesn't matter if she's pregnant, she can do anything. Excuse me while I give myself a smack."

Savich laughed. "Lucy said her only drawback is having to pee more than usual, but she assured me she's got it figured out. Yeah, I was a bit concerned, too, but she gave me the *don't you dare say anything* look. She'll keep Ms. Bexholt well covered tonight. If Bexholt goes home, goes to bed, Lucy will leave for the night and Ollie will take over tomorrow morning."

"Okay, that's good. It was smart you didn't tell Nikki Bexholt we have Justice Cummings. You left her not knowing what's happened to him. I can see the stress of wondering about him, wondering what could happen, might lead her to make a mistake, or close up shop, cover up as best she can. Or run."

Savich said, "Yes, any of the above. And Mr. Maitland's agreed we're not going to tell Farriger about Justice, either, not yet."

58

Griffin pulled up to the gate to Eagle's Nest, pressed the intercom. "Good evening, Mr. Bodine. I would like to speak with Rafer."

There was a moment of silence, then, "I told you not to come here again, Agent Hammersmith. We do not have to speak to you. Go away."

Griffin said easily, "Believe me, Mr. Bodine, this short interview with your son would be far preferable to me bringing a warrant and taking Rafer in for questioning under federal custody."

Quint Bodine didn't answer. The gate opened and they drove to the house. Quint was standing in the open doorway. Behind him stood his brother, Sheriff Booker Bodine.

Griffin pulled up in front. He said as he got

out of the Range Rover, "As I said, I'd like to speak with Rafer."

Quint raised his hand to keep Booker quiet. "I'm afraid it isn't possible, Agent Hammersmith. My son is sleeping. He had a bad day. He took a good deal of pain medication, as you can well imagine, since it was you and this woman who hurt him so badly." He looked past Griffin to Carson, now standing beside him.

Griffin said, "Unfortunately this is of great importance. Please wake him up, Mr. Bodine."

Quint Bodine didn't move. He crossed his arms. His voice was controlled and smooth even as his anger radiated off him in waves. "You will listen to me, Agent Hammersmith. I'm sure if I call Mr. Jobs, our attorney, he will agree you have no justification for being here, harassing us. Once again, you have no proof my son was involved in any of the kidnappings. You have no reason for coming."

Griffin said, "Another sixteen-year-old girl, Linzie Drumm, disappeared today, assumed kidnapped from Whytheville."

Booker looked like he'd been kicked in the gut. He was slowly shaking his head. "That's Sheriff Cruisie's town. Nobody called me. But how could this happen? Everyone was on the alert in this area, parents, all law enforcement. Every family with a daughter should have been watching over her."

Quint said, "My son has been here since we brought him home from the hospital. He has not left the house." He looked at Carson, and his mouth seamed. "What are you doing here?"

Griffin said over him, "I have questions for him, Mr. Bodine. As I said, I can talk to him here, or I can take him into custody for questioning."

Booker laid his hand on his brother's arm. "It's okay, Quint. You told me Rafer hasn't left the house. Cyndia can verify that. Let him speak to Rafer. It doesn't matter."

Quint Bodine didn't say anything more, simply stepped back. "My wife and Jessalyn are making dinner, so be quick with your questions. I'll go wake my son."

Griffin studied Sheriff Bodine's face. He saw no particular dislike, but he did see lots of questions, and something more—surprise. The sheriff said slowly, "You must have some reason you came here, something you found out about the girl in Whytheville. Come in, I don't want Rafer talking to you in the doorway."

Griffin and Carson followed Sheriff Bodine down the steps into the great room and seated themselves on one of the oversize leather sofas facing the huge windows and the darkening mountains beyond. It was magnificent, the sky turning a soft pearly gray. They smelled beef stew.

Cyndia and Jessalyn came out of the kitchen, walked through the open dining room and into the great room. They stopped close together, wary and stiff. Cyndia said to Carson, repeating her husband's question, "What are you doing here? You have no business here."

Carson gave them a friendly smile, waved toward the glass. "Agent Hammersmith insisted. Isn't the view something? Like a painting. You're very lucky to see it every day."

They both ignored her. Jessalyn watched her husband walk to stand in front of the immense fireplace, legs spread, his thumbs hooked inside his wide leather belt, an old habit, one she'd thought was sexy before he'd gained thirty pounds. She said, "Booker, we heard the agent say there's another missing teenager. That's very upsetting. But why do they want to see Rafer?"

Booker locked eyes with Griffin, then his slid away, and Griffin wondered if he was remembering the duct tape removed from Rafer's basement. Had he removed it himself? Did he have any doubts about his nephew's guilt even now, with another young girl gone? Booker said to his wife, "It's an investigation, Jess. He needs to speak to a lot of people."

"But it happened in Whytheville! What is he doing here?" As she spoke she turned to give Griffin a long look. He felt the hair stir on the back of his neck. He focused back on Jessalyn Bodine's strong-boned face, looked directly into her eyes and said clearly in his mind, *Your nephew is very*

*probably a killer. You know it, I know it. Will you
ignore it forever?*

She jerked back, shock on her face. Without
a word, Jessalyn Bodine turned and walked back
to the kitchen. Cyndia said, "What did you do to
her? What?"

Griffin smiled at her. "You've been here,
I haven't said a word to your sister, haven't
moved from this spot. It's like you and Agent
Sherlock—you didn't say a word to her, either,
did you, Mrs. Bodine? And you were even across
the room."

She looked like she would blast him, but
Quint Bodine came into the great room with
Rafer, his hand under his elbow, as if to support
him. Rafer looked in no need of his father's help.
He looked tough and hardy with the dark beard
scruff, tight jeans, black T-shirt, and scarred black
boots. Then Rafer spotted Carson and took a
quick step back.

"Hello, Rafer, how's tricks?"

Rafer stared at her, said slowly, "Dad said
Agent Hammersmith was here to question me
about a missing teenager in Whytheville. Why are
you here? You're sleeping with him, aren't you?" He
gave her a knowing, hungry look that was potent
indeed. He looked at Griffin. "Look, I don't know
anything about it, do you hear me?"

Carson took a step toward him and he stumbled back against his father, no lust on his face

now, only fear. "No, don't you come near me. I don't want you looking into my head again."

Quint Bodine's voice was soothing. "Stay calm, Rafer, stay calm. She can't hurt you, you know that." He said to Griffin and Carson, "He's still confused because of the pain medications. Let's get this over with. Agent, I expect you to be professional."

Carson said, "You don't look confused to me, Rafer. You look ready to play some pool down at the Five Star Bar. Well, maybe you could use a shower, a shave first."

"Bitch."

"Rafer!"

Rafer glanced at his mother, who was holding a spatula in her hand. He shrugged, said nothing. He let his father lead him into the room, ease him down into a chair. Quint moved to stand behind him, his hand on his shoulder. "Ask my son your questions, Agent Hammersmith, then leave and take her with you." His gaze flicked over Carson.

Cyndia came to stand beside her husband, her hand on Rafer's other shoulder. She still held the spatula.

Griffin told them how and where Linzie Drumm had been taken, as if he needed to.

Rafer shook his head. "You can't believe I took her, I was here at the house, right here, loaded up with meds."

Griffin said, "Rafer, how familiar are you with Whytheville?"

"It's a dip-crap little town, even less nightlife than Gaffer's Ridge. I don't go there often."

"When was the last time you visited the dip-crap little town?"

"A long time ago, so long I don't even remember—" He stopped cold, gulped, and shook his head. "Well, okay, maybe I did stop by Whytheville a while back, not that long ago, I don't really remember what day."

Griffin said, "What did you do in Whytheville that day you don't remember?"

Rafer sent an agonized look to his mother, not his father. Interesting. Cyndia said smoothly, "Yes, I do remember. You told me you were going to Whytheville to check out a special lumber shipment you'd heard about at McComber's Lumber Yard. You were thinking about ordering some for Mr. Zingara's new addition since you couldn't get it easily, right?"

Griffin said, "That was very good, Mrs. Bodine, very fluent."

"That's it exactly," Rafer said. "Look, my brain's all fuzzed up. I would have remembered."

"What is the name of the person you spoke to at the Whytheville mill?"

"I don't remember, I—"

Cyndia said quickly, "I believe you said you were going to deal with Pete Crosby, the manager."

Griffin said, "Did you buy the lumber you wanted for Mr. Zingara's addition?"

Rafer shook his head. "No, the quality wasn't what he was looking for."

"Did you have lunch in Whytheville?"

"No," he said immediately, then shook his head. "Wait, now I think about it, I might have stopped somewhere. What does this have to do with kidnapping?"

Carson said, "According to Mrs. Buffett, owner of Buffett's Hamburgers, you don't have any manners, Rafer, which must disappoint your parents. She told us you were staring at a group of teenage girls while you ate your hamburger. Then you tossed your wrapper on the ground, not in the garbage can, which may be why she remembers you."

"The old hag's always making stuff up—"

Cyndia squeezed her son's shoulder, and he added, "Yeah, I remember now. I didn't much like the hamburger, and that kind of made me mad, so maybe I did toss the wrapper on the ground."

"Was that the first time you ever saw Linzie Drumm?"

Griffin saw it, plain as neon lights. Rafer was scared. "I don't know who you're talking about. I don't know anything about this girl." He dashed his hand with the splint on the wrist over his forehead. "I don't feel so good, Ma."

Cyndia looked at Griffin. "Is there anything

else, Agent Hammersmith? May I put my injured son back in bed now you've browbeaten him?"

Carson laughed. "It must really frustrate you when your injured son here screws up his stories, and you have to feed him his lines."

"Get out of my house!" Cyndia Bodine lunged toward Carson, death in her eyes. "Get out before I hurt you! Get out!"

Sheriff Booker Bodine walked to stand in front of Cyndia. "That's enough. Are you done, Agent Hammersmith?"

"For the moment, Sheriff. But you know Rafer isn't acting alone, don't you? It's both of them." He nodded to everyone, took Carson's arm, and they walked out of Eagle's Nest.

59

Yet again Savich saw Sherlock looking at their bed. She was wearing a robe over her tiger stripes, a rarity.

She turned slowly to him. Her face was scrubbed clean, her blue eyes were shadowed. She'd combed the rich red nimbus of hair back from her face and he saw the small Band-Aid over her left temple. Savich said from the bathroom doorway, "You look like a teenager, which has to make me a dirty old man."

She blinked. To his surprise and pleasure, she laughed. "Nah, not with you looking so hot in those black boxers and black T-shirt. Hot and buff. Do I tell you that a lot?"

He wanted to jump her, truth be told, but he

didn't move. "Yes, you do. Do you know we always try to go to the gym together?" The shower, too, but he didn't mention it. "You're getting good at karate. You've moved smartly forward for six years."

"What belt am I?"

"Well, we haven't formalized your belts, since I'm your teacher, but I'd put you right up there in a solid gold."

"Gold belt? I never heard of that."

"It was created only for you."

She smiled, but it fell off her face. "I didn't recognize Sean's voice."

He saw misery in her eyes. They'd spoken to Sean together for the first time, an hour before. His grandmother had let him stay up late to watch a Spider-Man movie with her and Senator Monroe, who'd asked Sean to call him Uncle Bob. And when he'd left, Savich's mother had allowed Sean to call them to say good night. To Savich's ear, Sherlock had sounded natural, pleased to hear from her son, telling him he'd be staying with his grandmother a bit longer, she was still contagious, and no way would she take the chance of making him sick. Yes, she was better now. Not much longer. She missed him.

He said, "You'll remember his whining before bedtime soon enough. Are you ready for bed?"

"What about Justice?"

"I checked him before I took a shower. He

was sound asleep, blissed out on the pain meds Dr. Breaker gave him. Ned said they could hold him for the night."

"Having a doctor willing to come here to the house. Now that's impressive."

"I keep telling Ned the debt—if there ever was one, which there wasn't—was paid in full years ago. He tells me to shut up, that when I call him for help, he knows he's in for some excitement. He said Justice will be fine in another couple of days. He also thought Justice will be thinking more clearly when he's not so distracted with pain. He seemed well enough at dinner, didn't he?"

"Yes, but I wish he'd eaten more. Dillon, he was so frightened and paranoid this afternoon, inviting him here was a great idea when he turned down going to Quantico. Have we ever done this before? Brought someone to stay with us?"

"Before we were married, I brought you here, but that's another story." He paused a moment. "Thank you for letting Ned check the stitches in your head and do a quick neurological exam."

Sherlock nodded, touched the fresh Band-Aid over her temple. "He's kind, a good doctor. It's nice to get a clean bill of health. Well, almost."

"You told him the truth? No more headaches?"

"Only a few, but they're less and less and not nearly as bad. Don't worry, Dillon."

Savich's cell chimed with a text. He walked over and read it quickly. "Good. That's the message

I've been waiting for. MAX broke the encryption on Bodine's file." He picked up his laptop. "Shall we take a look together at what MAX has got?"

She fluffed up four pillows, something she'd always done, and climbed in bed. She patted the space beside her.

Savich typed in his access codes, opened to Quint Bodine's Documents file. He scrolled through only briefly before he saw one labeled Project C. He settled in beside Sherlock, opened the file.

> July 2: *Subject K starts to show a bit of promise, with the new combination of drugs. At least she is willing to interact with Cyndia, watches old movies with her. She is rewarded, of course, with her favorite kettle corn and a movie of her choice, usually one of those absurd horror films. I pray she will be able to move forward as Cyndia expects, but I have strong doubts. She responds well to the medications, they keep her settled and calm, and I hope they don't mask her abilities, if indeed she has any. Whether Subject K understands what Cyndia expects of her is another question entirely.*
>
> July 27: *Subject M continues to be mutinous, won't cooperate, refuses to make eye contact, and continues to stare straight*

and ignore us, even Cyndia. She doesn't
seem to care about any pain and the drugs
knock her out, so there's no benefit at all.
A poor choice, despite rumors of her odd
abilities. She tried to escape yet again. Must
decide what more we can do with her. I am
not certain—

Sherlock said, "These aren't minutes, they're personal notes on experiments. They call the file Project C. I wonder what that means? Dillon, wait. What's happening? Look, the text is disappearing. What's going on?"

Savich cursed, began typing furiously. Bodine had installed a wipe program that kicked in if the file was opened without following a special series of passcodes. Even if Quint Bodine wouldn't ever realize someone had copied and decrypted his files, he had yet another fail-safe. Who had installed it for him? It was sophisticated. Savich tried everything he could to stop it, but still, line by line the file disappeared. He watched as *Subject K* simply faded from the screen. There was nothing left, nothing at all. Only a blank screen, and no way to retrieve the deleted file.

Savich slowly closed MAX down. He sat back, rubbed his eyes. "Well, that stunt was worthy of Nicholas Drummond. Where did Bodine find an expert to install that wipe program? Even if we get a warrant for his computer, he'll make certain that file is blank before we can access it."

"There was no way for you to know the file was booby-trapped?"

He sighed, dashed his hand through his hair. "It didn't even occur to me. If I'd known, maybe I could have figured out how to deal with it. I don't know, Sherlock."

"Subject K and Subject M—they're two of the missing girls. They must be the first two. Remember, Latisha was only taken in late July. And Rafer Bodine thought 'Amy died hard'? Maybe she's Subject M, maybe she tried to escape again and they killed her. What was the date he wrote about her?"

"July twenty-seventh."

"The others could still be alive. All of them are subjects in some kind of experiment? Cyndia wants them to behave in some way and they're using drugs on them—to do what? Control them, certainly, but what else? Drugs Bodine hopes won't mask their abilities? What abilities? But the way he writes, I don't think he believes they have any."

Savich reached for his cell on its charger, punched in Griffin's number.

"Griffin here. What's up, Savich? You get Bodine's computer files decoded?"

"Yes. I'm putting you on speaker."

"Carson's with me. Let me put you on speaker as well."

When Savich finished telling them what he and Sherlock had read, he paused a moment, then added, "The way Bodine wrote his notes, it didn't seem to us he believed what he and Cyndia were doing to the girls would gain them anything. And it was about what Cyndia hoped and wanted, not Quint."

Griffin whistled. "And even with the wipe program installed on top of the encryption, Quint didn't use their actual names. Talk about paranoid."

Carson said, "And *K* and *M* aren't the initial letters of any of the girls' names. I'll bet Subject K is Heather Forrester, from Gaffer's Ridge. Dillon, why didn't the program wipe when MAX was decoding it?"

"Different process," Savich said. "It didn't trigger the program."

Griffin said, "Okay, back up a minute. All the girls are sixteen. Wasn't their daughter, Camilla, sixteen when she disappeared? And the file name, Project C. I'm wondering if it has anything to do with their long-missing daughter."

Sherlock cocked her head, said, "That's brilliant, Griffin. And I had a thought. The Bodines' missing daughter, Camilla—do you happen to have photos of the missing girls?"

60

Savich divided MAX's screen into four quadrants, a photo of a kidnapped girl in each quadrant.

Griffin said after a moment, "The four girls do seem to resemble each other a bit, their general build, their coloring, but not enough to grab your attention. So I doubt those similarities are much of a factor. Now we need a photo of Camilla Bodine. Do you have one, Savich?"

"Yes, from a local newspaper when she disappeared." The four quadrants became two, one divided into four smaller squares, each with the photo of a kidnapped girl, the other half of the screen Camilla Bodine's face.

Savich said, "Anyone see a resemblance between Camilla Bodine and the four girls?"

Carson said, "Not much, though the shapes of their faces are a bit similar. But wait—their eyes. Look at their shape, their color. Does anyone else see it? They've got what I'd call dark, brooding eyes. Camilla, too."

Savich said, "Yeah, okay. There's the hair and eye color, but nothing else I can see to tie them physically to Camilla Bodine. Linzie Drumm, now her eyes are a very dark green, something like Cyndia Bodine's eyes."

Sherlock said, "So you think their eyes might have something to do with why they were taken? That seems a bit thin. Has there been any hint these girls were thought by their friends or families to be different or unusual? To have anything like psychic gifts?"

Griffin said, "Nothing like that appears in any of the police reports, not even in Sheriff Bodine's notes on Heather Forrester, and you'd think he'd have heard if she was considered in any way psychic." He shook his head. "If the girls were gifted, no one would say anything because of the parents, so who knows?"

Carson said, "So we're left with thinking these specific girls were taken because Cyndia and Quint believed their eyes are like their missing daughter's and because they believed it meant the girls could be gifted? Like their daughter?"

Sherlock said, "It sounds crazy, but it might make sense, given our meeting with Cyndia and what happened."

Savich said, "Quint drugs them to keep them calm. They interact with Cyndia, watch old movies with her. Why? Because Cyndia wants one of them to replace her missing daughter? That's over the top."

Griffin said, "Yes, it sounds flat-out crazy. I mean, you want to replace your daughter so you commit a federal crime by kidnapping four girls who vaguely resemble her?"

Sherlock said, "Guys, remember when Cyndia hurt me that first time we visited Eagle's Nest? I was coming back to the house to tell Dillon I thought something was off with the garage. I'll bet they've built rooms, apartments, under the garage, and that's where they're keeping the girls. Can we get the plans? Someone had to have done the building."

Savich said, "That makes sense, Sherlock. You'd need to have the girls close to have full control, to study them, to monitor them, give them drugs, whatever. I'll set MAX on it, see if he can find plans." He typed in instructions as he listened to Carson. "Don't forget Jessalyn, the sheriff's wife. Is she involved?"

Griffin said, "We'll have to consider all of them involved until proven otherwise. Savich, Sherlock, please write down everything you remember reading before it was erased. We need all the ammunition we can get. Any chance we can get a warrant?"

Savich said, "Unfortunately, a warrant went out the window with my hacking Quint's computer, a primo illegal search. We knew that going in. But it leaves no doubt where we're headed."

Sherlock said, "You know what I think? Even though Quint wrote that journal, and he probably administers the drugs, my bet is it's Cyndia who wanted this, it's Cyndia who's driving the bus. I'll bet she's the one with the power to control all of them."

Griffin said, "I will say after our interview with them this evening, it was obvious she has complete control over Rafer."

Savich said, "Okay, quick search. MAX didn't spot any plans immediately for construction under the garage, which means either they weren't ever filed, or Quint had them destroyed. Griffin, anything to report on Linzie Drumm's kidnapping?"

Griffin told them about the little girl seeing Rafer Bodine in Whytheville at the burger place, and gave them more detail about their visit to Eagle's Nest. "After what happened at the Bodines' this evening, I have a feeling time's running out." He stopped. He wasn't about to tell his boss he knew he had to act quickly now or those girls might die. He wasn't about to lay this on Savich.

He would call Bettina Kraus at Richmond, arrange for backup. For tonight.

Griffin said easily, "Sounds like I need to do interviews tomorrow with each of the kidnapped girls' parents, verify if they were considered different, had special abilities. Don't forget to send me what you remember from Quint's file before it was erased."

After Savich punched off, he and Sherlock recorded everything on MAX they could remember before the wipe program had erased the words, emailed it to Griffin. Savich turned off the light and eased a bit closer to Sherlock.

He felt her warm breath on his shoulder, said against her hair, "It's coming together. Don't worry about Griffin. He's not stupid. He'll do what's smart and needful."

Savich also trusted Griffin to arrange for backup. "Now we figure out what's going on with Justice. At least he's with us and as safe as we can make him. Justice made me promise no one would know where he is, not even Mr. Maitland, which will piss him off, royally."

Sherlock said thoughtfully, "I wonder what 'smart walls' means?"

He loved her brain, the way she looked at things, made leaps and connections. "We'll ask Justice more about all of it tomorrow. You ready to sleep, sweetheart?"

Sweetheart. Was that his usual endearment for

her? She swallowed, took a leap. "Maybe you want to kiss me, Dillon?"

Did he want to kiss her? Was she nuts? He'd like a whole lot more, but it was a wonderful start, and it was her idea. He turned his head to smile into her beloved face. "I don't know," he said slowly. "What if you start singing and wake up Justice?"

She was dead silent for only about two seconds, then she laughed, her warm breath fluttered against his cheek. "You willing to chance it?"

"Yeah, well, maybe." Control, he had to keep control, he couldn't scare her. Start slowly, let her take the lead.

She did. She kissed his cheek, his nose, his chin—light forays, then at last she lightly touched his mouth, her lips seamed. She touched her forehead to his. "That was nice."

An understatement. "Yes, nice," he repeated as he lightly stroked his hands up and down her back over her tiger stripes. He wasn't going to lose it, wasn't about to let that happen. He stilled his hands. "So what do you think? Maybe another kiss?"

"I can't imagine having a lover since we've been married. I mean, look at you."

"No, you haven't. Neither have I. You and I— we're a team, Sherlock, a unit."

She was silent a moment. They were a unit. That sounded right. She put her palm flat on his chest, wished he didn't have on a shirt, wished for a moment his boxers were on the floor. She pressed him back onto his back, bent over him, and kissed his chin. "If we made love, it would be like taking a lover. I know that sounds weird, but I don't remember us as a unit, and I see you as a kind of hot stranger—"

"Sherlock? Savich?" Their bedroom door burst open and there stood Justice Cummings, sounding both scared and excited.

Sherlock snapped to immediately, jerked up. "What's wrong, Justice?"

He realized what he'd interrupted and took a quick step back, stammering, "I'm sorry, I shouldn't have barged in like this, but I remembered something and I knew it was important and you'd want to know right away. I remembered because of my dream."

61

Savich turned on the bedside lamp to see Justice Cummings in the pair of blue pajamas Savich's mother had given him the previous Christmas. They were too big for Justice, but the drawstring kept them up. He was pale, but his eyes were bright and focused. He was very nearly vibrating.

He gulped, took a quick step back. "I'm sorry, really, I'll leave—"

"It's all right, Justice," Sherlock said, and pulled the sheet up to her shoulders. "Come sit down on the chair by the dresser. How is your leg?"

"I took another of Dr. Breaker's pain pills, so it hardly hurts at all now." Still, he walked carefully to the chair, pulled it closer to the bed, and sat down. He lightly touched his fingers to his bandaged nose and smiled. "My nose doesn't hurt, either."

"Tell us about the dream," Savich said.

"Okay, but I've got to back up first. Maybe a week and a half ago, I was having lunch with one of my co-workers, Peach—that's what everyone calls her because she's from Atlanta—and all she wanted to talk about was the upcoming NFL season and if I was going to play fantasy football. Finally, I told her I really don't like sports very much, even football, sorry, and I went back to my workstation early. And there at my workstation was my boss's boss, Assistant Director Claire Farriger. She looked up, saw me, and nodded, told me she wanted to read that Russian hacker's commentary I'd flagged about that new surveillance technology I'd reported, and could I show it to her. I did. She thanked me and left. I didn't give it another thought."

He drew a deep breath, whooshed it out. "Then I saw her in my dream tonight, sitting at my computer, and she wasn't trying to access that file, she was actually downloading something. And when she looked up at me, her expression was—well, furtive—I guess that's the right word. Furtive, like she was doing something she shouldn't be doing, not looking for that chatter like she'd told me. Then in my dream she ran her hand along the base of my workstation and pulled something out of the USB port, had to be a jump drive. She flipped it in the air, caught it. As she walked away, she started singing that song 'Don't

Worry Be Happy,' but not those words. She belted out, '*Sorry, sorry, but you're the best goat I've got.*'"

He looked embarrassed, but plowed ahead. "You know how dreams are, they're crazy-sounding when you think about them the next morning, if you even remember them, but those words—I jerked awake and I knew something was real about the dream. I can't get the words out of my head, the way she sang them, like she was really pleased with herself. And I wondered if my subconscious was trying to tell me something. Did I really see what she did, but not realize it?" He finished in a rush and stopped, stared at them.

Savich said, "I agree, Justice, your subconscious is banging on the door. You saw things you didn't pick up on at the time and your dream clarified them. Now you're remembering details you dismissed earlier. Relax and close your eyes a moment. Yes, that's good. Now go back and see yourself at your workstation. You see Farriger at your computer."

Justice kept his eyes closed, slowly nodded. "Yes, I see Farriger sitting there, her head is down and she's focused on something on my computer and yes, she's authorized to be there, but why wouldn't she call me if she wanted something?"

His eyes popped open. "Yes, she was typing, and yes, she did take a jump drive out of my computer. I really didn't think about it at the time because she was so calm, so matter-of-fact. Did she input something classified I'm not authorized to see? Did she create a cyber trail that would burn me? But what? Why me? I was the best she had? The best patsy?" He repeated her words from his dream. "The best goat she's got? For what? And then someone knew where I'd be and tried to catch me, someone murdered Eleanor Corbitt. Do you have any idea what's going on here, Agent Savich? Why these people want to kidnap me, or kill me?" He stopped, shook his head, lightly touched the bandage across his nose to make sure he hadn't dislodged it. He whispered, "Could she have been trying to make me look like a traitor?"

That was the bottom line.

Savich said, "My boss Mr. Maitland, Sherlock, and I went to interview Assistant Director Farriger after you went missing. She tried to cut us out completely, even Mr. Maitland. She implied it was your own doing, maybe even a personal matter. All of us agreed when we left Langley she was involved in something we didn't understand yet. You said in your dream she looked furtive? I'd say that's close to our own impression. Let's go downstairs and talk this over."

Sherlock said, "Justice, there's a robe and slippers by your bed. Go to the kitchen and turn on the coffeepot. We'll be down in a minute."

When Savich and Sherlock stepped into the kitchen, MAX under Savich's arm, Justice was whistling and taking down three mugs from the cabinet. He'd pulled the drawstring tighter on his pajama bottoms.

Sherlock said, "I'm the blue-and-red Wonder Woman mug, Dillon's is the Mickey Mouse mug, both twenty ounces." She started, blinked. She knew about the frigging mugs?

Justice grinned at her, making him look very young. "I've got a giant mug that says *Hogwarts Forever.*"

While they waited for the coffee to brew, they sat at the kitchen table. Savich said to Justice, "Do you normally have remote access to the files you're working on at Langley?"

"No," Justice said, "not outside the firewall. There are some unsecured CIA databases I can access with my passcodes."

"All right," Savich said. "I'd like you to try."

Justice navigated to the sign-in page on MAX, entered his passcodes.

"As I thought," Savich said, "access denied. I'd say the CIA thinks you went rogue, and whatever it is Farriger both downloaded into your work computer and copied is more than likely the reason you're now locked out."

Sherlock poured the coffee, handed them their coffee mugs. "Justice, why didn't Farriger simply enter your computer remotely? Why did she come to your workstation? If someone saw her, wouldn't they wonder?"

He stared at her a moment, said slowly, "She came to my workstation because all correspondence, emails, reports, whatever, always identify the computer used, and I guess she didn't want anyone to see she'd used her own computer to access mine. Although who would even wonder, I don't know. May I have some milk, please? No sugar."

Sherlock nodded, handed him the carton from the refrigerator. She said, "It means it had to be important. She didn't want to take any chance of it coming back on her, no matter how unlikely. Justice, what day did you find Farriger at your computer?"

"It was the very next day after my chief spoke to her about the chatter, and he closed me down, reassigned me. Now I'm thinking it was Farriger who told him to reassign me. Then on the following Tuesday, I hit your car, Agent Sherlock."

Sherlock sipped her coffee. "What day did you meet Ms. Corbitt?"

Justice looked startled, slowly nodded. "I see where you're going. I met her in the parking lot the same day Mr. Besserman reassigned me, when I was leaving for the day."

"That's fast work," Savich said. "You saw Eleanor Corbitt again when?"

"Two days later, in the cafeteria, like I told you. We chatted and she was very nice. And then she called me on Monday, wanted to meet at the Blaze Café on Tuesday. That's when the man and woman chased me and I ran out of the alley and into your car, Agent Sherlock."

"Only Sherlock, please."

He nodded. "And then they murdered Eleanor while I was still hiding out in the warehouse district in Alexandria Thursday night. She seemed so interested in me, but she had to be involved, didn't she?" His hands were shaking as he picked up his mug. He didn't drink, only looked down into it, as if searching for answers.

Savich said, "Justice, somebody at the CIA had to arrange for Eleanor Corbitt to get through security at Langley the day she talked to you in the cafeteria. She needed an invitation, and a guest pass, maybe a fake CIA ID tag for you to see. I'm thinking it was Farriger who arranged it. What about your chief, Alan Besserman? Do you trust him?"

"Trust? He's my boss, a career CIA guy. I never even thought about not trusting him." Justice fell silent, drank some coffee, then looked at them and slowly shook his head. "Do I trust him now? Given what's happened? I don't know who to trust. But Besserman? He's always been fair with all the analysts. Yes, if I trust anyone now, it would be him. This is all so crazy."

"There's someone else who had to know Eleanor was at Langley—Nikki Bexholt, a vice president in the Bexholt Group," Savich said. "She and Jasmine Palumbo, also at Bexholt and driver of the car that hit Sherlock, both seemed to know Eleanor quite well. Did you ever work with the Bexholt Group, have anything to do with them?"

Justice said, "Everyone in my unit's heard of them. We make use of firewalls occasionally, license some of their portable security software, but working directly with them, that would be way above my pay grade."

Savich rubbed the beard stubble on his jaw. "Still, it can't be a coincidence Claire Farriger put a stop to your sleuthing out that new surveillance technology and then set you up to disappear and get locked out of your own workstation. Communications security is the Bexholt Group's main line of business. Do you know if Farriger is currently working with Nikki Bexholt on some project?"

Justice shook his head. "Sorry, really, I'm only an analyst, not a CIA mover and shaker."

Sherlock checked the kitchen clock, a dragon with a purple tail and numbers, a Christmas present from Sean, doubtless assisted by his grandmother. "I think Besserman would be real interested in what you have to say, Justice. It's not yet eleven o'clock. What do you say we pay him a visit? Are you up for it?"

He gave her a grin. "I need more coffee first. With the pain meds Dr. Breaker gave me, I can hardly feel my toes."

"Take your time," Savich said. "I'll see if MAX can find out how well Claire Farriger and Nikki Bexholt know each other." He looked up. "There's no doubt in my mind they've worked together, and they're working together now."

62

MCLEAN, VIRGINIA
ALAN BESSERMAN'S HOUSE
FRIDAY NIGHT

Besserman's house was in a comfortable, older middle-class neighborhood with lots of mature trees and good-size yards. There was a single black SUV in his driveway, a single light on in what was probably the living room.

Sherlock sat on Justice's lap in the passenger seat of the Porsche. They were grinning by the time they'd gotten settled. Neither Savich nor Sherlock had thought yet about a rental car to replace Sherlock's demolished Volvo.

As they walked toward the house, they heard Humphrey Bogart's distinctive voice.

"Mr. Besserman mentioned once he really likes old action movies," Justice said. "He likes to quote Bogart—*African Queen*, sounds like," Justice added when they reached the front door. "He's divorced, alone now for about four months, says he likes the peace and quiet, but he hasn't looked too happy lately."

Savich pressed the doorbell. He could picture Besserman checking the late hour, perhaps picking up his Glock if he'd been an operative in the field for a while. He saw the living room curtain twitch. Then they heard footsteps coming toward the front door.

A deep voice, no real concern, a bit of impatience. Yes, he was very probably holding his Glock. "Who's there?"

Savich said, "Mr. Besserman, I'm Agent Dillon Savich, FBI, here with Agent Sherlock and Justice Cummings, your analyst."

A moment of silence, then, "Justice?"

"Yes, Mr. Besserman. May we speak to you, please?"

Sherlock said, "We're sorry it's so late, but Justice has remembered certain details we hope you can explain to us. We could use your help, and perhaps you could use ours."

The door opened. Besserman held his Glock pressed against his thigh. He was tall, on the thin side, with thick black hair, his temples sprinkled with white. He was a good-looking man, with an aesthete's face, long, narrow, hollow cheekbones. He was wearing chinos and a white short-sleeved T-shirt, and his feet were bare. His eyes were an unusual pale gray and looked like they'd seen too much and he was tired of it all.

He stepped back, waved them in. "Come in, all of you." He looked Justice up and down, saw the too-big sweats he was wearing, looked at Savich. "We've discovered Justice illegally copied and removed intelligence reports from the Ukraine he wasn't authorized to see. I'll have to take him to Langley for questioning."

"Let's stipulate for now Justice is already in my custody," Savich said. "You might want to change your plans once we've had a chance to talk."

They heard a friendly woof. A black Lab appeared in the living room doorway, tail wagging, tongue lolling. Besserman said, "He's a sucky guard dog, but he sure keeps me warm in the winter. Come and lick hands, Buzz, you know you want to."

63

COVERTON, MARYLAND
BEXHOLT GROUP CAMPUS
LATE FRIDAY NIGHT

Agent Lucy McKnight got out of her small Toyota and stepped behind a lovely thick-leaved oak tree. She was parked a half block from the entrance to Bexholt, out of sight of the security guards in the lighted entrance kiosk. She'd already called her husband, Coop, camping near one of the gazillion lakes in Minnesota with his fishing buddies. She'd started to tell him what she was doing, namely surveillance, then decided he'd worry, despite the fact she could take him down at the gym on a good day and outshoot him at the firing range on most good and bad days. His cell cut out. She sighed and rubbed her rounding stomach. At least her pants had a very stretchy elastic waist, a gift from a group of her friends, given to her even though they'd canceled the party because of Sherlock's accident. "If we wait," Ruth had said, giving her a big hug, "we might have to skip these pants entirely and get you a bigger pair." Lucy, like every other agent who worked with Sherlock, was worried sick. Imagine not knowing who you are. When she'd briefly seen Sherlock at the hospital, she'd hoped it would be her face that brought back Sherlock's memory, but that hadn't happened.

She stared back through the leaves toward the entrance. How late would Nikki Bexholt be working? Everyone else had left. Was there a back way Dillon hadn't known about? No, she wasn't going to second-guess herself. Surely Bexholt was getting hungry. Lucy was. *Some sweet fried sausage with peppers and onions, oh goodness, that sounds heavenly. No white wine with that lovely sausage. Bummer.* Lucy was momentarily distracted by that visual, but jerked back when she finally saw a single car come toward the kiosk. A security guard stepped out, leaned down to speak to the driver. It was Nikki Bexholt, her face clear in the guard-house lights.

There you are, Nikki. Can't wait to see where you take me. We can all dance. Lucy slipped back into her Toyota and started the engine, let it purr quietly, and waited. She knew where Nikki Bexholt lived, not quite a mile from the Bexholt campus. Would she go home?

Ten minutes later, with Lucy following discreetly, Nikki Bexholt left-turned her silver Audi onto Morning Glory Drive in a seriously ritzy neighborhood with large houses and manicured yards. Bexholt drove slowly, then steered into the driveway of a painfully modern two-story brick-and-glass house in a cul-de-sac. There were no trees in Bexholt's front yard, only a half dozen shrubs, with gravel surrounding them, cold and stark, to Lucy's eye. She pictured a small child stumbling over the gravel, scraping a knee. *There'll be nothing like that for you, Junior, I promise.* Bexholt didn't open the garage door. She got out of her Audi, walked quickly down a flagstone path sided by more gravel to a lighted front door. When she was in, the lights went on downstairs. After ten or so minutes, the downstairs lights went off, and on went the lights upstairs. Most likely her bedroom. Lucy had hoped Bexholt wouldn't come home, that she'd meet someone in some dark, out-of-the-way restaurant where Nikki wouldn't want to be seen. It looked like she was in for the night, but if so, why hadn't she garaged her car? Maybe she still planned to go out. Lucy decided to give it an hour, then call Ollie at the scheduled time and tell him all was clear and she was headed home. He'd pick up Bexholt in the morning.

Lucy was drumming her fingers on the steering wheel, waiting, watching, waiting some more, when the front porch light went on, the front door opened, and out came Nikki Bexholt. She was wearing tight jeans now, a white short-sleeved top, a light red jacket over her arm. She walked quickly to her Audi. Lucy heard the powerful engine kick in, watched her back out of her driveway.

Lucy's fingers danced the rumba on the steering wheel. The excitement of the chase. She kept her lights off, pulled out, and followed Nikki Bexholt through Coverton to 495. Where was she going?

She punched in Ollie's cell phone number.

"Lucy? What's happening?"

"Bexholt's on the move, Ollie. I'm hanging back a good ways, have to since there's very little traffic. She's headed south on 495 to Virginia. You can track me, right? Both my watch and phone are registering my location?"

"Yes. Both GPSes are loud and clear. I'll call Savich, tell him you're following Bexholt. Since we have no idea where she's going or what her purpose is, stay well back. Lucy, don't be a hot dog, all right?"

Lucy thought of the baby growing in her belly. "Honestly, I doubt I'll ever be a hot dog again, not good for Junior's nerves."

"I was thinking about Coop's nerves, too. Don't want him to have a seizure. Keep back, Lucy, all you're doing is surveillance, okay?"

Yeah, yeah. She followed Bexholt across the Potomac into Virginia, turned onto 193, and headed northwest. Still not much traffic, so she had to continue hanging back. Bexholt drove past the exit for Great Falls, then turned onto 7. Was she headed to Potomac Falls? As far away as Leesburg?

Fifteen miles before Leesburg, Bexholt took the exit marked MORGANTOWN. There were few cars this time of night in the middle of nowhere. Houses were set far apart, and the towns she drove through were small and dark. Thank heaven there was a full moon. Lucy could turn off her car's lights and still make out Bexholt's Audi in the distance. She'd never been this way before and she imagined the countryside was beautiful in the sunlight, the trees thick and lush, nearly canopying over the two-lane road.

Lucy saw Bexholt's lights turn sharply, and she slowed. She reached the white gate the Audi had entered, then continued to drive forward. She parked thirty yards up the road and walked back to the white-fenced property, ducked through the wooden bars, and continued quickly up the graveled drive to a lovely old white colonial house. There were four cars parked in the large driveway. Bexholt had left her house late to come to a meeting of some kind in the boondocks? Whose house was this? She saw a light in a front window, probably the living room. She walked quietly to the side of the house and crouched down, rising only when she reached the edge of the window. There were drapes covering the window, but thankfully, a bit of open space. She looked in to see a long, narrow low-ceilinged room, like in many colonial houses she'd visited, with wide dark oak planks on the floors. What was happening in this living room now wasn't colonial. It was a workspace, with rows of computer equipment, monitors and cables, and large opened cardboard boxes labeled BEXHOLT GROUP. In the middle stood five people in a conversation Lucy couldn't hear. Other than Nikki Bexholt, Lucy recognized Jasmine Palumbo, the woman who'd struck Sherlock's Volvo on Tuesday, but the other three she didn't know. The young man was slight, bald with brown eyes, and he sported a Fu Manchu mustache. To make him look less nerdy? The young woman couldn't be more than five feet tall with short spiked red hair and large black-framed glasses that dominated her small face. Bingo. She'd bet these two were the ones who'd chased Justice Cummings on Tuesday. And an older woman, in charge, powerful, that's what Lucy thought when she looked at her. She didn't know who she was. What was going on here?

She watched Bexholt motion for them to sit down at a circular table and conversation continued. Lucy still couldn't hear them, but she did feel the tension coming from the group.

Should she call Ollie? And tell him what? She was thinking it through when the meeting broke up. She quickly snapped some photos of all of them standing up, ran down the long drive back to her car, climbed in, turned the car around, and waited. Soon, three cars turned left out of the driveway. Finally, she saw Bexholt's Audi.

Lucy waited until she'd turned, gained some distance. Then she followed.

They traveled fifteen miles on 7, then Bexholt suddenly pulled off onto a frontage road. Lucy slowed down, saw her turn into a four-bay gas station with a well-lighted Quick Mart. The lights were bright, gave her an excellent view. One older guy was pumping gas into a Chevy long bed. She saw three people in the Quick Mart. She exited slowly, drove a half block past the gas station, and eased off the road, cozied up to a copse of oaks and maples. She got out of the car, walked around the slight curve, so she could see what Bexholt was doing. Duh, she was pumping gas, nothing more. But Lucy frowned. She hadn't pumped very much. Why? Lucy watched Bexholt reset the pump and walk quickly into the store to pay. When she came out, she walked briskly to her car.

Lucy hurried back to her Toyota but didn't get in. She waited for Bexholt to pass her on the way back to 7. And waited. Where was she? Finally, Lucy walked back until she could see the gas station. She saw Bexholt's Audi parked at the side of the station. Was Bexholt in the women's room? Lucy moved closer. Maybe she'd slipped into the

Quick Mart. The long-bed truck passed her, heading back to 7. Where was Bexholt?

She heard a noise. She pulled her Glock from her waistband, stilled and listened. Had she heard an animal? Okay, probably. There were lots of trees pressing against the frontage road, which meant there had to be wildlife roaming around. It was odd. The night was warm but she felt a sudden chill on her bare arms. She began to walk slowly, quietly, toward Bexholt's Audi.

She heard another noise close. It was faint, but she knew it wasn't an animal. It sounded like feet moving, trying to be quiet.

She whirled around, but she wasn't fast enough. Something struck her on the back of her head and she was down.

64

There was a full moon overhead, so bright Griffin could see the road and the mountain clear as day. He left his Range Rover against the side of a cliff within sight of the Eagle's Nest gate. He looked over at Carson. "Listen, I've given this a lot of thought. You're a civilian, you're not trained. The last thing I want is to take a chance of your getting hurt. Bad enough I'm going in like this, without a warrant. Your coming with me only raises the stakes."

Carson laid her hand on his arm. "Griffin, this all started with me. Rafer attacked me. He might have brought me here, with those girls. You know the girls are here, I know they're here. In what shape? I can help. You'll need me." She paused, looked at his stone face. "We started this together, we're going to end it together. I won't do anything stupid, I'll do exactly what you tell me to do."

Still, he shook his head.

Okay, time for the big threat: "Here's the deal, Griffin, unless you handcuff me to the Range Rover, I'll sneak in after you."

He knew she would, too. He'd let her talk him into coming this far and now he knew there was no going back, no matter what he said. He remembered Carson smacking Rafer on the head with the pipe. She had guts, showed she could handle herself. Still, he worried. He saw himself handcuffing her, then sighed. He reached down and pulled the small Colt from his ankle holster. "You told me you could shoot."

She gave him a blazing smile. "Yep, I still go to the gun range with Dad every few weeks whenever he's home. Up close I'm great. Maybe not so great from farther away, but I won't shoot myself in the foot, or you." She slipped the Colt in her jeans pocket. "This is right, Griffin."

They both wore black from head to toe, hoping to avoid being picked up on cameras. He shrugged on his backpack and they climbed the fence, dropped to the rocky ground, and stayed low, walking upward on the edge of the paved drive toward the top, toward the house.

Minutes later, they rounded a slight bend and saw the large black monolith that was Eagle's Nest, backlit by the full moon. The garage stood to the side, some twenty feet from the house. There were no lights anywhere, only the moonlight, but it was bright enough they could easily be seen if they weren't careful.

They quickly walked inside the edge of the thick forest to within twenty feet of the garage. Griffin knelt and pulled off his backpack. He assembled the portable parabolic microphone, checked to make sure it worked properly. They listened, heard nothing. He set his cell phone camera to low light mode and walked behind the trees, taking pictures. He came back, dropped to his knees beside her. "Our range is about fifty feet, and that's about what we've got. If there are rooms beneath the garage, there's got to be access, a stairwell, probably hidden inside."

They heard nothing from the garage. Griffin panned the parabolic microphone toward the house, and they hunkered down and listened. They heard very faint, low voices—adults, a man and a woman talking on the other side of the house. He shifted the microphone, but the voices were still too faint. Then they heard Quint Bodine's voice rise with impatience. Griffin turned on his cell phone recorder and set it close to the microphone.

"You shouldn't have sent Rafer out to get Subject S today without talking with me, Cyndia. It was far too dangerous. And look what happened, that FBI agent was here like a shot."

They heard Cyndia's voice now, higher, too, anger simmering. "Her name is Linzie Drumm, Quint, not 'Subject S.' I agree with you, the other two girls aren't going to work, and we'll have to figure out what to do with them. But maybe Linzie will be the right girl. There was something about her, I could feel it. So stop complaining about what's already done and go get Rafer. I think he went to their quarters, and it's late."

Griffin whispered, "We've got it all recorded. Legal or not, we've got proof, and there's a question of life or death here. Savich can get a search warrant with this tonight and we can be back here with Kraus before morning."

They heard nothing else, but a minute later, the front door opened and closed. Griffin quickly took apart the parabolic microphone, put it into his backpack. He and Carson pulled back farther into the trees and went down on their knees. Quint Bodine came out of the house. Even the frown on his face was clear beneath the brilliant moonlight. He was wearing an ancient dark blue robe and western boots on his feet. He stood on the top step a moment, looking out toward the mountains. Then he stopped and looked directly at them.

Carson felt her heart gallop though she knew he couldn't see them, even in the bright moonlight. They were on their knees, well back, well hidden. She jumped at the sound of Rafer's voice.

"Pa, what are you doing up? I thought you and Ma were in bed."

They saw Rafer come out from the side of the garage nearest the house. "I was just coming to bed," Rafer continued. "Everything's okay. Linzie's asleep—sorry, Subject S. She was tossing around from the drugs or maybe a nightmare, I don't know, but she's fine."

Bodine said in an emotionless voice, "I know you're concerned about her, Rafer. You worry about all of them."

A brief pause, then, "I only wanted to check on her. I didn't look in on the other girls—subjects. I guess they're all sleeping, since I didn't hear any music or TVs playing." He scuffed his booted foot into the gravel.

"I'm sorry about this, Rafer. But you know your mother is desperate. This is what she wants. Badly. Her vision, you know she believes in it completely." Quint paused, sighed. "I fear it's pushed her over the edge, and we can only hope all this passes. You know what will happen to both of us if we don't do as she asks."

Rafer looked back toward the garage. "The FBI agent, he knows I took her. He's not going to stop."

"Yes, yes, let him try, but it doesn't matter. Rafer, if he gets too close, well, it will be handled."

"Handled? What is Ma going to do?"

"It doesn't concern you. Come along back to bed. We all need our rest."

Rafer said nothing more and fell into step beside his father. Quint Bodine paused once more on the top step and looked out toward the mountains. He stilled, breathed in deeply. "It was a full moon the very first time I hiked up this mountain decades ago, when I came up here with my father. It wasn't quite this bright, but close. The mountain was wilder then, not a single trail, but I knew that night this mountain would belong to us, knew this was where my father would build his house, raise his family. This will always be my home, my castle." Then Quint turned and looked directly at where Carson and Griffin were hidden in the trees. He frowned a moment, and walked into the house, his son following him.

When the front door closed, Carson whispered, "He stared right at us again, Griffin. I know he can't see us, but do you think maybe he sensed us?"

Griffin shook his head, he had no clue.

"Sounded like the three girls are okay, well, other than being drugged to their eyeballs. I want to know how we'll be 'handled.' What do we do now, Griffin?"

"They're safe enough until morning as long as he doesn't realize we were here listening. I'll call Bettina Kraus first thing, get us a warrant and agents here."

They made their way back downhill, keeping low and to the shadows, climbed the fence, and walked to the Range Rover. He shot her a grin. "Fear not, I've got all this great moonlight to help me make my signature K turn."

Griffin cut it as close as he could, but the road was too narrow and he couldn't make the turn. He cursed under his breath, managed to make a K turn on the third try, but he was still too close to the edge, his Range Rover stopping not six inches from the cliff. He prayed the earth wouldn't crumble and send them over the side. He didn't say a word until they were once again in the middle of the road, facing downhill. He was about to tell her that was the last time he would make a hairy turn like that one when there was a huge explosion above them, like a blast from a thousand shotguns. There was a tremendous rumbling, then rocks and soil came plummeting down the side of the cliff, slamming across the road in front of them, bouncing off into space and over the cliff edge to the base of the mountain hundreds of feet below.

The road shook and shuddered, making the Range Rover slide toward the cliff.

65

FRIDAY, MIDNIGHT

Lucy woke up with a throbbing head and a roiling stomach. Automatically her hand went to her belly and she prayed she hadn't hurt the baby. She waited a couple of moments, pressed lightly, but there was no pain, no cramps. She closed her eyes, said a prayer of thanks. She turned her head toward a narrow beam of moonlight coming through a small window with half-drawn blinds. The window was set high in the wall, not where it should be. She realized she was lying on a single bed in a room lit only by the moonlight from that small window. She had no idea where she was.

She sat up slowly, fell back again at a wave of nausea and dizziness. She lay perfectly still and tried to think. She saw a gas station on a frontage road, saw herself following Bexholt off the exit. She remembered wondering where Bexholt was, then a hit of pain and she'd been gone. Nikki Bexholt, or someone she'd arranged to meet at that gas station. Lucy couldn't believe it. A fricking civilian had struck her down, which meant Bexholt had spotted her and set a fine little trap and Lucy had walked right into it. She squeezed her eyes closed at the humiliation of it. She'd been so careful, but not careful enough. Dillon had trusted her to do something important, and she'd screwed it sideways.

And now she was paying for it. She raised her fingers and touched the back of her head. She found the small wound, still bleeding sluggishly, and pressed down hard on it. She tried to concentrate. So what now? Where was she? Then she remembered being dragged into a room, barely conscious, a different room, not this one. She had been about to say something, to move, but then she saw two people walk briskly back toward her— two women?—maybe, the light was very dim and she couldn't be sure. She'd felt the weight of their eyes on her. Were they going to kill her? Her baby, Coop— She'd gone perfectly limp, hoped they'd believe she was still unconscious.

There had been more talk above her head and she'd strained to listen. She'd felt hands move her hair, then she'd felt a needle slide into her neck. She'd nearly flinched, but managed to keep still. Their words quickly became nothing more than jumbled sounds, with no meaning at all. She'd slitted her eyes open to try to see them, but they were blurred. Everything was blurred. She'd had the oddest feeling she was falling down a hole and the voices were a thousand miles away. Then there was nothing at all.

She'd awakened here, so they'd only knocked her out, hadn't killed her. Of course, if they had killed her, she wouldn't be thinking about it now.

Concentrate, Lucy. So after they'd drugged her, they'd brought her here, where she'd awakened, alone, in this strange dark room with only a single bed and a high window to let in a little of the bright moonlight. She lightly laid her hand on her belly again. *Think, Lucy.* All right, no bedroom had a single high window. She had to be in a basement. They hadn't tied her down. Why? Because they hadn't expected her to wake up so soon? Slowly, she swung her feet to the floor, held herself perfectly still to let the pain in her head and a wave of dizziness pass. She stilled, waited for her brain to clear.

When the world righted itself again, Lucy slowly rose and walked to the door. It was locked. To her relief, there was a small half bathroom off the room. She used the facilities and walked carefully back toward the bed, thankful for the sliver of bright moonlight since there weren't any lamps. She saw a light fixture in the ceiling, flipped the switch on the wall, but nothing happened, they'd taken out the light bulb.

She felt for her cell phone, but it wasn't in her pants pocket. Had they found her wallet with her ID tucked under the passenger seat? Did they know she was FBI? Bexholt had to have guessed who she was. Was that good or bad?

Relief swept through her and her brain fired sharp when she remembered—she reached down to the watch Dillon had requisitioned for everyone in the unit six months before, the watch with its own GPS. Ollie knew where she was, even if she didn't, and he would have called Dillon. He'd come for her very soon. There had to be something she could do. She felt strong enough now, her head clearing from the effects of the drug. She walked a fairly straight line to the door, called out, "Who's there? Come let me out, let's talk this over. I have no idea what's going on."

There was no answer, no movement she could hear. She called out again, trying to sound scared, voice trembling a bit.

Still nothing. Had they simply locked her in and left?

Did they intend to come back and kill her? If they'd wanted to kill her, they could have given her an overdose and dumped her in some woods somewhere, no muss, no fuss. No, Bexholt had to know if Lucy was found dead, she'd be the main suspect and Dillon would hound her to the gates of hell. So, they hadn't killed her. Not right away. They had to think of something less obvious. An accident of some kind or simply make her disappear. Did Bexholt, and her group, really think getting rid of her would make any difference? Did they believe she saw or heard something at that house that made Bexholt desperate enough to attack her?

Lucy sat down on the edge of the bed, let her brain continue to settle and sort things out. She looked at her watch—midnight. What could she do? There wasn't any furniture she could pull over to that window, maybe jump up, see if she could escape. The bed was too heavy. She eyed the window again. She could squeeze through it, but no way would she take the chance of hurting the baby. No, she had to sit like a fricking damsel in distress and wait for the prince to come rescue her. It was mortifying, everything about this night was mortifying.

66

Savich, Sherlock, Ollie, and Ruth made their way quietly to the small single-story house set a bit apart from its middle-class neighbors in a quiet neighborhood in McLean, Virginia, the address Lucy's GPS signal had led them to. It wasn't more than two miles from Alan Besserman's house. It was as dark as all its neighbors. There were no street-lights. A single black SUV sat in the driveway. They paused twenty feet away, behind a thick maple.

Savich pulled out his cell, pressed in a number, said quietly, "Savich here. I have a license plate. Let me know who owns it. It's urgent."

Not a minute later Savich's cell vibrated. He answered, listened, then, "You've got to be kidding me. Well, it's not a complete surprise," and he punched off, looked at the three of them. "It's a company car, assigned to Mr. Lance Armstrong, Ms. Claire Farriger's admin."

Ollie stared. "The fricking CIA is holding Lucy?"

Ruth said, "Someone's got to have gone round the bend to kidnap an FBI agent. It's crazy."

"There's a lot more to this than any of us know yet. But I do know it's one specific person with the CIA—Claire Farriger. Armstrong not only works officially for her, it now seems he's also her accomplice. Whatever rogue operation Claire Farriger and Nikki Bexholt are involved in, we know getting Justice Cummings out of the way was crucial. To make him the goat."

Ollie said, "Did it come from Farriger or from Bexholt?"

Sherlock said, "Let's find out. I guess it's probably not the best idea to knock on the front door and identify ourselves."

Savich grinned. "Probably not. Sherlock and I will go around to the back, see what we can see. Ollie, you and Ruth stay here out front. We don't have our comms units, so if anyone comes or goes, call me."

Sherlock suddenly saw herself again hugging an insanely happy Lucy McKnight, in the CAU, laughing, congratulating her. Lucy was smiling a jaw-splitting smile. She'd just told Sherlock she was pregnant.

"What?" Savich whispered against her hair as they walked around to the back of the house.

She shook her head. "Another flash, of Lucy. I'm sorry. Dillon, I'm wondering how deep this goes in the CIA, or does it begin and end with Farriger and Armstrong? It has to mean Farriger met Nikki Bexholt when the CIA hired Bexholt for a project." She stopped, grabbed his hand, listened. They waited. She whispered, "For a minute I thought I heard footsteps inside."

"Keep listening."

"Is being an FBI agent always this nerve-racking?"

"Only sometimes." He looked down at her, cupped her face in his hand. "But for you, the hairier the better—you love it."

Oh my, it sounded like she was a wild adrenaline junkie. She gave him a huge grin. "Maybe I do."

They moved silently past the darkened kitchen windows, around to the back kitchen door. No surprise, it was locked. Savich started to pick the lock, then motioned her on. He whispered next to her ear, "Dead bolt."

They paused at two of the back windows, took quick looks, saw no movement. Then Savich saw a pinpoint flash of light. They snugged up against the window, saw a small beam of LED light cross what was probably a bedroom. They saw a door open, and a bathroom counter beyond it. The beam of light was cut off as the bathroom door closed. Time to move, fast.

Savich pried up the bedroom window with his knife and climbed in. "Stay here," he whispered to Sherlock. "Be ready." He walked on cat's feet to stand beside the closed bathroom door. He knew he had to bring Armstrong down fast, and quietly. It was possible there were others in the house.

He slowed his breathing, waited. His cell vibrated in his jacket pocket.

67

Griffin prayed the road wouldn't crumble beneath them with the landslide of heavy boulders slamming onto it and bouncing over the cliff. He had no control of the Range Rover, now tilting toward the edge.

The rocks continued to crash down, luckily, none hitting closer than about six yards in front of them. The Range Rover continued to slide toward the cliff edge.

"We're going to jump, Carson!"

He grabbed her arms and pulled her across the driver's side after him. They stumbled back toward the gate and landed on their knees in the center of the narrow road. They watched from well back, frozen, as the earth beneath Griffin's Range Rover split and crumbled.

Griffin watched his car plow down the bushes and slide over the edge. They heard the SUV bouncing against the cliff wall, heard it land with a loud boom at the base of the mountain. Griffin ran as close to the edge as he dared and looked down. He saw his beloved Range Rover crushed against rocks, one wheel slowly spinning. Suddenly, the earth beneath his feet ripped apart and he slid into an ever-widening crevasse. There was nothing to hold on to, nothing to save him. He knew he was going to die, and how to make peace with that?

"Griffin! Grab my hand!"

He flailed his arm upward and he felt her grab him, and she was pulling him up? But how? No, he would pull her over with him. He yelled, "Let me go, Carson!"

"Griffin, I've got this bush between my legs. Pray it holds our weight. Come on, pull yourself up. No way are you going to fall." She pulled as he climbed upward, his feet scrabbling to find purchase. He managed to fit his boot against a rock that hadn't yet pulled loose and heaved himself up, so slowly it felt like eternity. "Come on, Griffin, pull, pull," she said over and over, her litany, until finally he reached solid ground. He fell next to her, breathing hard, his heart galloping. But only for a moment. They crawled backward until they hugged the mountain. Carson grabbed him around his chest, squeezed him hard, then pulled away, stared at him a moment, then began laughing like a loon. He pulled her back against him, his heart still kettledrumming, but he was alive, she was alive, and he was so grateful it nearly swamped him. She hiccupped and eased away from him to lean back against the mountain wall. She wasn't laughing any longer. "I was so scared, I thought you were going to— No, forget that—we're both all right, we both survived. I didn't think, just acted." She looked toward the lone bush still upright at the edge of the cliff. "May all of heaven rejoice at the strength of that precious bush. I want to take it home, take care of it, maybe add a dollop of vodka in its water."

Griffin's heart was slowing enough so he could catch his breath. He leaned in close, said against her tangled hair, "Thank you for my life, Carson."

She hiccupped again, swallowed. "You're welcome, but please, don't ever do anything like that again. I don't want my heart to stop. It might not reboot next time."

If she hadn't been with him, if she hadn't been such a quick thinker— No, he wouldn't go there. He was alive, they were both alive. He hugged her once more, and turned to watch a huge boulder hurtle down the mountain, hit the road like a bomb, then bounce high like a basketball to hurl itself over the cliff.

"It's probably going to land on top of my Range Rover." He popped his ears. "There, that's better. I wondered why I was having a hard time hearing you."

Carson popped her ears. "Yes, good."

"Are you okay, Carson? Really?"

"I—I, that is, yes, other than not having any spit in my mouth and my heart wanting to leap out of my chest, but, hey, who cares? We're alive, Griffin, we're alive."

Griffin drew in a steadying breath. He finally said, "I bet Quint's had the explosive in place for a while now."

"That's how he was going to handle us? Even though we were really careful, it's gotta mean he saw us on a camera. But why did he have it already in place?"

"To take care of unwanted guests and claim it was an act of God? Still, it was sloppy, hard to time a landslide at exactly the right time, has to take some luck, which he didn't have with us. He should have gotten out his shotgun and drilled us clean, over and done. Thank the powers that be he wanted to be cute about it, turn it into an accident, no dead bodies on his property. Still, it was close."

He took her dirty hand and they sat quietly. The night was silent again.

"Griffin."

He felt her hand on his forearm. He pulled

her in. She was shaking, no surprise, she was overloaded with adrenaline from the shock and fear, the fight for his life, and the aftermath, finally knowing they weren't going to die. All of it made a wicked brew. She said against his ear, "I'm sure glad you're a crappy driver. If you'd made that first K turn, we'd be dead. Smashed really dead. Do you think Quint will come down and check?"

"I would," he said, gave her another hug, and pulled out his cell. "I am now officially pissed."

Savich whispered, "Griffin? What's up? Sorry, but you've got to make it fast."

And Griffin told him what had happened.

"Good, you're both all right. I can't talk, I'm up to my eyeballs in trouble here. Get off the mountain, Griffin, now, before Quint Bodine gets down there to see if you're both dead. When you can, call Bettina Kraus. She'll bring the troops."

Griffin was shaking his head as he said, "I was going to wait until morning to call Bettina, Savich, but not now, not since Quint knows we were looking around. You know as well as I do the girls' lives are on the line. He might kill them, bury the evidence. I can't let him do that. I'll call Bettina, tell her the situation. We'll wait here for her and her troops."

"Be careful, all right?" Before Griffin had a chance to say anything more, Savich had punched off.

Griffin said, "Savich is in trouble himself." He

immediately called Bettina Kraus, woke her up. He talked faster than he'd talked to Savich. When he rang off, he said, "She'll be here with agents as soon as she can get everyone rounded up. Say two hours."

"Good. No, Griffin, I know you're going to say something stupid like I should walk to the bottom of the road and wait. No way." She stood up, brushed the dirt from her pants. She shook a teacher's finger at him. "Don't even try it. Consider me your second skin until this is over." She sighed. "To think I came to Gaffer's Ridge to do a human interest interview, and look what happened instead. No, keep quiet. I'm not about to leave those girls. We'll be ready for him. I've still got the gun."

"You nearly died—twice."

"And you were very close yourself. Now, we're wasting time. What do we do?"

He got to his feet. "I doubt we have much time before Quint gets here to see what's left of us after the landslide."

Carson pulled the small Colt Griffin had given her from her waistband, said in a calm voice she didn't recognize as hers, "Let's get the murderous bastard and rescue those girls."

They walked back toward the gate.

68

MCLEAN, VIRGINIA

The toilet flushed, the tap water ran, then stopped. Savich pictured Armstrong wiping his hands. The door opened, but there was no light this time. Armstrong was confident enough he knew where things were in the room. Savich jerked Armstrong back against him, squeezed his arm tight around his neck, his Glock against his temple. He said into his ear, "Armstrong, you're a long way from Langley."

Armstrong didn't say a word. He twisted to grab Savich's elbow and pressed his fingers hard on his ulnar nerve. Fire flashed down Savich's forearm and his hand went instantly numb. His Glock fell to the hardwood floor.

Armstrong was on him. He was well trained, hard as a seasoned fullback, and out to maim.

Savich felt a rush of adrenaline. It had been a long time since he'd mixed it up, and this guy was a brawler. Armstrong jumped in close, pummeled him with his fists, grabbed Savich's left arm with both of his and twisted it sharply behind him. Savich knew he had only a second before the bone snapped. He ignored the pain and his numb right hand, managed to feint and turn to the side to gain a bit of space, and kicked Armstrong in the belly. Armstrong sucked in a breath, let him go as he stumbled back. "You're going to pay for that, you FBI prick."

"Yeah? Show me what you've got." Savich jumped back a step to get the leverage he needed, whirled, and kicked Armstrong hard in his kidney, whirled again and kicked him in the groin. Armstrong grunted, went down on his knees, grabbed himself as he rolled over onto his side, keening. Savich flipped him onto his belly, jerked the flex-cuffs from his belt, realized he couldn't fasten them with his numb hand. Then Sherlock was there. She bent down next to Armstrong, whispered in his ear, "All right, moron, enough fun and games. Don't move or I'll shoot your ear off and make you eat it. You got that?"

Armstrong was breathing hard, fighting nausea from the blow to his crotch, the hot pain in his kidney.

Sherlock pressed her Glock into his ear. "Say it out loud. You understand, Armstrong?"

Finally, he managed, "Yeah, I understand."

In that instant, Sherlock saw the Glock in his belt holster. She made a grab for it, but Armstrong was fast, clamped her arm against him. Savich calmly stuck his own Glock into Armstrong's other ear. "Let her go or you're a dead man."

Armstrong let her go. Sherlock pulled Armstrong's gun free and slowly rose, shook her arm. "I'm okay, Dillon. Step away while I cuff him. How's your arm? Can you use it?"

"It's coming," Savich said. He rose, shoved his Glock back into his belt clip, and watched Sherlock fasten on the flex-cuffs. He looked up to see Ruth and Ollie in the open window, their weapons drawn. "We're secure here," he said to them.

Ollie said, "No one else is here. Only this guy, Armstrong."

Savich walked over to the door and flipped on the switch. Light flooded the small bedroom. There was a closet, a bathroom, a dresser, and a double bed covered with dark blue sheets. He walked back to Sherlock and looked down at Armstrong, his legs drawn up, his face against the floor.

Savich said to him, "You going to heave?"

Armstrong whispered, "Bastard. What are you doing, attacking a CIA safe house?"

Sherlock pressed her foot against his ribs,

hard enough to get his attention. "You're calling him a bastard when you're holding an FBI agent prisoner here? Where is she? In the basement? She'd better be all right, or believe me, this won't be your lucky day."

Armstrong raised his clammy face. "I don't know what you're talking about. Yeah, I have a detainee in the basement. She isn't FBI, she's a suspected foreign agent. I was assigned to keep guard over her until the morning, when she'll be picked up and interrogated. I'm only babysitting her. I was told she's violent, and so they drugged her. Last time I checked, she was still out."

Savich said, "Sorry, Lance, that story isn't going to fly."

Sherlock said, "Did you people ever hear of checking a wallet for ID? You'd see she's FBI."

"I was told she didn't have a wallet, par for the course. Even if she did, it would be fake."

Savich said, "Who told you to hold her?"

"None of your freaking business. Let me go. I've got calls to make. This is your mess to figure out, not mine. Get these cuffs off me!"

Sherlock said, "You want to call your boss, Claire Farriger? I can tell you right now, Lance, she isn't going to be happy with you. She gives you one simple assignment and look what happens. The FBI rides to the rescue and you end up on the floor whimpering like a little boy."

Savich said to Ollie, "You and Ruth get down

to the basement and see that Lucy's all right. But be careful, it's possible there's another one down there with her. We'll take this one to the kitchen."

Armstrong was no longer thinking he'd die. He was wishing his hands were free and he could have another go at these two. "Let me loose. I'm entitled to a phone call."

Sherlock said, "Sorry, Lance, you're not entitled to anything at all. Tell us exactly what Farriger and Nikki Bexholt are up to or I might let the big man here at you again."

"He was lucky. Let me loose and I'll show you."

Sherlock laughed. "If I let you loose, what I'd see is him tying your legs around your neck. Now, what did you do to her?"

"I didn't do anything to her, simply carried her downstairs and put her on a bed. She was out cold. I was told she was given a dose of ketamine to keep her out. No one wanted any more trouble out of her."

Savich dragged Armstrong to the wall so he could sit up. He left his hands cuffed behind him. He looked into Armstrong's hard face. Could he really be a dupe? He knew Armstrong and Farriger were close. It was more likely he was her hench-man, perhaps her lover. Had he murdered Eleanor Corbitt?

Armstrong said, "You haven't told me how you found this house. You had no way to know."

Savich gave him a grin. "Would you believe I'm psychic?"

They heard Ruth shout, "We've got Lucy. She's okay, well, she's so mad she's frothing at the mouth. She's got some pain from the blow to her head, and there's some bleeding, but not much now. She's a little dizzy from a drug they gave her. No one else is here, only the bozo you guys found. We're bringing her up."

"I am not a bozo."

"Maybe not," Sherlock said slowly. "If you're a dupe, that means Farriger has roasted you." She pulled Armstrong's Glock from her pocket, studied it a moment. "Dillon, I'm thinking this could be the same gun that murdered Eleanor Corbitt."

Savich watched Armstrong's face, saw the brief flash of knowledge in his eyes, but he shook his head. "I don't know any Eleanor Corbitt. You want to know anything else, you can talk to my boss." He didn't say another word.

69

EAGLE'S NEST

Quint Bodine didn't come with a shotgun. He didn't come at all. It was Cyndia Bodine, running toward them, her bathrobe flapping around her ankles, flip-flops on her feet. She saw them and stopped, breathing hard, and there was something dangerous in her eyes. Just as suddenly, her features smoothed out. "I'm relieved you're both alive, but how are you here? You shouldn't be here. I heard the landslide and I came running."

Griffin didn't move. "Why? How did you know anyone was down here, Mrs. Bodine?"

She said, "I didn't know. These landslides sometimes happen, do some destruction to the road, but what scared me was my husband wasn't in bed and I was afraid something had happened to him."

"Your husband isn't here, but we were. Sorry, but the landslide didn't crush us under a ton of boulders coming down off the mountain. Didn't you hear the explosion?"

She said nothing. She kept looking at him, but Griffin saw her eyes go vague, fixed inward, as if she was focusing on something he couldn't see. Or someone. "Oh no you don't!" He ran to her, grabbed her arms and shook her, hard. "Snap back, Cyndia. Whatever you're trying to do, stop it."

She hit his chest with her fists, tried to score his face with her fingernails. "Get away from me! I don't know what you're talking about. Go away, there's nothing here for you. Let me go!"

But Griffin wasn't about to let her go. He shook her again. "Listen to me, we know you're holding three girls in your underground—what? Lab? Apartments? Under the garage. We know you had Rafer kidnap them, you gave him no choice. And do you know what? We've finally figured out why you kidnapped the girls. All of them are sixteen years old, and you think they're perhaps gifted, like you are, like your missing daughter. This is all about Camilla, isn't it? She's at the center of everything you've done, the excuse. But I don't understand why, Cyndia. Were you hoping the drugs would enable you to coerce one of them into playing the role of your long-lost daughter? You wanted one of them to take Camilla's place? And your husband has been drugging them, recording their behavior. Yes, we read about Subject K and Subject M. Do you know how sick that is? How crazy?"

She screamed in his face, "You're a fool! How could you ever believe any of those girls could ever take my Camilla's place? That I would want one of them to take her place?" Her eyes turned nearly black. She was panting now, locking her eyes on his face, and again, Griffin shook her hard.

"What you've done—kidnapping, using drugs, imprisoning these girls, murdering Amy—"

"Let her go, Agent."

Griffin slowly dropped his hands at the sound of Quint Bodine's calm voice. He had a shotgun aimed not at him, but at Carson. Rafer was behind him, his hand outstretched. To stop his father?

Griffin felt a sudden tearing pain in his chest, a pain nothing like he could ever have imagined. It was agony, he knew it had to be a heart attack and he was dying. He staggered back, slapped his hands to his chest, and fell to the ground.

Carson yelled, "Stop it!" She fired once, kicking up dirt a few inches from Cyndia's foot, but Cyndia didn't stop.

Griffin had to stop her or he knew he'd die. He looked straight at Cyndia, pictured her lying on the road, a huge boulder on her chest, her eyes rolling back.

Cyndia screamed, leaped back, and Griffin

was free. The pain in his chest vanished, he could breathe again.

Quint Bodine fired his shotgun at the same time Carson fired hers. His bullet struck the road in front of Griffin, spewing up rocks and dirt. Carson didn't see where her bullet hit, but she didn't need to. A fountain of blood spurted from Quint Bodine's head. He fell to his knees, then over onto his side.

"No!" Rafer fell on his knees beside his father.

Cyndia leaped at Carson, hit her with her fists, kicked her. Carson grabbed her around her neck and pressed the small Colt against her cheek. "Stop it. You tried to murder Griffin, just like you hurt Sherlock, but you failed this time. Your husband was going to shoot Griffin. I had no choice. Now stop it!"

Cyndia was cursing, struggled frantically to get free. Carson swung the Colt against her head, watched her crumple to the ground unconscious, one flip-flop falling off her foot. She didn't move. Good.

Carson yelled, "Rafer, don't you dare pick up that shotgun or I'll shoot you!"

Rafer jerked back his hand, pulled his father up in his arms, shook him, but Quint was gone. Rafer screamed at Carson, his voice high and broken, like a little boy's, "You shot my pa in the face! All the blood, too much blood—he's dead. Do you hear me? My pa's dead!"

Carson felt roiling nausea, swallowed convulsively. She hadn't meant to shoot him in the face, she'd been aiming lower. Hadn't she? Carson's world shifted, what was real and what seemed like a mad nightmare mixed together, a toxic brew spewing real death at her, swamping all sense of control. She'd killed another human being. No, no, it didn't matter, nothing mattered except Griffin. She'd had no choice. Quint would have killed him. No way would she let that happen. She saw Griffin was sitting up, staring at Cyndia Bodine, still lying unconscious on the rocky ground, her robe tangled above her knees, the single flip-flop on the ground beside her. She moaned, shifted, fell onto her back, but stayed down.

Carson called out, "Rafer, I'm sorry, I didn't mean to kill your father, only stop him. Stay there and don't move."

She went down on her haunches beside Griffin, put her Colt on the road, and shook him. "Are you all right? What did Cyndia do to you? How did you stop her?"

He struggled up to his knees. "It was my heart. I thought at first it was Quint trying to kill me, but I realized it wasn't Quint at all—"

"You're right about that, you stupid man, it wasn't my poor husband."

They turned to see Cyndia Bodine on her knees facing them, her bathrobe fanned around her, a Beretta in her hand, pointed at them. "I'm an excellent shot. Either of you move and I'll finish what my husband started. No, don't pick up the gun, missy. Leave it on the ground. Good." She turned to stare at Griffin. She shook her head, looking confused, uncertain. "I don't understand. I thought I'd killed you, but something happened."

Griffin said, his voice infinitely calm, "Yes, you tried, but I stopped you."

She shook her head as she rose to face them. "No, no, it was something else, something you did psychically. And now Quint's dead. I told him the explosion, the landslide, it was too uncertain, but he told me he knew it would do the job, send you both over the cliff. He'd worked on it for more than a year, a fail-safe to deal with any threat to us, to his house. When I saw you making the K turn on the camera I told him to set it off, but you were too slow, you kept missing the turn. Then it looked like you were going over the edge anyway, and I came running to take care of her."

Her hand shook as she turned the Beretta on Carson, gave her a mad smile. "I don't need a gun to destroy you, but after his little trick—you surprised me, is all."

Griffin got slowly to his feet. "The kind of little trick you use to control everyone around you, Cyndia? Face it, I'm stronger."

She laughed. "Who cares? I'm the one with the gun now. You're no longer important. She is." She turned to Carson. "You murdered my husband!"

Griffin tried to shove Carson behind him.

Cyndia laughed. "Hero to the end, aren't you? Well, it's too late."

"Ma! Stop!"

Cyndia turned to see her son running toward her. She didn't move, kept the Beretta aimed at Carson. "Rafer, you saw her, she killed your pa. Don't get near them, stay back." She sneered at Griffin and Carson. "You both think you're so smart, but in the end Rafer's going to bury both of you."

Griffin watched her finger tighten on the trigger and said in the next breath, "I called Agent Savich. He knows exactly where we are, what you, Rafer, and Quint have done, how you tried to kill us with the explosion. Agents are on the way. You can't get out of this, Cyndia, even if you manage to kill us. Don't make it any worse. Lower the gun."

Rafer grabbed at her arm, but Cyndia jumped away, panting, beside herself. "Listen, Rafer, I can't give up, I have to make them pay for murdering your pa."

Tears were streaming down Rafer's face, pain radiating off him in waves. He held out his hands to her. "Ma, please, you've got to stop this. He's right, it's over, Pa's dead, do you understand? He's dead! He never wanted this, he thought it was crazy, impossible, but he knew he had to do it for you, but now even he'd say it was over. He wouldn't want you to kill them. And me? I knew I had to go along with what you wanted, knew if I didn't you'd shine me and make me do it anyway, just like Pa, but now it's finished and I'm glad. Yes, I know you've said over and over for years you knew your precious Camilla was alive, you dreamed about her calling to you, begging you to come to her, that she needed you, that without you, she'd die. But, Ma, why didn't she ever tell you where she was? She didn't, did she?"

70

"**C**amilla would have contacted me, Rafer, but she couldn't, someone was keeping her from me. All these years I've known that, tried and tried to get through to her, but I couldn't. I could hardly stand it. But then I had the dream, no, it was a vision. You know about the vision, Rafer. Camilla came to me, yes, she came to me just as I told you and your father. I saw her clearly. She told me there was a girl nearby, a girl her age, dark, like her, with eyes like hers. She told me to find her, Rafer, and bring her to Eagle's Nest, get close to her, that I would know when I found the right girl. Then Camilla could use her to help contact me, to tell me where she is. She said she wasn't strong enough herself to get through to me, she'd tried and tried. It was up to me.

"Don't you see? I had to find that girl. I prayed we'd find the one girl who'd be perfect and help Camilla contact me. None of them was right until this new girl, Linzie Drumm. She's the one, Rafer. I looked into her eyes and I saw something I didn't see in the others. I saw strength, like Camilla's strength, Camilla's power. I know she's the one. I have to try with her, Rafer, I have to. It will still be possible, if the two of us work together, to find Camilla, finally. You do believe that, don't you?"

Rafer swiped away the tears. Suddenly, he looked utterly calm, in full control of himself, and he sounded like the father, not the son. He said to his mother, his voice gentle, "No, Ma, none of those girls are going to be able to help you find out where Camilla is, not even Linzie Drumm. They aren't going to add to your strength, none of them are going to help you hook up with Camilla. Don't you understand? It's impossible and Pa knew it, yet he did this for you." He paused, then added quietly, "He was afraid not to do what you wanted, just as I was." *And now he's dead* hung silent in the air.

Cyndia was shaking her head. "You're wrong. You make it sound like your pa was afraid of me. It isn't true, your pa wanted Camilla back, too."

Rafer shook his head. "Listen to me, Ma. Camilla's not in Paris. She's not in New York. She's not even in bloody Florida. She's not anywhere. She didn't leave you when she was sixteen because she was angry at you. She didn't leave you at all. Don't you understand?"

Cyndia stared at her son. She whispered, "What are you talking about, Rafer? I always knew my Camilla was somewhere, knew it to my soul. And I was right, she came to me in my vision and told me exactly what to do. She was sixteen when she left, a rebellious age, and she was so independent, always defiant. Like every teenager, she wanted to do the opposite of what was good for her, what I wanted her to do. My perfect gifted child. She was all I could ever want. I must have her back, Rafer, or I'll go mad.

"Don't you understand? Once I connect with Camilla, I can go to her and bring her home."

Rafer said quietly, gently, "Ma, in your vision, when Camilla came to you. Did she actually appear to you? Did you actually see her?"

"Of course I did. I saw her clearly, my beautiful Camilla, so talented, so ready to live life to the fullest. I love her, Rafer, your father worshipped her, everyone admired her. She will come to me, she'll tell me why she ran away. Remember all those worthless investigators your father hired over the years? They claimed they couldn't find any trace of her, the idiots. In my vision Camilla said she'd had to hide herself from them, from all of us, that she was in danger, but she needs me now." She stopped a moment, searched his face. "Don't you see? Linzie Drumm, she's the key to finally seeing Camilla again."

"Ma, how old was Camilla when she came to you in your vision?"

Cyndia stopped cold. She shook her head back and forth. "No, no, that doesn't matter."

"She was still sixteen, wasn't she?"

Cyndia said nothing, kept shaking her head.

"Not everyone loved her, Ma."

Cyndia's head snapped back. "That's not true. Camilla was magical, she'd come into her gift, she was testing her limits. She was so happy with what she was, ready to conquer the world. No matter why she left, no matter what she's done over the years, she deserves to be happy, deserves to be someone important. She wants me to find her now, Rafer, she wants me to bring her back."

Rafer straightened, taller than his father, but young and fit, strong. "You want the truth about your precious Camilla? Oh yeah, she was happy, you're right about that. She was deliriously happy with her gift, with what she could do. She loved to rub my nose in it, me, the little brother who didn't have any gifts, the little brother who didn't count, who couldn't protect himself, whose parents didn't even see him. How could you not know how she made me her slave? That she tried out her powers on me? Experimented on me. On me, Ma. I was only eleven years old. She made me do things, stupid things, awful things. She made me hurt the boy who broke up with her—made me steal the car he loved and wreck it, and I almost killed myself doing it. She told me she'd make all the blood in my body burst out of my mouth if I told you or Pa or anyone. She called me her little toy.

"You didn't see what she was, what she was doing. I don't think you wanted to see. She was the only one who was important to you. I was nothing at all, worse, a failure because I didn't have your gift.

"I bet you didn't know she hated the name Camilla, but what could she expect with you as her mother? She made fun of you, Ma, and Pa, too. She said Pa was just one of your tools, just like I was one of hers. She'd laugh, tell me she was only waiting until she was stronger than you, then she'd rule you like she ruled me.

"I think Pa knew Camilla was bad, but he couldn't admit it to himself or say it out loud. He knew, but he never did anything to keep her away from me, to keep her from hurting anyone she wanted. Do you know, I think Pa was afraid of her, like he was afraid of you.

"And Aunt Jessalyn knew what she was. She found me one day after Camilla had made me hit myself over and over with a rock, laughing as I cut myself again and again. She called me a pathetic little loser and she left. I was sitting cross-legged on the ground, crying, rocking myself, and Aunt Jessalyn came. She tended me, comforted me, and

I told her everything. Like Pa, she knew, knew deep down, and now she had proof. She promised me that day she'd deal with Camilla.

"But I couldn't wait, I was afraid to wait. Camilla knew Aunt Jessalyn had taken care of me and she was furious. I knew in my gut she could kill me, and then she could go after Aunt Jessalyn, there wasn't a doubt in my mind. But you, Ma, you refused to see what she was—a demon from hell. She was evil, evil to her rotten heart." He paused a moment, searching his mother's face. "You noticed I was hurt, since Aunt Jessalyn had put bandages on me and my face was so bruised. Do you remember what you said? Of course you don't. You said I should stop fighting with the other boys at school, nothing more. Camilla heard you. You know what? She laughed, said when she was strong enough, she wouldn't be stupid and blind like you, her lame mom.

"Time was running out and I was scared, so scared, but I had to act. I waited until I knew she was asleep and I snuck into her bedroom. I remember standing over her, looking at her face in the moonlight coming through the window, and I wondered how such a pretty face could hide such evil. I watched her face as I rammed the knife through her neck. Her eyes flew open and she tried to speak, to curse me, to destroy me, but blood was pouring out of her mouth and her neck and she only made garbled sounds. But I was still afraid, so afraid. I pulled the knife out of her neck and shoved it in her chest. I watched her eyes go blank and empty. I didn't know what to do then, and so I just stood there, frozen with fear, but relief, too, simple relief. She would never hurt me again. She wouldn't kill me, she wouldn't kill you or Pa. And then I saw Aunt Jessalyn at the window. She's never said, but I know she'd come to kill Camilla. I just beat her to it. She told me to take off my bloody pajamas and bury them deep, then take a shower and go back to bed, she'd handle the rest. She placed her hands on my head and looked into my eyes. She told me to forget. I know she's got some gifts, but the fact was, I never forgot, any of it.

"But I didn't do what she told me. I wanted to be sure. I watched her carry Camilla away, over her shoulder, and I followed her. I watched her bury Camilla deep in the forest underneath an ancient oak tree. She never knew I was there, watching, and I never told her. I always pretended I'd forgotten. Do you want to know what Aunt Jessalyn said while she was shoveling the dirt over Camilla's body? Something I'll never forget until I die. 'You're gone now, you nasty little witch, dead and gone. Your sweet little brother will never remember. You shouldn't have shined Booker, made him sleep with you. I found out, you know. He dreamed it one night and shouted it out. Your own uncle. You had sex with your own uncle.'

"How could I ever forget that? I mean, Uncle Booker was old, like Aunt Jessalyn. But that's what she said about your sainted Camilla. Then she came back and packed Camilla's favorite clothes and buried them, too. She cleaned all the blood off the bed and floor until there was nothing left of Camilla, nothing at all. And I was happy, Ma, happy she was gone. And for the first time, finally, you and Pa started to look at me, to actually see me.

"Camilla's been rotting for eighteen years in the grave Aunt Jessalyn dumped her in. She's not torturing people like she did me, she's not forcing them to do what she wants or she'll make the pain so bad they'll want to die, like she did me, like you just did to Agent Hammersmith. Camilla's not anywhere, Ma, except in hell, where she belongs. Do you think she sent you this vision from hell? Do you think she wants you to get her out of the flames?"

Cyndia stared at her son, whispered as she shook her head back and forth, "No, you were only a little boy, she loved you, she had to, didn't she? It's a lie, my dear sweet girl—no—"

"No, Ma, I'm not lying and deep down you know it, too, you know what she was. Just like Pa knew but chose not to believe it."

She looked at her son, her eyes blind, and kept shaking her head back and forth. Then she stopped. Her eyes went vague. She whispered, "I'm sorry, Rafer."

Rafer dove for her but he wasn't fast enough. Cyndia put the Beretta in her mouth and pulled the trigger.

71

MCLEAN, VIRGINIA
CIA SAFE HOUSE

They were drinking coffee strong enough to launch a rocket when Savich said to Lucy, "Nikki Bexholt's group had to think you overheard what they said at the house and lured you to that gas station. One of them, probably Bexholt, knocked you out. They brought you here to a CIA safe house. Have I got this right, Armstrong?"

"No, of course you don't. I've told you what my assignment is."

Savich continued, "Not a good solution, but it would buy them some time. Maybe enough time to clean everything incriminating from that house?"

Lucy said, "I saw boxes in what was the living

room, and computer equipment, obviously the place was where they were working. But on what, Dillon?"

"I have some ideas, but nothing solid." He tapped his fingers on the kitchen table, rose suddenly. "We need to get to that house, Lucy. They're not stupid, they're going to be tearing down the operation and removing evidence as fast as they can. Can you show us where it is?"

"Can I borrow your cell phone, Dillon?" She opened his Google Earth app, pinpointed where she was, and followed 7 back to the exit Nikki Bexholt had taken. Half a minute later, she zoomed down to street view. "Here it is. That's the house. Right there."

"Take us closer, Lucy. Good. Show me where you were standing."

"Right here, by the living room window."

Sherlock tracked down the address on her own cell. "Listen to this. It's listed as a protected historical property called Redemption House. It was a part of the underground railroad for escaping slaves. Now, the owner—" She searched, then, "It was purchased three years ago by an LLP, a limited liability partnership, owned by an offshore corporation. In other words, difficult to connect to Nikki."

"Let's go, then," Lucy said, and bounded to her feet, swayed where she stood, and sat down again.

Savich said, "Ollie, I want you to take Lucy to the hospital, get her checked out."

"It's nothing, Dillon, really—"

"Lucy, you were hit on the head and drugged, and you're pregnant. We're not going to take any chances with your health."

Armstrong stared at Lucy. "You're pregnant?" He shook his head. "I thought you were fat."

Lucy smacked him in the head.

Savich said with a straight face, "What I want you and Ollie to do is take Armstrong with you and contact Mr. Besserman, tell him what's happened. He'll take care of Armstrong. Ruth, you and Sherlock are with me. Let's move out. Ruth, get us some backup."

72

REDEMPTION HOUSE

Claire Farriger wished she'd given the FBI agent enough ketamine to kill her on the spot, but of course she couldn't, not with Nikki Bexholt and the others standing right there, watching her every move. She didn't know what McKnight had overheard, what she'd seen, but even if she'd only seen Redemption House itself, she'd signed her death warrant, just as Eleanor Corbitt had when she'd let the CIA agent see her. Farriger could only hope McKnight hadn't already called for backup or revealed what she'd seen.

McKnight would have gotten away clean if Craig hadn't happened to look at one of the monitors and see her on the property. It was only luck Claire herself had been there to set a plan in motion, or she had no doubt it would have been a disaster with the amateurs trying to figure out what to do. Nikki had led her away from the house and McKnight, as she'd expected, had followed her. And when Nikki had turned off at the isolated gas station, the agent had exited with her. Farriger had followed them both and taken care of the agent. She'd hoped her blow had killed her, but unfortunately it hadn't. Thankfully, the agent had stayed unconscious after Nikki had insisted they bring her back to Redemption House. Farriger couldn't very well fight with Nikki right there on the road. Back at the house, she called Lance and told him to come and pick her up, so little time was wasted. She had to call with everyone listening, so she had to tell him loud and clear to take the agent to a CIA safe house until morning.

By now Lance was back in McLean at the safe house. She watched Cricket Washburn, Dr. Cook, and Nikki work for a moment, then slipped into the hallway and called him on her burner phone. She got his voice mail, frowned. No, she wouldn't worry. Lance was a pro. She said into her cell only "It needs to look like an accident." She walked back into the living room, where they were still all busily breaking down equipment, Nikki giving them orders. She studied them a moment. It amazed her how their collective greed overcame breaking more laws than she could count, yet they weren't willing to do what was necessary to save themselves, save the project. They had to know the FBI agent threatened their very lives, yet they wouldn't hear of killing her.

And that's why she'd never admit to them she'd had Armstrong kill Eleanor Corbitt. In her case, there'd been no time to stage an accident. She wondered, at odd moments, if killing Corbitt had been a mistake. Perhaps if she'd left her alone—but no, she'd spotted Corbitt as the weak link, and Corbitt had proved it when she panicked and drove off. Water under the bridge. Now the new threat was from Agent Lucy McKnight. This time she would do it right.

She'd known working with amateurs meant screwups were inevitable—even with pros you never knew when things would go sideways—but she'd figured she could manage any amateurish mistakes. The only thing she hadn't counted on was the FBI making connections so fast. They'd managed to scare the crap out of Palumbo and Nikki. Almost enough to give them all away.

As for Justice Cummings, being dead was the only thing she wanted from him. The incriminating data theft from his computer would prove him a traitor. If anyone was going under the bus, it would be him.

When she walked back into the room, Dr. Cook stopped his packing and gave her a long look. "I was telling Athena you would have the FBI agent killed if we let you, like you had Ellie killed. We all saw you go into the hall just now—in the mirror." He waved back to the large mirror over the fireplace. "You pulled out your cell. Did you call that goon of yours and order him to kill her?"

Farriger shook her head, sighed. "Craig, we've worked together for months now. I told you I didn't have anything to do with Eleanor Corbitt's murder. But now, you must listen to me, all of you. I will be honest. The FBI agent is another matter entirely. She could and would bury us all so deep we wouldn't see the outside of a cell for the rest of our lives. No, don't look away from me. They know the agent was following Nikki, they most assuredly will find out she came to Redemption House, and that's why we're removing every trace of our work. If she isn't around to accuse us, and nothing is here to be found, we might still get out of this whole-hide. We can't let her get back to them, she'd identify us all. I'll arrange a fatal car accident. There will be questions, sure, but if it's done right, there will be no proof. We can all go quietly back to our lives."

There was dead silence, then Cricket said, "They will know it wasn't a real accident."

Nikki said, "Even if they can't prove it, they'll never stop if they think we killed one of their agents in a staged accident. And they will, you know it."

Farriger looked around the group, her eyes resting a moment on Jasmine Palumbo, responsible for the biggest screwup. She hated amateurs. "Yes, of course they'll suspect, but I'll see to it there is no compelling proof. Listen to me, all of you. If we're very lucky, they may never find this place. In any case, I've managed to buy us perhaps twelve hours.

We can't waste more time on these senseless debates. We've got to empty this house and get out of here."

Nikki took a step toward her. "No, Claire, there will be no more killing. If only you'd asked me about Ellie, I could have told you she could talk her way out of anything. Here's what we'll do. We'll clean out the house, and they'll have no way of knowing why we were here. If we stick together, we'll get through this. When they find the agent, maybe she'll be wandering around, still confused from the drug you gave her. Let her say whatever she wants, there'll be no proof."

Farriger wanted to draw her service weapon and shoot all of them. Instead, she drew in a deep breath. "I don't care what you believe about Corbitt, but if the FBI agent simply shows up, confused or not, the FBI will not stop, do you understand? They. Will. Not. Stop. We have no choice."

She saw a moment of indecision on Cricket's face, saw Jasmine shake her head. She said to Nikki, "If we don't kill her, your father wins, you'll have proved him right—you're a girl, inferior, a failure. And your brother? Can you imagine how happy he'll be when you're hauled off in your orange suit to federal prison?

"Listen, Nikki, when you told me about Dr. Cook's invention, we both knew it was our big chance. I could wipe the CIA muck off my shoes and we could both live the lives we wanted. You were so excited, anything to pay back the father you hate and your prick of a brother. Let me point out you were the one who led that FBI agent here to the house, like Jasmine blundered and hit Agent Sherlock's car. Your fault, not mine, all the mistakes, the missteps. I'm the one who can save you, the only one. You've got to let me do what we have to do to keep us safe."

"No, Claire," Nikki said, "you will not kill anyone else. We all talked about this, we're all agreed."

Farriger was sick of all of them. More blah, blah. She stopped listening. She moved to stand next to a wall with shelves holding dozens of old leather books from before the Civil War. She splayed her hands in front of her. "Very well, trust me, the agent will be freed."

Dr. Craig Cook pointed a finger at her. "Trust you? You gave her over to that bulked-up trained ape of yours, Armstrong, after you drugged her. We all know you called him a few minutes ago. You told him to kill her, didn't you? It's easy for you, like pinching out a candle."

"Dr. Cook, get ahold of yourself." Farriger walked slowly toward him and he flinched, she saw it. Good, the little worm was afraid of her. And so he should be. She stopped, clapped her hands together. "We must stop with these senseless accusations. We have to get to work."

Nikki said, "Make the call to Armstrong. In front of us. Now."

73

Savich, Sherlock, and Ruth crouched over as they moved quickly away from the long driveway to skirt the big colonial house. Savich nodded to Sherlock and she slipped around the side of the house to look through the front window. She backed up, whispered, "They're packing up, moving fast. A man and a woman just walked out of the living room carrying boxes."

They watched the man and woman carry out two boxes each and lift them into a large white van, the Bexholt logo on the side.

Savich whispered, "Let's get these two out of the way, then we'll deal with the others inside."

Cricket squeaked when she felt Sherlock's gun pointed at her temple. Sherlock whispered in her ear, "Don't move. Do as I say and you won't get hurt."

"Wh-who are you?"

"I'm FBI. Who are you?"

Cricket shook her head. "I could tell you, but I know I shouldn't."

"I guess that makes sense from your point of view, but not much," Sherlock said. "Walk with me and don't make another sound or I will have to hurt you." She looked over to see Ruth perp-walking the man toward the back of the house. They flex-cuffed their wrists and set them down behind a maple tree. Savich said to them, "Tell me now, what are your names?"

Craig gave Cricket a look, then, "I'm Dr. Craig Cook. She's Cricket Washburn."

"You both work at Bexholt?"

"Yes."

"Does anyone have a gun inside?"

Cricket whispered, "Claire Farriger does, she always has a gun. Are you arresting us? Craig and I haven't done anything, well, hardly anything."

Ruth said, "Yes, you're under arrest." And she read them their rights. "Now, if you try to warn them, like yelling, you'll be charged additionally with obstruction and have gags stuffed in your mouths."

Craig said, "No, please, we won't say anything."

She stood over them a moment, shaking her

head. "I guess it's because you two are so young it pains me to see what bad decisions you've made. We're all going to stay right here until more of our people arrive. Very soon now."

Sherlock crept back to look through the window again. Nikki Bexholt and Claire Farriger weren't working any longer, they were arguing.

Jasmine Palumbo suddenly shouted, "Look, on the security camera! They're here!"

"No choice, we're going in." Savich was fast. He backed up and sent his foot into the front door. It was unlocked and the door flew inward. They rushed through the entrance hall, their Glocks at the ready. "FBI! None of you move! Farriger, drop your gun. Now. Bexholt, Palumbo, down on the floor, hands behind your heads."

Farriger grabbed Jasmine, hauled her up against her, one arm tight around her neck, her other hand holding her weapon pointed at Jasmine's cheek. Farriger's face was set, her expression hard, her eyes filled with determination. "Not you two again. How?"

Sherlock said, her voice infinitely calm, "You don't want to die, Ms. Farriger. Put down your weapon and release Ms. Palumbo. There doesn't have to be any violence. You have no backup. Lance Armstrong is now in custody. Cook and Washburn are bound outside. Oh yes, Justice told Alan Besserman everything you did to him. He's safe as well. To round it all off, Agent Lucy

McKnight is fine. It really is all over, Ms. Farriger. Let Palumbo go."

Farriger tightened her grip around Jasmine's neck. "It will be proved Cummings is a liar. Now, Jasmine and I are leaving together. Any move on your part, and she's dead. I know you're well trained, but so am I. I will kill her. Do you understand me?"

Savich said, "Even if you manage to get away, there is no place for you to hide. Your best move is to try to make a deal with the federal prosecutors. You haven't killed anyone, have you?"

Nikki said, "All of us believe she killed Ellie or had her killed by that lover of hers, Lance Armstrong."

"Shut up, Nikki! Now, I know you're never supposed to give up your weapons, but if you don't, I will shoot Jasmine dead right now, in front of you. Glocks on the ground. Get down on your bellies, hands on your heads. Do it, now!"

Savich and Sherlock knelt down, placed their Glocks on the hardwood floor, then went down on their bellies, hands laced behind their heads.

Jasmine was white as a sheet. She knew Farriger would shoot her as soon as she got her into her car, maybe sooner. She had nothing to lose. She kicked down with her boot, got Farriger hard in the shin, grabbed her arm with both hands, and jerked with all her strength. Farriger shouted, "Stop it or I'll shoot you right now!"

But Jasmine wasn't about to stop.

Time slowed. Savich went for his Glock as he saw Farriger's finger tighten on the trigger, saw Jasmine trying to free herself, panting, her face turning red as Farriger's arm tightened around her neck. He wouldn't be in time. Then, to his surprise, Nikki Bexholt whirled about, grabbed a laptop from a table, and brought it down as hard as she could on Farriger's head. Jasmine jerked away from her just as the gun fired. Jasmine went down. And so did Farriger.

Savich moved to Farriger, peeled one of her eyelids back. She twisted, tried to grab her gun from the floor, but Nikki was faster. She bashed her on the head again with the laptop.

Jasmine Palumbo moaned, slapped her hand to the side of her head. Nikki was at her side in an instant. "Jasmine! Oh no, Jasmine!"

"No, Nikki, keep back." Sherlock pulled Jasmine's hand away, studied the wound. "You were lucky, Ms. Palumbo, it's only a flesh wound." She stilled, then turned to blink up at Savich.

74

GEORGETOWN
SAVICH HOUSE
VERY EARLY SATURDAY MORNING

Savich locked the front door, set the alarm. He turned to see Sherlock yawn, then she gave him a huge grin. She'd been mostly silent on the way home, as if deep in thought. She hadn't said anything when he'd stopped briefly at the National Mall and they'd watched the sun rise.

He touched his fingers to her chin. "You've been so quiet. And your eyes—I can see it now, you're starting to remember, aren't you?"

Sherlock raised her face. "Yes, but not every-thing. The most important thing is I remember me, who I am—I remember both of us holding Sean. I'd hoped it would all come back by the time we got home, and I was worrying it like Astro with a bone, but no, not yet. But, Dillon, you're not a stranger anymore, you're you. And I miss Sean."

He gathered her in, held her close. He felt such relief, felt so grateful, he swallowed, said against her cheek, "You remember all about me? Us?"

"Yes, you're front and center."

"How? Did something happen to trigger your memory?"

"It was something so simple, so small, that set it off. When I looked at Jasmine Palumbo's head to see how badly she was hurt, I told her it was only a flesh wound. In that instant, I saw Porter Forge. You remember Porter."

"Oh yes, I remember Porter."

"During a training exercise in Hogan's Alley at Quantico, he was assigned to be one of the bank robbers and it ended up he tried to escape and I had to shoot him. When it was all over, I looked down at his face and head covered with too much fake blood and I told him it was only a flesh wound. I saw everyone laughing. It happened at the academy, over six years ago, Dillon. Can you imagine? The image from so long ago, and what I said, and suddenly there you were, with me. And Ruth."

She shook her head, laughed, threw herself against him, and held on tight. "I looked over at you then and the world began to right itself. This was my life again."

She leaned back, still holding on. "There are these strange gaps in time, but I know, deep down, the blanks will fill in."

"Yes," Savich said. "Yes."

She touched her fingers to his face. "It was scary, Dillon, really scary, but now, being here with you again, it's so very fine."

He pressed his forehead to hers. "I fully intend to email Porter Forge and thank him, maybe ask when his birthday is, send him a present."

They stood in the entry hall holding each other. She whispered against his neck, "I want to bring Sean home, watch him eat his Cheerios with a sliced banana on top. Now, about his wanting a three-speed bike for his birthday next week—"

EPILOGUE

Executive Assistant Director James Maitland began reading the report Goldy, his gatekeeper assistant, handed him. Goldy had read the report first and now she listened to her boss's usual grunting, a couple of *great*s occasionally interrupting his humming silence.

Maitland read:

> *Lance Armstrong, former field operative and Claire Farriger's lover and longtime assistant and collaborator, is in custody, charged with assault and detention of Special Agent Lucy McKnight. It's unclear whether he can be indicted for the murder of Eleanor Corbitt unless*

compelling evidence can be found. The
CIA is scrambling, as you can imagine,
and Director Lindsey is demanding a full
investigation into any and all of Farriger's
activities that might have exposed or
compromised CIA operations in her
theater of activity. He is not a happy
man, an understatement. Lindsey has
temporarily assigned Alan Besserman,
Justice Cummings's boss, to Claire
Farriger's position at the CIA. Perhaps we
can benefit from cooperation from him in
the future if he remains in this position.
Farriger was released from the hospital this
morning and taken into federal custody.

Maitland made a mental note to follow up on
Armstrong. There had to be a case against him in
Eleanor Corbitt's murder he could convince the
district attorney to make. He continued reading:

Nikki Bexholt and her cohorts, Jasmine
Palumbo, June (aka Cricket) Washburn,
and Dr. Craig Cook, creator of the "smart
wall"—all Bexholt employees recruited
by Ms. Bexholt—are in custody. Garrick
Bexholt and the Bexholt Group have so far
been spared the collapse of the company
stock that very possibly will follow public
disclosure. Mrs. Bexholt is the only one in

the family championing Nikki Bexholt, her daughter.

Exactly how Claire Farriger and Nikki Bexholt came to work together remains unclear, as both refuse to answer any questions and deny all charges. We do know they met in their official capacities on several occasions (a project the Bexholt Group did for the CIA) and were also identified as taking the same weekly aikido classes at the Maru Dojo in Dupont Circle. It appears Farriger's role was to make use of her European and Russian contacts to sell the smart wall. Needless to say, the meeting room for the upcoming negotiations between the Federal Reserve and the European Central Bank has been double-checked to ensure nothing remains of Dr. Cook's smart wall. One of Farriger's contacts was probably the source of the chatter Justice Cummings came across a little over two weeks ago.

We are only beginning to examine the listening device itself. It appears to be a material they were installing in place of conventional acoustic tiles. In essence, the material absorbs and transduces sound waves into a faint electromagnetic signal that can be amplified and analyzed using their own algorithms to bring

out the signal in the electronic noise.
In other words, it is an undetectable
microphone that allows for old-fashioned
eavesdropping. What's new about it is
that you would never know you were being
bugged. The negotiations between the
Federal Reserve and the European Central
Bank were to be the test run of their smart
wall, believable proof it worked as every
word spoken would be recorded.

Knowing the outcome of those
banking negotiations before their public
release would have allowed Bexholt
and Farriger to make a killing in the
financial markets, betting with that inside
knowledge on anything from interest rates
to oil and commodity futures to individual
government bonds. And it seems that
was only one relatively small part of their
plan. Once they had proof the smart wall
worked, they would have sold or auctioned
the technology itself to the highest bidders,
to any oligarch or foreign government
willing to pay for it. Bugging safe rooms
at embassies, top-secret government and
international meetings, financial industry
and corporate boardrooms—there seems
to be no end to the clients who might have
paid them a fortune for their smart wall.
We are very fortunate we have prevented

any adversarial foreign intelligence service from purchasing it without our even knowing of its existence.

Justice Cummings, the CIA analyst whose work led to our discovering this labyrinthine plot, has told us he's decided to leave the CIA and enter the private workforce. I imagine his wife will be pleased, as I'm sure he can name his own salary. He is a very lucky man and he knows it.

Turning to developments in Special Agent Griffin Hammersmith's case in Gaffer's Ridge, Virginia, the three living kidnapped girls, Heather Forrester, Latisha Morris, and Linzie Drumm, have been reunited with their families. Their memories are hazy from all the drugs, but fortunately they are physically unharmed. Amy Traynor, the teenager kidnapped from Radford, was evidently killed when she tried to escape.

Rafer Bodine is in custody. He has confessed to murdering his sister when he was eleven years old, but his more easily provable crimes are the kidnappings of the four girls and the assault and kidnapping of Dr. Carson DeSilva. He denies killing Amy Traynor, but refuses to name either his father or his mother as the killer. He

denies knowledge of where she is buried.
The State of Virginia and the federal courts
will determine his future.

Jessalyn Bodine, his aunt, buried his
sister, Camilla, according to Rafer. He
claims not to remember where Camilla
is buried and Jessalyn Bodine denies all
knowledge. Unless a body is found, there is
no evidence to charge her.

Booker Bodine remains sheriff
of Gaffer's Ridge. Someone removed
evidence at Rafer Bodine's house, but
we have no proof of his involvement.
Agent Hammersmith is satisfied with the
outcome. Let me add he and Dr. DeSilva
were able to spend time with Dr. Alek
Kuchar, the Nobel Prize laureate she
had come to interview. I believe Agent
Hammersmith will be in New York City
for the rest of his vacation time.

There will be further developments,
there always are. I will keep you apprised
as they come to me.

Special Agent Dillon Savich, CAU

1

Marsia Gay would be living like a queen, not like an animal locked in a cell, if it weren't for FBI agent Dillon Savich. He was the one who'd screwed her perfect plan sideways, the man responsible for her being locked in this soulless circle of hell. Of course, that bitch Veronica would pay for her betrayal, too, no doubt about that, but he was the one who'd rained this misery down on her, the one she wanted most.

Savich was a dead man walking—but not yet, not just yet. She wanted to savor his downfall. He would die only after she killed the two people closest to him, the two people whose deaths would hurt him most.

She knew she had to snag his interest with

something unique, begin with only an oblique threat, nothing too over-the-top, but something enigmatic and bizarre enough that Savich wouldn't be able to resist. And suck him in. She wouldn't underestimate him, not this time. He'd proven he was smart, but she was just as smart—no, she was smarter, and she was going to prove it. She'd make sure Savich knew it was Marsia Gay who'd set everything in motion, who'd had her final revenge. Halloween was coming up. It was the perfect time.

She heard her mother's vodka-slurred voice whisper, *Even as a child, when you wanted something, you grabbed for it, didn't think. Didn't work out for you this time, did it?*

"I won't fail this time!" She didn't realize she'd screamed the words until the guard, a big lummox named Maxie, appeared at the bars and stared at her. Marsia wished she could tear her face off. "A nightmare, sorry."

Maxie didn't point out it wasn't dark yet, too early to sleep. She only shrugged and walked away. Marsia went over to the narrow window that looked out over the desolate exercise yard with its scarred, ancient wooden tables and benches, the pathetic torn basketball hoop where she usually won playing Horse—cigarettes, a small bar of soap from a Holiday Inn, an offer of a prison tattoo made from soot and shampoo or melted Styrofoam, no thank you. She saw Angela lounging against a wall, probably giving orders to her minions. What a sweet name for a mean-as-a-snake muscled gang leader awaiting trial for the murder of her boyfriend and his lover. It hadn't been difficult to seduce Angela into her orbit. She'd been even easier to manipulate than Veronica. Angela had taken to Marsia right away, told her she'd see to it no one would harm her, if Marsia was nice to her. Marsia had shuddered when Angela lightly touched her arm, but, well, Marsia had been nice. Angela always stayed in sight and took care of whatever Marsia wanted. She kept the other bullies away from the pretty artist girl who spoke so beautifully and was always so polite, so of course they hated her instinctively. Angela never tired of hearing about Marsia's sculptures, how she worked with this metal and that. Marsia missed her sculpting, of course, but now she looked forward to returning to her studio once she was found not guilty at her trial, and of course her studio would still be waiting for her. After all, she owned the building.

The wind had stiffened, whipping up the dirt into dust devils. She saw a dozen women wandering around the yard, doing nothing in particular, and one lone prisoner, head down, pacing back and forth, apart from the others. It was Veronica. She'd rarely seen her here. The guards made sure they were kept apart, but soon that wouldn't matter. Marsia knew Veronica well enough to know she felt guilt, awful guilt, about striking the deal as the prosecution's star witness against Marsia in exchange for the safety they'd promised her. Sorry, Veronica, that isn't going to happen; it's going to get you killed. With no witness to testify against Marsia, the evidence would be more circumstantial than not. No, not enough to convict her.

Veronica, I'm going to choreograph a special dance for you to mark your exit from the planet. Thank you.

Later, on the edge of sleep, she heard her dead lush of a mother speaking in her ear. *I could tell you things you haven't thought of yet, wormy things you could do. I could help you.*

She didn't scream out this time. She lay there and whispered, "Okay, Mom, talk to me."

2

WASHINGTON, D.C.
HOME OF ZOLTAN
WEDNESDAY EVENING
OCTOBER 28

The last place Rebekah ever expected to find herself was in the home of a medium. Zoltan the Medium was how the woman had introduced herself when she'd called Rebekah. But how do you say no when a medium tells you your grandfather who died only a month ago wants to speak to you? Wants you to forget he's dead and calling from the afterlife? Rebekah almost hung up, almost said, if he's in his afterlife, doesn't that mean his life here on earth is over? As in he's dead? But Zoltan had said her grandfather wanted to speak to his Pumpkin, maybe to warn her about something. Zoltan wasn't sure. Rebekah hadn't wanted to believe any of it, but Pumpkin had been his favorite nickname for her, and how could this self-proclaimed medium possibly know that? She'd felt gooseflesh rise on her arms. She'd had no choice, not really. She knew she had to find out what this was all about, and so here she was, walking behind Zoltan, a woman not that much older than her own twenty-eight years, into her living room. Rebekah had expected to see a table with a long red tablecloth covering it, primed to levitate on command, but there was no table everyone would sit around, only a small coffee table. She saw a long, narrow, high-ceilinged room lit only by one standing lamp in the far corner and draperies rippling in the breeze given off by a low-humming portable fan beside the large front window. Curiously, not far from the fan, a fire burned in the fireplace, low and sullen. However strange the mix, the room was pleasantly warm.

Zoltan wasn't wearing a flowing caftan and matching turban or big shiny hoop earrings in her ears. She was wearing a dark blue silk blouse, black pants, and low-heeled black shoes. Her hair was dark, pulled back in a sleek chignon. Her eyes were so dark a blue they appeared nearly black. She'd looked and seemed perfectly normal when she'd greeted Rebekah. She asked her to be seated on the sofa and offered her a cup of tea.

The tea was excellent: hot, plain, no sugar, the way she liked it. Zoltan smiled at her, sipped her own tea. "I know you don't believe one can speak to the Departed, Mrs. Manvers. Actually, I far prefer a skeptic to blind acceptance. I'm pleased you decided to come. I will tell you what happened. As I said when I called you, your maternal grandfather came to me very unexpectedly while I was trying to contact another Departed for his son. Your grandfather was anxious to speak to you. He called you Pumpkin, which you recognized. Do you wish to proceed?"

Rebekah nodded, drank more tea, and kept any snarky comments to herself.

Zoltan nodded. "Good. Let us begin. I want you to relax, Mrs. Manvers—may I call you Rebekah?"

Rebekah nodded.

"And you may call me Zoltan. I know this is difficult for you, but I need you to try to keep an open mind and suspend judgment. Empty your mind, simply let everything go. Begin by relaxing your neck, your shoulders, that's right. Breathe slowly and deeply. Good."

They sat in silence for a minute or so before Zoltan spoke again, her voice low and soothing. "Rebekah, when your grandfather crashed my party, so to speak, all he told me was he had to speak to you. I don't know why he was so anxious, he didn't say. On his third visit, three nights ago, he finally identified himself and you by your married name so I could contact you. He always came when other clients were here. Why? I don't know. Maybe it was easier for him to reach me with the pathway already open. His message was always, 'Rebekah, I want Rebekah, I want my Pumpkin. I must tell her—' A warning? That's what I thought, but I really don't know. I asked you to bring something personal of his with you."

Rebekah opened her handbag and pulled out a letter and a photograph of her and her grandfather standing on the steps of the Capitol building, people flowing around them. He was smiling, eager to get on with his life, and beside him Rebekah, just turned eleven, was clutching his hand and looking as happy as he was. He had no way of knowing what would happen to him, but of course, no one did. The photograph had been taken a year before the series of strokes happened and effectively ended his life, leaving him in a coma for sixteen years. He'd finally died last month and been buried in Arlington National Cemetery with all due pomp, with Rebekah's husband standing next to her, his arm around her. Rebekah felt tears swim in her eyes as she handed Zoltan the photograph and the letter.

Zoltan took the letter, didn't read it, but seemed to weigh it in her hand. She took the photograph, glanced at it, then placed it faceup over the letter, in front of Rebekah.

"Rebekah, please place your left hand over the letter and the photograph and give me your right hand."

Rebekah did as she was asked. She no longer felt she'd fallen down the rabbit hole. She was beginning to feel calmer, more settled, perhaps even receptive. She let her hand relax in Zoltan's. "Why my right hand? Why not my left?"

Zoltan said, "I've learned the right hand carries more latent energy than the left. Odd but true, at least in my experience. Good. I want you to think about what your grandfather said to you that day the photograph was taken, think about what you were feeling in that moment. Now picture the man in the photograph. Tell me about him."

"Before the strokes and the coma, he was in Congress, always on the go, always busy with his political maneuvering against the incumbent majority. I remember that day he was happy. A bill I think he'd authored had passed." She paused a moment. "As for the letter, it's the last one he wrote me. It was chatty, nothing serious. Grandfather rarely emailed me; he preferred to write his letters to me in longhand."

"Now, lightly touch the fingers of your left hand to the photograph. Let them rest on your grandfather's face. Excellent. Close your eyes, picture his face in your mind, and simply speak to him as if he were sitting beside you on the sofa. It's all right if you think this is nothing more than a silly exercise, but indulge me, please."

Rebekah didn't resist. She was feeling too relaxed. Zoltan poured her another cup of tea from the carafe on the coffee table. Rebekah drank, savored the rich, smooth taste, and did as Zoltan said. Oddly, she saw her grandmother's face, cold and aloof, not her grandfather's. Gemma had been a séance junkie all her life, something that made Rebekah's mom roll her eyes. Grandmother was talking to dead people? No, her mother had said, talking to the dead was crazy, meant for the gullible. Rebekah wondered if her grandmother had tried to contact her husband since his death. Why would she? To gloat that he was dead and she wasn't?

Zoltan said again, "Rebekah? Please speak to your grandfather. Picture him here with you. Speak what's in your heart. Be welcoming."

Rebekah said, her voice clear, "Grandfather, I remember you when you were well and happy before you fell into a coma. I loved you so much and I knew you loved me. Everyone called me your little confidante, and it was true. You trusted me with all the stories you called your secret adventures, even when I was a kid. Do you know I kept my promise to you never to tell anyone the stories, not even my mother, certainly not my grandmother? They were always only between us. You made me feel very special." Her voice caught. "I miss you, Grandfather. I think of you every day and pray you're at peace." She knew, objectively, when he'd fallen into the coma, his life was over, though his body held on. She knew she should have been relieved when his body finally let go, but the reality of his actual death still broke her. She swiped away a tear, swallowed. "Zoltan said you want to speak to me. If you can hear me, I hope you can come— through." Her voice fell off. She felt a bit silly, but oddly, it didn't overly concern her.

The draperies continued to flutter in the breeze, the fire stayed sullen. The lamplight, however, seemed to dim, then brighten, and dim again. Zoltan's face was now in shadow. She said in the same gentle voice, each word slow and smooth, "Keep talking to him, Rebekah. I can feel a presence hovering close, and it's familiar."

Rebekah didn't feel anything different. Well, except for the dimmed lamplight. Zoltan's right hand held Rebekah's, and her left hand lay palm up on her lap. Rebekah knew she should feel like an idiot, but she didn't. She felt relaxed, curious to see what would happen. "Perhaps it isn't really Grandfather you're feeling, Zoltan—"

Zoltan suddenly raised her left hand, and Rebekah stopped talking. "Is that you, Congressman Clarkson? Are you here?"

The draperies grew still, though the fan continued to churn the air. The fire suddenly sparked, shooting up an orange flame, then the burning wood crumbled, making a soft thudding sound. The lamplight grew brighter, then flickered and went completely dark.

Only the dying fire lit the room.

All tricks, she's pressing some magic buttons with her foot—

She felt Zoltan's hand tighten ever so slightly around hers. "Someone is here, Rebekah," Zoltan said calmly in her soft, even voice. "I can't be certain until the Departed talks to me, but the feeling of his presence is, as I said, familiar. Do you know of a nickname your grandfather was called? Or did you yourself have a special name for him as he did for you?"

She remembered her grandfather's face, clear as day, saw him throw back his head and laugh at something she'd said. She whispered, "Methodist, that was his nickname. He told me his cohorts in Congress called him Methodist, too. The name got out, and even his own staff began calling him that—'Methodist believes this, Methodist said that.'" She swallowed tears again, hating they were so close to the surface. "I remember hearing Grandmother say he'd made up the name himself. When I asked him, he admitted it, said he didn't want anyone else making up a name for him, particularly the opposition, and Methodist practically made him a poster boy for God, full of probity and sheer boring honesty. A lot of people called him that before his first stroke."

"Call him by his nickname."

Very well, play along, why not? At best, it's entertainment, but you're here, so why not go along with it? But is it only entertainment? Grandmother would believe it, maybe, but not me.

She felt foolish, but she cleared her throat. "Grandfather—Methodist?—it's Rebekah, your granddaughter. If you are here, tell me what's so important."

A puff of dense black smoke plumed up from the fireplace embers, making an odd sucking sound. The lamp brightened, then darkened again.

Rebekah's throat was dry, and she drank some more tea, then placed her right hand back into Zoltan's. She knew the lamp, the fire, the billowing draperies were simple stage props, but she didn't really care, it wasn't important. She had to know what her grandfather wanted to tell her or what this woman wanted her to believe he did. Rebekah was surprised how calm she felt, her body and mind relaxed. Still, how could any of this be true?

Zoltan said, "I'm not sure if it's your grandfather I feel. Is your grandmother alive, Rebekah?"

"Yes, she is. Her name is Gemma Clarkson. She's in her late seventies. She continues to run all of Grandfather's businesses in Clairemont, Virginia, west of Richmond, where she and my grandfather lived all their lives. Clairemont was in his district."

"Did your grandfather and grandmother have a strong bond? Would speaking about her to him perhaps make him come through the Verge? That's what I call the threshold the spirits have to cross back over into our reality."

"No," Rebekah said, nothing more. It was none of Zoltan's business. Even Rebekah couldn't remember a time when her grandparents had shown any affection for each other, and her memories went back a very long way. She'd never seen her grandmother at the Mayfield Sanitarium during those sixteen long years her grandfather had lain there helpless, his only sign of life his still-beating heart. She'd asked her grandmother once, back in the beginning when she'd been young, why she didn't visit Grandfather. Her grandmother had merely said, "Perhaps I will." But Rebekah didn't think she had.

"I think my grandmother was glad when he died. She did go to his funeral, but she had to, didn't she? I doubt she'd want to be here in my place if she thought her husband would show up. Even though she'd believe it."

"Your grandmother is a believer, then?"

"Yes, but she's always careful because she thinks most mediums are frauds. That's what I heard her tell my mother."

She wanted to ask Zoltan if she was a fraud, but when she looked into Zoltan's eyes, darker now in the dim light, and felt her intensity, she let the thought go.

"Your grandmother is perfectly correct. There are many frauds." Zoltan began to hum softly, then she said, her voice barely above a whisper, "Congressman Clarkson? Methodist? Are you having trouble coming through this time? If you are, reach out to me, and I will speak for you to Rebekah. Come, I am open to you. I am your conduit. You've already connected with me, you know you can trust me. Your granddaughter is here. You must try again."

The lamp bulb burst into brightness that reached the far corners of the living room. Thick black smoke erupted upward from the fireplace embers, and the draperies began to move again.

Rebekah held perfectly still. She heard her own voice whisper, "Grandfather, is that you?"

Zoltan said in the same soft chant, "Come in through me, Congressman. Let me speak for you. Give me your words so I can tell Rebekah what concerns you so greatly. Come through me."

Nothing happened. Rebekah took another drink of her tea, realized she was perfectly content to wait. The air was warm, and she felt calm, open, expectant, which she should realize was silly, but it didn't seem to matter.

Suddenly, Zoltan whooshed out a breath and stiffened. Her eyes closed, and her hand tightened around Rebekah's again, then eased. Rebekah felt a fluttering of movement, a brush against her cheek, and jumped. What was that? The hair lifted off the back of her neck as if there were electricity in the air. She whispered, "Grandfather?"

The room grew dim again, the embers quieted. Zoltan's lips began to move, and out came a flat, low voice, not quite like Zoltan's own voice, but deeper, sounding somehow distant, and older—like her grandfather's voice. "My dearest Rebekah. To speak to you again, even through this woman, it brings me great joy. You visited me when I still breathed earthly air. I knew it was you, always, and I understood you when you spoke to me. You came nearly every day, and I loved you for it. You held my hand, talked to me, and I savored each of your words, your loving presence. Everyone believed I was gone, even the doctors believed I was locked helpless into my brain, nothing left of my reason, nothing left of me, no awareness, no consciousness, and some of that was true. But even though I was unable to speak to you, unable to respond to you, I heard, yes, I heard everything, heard everyone. Do you know, I remember when Gemma came, only once, at the beginning, and she whispered in my ear she wished I'd just hang it up once and for all and stop wasting everyone's time. She punched my arm; I felt it. But your visits were the highlights of my day, and you came to me throughout the long years I lay there like the dead, which, thankfully, I finally am. It was only a month ago, wasn't it?"

Zoltan paused, her eyes flew open, and she stared at Rebekah. Time froze. Then Zoltan spoke again, her voice still deep, another's voice, still blurred, still distant. "Look at you, so beautiful, like your mother. I remember how proud you were when you told me you had earned your master's degree in art history at George Washington, that you knew you had the 'eye,' you called it, and you had decided to make yourself an expert on fraudulent art. You couldn't wait to start consulting with museums and collectors. You'd already begun your search to find a partner, someone who could work with you to identify stolen originals. And you told me you found the perfect person."

Yes, yes, my new partner, Kit Jarrett, now my best friend, a perfect fit, my lucky day. But wait, finding out about Kit Jarrett was easy enough. It wasn't a secret.

"Your excitement made me want to smile, on the inside, of course, and you couldn't see it. And now you are married, to another congressman. Manvers interned for me a very long time ago. I always found him a real go-getter. I think he was born knowing how to play the game. He's playing it well. Other than being a politician, Rich Manvers is a fine man, but isn't he a bit old for you, Pumpkin?"

"Perhaps, but what's important is he understands me, and he loves me." Rebekah licked her lips, drank more tea to get spit in her mouth, and managed to say, "Pumpkin—that was the nickname you gave me when I was six years old. Not many people know that."

Zoltan's brilliant dark eyes opened and fastened onto something beyond Rebekah. Rebekah turned but didn't see anything. Zoltan's lips moved, but no sound came out. There was no expression on Zoltan's face, only smooth blankness. Then her grandfather's voice again. "Yes, I remember the Halloween you carved a pumpkin to look like me. You nearly burned the house down."

Rebekah heard herself say, "Yes. I still have a picture of the pumpkin, and you're standing behind me, your hands on my shoulders. I have so many photos of us together over the years. Of course, I came to see you as often as I could in the sanitarium. I loved you. Grandfather, I will love you until I die. I know this sounds strange, but are you well now?"

The distant deep voice seemed to laugh. "Yes, Pumpkin, of course I'm well. I'm always well now. There is no more pain since I died—well, there was hardly any even before I died. I remember you were such a brave girl, never left my side during those long, final earthbound hours. You held my hand until I was able to depart my tedious life."

She remembered, too clearly, the shock, the pain, and the relief, too, when he drew his last breath. Dr. Lassiter, a kind, attentive man, had stood beside her, touching her grandfather's other hand. "John is at peace now," he'd said when it was over, and she'd finally known what that old chestnut really meant.

Rebekah said, "Yes, I remember. What is it you want to tell me, Grandfather?"